DEATH ON THE TIBER

DEATH ON THE TIBER

Lindsey Davis

HODDER &
STOUGHTON

First published in Great Britain in 2024 by Hodder & Stoughton
An Hachette UK company

3

Copyright © Lindsey Davis 2024

The right of Lindsey Davis to be identified as the Author of the Work has been
asserted by her in accordance with the Copyright, Designs and Patents Act 1988.

Maps by Barking Dog Art

A CIP catalogue record for this title is available from the British Library

Hardback ISBN 978 1 399 71958 2
Trade Paperback ISBN 978 1 399 71959 9
ebook ISBN 978 1 399 71960 5

Typeset in Plantin Light by Hewer Text UK Ltd, Edinburgh
Printed and bound in Great Britain by Clays Ltd, Elcograf S.p.A.

Hodder & Stoughton policy is to use papers that are natural, renewable
and recyclable products and made from wood grown in sustainable
forests. The logging and manufacturing processes are expected to
conform to the environmental regulations of the country of origin.

Hodder & Stoughton Ltd
Carmelite House
50 Victoria Embankment
London EC4Y 0DZ

www.hodder.co.uk

This book might never have been written.
It is dedicated to two dear friends,
one who made me fit enough to survive
and one who saved me on the day:
with thanks and love, for Marcus and Simon.

DEATH ON THE TIBER

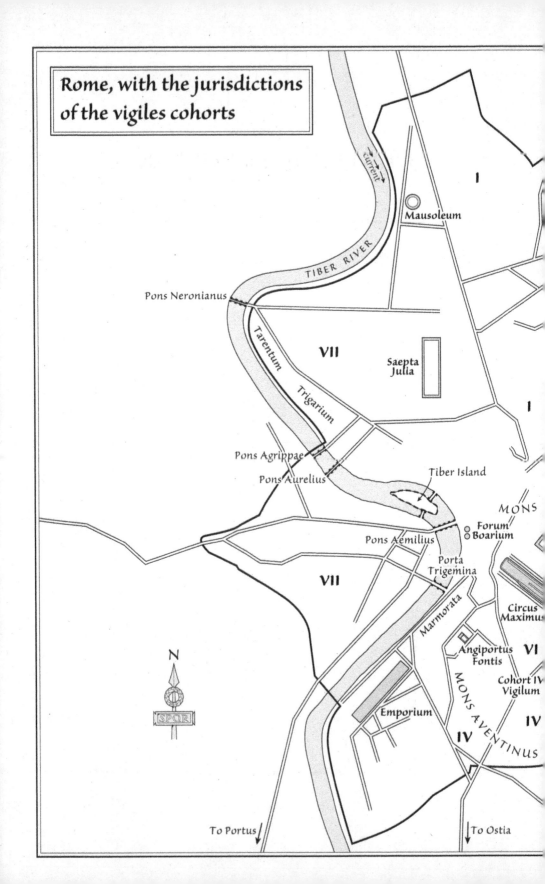

Rome, with the jurisdictions
of the vigiles cohorts

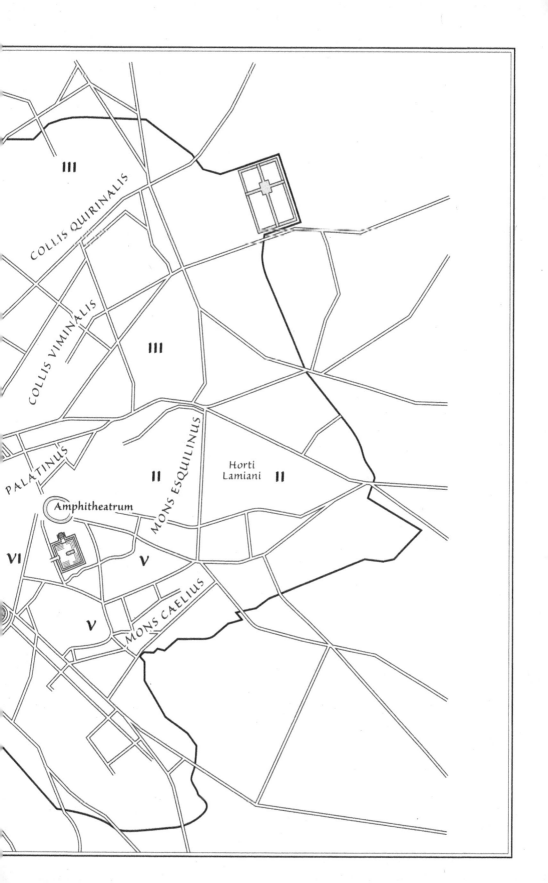

Rome and Ostia, February AD90

Colourful Characters

Family, drifting along

Flavia Albia	a talented informer, needs a commission
Tiberius Manlius Faustus	her tolerant husband, needs a column

Their household: Gaius and Lucius the dear little nephews; Gratus the smooth steward; Dromo the dim slave; Paris the cheeky runabout; Fornix the celebrity chef; Suza the hopeful beautician; Barley the shy dog; Mercury the placid donkey; Glaphyra the diligent nurse; Rodan the seedy door-keeper

Their workmen: Larcius the clerk-of-works, Sparsus, Serenus, Trypho, and Drax the watchdog

No name	the pet who has to go
Kicker	the auction-house mule
Piddle and Willikins	decoy chickens in Kicker's cart
M. Didius Falco	one-time hero; has he still got it?
Helena Justina	his wife, an absolute heroine
L. Petronius Longus	his old crony, retired from the vigiles (oh, yes?)
Maia Favonia	Falco's sister, Petro's wife, a tough woman
Rhea	Maia's daughter, noisy and determined
Petronilla	Petro's daughter, quiet and dogged
Tullus	an adorable baby (doomed?)
Marcia Didia	Falco's fearsome niece, the martial-arts supremo
Corellius Musa	her partner, a spy on sick leave

Others who bob up

Scribonius	a dredger captain who has scooped up:

Claudia Deiana	a floater, 'the Junia Delta', 'the Brittuncula'
Ulatugnus	her slave
Onocles	a priest, moonlighting as a tour guide
Cleon	his cousin in Ostia, a landlord
Tourists	thank goodness we don't meet them, except:
Margarita 'Agape'	writing intuitive *Scandi noir* (before her time)
Boy Bonivir	her Nordic hero, what a character
Itia	in property, a businesswoman, no ethics
Fundanus	dealing in death, no morals
Corneolus	a *designator*, funeral facilitator to the wealthy
Petrus	an ambitious slave, saving for his freedom
Struthio	a very big bird; keep him in his cage
Skyla	a miserable Agassian hound

On parade, riding the current
The Praetorian Guards
The Urban Cohorts

At the Castra Peregrina

a.k.a. 'Titus'	Princeps Peregrinorum, eight *phalerae*, ninth pending
Julius Karus	three gold crowns and a silver spear, imperial backing
The Varduloran cavalry	came in a package with Karus
Nicon	an undercover 'British specialist'

The Vigiles Cohorts

The First (Via Lata, Forum Romanum)
dodging the ruckus, if possible

Scorpus   enquiries, comes recommended

The Second (Isis and Serapis, Esquiline)
can't avoid it, apparently

Vergelius   tribune: close community
                                           relationships
Titianus   enquiries, just as useless as he
                                           seems
Juventus   special ops, not as useless as he
                                           looks

The Third (Temple of Peace, Alta Semita)
keeping out of it

The Fourth (Piscina Publica, Aventine)
landed with it, unfortunately: 'rigorous standards', 'honest', 'customary
thoroughness', 'competent and eager'

Cassius Scaurus   tribune: toothache and budgeting
                                           headaches
Titus Morellus   enquiries: rough and occasionally
                                           ready
Nicon   yes, him again, on secondment

The Fifth (Porta Capena, Caelimontium)
also keeping out of it

The Sixth (Palatine, Circus Maximus)
Absolutely right in it: 'those dodgy beggars', 'those sad boys', 'bunch of
idle bribe-takers'

The Seventh (Circus Flaminius, Transtiberina)
Passing it back if possible: 'those idlers', 'no reason to hurry'

Important Persons, well afloat
Prefect of the City
Rutilius Gallicus, a sick man

Prefect of the Urban Cohorts
a homeloving body

Prefect of the Vigiles
a delegator

A praetor
Corvinus: strongly worded traditional edicts

Underworld Professionals, on a turning tide
The Balbinus Pius Gang
(Circus Maximus and Aventine, expanding)

Balbinus Pius	a true villain, deceased
Cornella Flaccida	his widow, deceased
Balbina Milvia	their cute, innocent daughter, left at home by:
Florius Oppicus	her husband, recently 'abroad for business reasons'

The Ocellus Gang
(Campus Martius and Tiber South Bank, contracting)

Ocellus Gemellus	a once-violent twin, an old timer
Ocellus Gemellus	his brother, another old twin
Castor	their foot-soldier, with a contract on him

The Rabirius Gang
(Esquiline and Quirinal, expanding)

Old Rabirius	the criminal King of Kings, deceased
Rubria Theodosia (Pandora)	his sister, all too alive, a matriarch
Rabirius Vincentius	her son, recently 'abroad for business reasons'
Veronica	left at home, his embittered wife
Vincentius Theo	their talented son, deceased
Polemaena	Pandora's baleful retainer
Meröe and Kalmis	Pandora's beautiful beauticians
Young Roscius	the hopeful heir (hopeless)
Old Roscius	his ancient father, nearly deceased
'Legsie' Lucius	a runner, immobilised, deceased
Gallo	an enforcer, due for enforced sick leave
Anthos and Neo	out of sight, collecting rents
Turcus	an 'insurance agent' (the contract killer)
Mamillianus	a retained lawyer, keeping busy

The Cornellus Gang
(Aventine, doing very nicely)

Two brothers and their sister

The Terentius Gang
(Aventine, business suspended)

Two sisters and their brother	he's abroad 'for business reasons'

I

Nobody sensible takes a leisure cruise in February. Only idiots would do it: the kind of well-heeled tourists who turn up in oversized boats with music so loud that their crew cannot hear the protests from commercial craft they are swamping. Down at Ostia and Portus, outward-bound vessels are held up because the seas are stormy and unsafe, so the trippers hang around in the city, annoying the rest of us.

During the lull between Saturnalia and the big spring festivals, people here do not want them. They are too much trouble for too little profit. They catch fevers; they break ankles in potholes; they lose their cash through theft or their own carelessness. At least that makes the locals smile. Occasionally their illnesses or accidents are fatal, which is good for the funeral and carrier trade: embalming and re-patriation of corpses to distant provinces command a high price. 'Chersonesus Taurica? Ooh, that's going to come at a premium . . .' But sometimes visitors' disasters are not acci-dental. Then, if the authorities can be bothered, they may investigate. If they hire a freelance, it might even be me.

That winter, one group of emmets had arrived from northern Europe. I lived up on the Aventine tops so did not witness their disembarkation, but as a young girl I had been brought up in a house at the foot of the hill, so I had observed plenty of these characters as they paraded in their elegant travelling cloaks, pinned with *look at me!* brooches. Over the years I defined the people wearing them. The new group, I was later to learn, included the usual bigamists, blackmailers and spongers. Parents hated their children; siblings plotted against each other. Adultery was as catching as ringworm. Hanging on to those who possessed fortunes were hopeful remote relatives, bumbling doctors, cheating accountants and baleful secretariat staff. Some of the tourists had mysterious pasts – feel free to groan. All were extremely self-absorbed, and although they made a lot of noise, none seemed to be enjoying themselves.

It would emerge that the group included oddities: a would-be novelist, barred from a career because she was female; an engineer who yearned to see the Forum sewers; a man from Umbria who claimed he was interested in Egyptology, though he behaved like a spy; and a plump elderly person, who spoke in a mannered accent about a mystic search for truth. Possibly he was a druid. I had met one once. I don't waste my time on druids.

Along the way these characters had gathered up a solo female traveller wearing valuable ear-rings. She had an agenda of her own.

The main party was plodding the heritage trail. It would be too cold and wet to enjoy monumental sites, but they meant to try. In Rome, once deposited on the embankment, they strolled around, bumping into stevedores, then hurting themselves on bollards. They rebuffed hawkers, believing them to be pickpockets, but cosied up to real wharfside thieves. Porters, aiming to pick locks on jewel boxes, rushed up and offered to carry trunks, bales, lapdogs and invalid sedans; endless haggling ensued. A testy official moved the group on. They asked for the name of his superior; he answered with an obvious lie.

After these people had been led to lodgings, they complained about room sizes and the smell of drains, then hired a guide, who took the job because it was the low season, so he was desperate. At least he knew they would believe any myth he invented and they would eat lunch at his cousin's bar. He led them around the Flavian Amphitheatre, up to the golden Capitol and into the Imperial Palace with its tiring list of coloured marbles; every evening he shovelled them into more bars, where they were entertained by bare-bellied dancers and sold very nasty trinkets that fell apart in five minutes. They now owned faux-bronze lamps shaped like phalluses, and face creams with poisonous ingredients. What more could Rome possibly offer them? Time to move on.

Athens and Alexandria were calling. Off floated a river boat to take this load of cultured loafers back down to the port, where they hoped to find a freighter with passenger space, preferably with a cabin and cooking facilities. Everyone warned them no ships were likely to cross the Mediterranean for weeks, but these people were not big listeners. Tiber boats plied up and down all the time, after all. Dock workers, commercial traders, and customs officers went to and fro on legitimate business; foreigners who did not know the proper fare were always greeted with a toothless smile. I would guess that neither the captain who took them to the coast nor his half-drunk bosun bothered with a passenger headcount. Luggage may not have been properly assigned. Nor did the tourists pay attention to who came up the gangplank to board with them – or who did not.

One had been left behind.

She had not got out of bed too late to catch the boat. Nor was she smitten with a gigolo she couldn't bear to leave. She hadn't found long-lost relatives. She wouldn't be spending more time in our city because she adored its culture, cuisine and colour. She had passed her last day in Rome, though she was not leaving.

The lady with the ear-rings was now in the river, drifting among the sediment.

2

I had never thought much of the Tiber.

In Londinium, where I spent my childhood at the end of the world, the Thamesis flows wide and strong. It remains tidal as far as the new Roman capital, so shipping can move right up the channel, without prior unloading. A Customs House where traders pay their taxes stands on the north bank looking right up to the half-built forum, where bargains are struck, edicts pronounced, and where, in downsized versions of imperial temples, a mixed bunch of gods can be thanked for safe delivery. People who have survived the rough Britannic Strait often turn fervently to religion.

In Rome, as I had learned on my first arrival, the ocean approach had strong winds but was not as hellish as crossing between Britain and Gaul. Even so, landing or exporting goods involved a struggle. Everything had to progress nearly twenty miles inland from the sea by road across bleak salt marshes or via the tricky, meandering river.

Rome had come into existence at an unprepossessing spot where the river could be crossed by a muddy ford or ferry. The Tiber was two hundred and fifty miles long. It came winding down from the Apennine Mountains, crystal clear at first, then picking up as much loose material as old Father Tiberinus could suck in. Silt surged downstream, giving the molten-lead-coloured water a yellowish tinge. Fools called it the golden river; wise people never drank from it.

The Tiber pushed through the city bottleneck, its current sickly with alluvial sediment. In winter it rose and spread widely. The original habitation site had always been marsh-land, and parts remained squelchy for centuries after Romulus and Remus emerged from their hilltop huts. A couple of small historic temples had had to be built on tall perches to keep them out of repeated floods. However, in summer, there were also periods when the river was not deep enough for commercial shipping. At one point in historic times, a substantial and permanent island emerged in the middle of the stream; only bumboats could creep past, and transport beyond was operated by a guild of specialist navi-gators who were licensed for that part of the river. Bridges, bearing the names of ancient men of note, had hunched piers that caused worse blockages of sand, tree branches and any rubbish that feckless people further upstream had chucked in. Dead dogs, dumped horses and decaying human bodies were quite common.

Still, silt was the chief menace. This applied all through the city, above and below the bridges, continuing down to the sea. A new port had been built after Ostia became too sludged-up. This basin needed constant maintenance. A linking canal thickened like porridge if no one tended it. For miles out to sea, plumes of escaping silt changed the water colour from glorious blue to queasy green. To keep things as clear as possible, the authorities used dredgers.

One February day, in the glorious fifteenth consulship of our Emperor Domitian and the second of his decrepit colleague Nerva, one of these dredgers caught the attention of my husband and me. Tiberius Manlius, a building

6

contractor, had been at the great Emporium to see whether he could pick up a marble column on the cheap for a temple porch he was renovating. He was a mild man, currently seething.

Back at home we had left sick children who had passed on colds to their nursemaid, quarrelsome staff and unhappy visitors. We had run out of lamp oil and the doors to the dining room had jammed shut, just when the painters who sometimes showed up unexpectedly had indeed shown up, intent on doing a new triclinium fresco. Who ordered *The Battle of Salamis*, with dolphins on the dado? Who the hell was going to pay for it? What idiot had reckoned its rows of curly waves, trireme oars and fishy tails would dry out properly in winter? Because I, his feisty wife, was growing stressed, Tiberius had brought me out with him. He knew the adage that most murders happen domestically and he didn't want blood on our atrium mosaic. We had brought the dog with us, keeping her on a short rope because of the bustle.

In the hectic noise of the Emporium, Tiberius, too, became tetchy when a suitable piece at a suitable price could not be found. He was advised to visit the new imperial marble yard on the Field of Mars, an open-air treasure house where they might show him more useful offcuts; he dug in his heels because his grandfather, a marble importer, had never had to do that – and, besides, the word 'imperial' gave him indigestion.

We moved outside to the wharf, him chewing his lip and me now playing the tolerant partner.

'Calm down, darling.'

'I don't need to calm down.'

'Of course not . . .' Is that the oldest marital exchange in the world?

The river was crowded, which we came to realise was partly because of a hold-up caused by the cumbersome dredging vessel and a barge that took away the silt it scooped up; both were uncharacteristically moored on the Embankment.

'Hello! What's going on? Look at this!'

A queue of ferries, lighters and a few larger cargo boats were having to wait to reach the unloading wharf, though that could have been because the men who assigned berths had given up and gone for a break while they waited for a problem to be sorted. The big dredging boat was berthed at what ought to have been the busiest landing bay.

Beyond the dredger floated a flat-bottomed hopper barge, into which silt had been loaded – silt and something else. A grumbling dockhand told us the story, as he went off to get a hot toddy while everything was at a stop. The dredger had stirred up, and picked up, a corpse. This had been quickly tipped out into the hopper barge, perhaps with a view to losing it discreetly later. When people on other boats began shouting, the dredger came to shore.

No one was paying the body any attention when we arrived. On transports riding out in the river, crewmen leaned on rails with a grim patience that said they had seen this before; they hadn't been impressed on the other occasions and expected nothing better now. Lower in the water a couple of one-man skiffs had their oars laid up while men were fishing. If they had seen the corpse before it was picked up, they probably rowed around it on purpose. Don't drown yourself in the Tiber: you will be given no respect.

Someone must have called in the authorities. Milling around on the quay was a small group of vigiles troops in their red tunics; the law-and-order lads were acting officious on principle, which meant doing nothing to sort out the standstill.

I am a private informer, when home duties allow, so I noted what was happening, though with only mild curiosity. Drowned bodies were not new. I assumed this one was being dealt with as routine. Tragic, Legate. Someone fell in. Pull them out and call for a clearance cart.

Four men that I took to be the dredger's crew were being interviewed aboard by a vigiles enquirer. He was keeping them on deck, and had his note tablet out, though was not writing in it. The ex-slaves from his troop just wandered about on shore in case they found anyone to pin to a wall who might be a purse-thief, one who would hand over any stolen purses in order to be let off. Then it would be warm pies all round for the law-and-order boys.

The investigator was new. He was a moon-faced loon with a ponderous manner and I soon viewed him as useless. My uncle, Lucius Petronius, who had done that job before retirement, would already have had his troops on store-to-store enquiries all the way from here to the Aemilian Bridge – and because Petro could command respect, they would have done it properly and not have minded. One would have been singled out for finding a purse-thief while the rest diligently searched for witnesses to the death. Then Petro would have been included in the warm-pies round. Before he licked the last crumb from his beard stubble, he'd have had an idea of who the victim was and what had happened.

This new boy had much to learn.

Tiberius Manlius, in his usual way, was soon talking to the vigiles troops. They invited my ever-courteous husband to go onto the dredger. At once Tiberius strode aboard. He cut a lithe figure with good balance on the gangway and a cheery manner now that he had forgotten about his failure to find a column. He had worn his toga to the Emporium, hoping to look important if he had to haggle. It had the wide purple bands of his previous role as a magistrate, so anyone could see at once he was a man of authority. Even a courtesy title counts in Rome. He greeted the investigator, who looked baleful.

My role here as the wife meant I had to stay on land with the dog. The vigiles assumed I was scared of going up the plank onto the dredger's stern, so they offered steadying hands; I explained that, no, I had once been married to an ex-marine. I could do it. But the boat carried a rat-catcher, a short-legged, heavy-bodied, flap-eared, beagly hound, which had placed front paws on the rail and was looking down as if my genteel Barley would make him a good lunch. I had to keep them apart.

Tiberius disappeared out of view; he must have gone off the other side of the dredger and jumped down onto the hopper barge. For ease of movement, he had left his toga with a crew member. I saw the skipper break away from the enquirer and go with my husband as if he thought talking to Tiberius would be a better way to spend his morning.

I waited patiently. Wives learn to do this.

When they eventually reappeared, Tiberius called down to me that the dredger had fished out a dead woman. He added that her wrists were bound together; he had stayed on the boat in case I wanted to take an interest. He began fussing the ears of the beagly dog, which had barked at him loudly but now changed his attitude and reckoned Tiberius Manlius was the best friend he had met all week. Tiberius had that effect. He had pulled the same trick with me, so I ended up married to him.

There are various ways bodies can end up in the river: suicide, accident, people too mean to pay for a normal funeral – or murder. Bound wrists indicated foul play. Even so, I wanted to avoid being drawn in. I had recently finished a complex investigation and I had a load of domestic trouble waiting for me at home.

I knew it would be kind to identify the deceased, for her sake and that of her family. Of course that assumed it wasn't her own relatives who had done her in. Typically, your murderer is somebody you know. Where that happens, sometimes my role is to let the relatives know politely that suspicion has fallen on them.

The fact she had been tied up niggled me more than it bothered the officials. I could see they were not intending to do much. I also knew that if the boatmen were left with the problem, they would quietly tip the corpse back into the water. They would know where to drop her so the current would swing her across to the other side. Perhaps a different cohort over there would take more action, though more likely not. I had worked with the Seventh in the Transtiberina – those lads did not like putting themselves out any more than the Fourth did over here.

'Are you coming up?' asked Tiberius, not even bothering to grin at me. He knew I could not resist. I was already fastening Barley to a bollard. The vigiles, who *were* grinning, promised to look after our dog; they held out hands, but I skipped up the gangway unaided as my first husband had taught me. My second husband then received me on deck like a man whose day had improved. No doubt he imagined that if he could finesse the vigiles, I would acquire a new case with a fee from the Fourth's budget that would pay for those fresco dolphins of ours.

No chance. The Fourth Cohort's tribune was Scaurus, a notorious tight-fisted misery. He hated to lash out on consultants, even if their solutions beefed up his charge sheet for the Prefect of Vigiles. The prefect himself would rather spend petty cash on lady friends; this was a known fact. Scaurus could not afford a mistress: he was embroiled in a very expensive divorce. It had made him even more bitter. He saw freelance help as unnecessary; he would rather shove difficult case-notes under a pile of rope and forget about them. I was a particular bugbear. In my time I had impressed most of his colleagues with some quiet success, even though I knew none of them would want me around permanently. But every time Scaurus had a drink with one of the other tribunes, they chaffed him: 'Isn't Flavia Albia on your patch, that Falco's daughter? You must find her really helpful when your dopey squad gets in a mess!'

Scaurus would choke if I took on the dredged-up lady. That thought almost made it worth doing.

3

The barge felt quite firm at its moorings. It was something like thirty feet long, a solid, powerful working boat with a towing mast near the front; ropes would be fastened when moving the vessel by man- or ox-power along a river or canal, though the mast was currently folded down. Machinery on one end had lines that went to an open dredging well in the centre. There a strong straight arm descended through the deck, presumably with a scoop at its far end, now at rest from its job of lifting mud and scouring the river bottom.

The deck felt gritty underfoot. The crew, wide men in battered boots, looked full of grit too. River people. A different tribe from shore workers. Not necessarily compliant with civic authorities, but too canny to appear rebellious.

Without reference to my husband, I went straight to the vigiles enquirer. 'I am Flavia Albia, Falco's daughter, wife to Faustus.' I nodded at Tiberius. He let me do the introductions, easy with it. Giving a woman this much freedom in public was rare. As a social concept, the enquirer did not like it.

'Nicon,' returned the newbie, the least he could possibly give out. His one-word answer did not explain his position, nor acknowledge my mention of my male relatives and the suggestion they were important around here. Even so, his manner was ultra-polite, which to me meant slippery.

'Are you new to the Fourth?'

'Recent posting.'

'Working under Titus Morellus?' I pressed, still trying to establish my local credentials.

'You know him?'

'Oh, I taught him all he knows.' Morellus would probably say it was the other way around, but he wasn't on hand to contradict. Nicon conspicuously failed to clarify whether Morellus was his superior. Already I hoped Morellus took precedence. He had his sleazy side, but we had come to tolerate him and he accepted us. His wife brought their children to our house to play with the two boys we had fostered. I wouldn't mention that friendly relationship in case it made Nicon feel excluded. 'My husband recently stood down as a magistrate. We have cooperated with Titus Morellus on a couple of sensitive issues – the needle killer, the Terentius gang . . .' No reaction.

'I'm sure you'll soon settle in. Morellus is a good man,' I said.

Tiberius was gesturing me to go to the side and look over at the dead woman. Although Nicon stopped questioning the dredger-men and followed, standing fairly close to us, he made no attempt to survey the body in the hopper barge. He was watching Tiberius and me.

No question that the corpse below us was female; she was barefoot, though clothed in a good gown and stole. She was lying face up, slightly twisted, as she must have fallen when the crew tipped her into the barge. Water must have been streaming off the body at first, pulling away the stored grey sediment from immediately beneath her; now the flow had virtually stopped, simply pooling on the bed of silt. From her appearance she had not been in the river long before either the dredger banged into her as she drifted or it took her up from lying on the river-bed.

She looked about my age. Older perhaps, not younger. Mid to late thirties: life behind her, life still ahead.

She would have been good-looking. She had been healthy and well looked-after too. Dark hair had been fancily arranged, though pins had washed out in the river so tangling strands dragged free. Did she have a maid, or had she spent time on that hairstyle herself? Where was the maid now, if one existed?

A cloak in two colours had been pinned around her, but tide or trauma had pulled it diagonally down from one shoulder. The visible necklines of a white undertunic and the woollen *palla* over it were scooped, enough to allow sight of her neck, which had a thin red mark. Even from above, on the dredger, I could see the binding on her wrists that Tiberius had mentioned. She was not planning suicide: someone else had tied her hands.

'Do you want to go down?'

I shook my head. No point. He had inspected her. In confirmation of his basic search, Tiberius opened one palm. He showed me a single ear-ring that he must have removed: with a secure hook-and-loop fastener, it had a substantial oval setting that held a cabochon garnet, large and hardly flawed; the bezel was edged in gold granulation and a short ring system was suspended from the lower edge with a knobbly pearl of expensive size. 'Somebody provides pricey presents – or else he needed to compensate for a really big sin. Only one?' I asked.

Tiberius nodded, resigned to the loss of its pair, but the skipper, who had come to the rail on our far side (avoiding

Nicon), at once said something to one of his crew. The man sprang down into the hopper barge, then hauled the body to and fro so he could check under her for any other treasures, shaking her garments. He found a brooch, still tangled in the folds of her cloak, though it had been wrenched off and was only caught in the material by a badly bent pin. Shoving one hand down the neck of her tunic, he then brought out a broken chain; when it snapped, it had probably caused the neck mark.

'He's less squeamish than me!' Tiberius muttered.

'Wedding ring?' I called down. The man picked up her bound hands, checked all her white fingers, shook his head.

'No pendant? Nothing on the chain?' Tiberius tried. The crewman had a good feel again. The woman had gone beyond modesty. Still, I was glad when he stopped fumbling with her and clambered back aboard the dredger. He passed the brooch and chain to me. The brooch was small but gorgeous: copper, set with red, blue and yellow enamel, a coiled dragonesque beast created by an artist with a clearly northern imagination.

Tiberius put me in charge of the ear-ring too. Women's work. 'If these goodies were left behind when she was killed, the motive was not robbery.'

To cover distaste about how the tragic haul was recovered, I asked, 'I presume nobody knows who she is?'

'Never seen her,' confirmed the skipper, sounding bleak.

Nicon stood completely still on my other side, not speaking. I turned to him. 'She's not a bar-girl or a fishwife. Somebody is bound to miss the woman. She owned valuables, and you can see she had style.'

'Seems likely,' Nicon forced out.

'I want her off my barge!' The skipper finally vented his frustration. 'If you're not prepared to take her, just lose yourselves and we'll dispose of the remains.'

'Nobody is refusing you assistance, my friend,' Nicon assured him, with those unconvincing mild manners. 'We shall do whatever is necessary.'

I hated to think of this poor woman's murder being ignored. 'It looks as if identifying her will be next to hopeless. You could put up a notice in the Forum,' I suggested. 'Ask people to come forward.' Nicon gave me a look. I toughened up. 'My husband and I know your tribune. Would you like us to have a word with Cassius Scaurus?'

That would be a long shot. The Fourth's commander ran his cohort on a basis he would call 'hands off'. He might agree to my idea of a notice, assuming he could find a clerk who could write and who knew where the Forum Romanum was, but he would never suggest such a thing himself. For one thing, if an appeal brought in a response, someone would have to deal with it. He was bound to say he had no one available for the work – it might even be true. We'd gone a month since Saturnalia, but the vigiles had partied hard. They would still be short-staffed due to headaches, bad stomachs, and wives having sent them to drive Auntie Julia home to Praeneste after the holiday.

Taking his toga from the crewman, Tiberius backed me up. 'Somebody killed her. That cannot be overlooked. A small reward might help.'

'I don't imagine she will be a *Junia Delta* for long,' replied Nicon. 'Nice trappings, as you have pointed out.' He did not ask me to hand over the evidence. In fact, he gave a nod to the skipper, then set off back to the quay.

17

Skittering down the gangway after him, I kept up the helpful act. 'Fundanus is a funeral director the Fourth use for homicides.' I played it as if Nicon was so new that I supposed nobody had briefed him.

'Fundanus? Yes, we can bring him in on this.'

'He lurks near the Circus. Morellus knows where.'

'We can find him.' Nicon still made no response to my mention of Morellus. I had reprieved his name as a test; once again, the new man ignored it.

I kept playing nice, though it was becoming a strain. 'I'm sure you will do what you can for the poor soul, Nicon. Nobody deserves to die in this way – there are people out there who know how she went into the water, people who did it.'

'If so, we shall find them,' answered Nicon. He had all the complacency of a yelled-at rat, glaring as it promises to leave your rubbish heap.

'You know nothing about her, unfortunately, but at least you can give out a description of what she is wearing.'

That was a mistake on my part.

The vigiles who had been looking after my dog gave her back; they must have spent time talking among themselves about who I was and my past history. After Nicon said they must organise a corpse collection, his troops weighed in. A body that was so conspicuously well-dressed was beyond their expertise, they claimed. It showed they must have inspected her at some point before Tiberius and I arrived.

While I stared, they kept going. Since the woman's garments included a chequered cloak, it was decreed that no proper Roman wears plaid: the *Junia Delta* must be a visitor, *Junia Britannica*. Obviously I, Flavia Albia, the well-known adoptee from Londinium, was the right person to establish her fate.

Tiberius was keen, though I could see Nicon felt he had been pushed into this. He didn't want the anonymous woman investigated by anyone, certainly not me. Perhaps he was afraid I might do a better job than him. And I would do.

My husband was folding his toga over one arm, so the status bands showed. 'You could probably use local expertise while you're finding your feet in the cohort, Nicon. Is there any slack in the budget for inquiry expenses?'

'Not for me to say.' Nothing was for Nicon to say. We had gathered that.

I still felt resistant. My childhood had been bleak; I did not want to remember Britain.

But something else was niggling me. The vigiles never welcomed homicide inquiries, yet they would normally make a token effort to investigate. Their lack of curiosity struck me as suspect. Even the squaddies now gazed over the river, not wanting to meet my gaze, while Nicon's mix of smarm and reticence reeked of duplicity. I decided the Fourth Cohort knew more than they were saying.

4

Led by the dog, who felt we had been hanging about for too long, Tiberius and I walked home. Neither spoke. We were each considering whether to slip out alone to the station-house, to quiz Titus Morellus about his new colleague.

We did not need to. By the time I had sorted out domestic stress, and Tiberius had muttered to his clerk-of-works about the marble situation, Morellus arrived of his own accord. 'What naughty people have been upsetting our new recruit?'

'Your horrible nongle upset us, with his nonchalant style.'

'Oh, he's all right. Sharp as a claw once he gets going. People think the world of him, they tell me.' Impossible to tell whether this commendation was vigiles black humour, or if Morellus was even dimmer than I had always thought.

We took him into my small interview room, away from squealing slaves and truculent children. He had slimmed down after an illness but still carried himself with a wide-armed strut as if his body remembered being overweight; his head had been shaved with a blunt razor a week ago, there was no nap left on his sweaty red tunic, and he had a bruise by his left eye that might have been caused by a criminal lashing out or by his exasperated wife swinging a broom at him. He wouldn't care either way.

I dodged around furniture to escape his hideous hug. He lunged at me once on principle, then gave up, choosing instead to fall into the wicker chair that was supposed to be mine. I had to perch on the seat I kept for clients. Tiberius leaned in the doorway, holding one of his nephews on his hip, while he made a good job of nose-wiping. While we were out, my mother had taken away the boys' sick nursemaid because Glaphyra was a family treasure who needed to be properly looked after. It solved one problem but left us in sole charge of our three- and five-year-olds.

'Why are the Fourth ignoring the drowned woman?' I demanded at once. I hate to mess about.

'Forget pleasantries, Flavia Albia. *How are you these days, dear Titus, how is your lovely wife surviving, do your nippers all have snotty noses that they must have picked up from the snivellers here?* Answer: pissed off, out of her mind as usual, and, yes, they bloody do. I'm up to my eyes in porch-crawlers and arsonists, so don't bother me with floaters. The boys in red are supposed to be firefighters, not half-arsed criminalists. Some tourist gives herself a rope-and-gag thrill, then chucks herself off the Pons Aemilius, that should be her own lookout.'

'She was gagged?' asked Tiberius, quickly. He put down Lucius, giving him a pat so he scampered off. 'I never saw that.'

'In Nicon's notes. Some sort of neck scarf.'

'What notes?' I demanded. 'He took no notes when I was there.'

'You must have tripped along after he collected details. I think he's using the scarf to clean his scabbard.'

Crossly, I picked at more queries. 'Off the Pons Aemilius? Who said that? Were there witnesses?'

'No idea.' Morellus rearranged his tunic folds by giving a huge slobby shrug.

'The dredger crew told me the same, Albia.' Tiberius had arranged himself on a couch. 'They worked it out from where they found the deceased in the current. So she had been grabbed, immobilised and silenced. Does nobody plan to investigate?'

'We always do what we can, Aedile. Public service. Just up our street.'

'That's tripe,' Tiberius rebuked him bluntly. When I first met him, I had thought him pretty rude; now I generally chortled along with his verdicts. 'Nicon seemed to have finished asking questions.'

'He's a fast worker.'

'We didn't see any work occurring!'

'He wouldn't talk to you. He's funny like that. He nipped back up to barracks, like a gigolo up a skirt, screaming who in Hades were you two busybodies. I ought to have briefed him that you hang about making life difficult – as if clear-ups like this aren't hard enough.'

'All the more reason to accept help,' I said.

'He'll tie up any loose ends.'

'He won't!' I snorted.

'We all know how to do our job.'

'Oh, yes! You certainly know how to arrest innocent family members or pressurise business partners,' I chivvied Morellus scathingly. 'You can bully anybody into a confession, even when there is no proper suspect and all known associates have really strong alibis.' He might be wriggling at my assessment but remained unrepentant. 'Titus Morellus! "Making diligent enquiries" has always been the Fourth's watchword. All it means is someone pays a boy to yell, "Smoke!" so the troops can rush away with fire-buckets to avoid questions about their lack of progress.'

'Don't be like that, Albia. We never have to pay that boy. He does it from pure mischief.'

'From what I have seen,' Tiberius agreed in milder tones, 'when they have no fire to combat, and if your men are tired or bored, they quite like quizzing people about crimes.'

'All right.' Morellus finally caved in. 'It can be a bit of fun. It lets us batter suspects and sometimes brings in bribe money.'

'So what about the dredger woman?' I insisted. 'Nicon doesn't even care who she was, let alone who did for her.'

Morellus pretended he was watching a spider on the ceiling.

There wasn't one. Gratus had gone around with a sponge on a pole only that week. Now daylight was increasing, my steward was tutting over webs that had suddenly become visible. They didn't bother me. I had lived above the Eagle Laundry in Fountain Court. I never grow excited over any pest less than a foot long.

'You are hedging,' Tiberius told Morellus, back with his pleasant tone but unrelenting. 'Why don't the Fourth want to investigate?'

'That's just Nicon.'

'Is he incompetent then – or lazy?'

'Don't be fooled by the impression he gives. He'll be all over it, like mange on a donkey.'

I guffawed. 'You are saying he just took against us?'

'Unimpressed by our charisma and charm?' Tiberius joined in.

'He's new, Aedile. Nobody explained. Aren't you out of office nowadays anyway?'

'He can still be a concerned citizen. We were helping,' I argued, hard-nosed as a Forum statue. 'We picked up clues.

Made good suggestions. We even managed not to call Nicon a useless puffball.'

'We offered him the skills of a top-class investigator, with decent rates and proven experience,' asserted Tiberius.

'You got up his nose!'

'Apologies, if so. Where did this bum originate?' Tiberius slid in. 'Another vigiles cohort, or is he a legionary import?'

'Can't say.' Unfazed, Morellus gave the impression he knew perfectly well. He was prevaricating with the easy grace of a man who had been warned that his tribune would have him washing down the yard with a mouse's tail if he failed to warn us off.

Tiberius kept going: 'Relocated from snoozing in a fort in Galatia or Cappadocia? What will a frontier-watcher ever know about city crime?'

'Nicon comes with all his warts polished and a glowing résumé.'

'So, he's a turd.'

'Well, he does have a nasty whiff, Aedile . . . Look, we think he's been drafted in for an audit. The lads keep moving the esparto mats from store to store to stop him counting them, and Scaurus has put together a good story about why there are so many requests for new grapplers.'

'He wasn't imposed on you by Scaurus himself, then?' I shot in. Light dawned. 'This man is assigned to a special operation!' I let my disgust show. 'A bureaucratic exercise!'

'Some commissariat rubbish.' Tiberius caught on at once.

'What my father would call a time-wasting farrago, dreamed up by an ambitious no-hoper. Of course, the pea-brain Nicon will disappear before the pointlessness and cost of his ideas become too obvious.'

'Now, Albia, be fair!' Morellus shifted in my chair. I might have to have its cushions fumigated.

'That was the fair version. In your hierarchy, Morellus, does he report to you – or do you work for him?'

'Neither. Independent.' Morellus paused. 'Except where lines of operation may happen to cross.'

'And have they crossed over the dredger woman?'

'She is neither here nor there. The skipper reported her because of her being tied up like that. When word was brought up to us, I was out getting some salami rolls to keep me going, so Nicon took an interest. He's the type who brings in his own dinky packet of pickled radishes to peck at – what have we been landed with? Aren't soldiers supposed to forage in scary forests for grubs, or at least steal from bakeries? Look, Albia, one way or another, we'll do the necessary. Even for a visitor from weird Britannia.'

'How do you know that?' I demanded, on it like a whippet. 'She might be from anywhere. Don't give me the pathetic line that she wore a Celtic cloak – she could have bought that off an imports stall in the Market of Livia.'

Morellus had concentrated for too long. He forgot he was trying to be deceptive. 'She was as British as your pert arse – she admitted it shamelessly.'

'Admitted it?' I hid my triumph at extracting this. 'Are you telling me the Fourth actually met her? Did you talk to her yourself?'

'No, she went to the main barracks. Vicus Piscinae bloody Publicae. Some tour guide brought her up the hill a few days ago. Scaurus had a word.'

'*Scaurus?* Since when does your elevated tribune converse with female travellers?'

Morellus looked shifty, as if he wouldn't tell me the reason. 'He can be polite to women.'

'He's never been polite to me!'

'You're stroppy.'

'She wasn't?'

'She was teary, I believe. She was searching for her husband – well, that's what she called him. You know the story. A trader has lived abroad for years, then decides he's homesick. He packs spare tunics into his hand luggage and does a runner without telling his bedmate.'

'She didn't accept it?'

'She followed him.'

'She could afford the journey?'

'He must have left her a nest-egg. Presumably he regrets that now!'

'Was Scaurus sympathetic to her plight?'

'He's all right with plights – he's an officer. He took a few notes.'

'Oh, lovely! I didn't think he could write.'

'He got the clerk to scribble details.'

'Will he find the runaway husband?'

'Of course not. But he promised to look – he promised most sincerely.'

'I feel sick, just thinking of him lying like that!'

'Did she give him a bribe?' sniggered Tiberius, all man-of-the-world for Morellus's benefit.

'That I wouldn't know, my friend. She may not have been savvy enough. She thought anyone can come to the vigiles with a sob-story and file a missing-person claim, then nice men with consciences will turn up at her lodgings with her lost chick. We only follow up on runaway slaves. If she was Roman, she would have known that. Chase *them* down like a pack of lions.'

'You have to have rules in a civilised community,' Tiberius reflected drily.

'Too right! Plus we get a sweetener when we return slaves to their loving masters . . .'

'Who will undoubtedly beat them senseless. What lodgings was she at?' I asked sweetly.

'Some doss. How would I know?'

'Who's your scribe at the main station-house?'

'He's a nice boy. Don't you interfere with him, Flavia!'

'What's the husband?' Tiberius lobbed in. Though we each seemed to have our own ideas, we were working as a team.

'Businessman apparently. Property, import/export, usual crap. I believe she mentioned horse-racing. Middle ranker, she said. So Scaurus had to spell it out for her: an equestrian must be worth upwards of a hundred thousand sesterces to receive his gold status ring, so with that kind of collateral he's allowed to hide from any women he gets tired of. Free citizen's traditional right to dump and flit.'

'Naturally this duped girl suspected he had left a wife behind in Rome,' I speculated, 'which naturally was the truth.'

'You are not wrong, you darling. Bright as well as beautiful! She ought to have quietly let him go. Some women don't know how to follow the rules,' Morellus grouched. Then he sat up straight and formally addressed me with the vigiles' line: 'You see what it means, young Flavia, so do not trouble your clever self about who will solve it. Nicon won't need divining skills. We know everything already. Junia Britannica came looking for her man – and if she was drowned in the river by somebody, the verdict is, clearly, she must have found him.'

5

The notion that the Junia Britannica had been done in by the man she was chasing had logic; it was bound to appeal to the vigiles. Morellus even argued that this man posed no risk to society: suppose, in the course of his trading activities, he had abandoned women in provinces all over the empire, most would understand it was their role to be deserted. He kept moving on as traders do. His women would remain where he left them, condemned to poverty, no doubt, but safe in their humble hutments. There was no reason for this congenital flitter to bind their hands and drown them.

If he had a real wife in Rome, he had gone back to her. That would be what he had promised her years ago, and what he had always intended. She must be happy to have him – though she would not welcome a plaid-wearing floozy from overseas on the doorstep, especially if younger and prettier, as floozies by vigiles' definition always were. Sonny had had to get rid of the travelling girlfriend, and he'd had to do it quick. So he had thrown the Britannica into the Tiber to prevent domestic damage. With her gone, everything was sorted.

'He must have come home to be a good boy. Hang up his trophies. Count all the loot he's made. Settle himself back into Rome. Maybe he's getting on a bit now, creaking more than he used to. All he wants is a peaceful retirement.'

'That's gone wrong, then!' I sniffed.

When I asked if Junia Britannica had a proper name, Morellus went all vague on me. The same went for any identity for the husband. So, no handle on the wife in Rome either.

That wife could live anywhere on the Seven Hills – though why did the Britannica go to the station-house on the Aventine specifically? In Rome there were seven main vigiles barracks, with seven more out-stations attached to them, ensuring that all fourteen administrative districts were covered by law-and-order. It sounded as if the visitor had known where to look when she tried to make enquiries.

'I could help you find these people, Titus. I have methods.'

'No budget.'

'Come on, I'm good.'

'You are good,' he conceded. 'Just bloody hopeless at listening. We have got it sorted. SPQR. Amateurs, keep out.'

'If I could find the husband, you could pay me from the cash you are going to squeeze out of him if he wants to avoid the murder court. As a long-distance businessman, he is bound to be loaded with money chests.'

Morellus stood up to leave, making my wicker chair creak dangerously even now he had lost some flab. As he rose, he emphasised his point with a barely suppressed fart. 'We are not going to pay you, Flavia, because, like I told you, this man has disposed of his personal problem, so he now poses no danger to anybody else. I am telling you straight. We shall deal with him in our own time and our own way. Leave it alone.'

I didn't bother to retort there was no possibility I would do that.

6

Tiberius would be aware of my feelings. Since our door porter was feeling under the weather, which was Rodan's normal state, my husband took Morellus to the door. He came back fuming. He had tried to extract more information, but Morellus just fled.

That did not stop Tiberius Manlius Faustus, once a formidable plebeian aedile. His recent year as a magistrate had given him ask-a-favour rights with top men in Rome. He would play community activist and make a visitation. He expected the Fourth Cohort's tribune only to say the same as Morellus – indeed, it could have been the tribune who had ruled out further action. Scaurus called himself a details man: he would fiddle about with bath-house thieves, of whom there was always a rash, then believe that preventing a few stolen tunics made him worth a laurel wreath, without getting bogged down in murders. We had plenty of those too. Morellus normally dealt with them. As an inquiry chief, he was no more than adequate, but for most people adequate was surprising enough. We lived in a cynical neighbourhood.

My husband viewed Cassius Scaurus as cautiously as a cracked amphora of scallops. Scaurus was not worth approaching. He could not even decide whether rain was likely if water was soaking through his hat and dribbling into his gummy eyes.

Up a level: Tiberius was quiet at lunch. Then, without consultation, he took off in his toga and a warm cloak to inflict his qualms upon a higher personality. When his slave, Dromo, failed to appear in a timely fashion to escort him, Tiberius tossed a curse his way, then quickly went off alone.

I had guessed what he was up to. Tiberius Manlius was heading to the Prefect of Vigiles. This was the personage who, when criminals were apprehended, decided whether to make formal charges. I thought his well-trained staff would never let a man with a complaint through the front door.

They did. Tiberius must have used his charm.

In late afternoon he came home. He let himself in, threw his cloak onto a giant Greek vase we kept in the atrium, tore off his toga, walked into the courtyard with barely a snarl at Dromo, who was now moaning because he had been left behind.

I offered a cheek for a kiss. Then I slid one arm around him, holding him close. Since I had risen to greet him, I stood on his foot too. 'Where have you been, wanderer?'

'Out.'

'Don't answer like a five-year-old. We get enough of that around here.'

He worked his foot free, but once I grab a man I cling on. 'Seeing someone.'

'Who?'

'The wrinkled prune who commands all the vigiles cohorts.'

'Any good?'

'Everything is under control, he claims, so I should back off.'

'Same as Morellus. So?'

'When I wouldn't play nice, he sent me elsewhere.'

'To whom?'

'His grander colleague, in charge of the Urban Cohorts.'

'Juno! You went inside the Praetorian Camp?' That was scary.

Tiberius embroidered humorously as he kept trying to break free from me. 'No, he never bothers with the Camp. The Urbans' commander was having a snooze in his rather nice house on the Esquiline, as he does every afternoon while his riot-boppers keep order for him. He says he can't stand violence. He nearly received some from me because he tried to send me back to the Prefect of Vigiles. When I threatened to go over both their heads to the Prefect of the City, he did change his story and hurriedly said there was no need to bother poor Rutilius Gallicus.'

Gallicus was Domitian's virtual deputy. Pretending to look impressed, I tightened my grip again.

'Ow! Our Master may not see his godlike self as needing a substitute, which is fortunate because Rutilius is on furlough. It's known he is not a well man.'

'Overworked and heartbroken. His preferment dates from Vespasian. Liberal values. He hates to watch Domitian screwing Rome with his paranoia.'

'If Rutilius is having a nervous breakdown, I cannot harass the poor soul. I just mentioned to the Urbans' big rissole that your father, Albiola, is friendly with Rutilius. Implied that Falco knows him well. Tapped my nose and murmured that they share past history in North Africa and are fellow poets . . .'

'So the grand Urbanistus threw up his hands, crying, "Oh, you are Falco's son-in-law? Let me order a fresh bowl of nuts!" My pa will be thrilled by this recognition.' I chortled, not believing a word of it.

'Not quite. He wanted to know if I was the aedile who was struck by lightning.' That made sense. People were always fascinated. Tiberius admitted ruefully, 'Once I began telling him what that had felt like and how long the bruises lasted, we got along splendidly.'

'He told you everything?'

'I think he told me enough.' Tiberius was pretending to be diffident about his achievement. He was also about to be miserly with the truth.

What followed was a curious conversation, both for what was revealed and what was withheld.

The Urban Prefect had spilled enough to make the vigiles grumble at his openness. He did know of the case. The woman pulled from the Tiber had called herself Claudia Deiana. She had travelled from Britain to look for a man she had lived with for more than ten years, the father of her young children. She described him as an entrepreneur. He liked to install migrants he brought over from other provinces, some of them to do work no one had previously thought of.

I was able to explain to Tiberius that in Britain, where towns had been razed and burned in the Boudiccan Revolt, land that lay unclaimed was made available by the adminis- tration, seeking to revitalise the shattered province. It was what had happened after the Vesuvius eruption in Campania too. To make Britain Roman, people were needed – that is, not the people who already lived there, whose own culture had to be ruthlessly displaced so *they* could be given Roman values.

All kinds of tradesmen were being encouraged to take advantage of new opportunities in Britain: potters, glass- makers, leatherworkers, brickmakers, jewellers, wine and oil importers. Bath-houses were being built, which called for staff who knew how to run such places. Temples required experienced priests: Britons loved writing curse tablets and wanted shrines where, for a fee, they might deposit their furious denunciations. Building trades had flooded in. Lawyers and educators were sent, armed with scrolls of jurisprudence and literature, for use after they had worked through alphabet blocks for writing and teach-yourself-Latin playlets. With large numbers of troops stationed in the capital and on the frontier, civilians had also arrived in some numbers to staff the legions' places of entertainment: the amphitheatre, bars and brothels.

Remembering the brothels gave me a personal chill. If Tiberius noticed, he avoided the issue. 'Toga-makers,' he suggested instead. 'If you are encouraging tribes to come down from their windy hill forts to inhabit towns, speak Latin, bathe, start suing one another, then stand around chatting in forums, they must be properly dressed. Kitting out an entire nation that used to wear woolly shirts and fur must demand big warehouses of togas – or the cloth for them to be made to order.'

I agreed. 'Is that what the flitting husband did? Flooded the market with symbolic woollen garments?'

No. Tiberius told me Claudia Deiana had said her husband invested in urban property. This provided a healthy income, although they themselves lived quietly in a rural villa somewhere down south. The man might have preferred anonymity, but eventually he attracted notice from the governor's office. One day he was summoned to Londinium for a meeting about his business practices. He had to attend: they had sent an armed escort.

Word then came back to the villa that he had shipped out for Rome. 'Recalled for family business', he called it, although whoever was exerting pressure, it was not his British family. And if the governor's office had ejected him from the province, it sounded as if his return to Italy was not simply personal but permanent.

Once Claudia Deiana received word of the situation, she set off in pursuit. Expecting to come home eventually, she left behind her children, whose portraits she had on a plaque hanging from a chain – the gold neck-chain that had now been found on her corpse, broken and with the plaque missing. At the Fourth Cohort's barracks she had shown Cassius Scaurus her memento. Scaurus was not interested, but he sat up as soon as he twigged that her husband was someone on his persons-to-look-for list.

Why ever was that?

'Who is this man, Tiberius?'

'Some past villain who'd been away so long the vigiles forgot him.' The property investor had never been convicted of a crime in Rome, nor was he officially in exile; he had not been given 'time to depart' from the empire after a serious offence. So when he found himself in too much hot water in Britain, he must have thought he could return to Rome, his place of birth and original domicile.

'If he lived outside Italy,' I pressed again, 'why did he end up lingering on a list in Rome's Thirteenth Region?'

Tiberius thought the Fourth Cohort wanted to talk to him because he had connections in their jurisdiction and, presumably, his connections were of the wrong kind. Rome wanted him for worse, however. As the Urban Prefect had revealed, there was a good reason to look at this man: he was obviously prosperous – yet had never filed a head-of-household report for the Census. So he had paid no taxes.

Good grief, it was an outrage!

We lived in an empire with a highly developed bureaucracy. Rome was currently ruled by an emperor who had made himself Censor for life. That meant not simply counting heads nor even forbidding people to fornicate, all of which Domitian did with tyrannical zeal. The Censor's driving purpose was to assess everyone for tax. Dodging your assessment was criminal behaviour. Few people were charged with it, because if they were rich enough to make diddling the Treasury worthwhile, they could afford lawyers to fend off prosecutions. It is a tenet of democracy that any millionaire can make an accidental mistake, for which, if exposed, the sensitive oligarch should be let off with a gentle fine. Nevertheless, each citizen has a duty to keep full personal accounts and to make them visible when called for (even if a nice clean version is carefully written up for public view).

Roman bureaucracy worked, and it was never soft. On a large scale, neglect of fiscal reporting might offend the Censor's Office enough for them to put the squeeze on a suspect individual. Their agents possessed that favourite tool: draconian powers. An inquiry was to be fended off at all costs – 'cost' being a key feature of the pain those official agents could impose. My father used to help Vespasian with this. Falco loved the work and made substantial sums for himself, plus an uplift in his social rank as a reward. Father would never work for Domitian, but Domitian still inflicted swingeing punishment on defaulters. He would use informers, though not ones like Falco, let alone me.

Pursuing financial crimes was rare for the vigiles, who were firefighters first and burglar-catchers second. But an all-cohorts seek-and-find list for tax defaulters had been compiled. A couple of months ago, the Fourth had had a sighting of the dodgy entrepreneur from Britain. Superiors felt moved to act. Tiberius had been told that the man we met, Nicon, had been put in charge of a commission of inquiry. Nicon happened to be in Rome on secondment from a legion in Britain, so he was considered ideal. He knew at first hand how that remote province worked; he would have expertise in interrogating someone who had operated in that part of the world. At least he would, if he ever caught him.

So, on assignment to the Fourth Cohort, Nicon was now chasing down the culprit, the supposed husband of Claudia Deiana. She was a low priority. Drowning his concubine was of minimal interest, although if the vigiles believed that the husband was responsible they might perhaps use it as an excuse to call him in. For whatever reason the authorities in Britain had challenged him, his business affairs there were mainly irrelevant; what officials in Rome were eager to pursue was straightforward tax dodging.

'So,' suggested Tiberius, sounding typically reasonable. 'You and I have expressed our concern,' I liked his 'you and I', though not enough to be mollified. 'They seem to have answered us fairly. I do feel we can stand back and leave everything to take its natural course.'

I smiled at him like a meek partner who had been convinced by wise words. My tombstone would say I ran the home by never quarrelling. He was not fooled.

Neither was I.

For many reasons, including my work in the past, I understood how the drowned woman had felt when she saw that she was linked to a man she could no longer trust. I sympathised with the angry spirit that must have led her to follow him to Rome. Unless her husband was prone to domestic violence, she cannot have imagined that her journey would be the death of her. Even so, she might have begun to fear that their coming to this city would have tragic consequences.

She and I had things in common. I, too, was being forced to reassess the man I loved. Tiberius had given me a cogent explanation, yet I could see he was holding back: I believed he knew more. I had asked him at least one question that he had deliberately failed to answer. And when I uncovered the truth, Claudia and I would be joint members of a new kind of sisterhood.

7

I never supposed Tiberius was lying to me. Everything he had just told me would be true. But he was certainly capable of dissembling. Nowadays he was a man everyone liked, with a fine reputation for ethics and honesty, even for piety – yet when he was younger, he had been no stranger to shame. Crucially, his first marriage had ended after he cheated on his wife.

I had instinctively taken against Laia Gratiana, the superior, fleshless blonde he had married first. It gave me sneaky pleasure that Tiberius had once enjoyed extra-marital activities in sordid circumstances that had destroyed friendships and wrecked marriages. He had fibbed; he acted innocent; he spent time with other people, never taking Laia; eventually he had fallen onto a more voluptuous couch than he had at home with his wife.

He said theirs was a union purely for property reasons. I believed he had married me because I was a very different woman. Every bride thinks that, of course. So many clients of mine had claimed, 'He is totally changed, now he is with me. I am the one.' Fooling themselves.

Only part fooling, in fact, because they came to me when doubts bubbled up. In most cases I had to present them with damning evidence that their man had not changed at all. He was the usual, often serial, philanderer. Sometimes a deluded wife clung on, still convinced she would reform him, believing he would go along with it because, in the hackneyed phrase, she was the one.

I did not believe mine was womanising. He never raided the housekeeping; he wore no unusual unguents lately; with his new career in building renovation he simply did not have time for an affair. He loved me. Although nobody had expected it from me, he knew that I loved him.

What worried me was my feeling that Tiberius was keeping things to himself. I was the informer, he had his own interests, but we worked together. Solving a crime was how we had first met and quickly fallen in love. To be partners in all aspects of life had seemed inevitable. As a team now, we were close-bonded, frankly discussing anything.

His report made sense. The new material was closely argued. It was logical. However, there were puzzling holes that he seemed to ignore. It completely went against his usual habit, because he was often even more pernickety than me about details. Either the Urban Prefect was ill-informed (a possibility, of course) or else Tiberius Manlius had received more information than he had just passed on.

I did not ask him outright. As if I was going to compose a laundry list, I went into my workroom and compiled the queries that I myself would have raised with the Urban Prefect. I left my list on a side table, where Tiberius could come in and read it if he wanted. For emphasis, I headed and underscored it:

Points the most excellent Ti Manlius Faustus has unaccountably missed
- The entrepreneur. In a province where thrusting businessmen are eagerly welcomed, what circumstances

caused someone who had settled successfully for over ten years to be picked up by armed troops and kicked out? Isn't that very unusual?

- What commodities did he really import? Or export? Was he preying on the natives, double-dealing the army, exploiting the administration? Or all three?

- Why has his tax situation never been an issue before?

- Nicon. Why is he in Rome? If he is a serving soldier from Britain, how did he come to attention as suitable for a commission of inquiry into a civil matter? Does he have past experience in similar investigations? What is his legion in Britain? To what unit in Rome was he attached, if any, before being assigned to the vigiles – and does he still have the same reporting lines now he is with the Fourth? If so, who is his commanding officer?

- Who does Nicon know? He must have a patron. What person of influence pushed him forward? What gives Nicon this mysterious clout?

- The Fourth Cohort. Why them? Why did the dead woman choose the Fourth to call on? What connection does the entrepreneur have with the Aventine?

- Claudia Deiana. Who really killed her? What evidence supports the theory, held by the vigiles and presumably by Nicon, that she was murdered by her husband? Is there any proof that she found him in Rome? Are there witnesses to their meeting, or to whatever happened afterwards?

- Her husband. What's the secret? Simple question: WHAT IS THIS MAN'S NAME???

I did not see my own husband go into my room, nor reappear. After I had busied myself putting our two little boys to bed, perhaps talking them to sleep for longer than normal, I returned onto the upper balcony that ran around our central courtyard. There were other people in our house, all keeping out of sight as if they sensed tension. I wondered whether they had been given instructions to keep clear. Only my husband was standing below, quietly waiting for me there outside in the cold. He was making sure he would see me as soon as I emerged.

He had read my list. He went straight to the crucial question. First, he opened his arms in the universal gesture of surrender. 'I was trying to protect you,' he admitted. 'You know the man. I do not want his presence in Rome to upset you. His name is Florius.'

Holy crud.

From all that had been said, and not said, I was half expecting it. A few weeks before, I had had a private scare: I had thought I saw Florius locally. Since he was supposed to be in hiding and abroad somewhere, I had discounted the possibility.

I came down the balcony staircase, giving myself time to absorb this news. Stalling, I said quietly, 'If Fornix will let me into the kitchen, I am going to make myself a warm beaker of mint tea. Tiberius Manlius, would you like one too?'

'Well, it's better than a notice of divorce,' he answered.

8

Tiberius asked if I wanted to discuss it. I said there was nothing to discuss. He gave me the slow nod, accepting that *I* did not want this situation to upset him.

We drank hot tea together on our special bench, sometimes in silence, sometimes speaking of household matters. We touched on the painters: why did they have it in their heads that we wanted *The Battle of Salamis*, especially since neither of us remembered hiring these colourists in the first place? Apparently, they liked working here. Other people in the house began to move about: our interesting staff, two homeless relatives whose Saturnalia visit had become endless, the dog pattering to her kennel. Even the children peeked over the balcony, but when fixed with an index finger by Tiberius they scampered back to bed. I mulled over how we seemed to be good home-makers.

I took the beakers back to the kitchen. Tiberius began his nightly round of closing shutters and checking locks. I could hear him in the builder's yard, leaning over the stable door, talking to our donkey.

Gaius Florius Oppicus. That was his full *tria nomina*.

He was an equestrian, picked out by a master criminal to marry his only daughter, in order to provide a vicious underworld family with respectability. They lavished money on

Florius to fund his horse-racing obsession and so keep him sweet. During a period when racketeers were increasing their violence and intimidation in our district, my uncle Petronius Longus had tracked down the father-in-law, supported by my father. When Falco ended the racketeer's existence, the previously limp son-in-law inherited; he surprised everyone by learning very fast how to be a gangster himself.

He was never arrested. To escape unwelcome attention, he went into voluntary exile. By then much of the original crime empire had been dismantled officially, although the family had clawed back enough to finance Florius as he hid in foreign parts. His wife and his hag of a mother-in-law stayed here.

The Fourth Cohort, urged on by my uncle, continued their efforts to cleanse the city. Petronius led a special initiative against gangs. He even at one point travelled to Britain under cover to go after Florius because of what his henchmen were doing in Rome.

Florius had seized on the new province as ripe to exploit. In Britain, he controlled a vile web of protection rackets and he created a particularly filthy prostitution ring. He personally collected vulnerable young girls to work in his brothels. Sometimes poor families sold them as slaves, or else he picked up desperate souls on the streets. One day, he came across me.

I must have been born in Britain. In the Boudiccan Revolt, I had lost my family, together with all knowledge of who I was. I had ended up an unhappy, homeless starveling. I pretended to be tough and acted streetwise, yet I was little more than a child when Florius lured me with the usual promises of shelter and food. All over the world that is how pimps operate. I cannot even say he groomed me; I was not with him long enough. He never had to beat me either; exhausted by misery, I submitted. In the few hours that he had me in his clutches, Florius showed me what women in brothels have to do. As a street child, at least I knew enough already. Rape held no surprises. He was brutal. He wanted me to be afraid of what might happen if I refused to comply.

Against the odds, I was able to appeal for help. Didius Falco terminated my imprisonment; he had to fight off a ghastly brothel madam, but he rescued me. Helena Justina was moved to take over my care. They brought me to Rome. Whether or not they had intended it, they became my family.

As soon as Helena prised out of me what Florius had done, she told me that I should not let the experience dominate the rest of my life. I must deny him control. I had to lose my fear, refuse to feel guilt, and be as happy in my future life as the Fates allowed.

I do not remember ever telling my first husband details of my past. Lentullus, the carefree farm boy, ex-marine and ex-legionary, rarely questioned anything. We were young. He found everything in life wonderfully exciting; with him, I was able to share that thrill. After he was killed in a bizarre accident, I plunged back into a long despair, but I had been happy enough with him, for just long enough, to recover.

I worked. That was good. I expected no more from life. Then last year I met Tiberius Manlius Faustus. To start with, I did not like him. You can guess the rest.

Before we married, I explained what had happened to me. Tiberius was a serious man, a deep thinker and emotionally profound. I found out afterwards that Helena Justina, my adopted mother, had also quietly informed him. As she put it, this should not be a festering secret, darkly withheld until one day it was thrown up in some quarrel. It should be known, accepted, deplored – and put behind us. If he was the man my mother and I believed, it would not matter.

Tiberius never faltered. He accepted me, he *wanted* me, for what I had become. In the same way, I took him and trusted him, despite knowing – because he in turn had told me – that he had been unfaithful to Laia Gratiana. Tiberius was ready for a new beginning; so was I. By the time we met, we were equally level-headed and mature. We both wanted settled lives, where the past would only strengthen us for a happier future. We could each be private yet would never hide important secrets; that was genuine. Blame and shame were not our style.

However, I did have an unforgiving nature. Everyone knew it, me included. Tiberius had realised that seeing Florius again would shake me. On behalf of the sad child I once was, I had to want revenge. Being Flavia Albia, my promise to myself had always been that if I ever again had a face-off with Florius, I would kill him.

Tiberius would hate me thinking that way.

In fact, Tiberius must have been hoping I could ignore Florius entirely. For me, that was impossible – not only for the obvious reasons, but because of Claudia Deiana. I had seen her lying dead on a wet mound of silt in the hopper barge, a sight I could not forget. She was close to my age. Now I knew who her husband was, a grim idea surfaced: had her connection with Florius begun in the same way as mine? Had he bought her, kidnapped her, or otherwise gained control, in order to supply her as a young piece of meat to one of his brothels? Had he terrified and raped her too?

If so, had she won him over to save herself from worse? This was unbearable: if I had never been rescued on my first day in his power, could my fate have become hers?

No chance. I was too self-willed. I would never have been coerced.

Besides, maybe it was all different: when they met, was he looking for a permanent bedmate anyway? Any young girl who took his fancy? Even, perhaps, someone he met through his business? Did he choose a Briton, perhaps quite respectable in trading circles, who would give him a cover of normality? Was she content to be chosen?

Claudia could have lived through their years together never realising the source of his wealth. Many women manage it. Some will take the money, if they are given enough, not caring where it comes from so long as they are 'looked after'. *Oh, he never lets me know anything about bills, I just let him pay for everything. I couldn't order something for the house to save my life, he does all that. He's always been very good to me. He's always looked after me splendidly ...*

Just you wait, mindless *Domina*, wait until he has an unexpected heart attack on a hot day at the amphitheatre so you are unexpectedly left to do everything and the truth jumps out at you. Just you wait, until you find out he has been so tetchy lately because he is going bankrupt. Just you wait until the younger, prettier model that you had failed to spot on the horizon gets her beringed little hands on his legacy ...

Or there are those who absolutely know the truth yet always protest innocence. Women like Balbina Milvia: that petite pretty piece of nonsense, the gangster's daughter who now managed their businesses in Rome like any deputising wife with a husband abroad. The wife he had come back to.

His being in Rome gave me an unexpected quandary. Chasing down Florius should be nothing to do with me: no one was paying me to investigate. As various men were telling me, I should allow the authorities to conduct their own exercise. They would pursue Florius and bring him to justice. Then I might eventually feel I had a reckoning, even if it would never bring me peace.

But I could not stop myself being drawn in. I wanted to know about that woman from Britain, the woman who had pursued Florius Oppicus all the way to Italy. Everyone assumed he had abandoned her and then killed her, though doubtless she had never expected to die at his hands. I wondered if in fact she might have been intent on a different outcome. Did she have a similar motive to me? When Florius came back to his wife in Rome, perhaps Claudia Deiana was so furious that *she* had intended to kill *him*.

9

Next day, it was easy to act as though I had stopped thinking about the Florius situation. So long as I was unsure what to do about it, I could behave as though I was merely wondering why napkins had come back from the laundry still bearing salad-oil patches. (As usual, this was true.) When Tiberius went off with his clerk-of-works, searching for that marble column, I stayed in, played at being a housewife, raged about napery, told my cook to stop fighting the fishmonger and my steward to stop niggling the cook, then nonchalantly whistled up Barley and fell into that most innocuous task, taking the dog for a walk.

This is a chosen ploy of many: adulterers, skiving maids, kitchen hands who are selling stolen food via the back door, husbands who have been told by wives or doctors to stop visiting bars, also children who are breaking parental orders and, like informers, sneaking out. In each case lucky dogs get their exercise. They soon learn to go along quietly and not snitch.

Barley and I wandered across the top of the north-eastern Aventine, running the gauntlet of rat-like lapdogs, which we knew from experience were the most vicious biters, and fat-bellied mastiffs with spiked collars, which were glad to stop lying outstretched on atrium mosaics and come out to bark conversationally. Barley ignored most of them. She had one friend locally, the garland-maker's rough-haired, three-legged mutt, which smelt disgusting, but we didn't see him that day. She sniffed every discarded cabbage and lost sandal in the gutters, while fastidiously searching for a spot she felt was suitable to do her business. Fortunately, no cats crossed our path. I was too lost in thought to go through the procedure of hauling her back while she tried to belt up the road, threatening moggy-murder.

We were on a temple-trawl. I wanted to find a tour guide.

On the Aventine we could take our pick of shrines. I ignored those that were too far over the Hill: Juno the Queen, Mercury, Dis and Venus. Bona Dea was enclosed by a wall and supposedly home to free-roaming snakes. Since it was a dispensary for medicinal herbs, the tourists might have been drawn there; every travel group includes a hypochondriac, who usually acquires a genuine stomach upset – despite being told, 'Don't drink the water, don't over-indulge in low-grade wine, and avoid gigolos.' No luck with Bona Dea, nor Diana Aventina and next-door Minerva. Above the river on the north-east side, Flora was too little known. Luna had been burned down. Ceres was a patroness of travellers, but her enormously rich triple sanctuary was a haven for do-gooding women, like my husband's damned ex-wife.

After a very quick visit to Ceres, we arrived at river level where I walked Barley along the Embankment to the Aemilian Bridge. Linking the meat and fish market on this side to the Transtiberina and routes into Etruria across the river, the six-arched republican structure had been rebuilt by the Emperor Augustus as part of his master-plan to make himself unforgettable. I viewed it thoughtfully.

If this really was the scene of Claudia Deiana's murder, such a well-populated spot seemed ill-chosen. Had provincial living made Florius an idiot? Too much beer? Brain degenerated by end-of-world fog? As well as the markets, which never really closed, the Pons Aemilius was overlooked by the grand heights of the Capitol. River traffic would have ceased once it grew dark, but certainly people remained on the moored boats. At night there was bound to have been dubious activity in the shadow of the huge Hercules Victor altar, and probably loafers beside the replica of the sculptor Myron's statue of a beautiful cow. Beggars lurked under the arches, as they did at every bridge. All kinds of movement would have been going on in the long porticos of the Trigeminal Gate.

Was Florius, or whoever it was, actually wanting to have their deed witnessed? Was he one of those serial killers who aimed to be notorious? If the victim had been conscious enough to struggle or make a noise, she should have managed to attract attention. People in Rome were cynical. They might think she was enjoying herself, so assistance would be unwelcome, but even happy souls going home from parties should blearily recall an incident that, afterwards, was rumoured to be murder.

With trepidation, I approached the beggars below the bridge to ask if, while they were waiting to jump on laden delivery carts to steal anything grabbable, they had seen an incident. According to Latin grammar, I phrased it as a question expecting the answer 'yes'. They cannot have been taught syntax, because they gave me the answer 'no'. Education is not what it used to be. Half grunted at me to get lost, while others invited me to join them under the piers; their blandishments took me back to my bad days in Londinium.

Turning away towards the markets, I checked at the old Temple of Portunus: rectangular, high podium, Ionic columns, tetrastyle portico, stucco finish. Nearby stood the gorgeous small Temple of Hercules the Victor or Hercules the Olive-branch Bearer: even older, circular peristyle, Corinthian columns (some replaced with Luna), roofed cella with an oculus. It housed an unpleasant round mask of a shaggy-haired titan who was supposed to bite off the hand of any liar who stupidly inserted his arm between its lips. I say 'his'. Feel free to call that prejudice.

Portunus, god of keys, doors and livestock, stood on a bend in the river acting as guardian to cattle who were being brought up by boat and who, smelling blood from the markets, might stampede. Portunus proved doubly useless: the temple stood silent and, of course, was extremely well locked.

Cheery old Hercules did not let me down, however. A deadbeat priest was hanging around in the forlorn hope that some passer-by would pay for a sacrifice. Business was 'slow'. By that he meant religious devotees were all staying away.

I thought it was too soon after breakfast. People need to have woken up fully before they can face singed ox offal. You may want to plead for a favour from Hercules, but there is no point in buying a rite at the biggest, oldest, most historic open-air altar in Rome, unless the head-covered officiant passes you a cooked titbit from your hideously expensive sacrificial beast and you are hungry enough to enjoy it.

I had a reason for traipsing around all these temples. Visitors to Rome believe priests will be able to arrange private access to famous shrines, whose dim interiors are normally forbidden; they want to gawp at the gods' statues and any treasure on display. Bored priests don't miss a chance. They love being tipped for privileges and some actually offer tours.

As curator of the Mask of Truth – 'Want a try?' 'Honestly, I'm too virtuous. It would not be a real test' – this priest of Hercules had a part-time interest in travellers. His temple salary was minimal; he had to pay his rent somehow. At all the lodging houses within walking distance, he handed out advertising plaques for himself as a heritage marketeer.

A week ago, his efforts had been successful.

IO

His name was Onocles. I would have changed it. He was partially bald, and the rest of his coiffure consisted of long straggles. I would not have hired him.

We stayed on the marble steps beneath the slender Corinthian columns. Barley sat down beside me, her delicate front paws neatly together. Occasionally she looked up, as if whispering, 'This deadbeat is even worse than your usual witnesses, Albia.'

As we edged into our discussion, the priest dropped the toga veiling his head for sacrifice and freely admitted how he moonlighted. To bolster his cult stipend, he led city tours for people who never liked the food, the weather or the monuments. The worst of them only wanted to go shopping. They all annoyed local citizens by blocking rights of way. Once, a woman had fallen down on the Gemonian Steps on the Capitol, fracturing a leg bone. She would not give up but insisted on more site visits, having to be stretchered everywhere.

Onocles seemed depressed by life yet it had made him a vividly bitter speaker. He described to me his most recent group of travellers. They hailed from central Europe, so no Iberians or Africans, no one from the Danube, just a selection of wealthy white-haired women and overweight professional men, all immaculately dressed but short on manners.

Their home provinces were Gallia Lugdunensis, Gallia Narbonensis, Belgica, and the tiny Alpine territories. Even I, a Briton, found this list dreary.

Their entourage, Onocles griped, consisted of downtrodden companions, nurses and secretaries, none of whom he would have trusted. One doting mother had a wastrel son with her; another was cruel to a mousy daughter. A ruddy-faced ex-tribune was splurging his legionary discharge on this trip, while eyeing up single women. He ignored the pale girl whose father had been forced into bankruptcy by her bullying employer; that girl now had to fetch shawls and be insulted, dreaming of a better future while her snobbish mistress downed strong drink.

'What were these people's sources of wealth?'

'Corn chandlery featured, supplying the legions. Hides – Rome gobbles up leather. The cattle-ranching widow wore her pearls even at the baths, or so the others reckoned. I wouldn't know!' Onocles exclaimed, looking shy at the thought of naked widows even if they kept their jewellery on. 'There was a tax farmer's heiress from the Cottian Alps. She was being staked out as a marriage prospect by a failed gambler, though I thought the famous eye doctor had already been her lover – well, he said he was famous. If I'm honest, there was so much seething and loathing amongst the whole group, I was surprised to hear which was found dead. I had expected one of the others to end up drinking poison in their medicine or stabbed in the back with a nielloed dagger.'

In this group were some who wanted the safety of travelling in numbers. Claudia Deiana seemed to be there only for that reason, though she had taken an interest in where the group planned to go after their stay in Rome. She was travelling with a British slave. *Oh! What had happened to him?*

'Ulatugnus. Never spoke. Looked as if he sawed off people's heads. I suppose that made him good as a bodyguard.'

Claudia Deiana never said much either, though her reticence had seemed sensible.

'What was she like?'

'Self-composed.'

'Not bitter and angry?'

'No, generally calm. I thought of her as the quiet one.'

Onocles had felt she simply despised her companions; they in turn had little interest in her, due to where she came from. 'Well, Britannia, I ask you!' I smiled a little. I had learned to do that. 'Only the woman who wants to write fiction ever asked Claudia Deiana anything about herself. *She* calls herself Agape, because a Greek name sounds artistic. She's really Margarita. She quizzed all her companions whenever she could, and called it "gathering material". According to her, the nurse and the drains engineer were twins, while the impoverished Greek-and-Latin secretary was a disguised ex-consul. She wafted around like a dreamy fantasist – though I noticed she always got her spoon into the dinner tureens first.'

I said creativity could be hungry work. The writers' guild at the Temple of Minerva was famous for ordering in dinners. Yes, agreed Onocles, sounding bitter; his friends among Minerva's priests were always complaining about that. The writers presented themselves as unworldly, yet notoriously rushed off 'to see their patrons urgently' whenever any bills appeared.

It was the would-be novelist who had learned that Claudia Deiana was following her husband across Europe. Perhaps if I could find the group in Ostia, Onocles suggested, the inquisitive Agape could tell me more. If I did want to follow up, Onocles had recommended where the group could stay near the port (his cousin Creon's place). That was, if they had not already sailed on to foreign haunts.

While they were in Rome, Onocles had heard the defaulting-husband story. Then, at Claudia Deiana's request, he had taken her to the Fourth's station-house. She reckoned the Aventine cohort might assist her, although he was naturally sceptical. During her interview, Onocles lurked in the barracks shrine, overlooked by dusty busts of emperors, where a kindly firefighter brought him a cucumber roll; they sat on the pay chest and passed time debating why so many Greek epigrams had been written about that Greek sculptor Myron's bronze cow statue.

'Any conclusion?'

'Either they have a secret code – or epigrammatists can't find a new subject so they just copy each other.'

We gazed across from the temple to the replica statue. It was a very pretty cow, smoothly tactile and highly suitable for its position by the cattle market here in Rome. I boasted that I had seen the original in the agora at Athens.

'How was your tour guide?' demanded Onocles.

'We never had one. My mother always read up in advance and took maps with us. If you want to make your name, she believes a fortune is waiting for somebody who writes good guides for travellers.'

'Could be!' Onocles nodded. At that moment he looked keen to take up my tip, but if he ever attempted to create a voyager's compendium for Rome, I never saw the result; he certainly left Greece to Pausanius. I was right in the first place. The man was a dud.

As a witness, he had missed all his chances too. I've had more luck with piazza drunks. Claudia Deiana had remained tight-lipped after her vigiles enquiry, so Onocles could not tell me whether she ever found her husband as a result. She must have died the next evening. The group left Rome the following morning. A roll-call was not his responsibility. He had not even waved them off on the boat; he just went to pay his rent with his fee. 'It was not enough.' That was no surprise to me.

I felt obliged to consider all eventualities: I wondered aloud whether any of the people she had travelled with might have had a reason to drown Claudia Deiana. Onocles felt none of them really noticed her, let alone worked up a grudge.

So he was useless. At least I forced him to come good in one respect: I thought to ask how and where he had gathered up the group. He said a messenger had come to the Temple of Hercules in response to the flyer he had dropped around. Once they had hired him, Onocles had picked them up every day at their lodging house. It had had to be nearer lunch time than breakfast, so the tax heiress could apply her face paint and the corn-chandlery woman would have woken after her last night's sleeping draught.

Never mind all that. I was thrilled: he knew where Claudia Deiana had stayed. 'Holy crud, why didn't you say so?' Even though I had no commission, I would have paid him a copper for this fact.

'Is it important?'

'She may have said or done something useful – and I bet her luggage is still there.'

Even Onocles seemed surprised to discover he had given me a lead. He offered to show me the building, but lost interest when I said firmly that I would not tip him.

II

They called it Auntie Itia's. That had an ominous ring. I imagined the landlady would be a ghastly grasper who charged extortionate prices for mean accommodation where the cockroaches were as big as mice and the mice could chew into a tough leather pack in half a day – even if it contained no cheese. Overnight a rat would nest in your boot. These terrors would be nothing to the landlady, who was pure human vermin . . .

Undeterred, I told myself it was on my way home, so I should go along to have a look. I found it. The mournful place stood in twisting lanes on the Aventine side of the Circus Maximus. I identified an enormous, rambling old building that gave the impression it had probably been a brothel and still might be used for those purposes.

Once there, of course I was drawn in. A painted wall-sign had become too illegible to read, though a statue of Priapus was a clear clue. It looked a filthy antique – not one our family auction house would accept. Did the randy fertility god, who was a patron of sailors, indicate their customer base? Or did he have universal porno-graphic appeal? His upright organ offered a useful hitch-ing-post so I looped on Barley's lead. 'Stay!' She skit-tered about reluctantly. 'Don't be a prude, doggie. Just wait here.'

The entrance door was unlocked, though it had dropped on its hinges so I had to give a good push to open it. As I ventured inside, I wished I had brought Paris, my runabout, or that I had mentioned to Tiberius where I intended to go.

It seemed cleaner than I'd expected, quieter too. It did not have the clinging lamp-smoke-and-sex smell of a bawdy-house but a faint whiff of terebinthine. They had a guard-dog with a spiked collar, which could not be bothered to stand up. A sack-like lump suddenly moved, turning into a porter, but he ignored me too. There was no atrium, only a dingy corridor ahead.

A girl appeared abruptly. She asked if she could help me.

'Am I in the right place?'

'This is Itia's.'

'A travellers' rest?'

'It is. We have one or two single seniors staying long-term, but only with no pets and no need for medical attendance. Pay in advance. Clean beds, half board is extra, no cooking in the rooms. I'm afraid we don't have stabling.'

I said my donkey was fixed up, though I had visitors who might want a temporary rental. Cousin Marcia did not know yet that I yearned for her and her gruff partner Corellius to move out of our house, but it struck me I could pass this off as 'secret observation of a suspicious venue'. After all, they had run a government safe house, which meant they were used to spying. They needed their own place. Ours was so comfortable they might not have realised it was time to leave. I was ready to tell them.

The girl offered to show me rooms; I looked into a couple that were not in use. Basic bed, stool and side-table, small window, no floor rug; she said they had bigger and better for a bigger and better price. I wondered what a bunch of flash, moneyed people had made of this. Were they really looking for small dim rooms that came with racetrack pandemonium from the nearby Circus Maximus? Perhaps there was a peaceful Imperial Suite where, after a hard day stamping around culture, they could order tots of sweet red wine while writing up their travel journals – though I doubted it.

We passed a large hall, where I was told a previous building-manager used to hold 'symposia'. If this was ever an intellectual academy, I could imagine the level of discussion. Entertainment was no mystery either. The young woman, though neat and polite, looked as if she might well have learned Spanish dancing and could probably finger a tibia . . .

She had taken me back to an office, when Auntie Itia herself appeared.

Holy moly, magical herb! My first assumption had been just so wrong.

The young girl had taken a good look at me; Itia's scrutiny was much harsher. I gave back an equal open stare. To the girl we must have looked like lionesses having a growl-off.

This Itia was perhaps in her thirties, though so lavishly groomed it was hard to tell. I wanted to ask where she had her manicures. She wore the full respectable matron gear: long-sleeved leaf-green tunic with a fancy, flouncy hem; sleeveless brown over-tunic with narrow shoulder straps; lightweight stole with a shimmer that could be mistaken for silk. She had even perched a cloth turban on face-framing hair. She didn't bother to pose in the doorway when she came in; she took her own swank for granted.

Apart from very simple glass bead ear-rings, I saw no jewellery. Nor could I detect perfume. Everything otherwise shouted that this landlady never got on her knees to scrub floors. Just like the masculine toga, the gathered swathes of dress worn by women who have social standing indicate a life of leisure, with no physical labour even possible in such a get-up. She would be ordering someone else to do the work, then criticising any missed corners.

I reckoned she was iron-hard, but enjoyed herself. Auntie Itia might rob customers blind with her scaled-up price-list, but she arranged it from the elegant long chair of an expert professional businesswoman. She was passing herself off as the type who had been left a nest-egg by a doting father, then gathered a clutch of husbands who, one by one, had bequeathed her more premises, which she briskly ran. Daddy and the hubbies were long gone. In a provincial town, she would have donated a prominent civic building and the decurions would have given her a statue in the forum. In Rome she lived invisibly; I suspected she preferred that.

'I never accept single women,' Itia rasped at me. She must have tried to polish her speaking voice, but vowels from the stews were indelible. 'They attract the wrong kind of men.'

Raising my eyebrows, I waved my wedding-ring finger. Without discussing a professional role, I judged it best to inform Itia straight out that I was interested in the group who had stayed there recently. I even admitted wanting news of one in particular.

'Really?' sneered Itia. She could wield a one-word answer like a well-thrown spear.

'I may have known the family in Londinium, many years ago.' I managed to say that, not letting myself think about Florius. 'Claudia Deiana is her name, if you remember her – I presume you made an exception to your single-women ban.'

Itia acknowledged it. 'She was with the group. They seemed nice people.'

'Do you know that she died?'

'I heard something.' Itia showed not a flicker. She must have had a lot of practice in refusing to cooperate with authorities' questions.

'In the river. Very sad. Have you been visited by an investigating officer?' I threw in.

'No one like that.'

'He'll be here,' I assured her. 'I met him the day they found her corpse. He's a nurdle – but I am sure you will handle him.' Flattery made no dint. Still I kept going. 'She was abducted, you know. Grabbed and murdered.'

'Was she?' Auntie Itia gave the impression her customers might often come to sticky ends. So long as they had paid in advance, losing them failed to move her.

'It was the night before the group left Rome. Did anyone in your building see or hear anything?'

'I believe my staff did not.'

Oh! Had she asked them, then? That implied some interest on her part. 'I am sure your people are very attentive and would notice anything suspicious that involved one of your guests?' I dropped my voice to a more confiding tone. 'Is it possible I could see her room? And did she leave any luggage behind? May I look at that – or have you already sold it?'

I had made it jokey. Surprisingly, Itia took no offence at my suggestion they would sell off customers' property, though she refused either to let me see the abandoned luggage or to show me the room. According to her, everything left behind was being kept safe, in case anyone had known the deceased.

'Are you expecting someone to claim it?'

'I couldn't say.' I bet she could!

'I believe she had a slave with her. What has happened to him? Is he here?'

'Gone.'

He could have run away, either when his mistress was abducted, or afterwards, once he realised she would not be coming back.

'Can you give me a description?'

'He was just a slave.'

Itia did volunteer something intriguing. Claudia Deiana had told her she would not be leaving Rome with the group, so she wanted to keep her room longer.

'Did she pay you?'

'She had money.'

'You checked, of course! Did she strike you as upset?' I asked. 'Was she angry about her situation? Embittered?'

'Not that I could see. She seemed like a pleasant woman – who was in Rome to join her husband.' Itia sneered. I could not tell whether she despised the idea of a husband, or was gloating over me not seeming to know the relationship.

I rapped back angrily, 'If she could find him! That was the story she told you?'

'In my business,' opined Auntie Itia, gravel-voiced, 'you soon acquire a nose for people who are telling lies.'

That meant me.

There was nothing to gain by staying, so I took my leave. As I collected Barley, I was reflecting that, although Itia kept a clean, quiet house and comported herself like a middle-rank *domina*, she carried a darker aura. She never threatened me, but I felt she could have done. Instead, she had been confident she could get rid of me without.

Her made-up face failed to hide everything. Immaculate she might be now, yet give her ten years and she would look like the tyrannical gorgon I had first expected. There were lines that said the woman had had a hard past; she had risen

above it, but I saw the signs. I ought to: I had risen above my own hard past.

How long had Itia been in charge? I would guess her presence might go back even to the previous management. Had she taken part in 'symposia' in that entertainment room? What had happened to the earlier owner? Nothing good, I reckoned. Did Itia now own the building? Probably.

This place was pretending not to be a brothel, but perhaps only to avoid enforced registration and complaints from neighbours. The owner was hardly clean-living and innocent, merely shrewd and practical. 'Auntie Itia's' teetered on the boundary between what was decent and what was not. But I had just walked across that boundary, out of the light and into a shadow I recognised clearly. To me, the rooming-house reeked of long-term, professionally organised criminality.

12

Fundanus, the funeral director I knew of old, had a dank yard with a gloomy shack in this same area beside the Circus. Barley stopped dead outside. I went in alone to ask whether the vigiles had had Claudia Deiana brought here from the hopper barge.

That great flanneller wanted to pretend he knew nothing about any Junia Delta pulled from the river, anonymous and unlikely to be claimed. Fundanus made out I was being unreasonable when I set him straight: 'Two days ago, pulled out by a dredger. A bugbear called Nicon believes he is officiating for the Senate and People.'

'Oh, the wet lady! Yes, I've got her. Standard fee and no parade . . . What hole did that Nicon crawl out of? I don't like him at all.' To be despised by Fundanus was a low insult.

His premises stank of decay; he himself oozed depression, bad faith, bad breath and debauchery. I had found him leaning on a sarcophagus while he tore off parts of a loaf. He was a messy eater. Crumbs were dropping down inside the stone container. I did not look inside to see whether some dead soul was sharing the snack.

Fundanus was appalling in so many ways it was hard to excuse it by saying he had to deal with putrefaction on a daily basis. Live mourners could be problematic too; I coped with the bereaved in my own work, so I tried to be tolerant. Indecisiveness would be the best he could expect, while people loved to use grief to create family conflict. He had his nasty trade rites too: embalming, plugging orifices and padding out cheeks to look good. Then he must deal with professional wailers and musicians, keep his cart and its obstreperous donkey, beat off bath-house workers in bargaining for firewood. He always said suppliers of precious oils were his worst enemies: they knew that although time had ended for the departed, for him time was of the essence. He had none to waste on comparing prices.

I told him where I had just come from. When I asked if he knew Auntie Itia's, he growled that he wouldn't set foot in the place. 'Don't let that fine husband of yours know you went there.'

'I presume Itia is not as classy as she makes out?'

'She's a dangerous bitch, although I think she gave up working horizontally herself. At her place, they'd steal the hairs from your bum-crack. Used to be a thieves' kitchen and knocking shop, called itself the Bower of Venus. Very short on goddesses. The orgies were a legend – or so I believe!' It sounded salacious, yet surprisingly Fundanus lost interest. Even for a slug like him, Itia's had been and still was a place to avoid. He swanned into a new tack: 'Want a cheap urn, Albia? I just got a job lot from a cemetery clear-out.'

'You mean it's been used?'

'Only slightly.'

I said if he had obtained it for free, he ought to donate this repository to Claudia Deiana. I was startled when Fundanus replied there was no need. Claudia Deiana had her own pot, organised and paid for. Who by? A man had burst in, rudely demanded to see the body, checked her, gave instructions and handed over money. An urn had been paid for. Rather a fine one. With no quibbling.

Fundanus showed me. The elegant receptacle was a round, banded-agate piece on a shaped foot, double handles, lidded with a beautifully designed toggle. The striated stone was in delicate shades of oatmeal, grey and gold.

I whistled. '*Very* nice! That is some container. You could store a princess in it, and she wouldn't complain. When are you burning her?'

'When it suits me. No mourners will attend, I was told.'

'That's taking "private" a bit far. Where is she heading after the pyre?'

'General columbarium.'

'You said a man turned up. Who was he?'

'I asked. The individual never said.'

'You let it go at that?'

'Why not? I don't need to know a purchaser, only what inscription he wants on the memorial. If any.'

'So, what is to be said?'

Fundanus had to consult his assistant. He had a new one, about twelve years old as they tended to be. Anyone older would organise a better job for himself elsewhere. This lad had been sitting on a bucket, holding up a small dim mirror so he could paint his face with the cosmetics that were used to make the dead presentable. The mirror was probably employed to check that bodies really did have no breath remaining. A traditional courtesy.

The boy seemed oblivious to the fact the eye shadows and blusher had come direct from use, with no washing of the spatula. They only had one mixing tool. When it had been used for a particular colour, he spat on it to clear any residue.

I noticed he had made a rather lurid job of decorating his features. He saw me looking and gurned at me.

'Small plaque,' he piped up, not needing to consult a note-tablet. 'Plain scratched letters, red paint filling. *To the shades of the dead. Claudia Deiana, lived thirty-two years, well deserving.*'

'That cannot be all, surely? No mention that the memorial will be put up by some loving associates?'

'No, Domina.'

I sighed. 'Slaves receive better. Children a *lot* better – she did have children, I believe. Are you sure? No donor will be included?'

'Nope.' He checked off on his little rouge-stained fingers. 'No parents, no spouse, no siblings, no slaves, no nippers.'

'Do I gather, Flavia Albia,' demanded Fundanus, who had seen me at work, so he knew how well-informed I liked to be, 'you have poked around horrid alleys and found out the deceased's identity? So who was the grunt who barged in to see about her?'

'It might have been the husband. Did he behave that way?'

'No emotion. Clipped as a topiary tree. One with poisonous berries.' If it was Florius, that fitted. 'He wouldn't allow me to get a word in either,' Fundanus complained. He loved to pontificate with those who were too helplessly grieving to shut him up. 'Gave his orders, picked my best urn, cash buy. So I am stuck with her.'

'Well, you're paid, so stop moaning ... Anything you can say about the body? I know she had been tied up, then drowned.' I braced myself. 'Would she have been already dead before being thrown off the Pons Aemilius?'

Fundanus for once spared me any grisly details. 'Most likely she was alive.'

He assumed a solemn attitude. We were silent for a moment. Then I wondered, 'Did your visitor ask that question?'

'He did.'

'When you told him, was he upset?'

'Wouldn't show it. He did mutter something to the slave.'

'What slave?' I exclaimed, in high annoyance. 'You never mentioned a slave.'

'Red hair, northern-looking type. Just his escort, I supposed, though why he would have some ugly Celt in barbarian trousers, I don't know.'

'Spare me your bias. I have bad news for you, Fundanus.' I knew every prejudice Fundanus harboured. 'I presume you hated the deceased for being a woman – but there is worse, from your miserable perspective. Did the mystery man tell you she was foreign? She came from Britain.'

Fundanus leaped back in theatrical horror. 'No, the villain did not confess that detail. Shit on a stick! A bloodthirsty druid? I don't want some moon-worshipping Britannica in here, defiling my premises.'

I gave him a look. He failed to catch on. That might have been deliberate.

'Describe the rude paymaster, Fundanus.'

'Ordinary. Absolutely bloody ordinary as a donkey's bollocks.'

'You are all charm. Toga?'

'Tunic.'

'Cloak?'

'Cloak.'

'Long?'

'Mid-thigh.'

'Age, class, hair, height? Come on, Fundanus, you ought to be observant. You measure bodies for a living.'

70

'Only dead ones. I can't be expected to notice people who are moving about.'

'Moving about? Was he fidgety?'

'As a flea's fart.' That the mysterious man had been agitated seemed to be all. Only when I was about to leave did Fundanus remember something. 'He had one urgent question. Had I taken any jewellery off her? I said if there ever was any, the vigiles must have palmed it.' The fat, flatulent old fraudster moaned in high indignation. 'He seemed to think *I* might have helped myself to something!'

'What – you? The noble Fundanus? He was an astute fellow! You would have, if she'd still worn her garnets . . . If he comes back,' I advised him gently, 'you can say that anything found with her has been collected. A respectable woman has it in safe-keeping. Tell the man with no name that I have it.'

'I don't want that domineering pig coming back. I can manage without seeing him again.'

If the pig was Florius Oppicus, I did not want to see him either, though I kept quiet.

I had crossed the yard and was almost with Barley in the street, when Fundanus bawled after me: 'I do know where you come from, Flavia Albia!'

I made a barbarian gesture, then kept going.

13

I decided I might as well continue to suffer Rome's seedier grade of person. Instead of taking my usual route home, closer to the river, I walked Barley down the Circus in the other direction, to the apsidal end with its big new ceremonial entrance. There I turned up the Aventine on the Vicus Piscinae Publicae, parallel with the leaky Aqua Marcia. It brought us to the main station-house of the Fourth Cohort. Aware that this was where the tourist guide Onocles had brought Claudia Deiana, I entered quietly through the huge gates. I wondered whether she had felt trepidation, because Onocles might not have seemed much of a chaperone. Was she timid? Or had living with Florius inured her to threats?

Once again, I ought to have brought Paris. Members of the public had a right to call, but a woman coming in on her own with a rather meek dog had to be braced for a lewd reception.

Red tunics were loafing in the yard. There was the usual lacklustre activity. Coiling ropes. Piling up buckets. Chasing a pigeon around with a besom; the bored bird seemed to be used to it and knew it was a game. I had to stop Barley running over to join in.

The first person I recognised was Titus Morellus. He must have checked in a sulky group of prisoners with the tribune. Troops were listening with evil smirks as he announced what fates Cassius Scaurus had decreed: 'Charge this ugly beggar and the next. Fine the pink tunic, beat the squint-eye, fine, beating. Read out the householder's duties to avoid fire – then you can let the dope go, but lash his balls off first, so he remembers in future.'

He saw me. 'Oh, here we go. It's the luscious Flavia come to bother us again!'

'Albia.'

'*Flavia Albia!* I didn't know you were our tribune's new girlfriend. Does your pious husband know about this?'

'Obviously not, or he would have to punch your tribune's head.'

'I wish he'd keep you at home.'

'Stop messing about, Morellus. I have information.'

Morellus mimed amazement for the benefit of his men, who were ignoring us as they set about their prisoners. 'Whatever is in that twisted little brain of yours, Flavia, cough it up.'

'I will, but only because I have gone into these matters and cannot proceed any further myself.'

'Give it to me,' ordered Morellus again. 'Act like a dutiful citizen.'

'Duty is for wimps. Will you pay me?'

'No.'

'I'll go home, then.'

'Close the gates, lads!' Morellus roared at the top of his voice, the level he used for issuing warnings that a roof was about to cave in during a fire. 'Flavia and I are going to snuggle in this portico to talk dirty, and we do not want to be interrupted.'

Luckily the troops only grinned at me sheepishly. They left the gates half open, though Morellus did haul me into a side colonnade. He had made so much noise that Cassius Scaurus peered out of his office. He then leaned in his doorway, listening to our discussion, but at no point did he speak. Nor did Morellus acknowledge the tribune's presence, though I knew he could see him.

There were stools, not too wonky. I hoped they were for vigiles to sit and read poetry, not to position suspects during cruel interrogations. I checked mine and could see no blood or other stains. Morellus just dropped onto his with a groan, as if he had been on his feet all day.

I reported my day's findings. Claudia Deiana, their Junia Delta, had been staying at Auntie Itia's. She had left behind luggage, though I had not managed to examine it. The vigiles ought to confiscate her property. I suggested they also take a look at the dead woman's room, which had been barred to me. Morellus nodded, on the verge of grumbling at me for telling him what to do. I said even more sternly that her slave was missing. The vigiles were specialists in finding runaway slaves so—

'I don't blame him for escaping!' interrupted Morellus. 'Itia's? It's a sleaze-hovel. As for her that runs it, she's a horror.'

'You know her?'

'Everybody knows her. They all wish they didn't. She has property all over the place. That's her personal headquarters.'

'Do you have it on a register? Or any women who work there?'

'Not our problem. It's in Region Eleven, Sixth Cohort – bunch of idle bribe-takers. Is that all you've brought?'

'No. You know Fundanus, that ghoul. He's had a surprising visitor, some standoffish man who financed funeral rites for Claudia Deiana. I wonder if it was her husband.'

Astounded, Morellus swore at this news. I prodded him, 'By the way, I know her man is Florius Oppicus.' Morellus gave no reaction. Maybe no one had ever told him my connection. 'Do you still believe he killed her?'

'Florius? That is our opinion. Who else in Rome would know the Brittuncula?' He used a derogatory term the legions had invented for the native people of my home province. 'Her turning up here must have been a huge nuisance. So he drowned her like an unwanted kitten.'

I refrained from argument. 'Make Fundanus tell you when the funeral is. He was being vague with me. He says no mourners will attend, but someone ought to monitor the event.'

'In case the killer shows? You know that's a myth, Flavia.' Despite this, Morellus added, 'Going yourself?'

'Depends when it is.' I did not really suppose Florius would appear pyre-side. 'I don't reckon our man will show. Florius has a wife to placate. She still lives by the Circus. Does that mean,' I offered cautiously, 'all this juicy information I've given you for free needs to be referred to the Sixth Cohort for forward action – or should it be handed to your colleague with the special project, Nicon?'

A crafty look applied itself to Morellus's face.

When he said nothing, I queried softly, 'Do you still have Nicon on detachment?'

'Oh, we do, Flavia. We still have that privilege.'

'Still cooperating with him?'

'Absolutely. Yes, we are! My tribune would never have it any other way.' His tribune, in the nearby doorway, stood with training-manual stillness.

I let myself be conspiratorial. 'I only ask . . . Titus Morellus, you are a neighbour and a good old friend so I hope I can speak freely.' He made a gesture of encouragement. 'I know how things work. That man is a creep. So, Titus my dear, I wonder if the Fourth, with their much more rigorous standards, might by now have come to loathe him?'

Morellus adjusted the set of the belt over his grimy tunic. He ran both hands back over his shiny shaved head. Though I never expected agreement, a slow grin was allowed to spread all over his face.

Neither of us looked over at the tribune. Scaurus made no attempt to intervene. I supposed he must agree that resentment of Nicon existed. Presumably there was nothing he could do about the man's unwelcome secondment.

'Where does Nicon come from?' I asked next. 'The Urban Prefect told my husband he had served in a legion in Britain. If so, who brought him here?'

Morellus considered whether to tell me, then admitted in a low voice, 'He's a Domitian nark. Special forces, on the dark side.' He tapped his nose. 'Brought to Rome to snitch on his province. Report dissent in his legion. Finger the governor – though someone had already done that! You would know, Flavia Britanniorum. Wasn't their governor topped for disloyalty?'

I nodded. Last year there had been a military revolt in Germania; Domitian, with his brooding fears of plots, had decided the then governor of Britain supported the mutineers. The revolt in Germany was crushed. Reprisals were ghastly. I never discovered specifically what had happened in Britain, but one thing was certain: Sallustius Lucullus, the luckless ex-governor, was never coming home.

'Done in,' I told Morellus grimly. 'A nightmare called Julius Karus was heavily rewarded for fixing it. Spearheads and crowns for his trophy cabinet. Details of the execution must have been so graphic they have been suppressed. Now Rome has the privilege of hosting the imperial favourite.'

'We know Karus,' Morellus assented. 'Only slightly – and we'd like to keep it that way. Operates out of the Castra Peregrina, that hideous place on the Caelian. Nicon too. It's dressed up as a base for army grain factors, but you don't want to know what goes on there.'

'I do know.' I smiled. 'I have been there.'

'Not inside?' gasped Morellus.

'Right inside. Do not ask me why. You know I have my contacts. Mention my name and the camp commandant will go all quivery. If ever the Fourth need to visit him – on this case, for instance – I'd better come along and hold your hands.'

Morellus raised his eyebrows, imagining me among that crowd. The Castra Peregrina contained picked soldiers from all over the empire. As he said, there was a pretence these 'strangers' organised the legionary supply lines. Possibly they did. But they had been brought to Rome to dish the dirt on their home provinces. Once here, they were otherwise tasked: spying on those of us who lived here.

Morellus resumed grumbling about Karus. 'Somebody stupid has put him in charge of anti-gangster measures. We keep tripping over him when he crawls out of the Castra, though he works mainly on the Esquiline and around the Campus Martius. He's mixing it with various gangs, at a time when we suspect there's trouble brewing. Mind you, he's welcome to that.'

'I can see what is going on here,' I said. 'Karus has come from Britain, so he rates as a British expert and takes a special interest in Florius. Perhaps he even had a hand in driving Florius out of the province. That sounds like his kind of activity.'

'Landing us!' complained Morellus.

'He had back-up for whatever he did in Londinium,' I went on. 'His team were honoured at the same time as him.'

'Yes, he rides around town with a little circus of auxiliaries.'

'Domitian loves them. So is Nicon a Karus trusty?'

'Blue-eyed boy,' confirmed Morellus. 'Why do you think we are being so polite to the darling?'

That all made sense now.

I stood up. Morellus stayed where he was. Behind me, so did Scaurus. 'So, this is the situation,' I mused. 'The inadequate Nicon, backed by the horrendously adequate Karus, is going after Florius. Florius is back in Rome so the hope must be to stop him settling down and re-establishing his old set-up. That's urgent. The Fourth Cohort is kindly assisting Nicon, on instructions from the Castra spooks. You won't cause Nicon embuggerance – that would be political suicide. Those Peregrini all think they are masters of intelligence-gathering. But you know your patch better than Nicon. You understand the criminal element. Here's an idea. How good would the glorious Fourth feel if they managed to arrest Florius independently – and if they snaffled him first?'

'Before Nicon? Now there's an absolutely huge idea!' Morellus concurred cheerily.

I was leaving. 'I could help you, but you won't pay me. I know, I know – no budget! All used up on reparations to Salvius Gratus when you naughty boys burned down his warehouse at your Saturnalia drinks party . . . Nothing left to cover informers, supposedly. But I am still your best hope. For one thing, I met Florius Oppicus. I met him once, Titus my friend, and let there be no mistake: I hate him.' When the silence continued, I kept nagging. 'He will take some catching. My father and my uncle tried to chase him down in Londinium years ago. Good as they are, he evaded them. Slipped away on a ship downriver, it was said. He could have ended up anywhere. But years later, it transpires he had stayed in Britannia all along.'

Morellus nodded his greasy head. 'An escape artist.'

'That's why you should appeal to the public, Titus.' He winced. Time to show I understood procedures: 'I bet you could dig out a little bag of treasure, if it would incentivise *the public* to point out Florius.' Hard to tell how Morellus, or Scaurus, received this suggestion 'Clearly you must convince your tribune.'

'My tribune,' said Morellus, sounding droll, 'is famously open to imaginative work with the community.'

We continued not looking at Scaurus, who continued to stand there, listening. 'He loves new initiatives,' I returned, in the same admiring spirit. It was true, in fact. Senior officials are always keen on 'initiatives', which make them sound energetic so they need not be. 'A public appeal isn't disloyal to the Castra Peregrina,' I said sweetly. 'Any tips received can in theory be passed to Nicon.' Morellus and I snorted. 'Though, of course, acting on those tips independently might help the Fourth to show him up. Go on, Morellus; beat him to it! I am not asking you for a commission. Offer a reward,' I spelled out. 'Then if I find your fugitive first, I can claim it.'

14

I went home. Dusk was half an hour away. Coming across the Aventine, shops and workshops had still been open; there was the faint stir of woodsmoke as bath-houses began firing up their furnaces.

Walking towards the Temple of Diana Aventina, where I had started my search for the tour guide only that morning, I smiled to myself. As I was leaving the station-house colonnade, I had observed a little scene. Barley had pattered over to look at Scaurus. She stopped a couple of feet away, considering what she thought of him. Except when chasing an animal not much bigger than her, she was never an aggressive dog. That was precisely why I had allowed her to adopt us: she would sit patiently, happy with the company of her chosen humans.

Scaurus, on the other hand, had jumped in alarm. He had vanished into his office, crashing the door behind him. It struck me that the self-assured tribune must be frightened of dogs.

At home, Rodan let me in for once. He had been anxiously watching the street, as if he had been left far too long until he was worried we had abandoned him. I should have shown that everything was still normal by cursing the sweaty mound of blubber, but I could not find the energy.

Barley went straight through the courtyard to her kennel, where she plumped down with a sigh. I, too, suddenly felt my weariness. I realised I had been wandering for hours, with no food or drink. I found Fornix in his kitchen. He offered me a dry caraway biscuit, after which I had to tantalise myself until dinner. At least we ate early because, although the children were compliant, our insubordinate hangers-on tended to complain when hungry.

Fornix never seemed to look out from the kitchen, yet he always knew what was going on. He told me Gratus and Paris were at the baths. Suza and Dromo had taken the boys down the hill to my parents', to allay their fears that Glaphyra had died, like their poor mother. Corellius, our convalescent visitor, was out walking on his false leg. Bored with having no one else at home to grouse at, my cousin Marcia had gone with him.

I had beaten the master home, but he arrived back from the Campus Martius, coming in from the yard then stomping straight upstairs without a word. When he failed to come down in his slippers, I sought out his clerk-of-works, Larcius. They had taken a cart to the imperial marble yard, but had returned empty-handed. As he stabled the donkey, Larcius shook his head at me: Tiberius was grumpy and should not be approached.

I went up and tackled him anyway: wifely privilege to court danger. 'Io, luckless company proprietor! Do I guess Domitian's marble collection is on special reserve, only for imperial projects?'

Still in outdoor clothes, Tiberius had been lying on our bed. He sat up on the edge, running his hands through his hair. He refrained from growling at me but seemed reticent.

'Long hard day, love?'

'Found the new stone yard. Closed all today.'

Something was bothering him. I sat alongside, wanting to share my own news but suppressing my eagerness. 'Isn't that unusual?'

Tiberius heaved a sigh. He swivelled to put both arms around me, kissed the top of my head, held me tight for a moment, then relaxed slightly. Whatever was bothering him, I knew he would tell me. He stood up, then began taking off his cloak, boots and belt. I found him his slippers and a comfortable old over-tunic, then waited.

'I managed to get inside, though they had nothing suitable. I did find an old fellow who remembered my grandfather.' The grandfather had founded the Faustus family fortunes as a marble supplier. 'We had a long chinwag, but he couldn't help. Work was stopped. The whole Campus was locked down. Troops were swarming everywhere, some odd unit, bullying everyone who dared look at them.'

When I asked why, I had to drag it out of him. 'Somebody died. A local criminal.'

There had been an upsurge in gangster violence. We had already heard that. Tiberius and I had had the occasional brush with a clan called the Rabirii. Today, one of their henchmen had been found dead, mercilessly done for and dumped in plain sight, clearly a message killing. Tiberius, who was tough yet a sensitive man, had been shown where it was done and how the man had been killed. Even talking about it while safely back at home was upsetting him.

'Your father found the body. He hauled me there to have a look.'

'One of his specials?'

'Truly ghastly!'

15

My mother always reckoned that if anybody died by foul play within a hundred strides of my father he would be the one to stumble upon the corpse. Today, said Tiberius, was no different.

We talked it through over dinner. On some nights we would have waited until afterwards, but not much else was going on. Marcia and Corellius were being tense with one another. Little Gaius and Lucius had been fed by my mother; happier now they had seen Glaphyra safe at the townhouse, they were put to bed by my maid Suza. Dromo must also have gorged at the parents' running buffet since he lay on his sleeping mat moaning that his belly hurt. Our other staff listened as Tiberius told his own disturbing bedtime story, one for adults only.

After his search for the elusive porch column failed, Tiberius happened to run into Falco outside the marble yard. Since they were both disgruntled, they marched together to the nearest bar where naturally the father-in-law offered drinks, intending to finesse his son-in-law into paying, although the son-in-law deflected him with a cry of 'Oh, thanks, Marcus Didius, that is very generous!'

Tiberius moaned to Pa about the column. Falco was unhappy because an auction he was running from his warehouse at the Saepta Julia had proved disappointing.

83

Personally, I sympathised. On a cool day at the start of February, no one wants statues so old they are wearing crowns of decayed pigeon guano. For most people it was still too early in the year to think about garden ornaments, even cheap ones sold by an auctioneer who told good jokes.

When his jokes fell flat, Falco stormed off. He strode away in a fug of foul language until the river stopped him. Watching the fast glide of the Tiber, foaming with silt and odd tree branches, he walked along the embankment between the bridges of Agrippa and Nero. That was where he found the body.

What he first noticed was an extremely large grey pot. Falco could tell that everyone else in the locality was carefully ignoring it. Their nervousness caught his attention.

Standing close to the river, on a wharf, was a ceramic container, a monster of very basic design and material. It was almost as tall as him. The dolium was of a type normally buried in the ground at a rustic villa for temperature-controlled storage; for some reason, this cumbersome example must have been in use for transportation. It had a wide access hole on top, with a plain round lid. Spillage all around it alerted Pa to curious facts: it had contained olive oil, but a quantity of this expensive commodity had been displaced. It had leaked out past the dolium's lid, even though that was roped tightly to two rough handling-lugs, then further weighed down by heavy roof-tiles. Being the man he was, my father boldly shoved aside the tiles and pulled off the lid to look inside.

The horrific Archimedes experiment he uncovered would have required several men. A desperate victim had been inserted head down, then his limbs forcibly folded in with him. The lid had been fastened with weights in case the occupant was still alive, though with his lungs full of oil, he could not have struggled long.

The incident presumably happened after dark, but even in daylight scared locals thought it best not to notice anything. They could tell what kind of people must have done this. Perhaps they even knew for sure which people it was, though none would ever say so. Even my father was not so crazy as to investigate a victim who must have been annihilated by dangerous thugs who might still be watching. He hailed a member of the Seventh Cohort to report his find. Let those idlers handle it. Mellowed by rotgut at their bar, my father insisted he should walk Tiberius to have a look. Both could pleasantly advise the Seventh on how to do their jobs, acting as citizens who both had high-status civic positions behind them. However, by the time they arrived, word of the incident had reached the Castra Peregrina. Julius Karus had rushed on scene, taking over the Campus Martius with an influx of paramilitary hard nuts. My menfolk agreed this would not solve the problem, though it would let people know how important and busy Karus must be. Or thought he was. Which was not their opinion. And, they congratulated each other (still exceedingly mellow), they were both experts in human nature so they knew.

Father and Tiberius could have gone quietly home, but neither was that kind of man. Back at the spot, the spilled oil was still causing bystanders to slip and slide, although poor people from hovels nearby were trying to scrape up this free fuel into chipped jars and bowls. The corpse had been dragged out. He lay beside the giant pot in a gloopy heap. From time to time, desperate paupers crept up close and wrung out accessible parts of his garments to extract more free oil. Men with Karus harshly ordered them to scarper.

Tiberius told me they had spoken in a foreign language: legionary auxiliaries. They were too arrogant even to attempt Latin, though their meaning was clear, their attitude frightening. They were armed. Inside the sacred city boundary this was illegal. No one was going to point it out.

Bullying failed to impress Didius Falco and Manlius Faustus. That solid pair sauntered over to see if they recognised the dead man. Neither did. A red tunic from the Seventh Cohort, literally the bodyguard, recognised Falco, a well-known local character. Defying the auxiliaries, the vigilis gossiped to Pa that this unfortunate belonged to the Rabirius clan, a certain 'Legsie' Lucius. He had been a runner for Young Roscius, the ascendant gangster heir; Legsie ranked low as a foot-soldier, yet he would be missed and mourned. Roscius was none too bright (Tiberius and I had once interviewed him about a burglary, so we knew that), but he had spunk, plus enough manpower to carry out reprisals.

No one had come forward to claim ownership of the container. It had presumably been unloaded from a river vessel at some time in the past few days. Julius Karus decreed that the Seventh should conduct routine enquiries: whose dolium it was, what boat had brought it here and its intended destination. It might have belonged to an entirely innocent trader, who would have lost a lot of money here. He ought to be hopping up and down in frustration, but was either terrified of the gang involved or perhaps keeping quiet because he had failed to pay the full customs duty. The Seventh would find him, though they saw no reason to hurry.

Karus and his own men zoomed around the Campus like het-up wasps as they obnoxiously sought witnesses. They had even closed the bridges. Such disruption was highly unpopular but Karus maintained it sent a message that gang warfare would not be tolerated. My menfolk said Karus was cracked.

It was being assumed officially that the dolium victim had paid a harsh price for his group, the Rabirii, moving into new territory. Their traditional area was the east side, mainly on the Esquiline and Viminal Hills, never much further across than the Quirinal. However, last year, spurred by the ambitions of Young Roscius and a powerful enforcer called Gallo, they began to creep across the Via Flaminia. Blood was spilled, a great deal of blood. In the process the incomers had wiped out most of another gang, who used to call the Campus Martius theirs. Now the Rabirii had successfully moved through the Campus and onto the riverbank north of Tiber Island – rich territory. The public monuments came under the eye of the authorities, but fringing the river were newish docking wharves and stores, half-hidden bars and other low dives. Then near the Neronian Bridge there was a very old training ground for racehorses that offered opportunities to mingle with breeders, grooms and jockeys, take over gambling, interfere with horseflesh or otherwise fix races.

The Seventh Cohort and Julius Karus were taking the line that Legsie Lucius had been pitched inside the dolium by the last remnants of the nearly defunct rival gang. Giving up their long-held rackets to the Rabirii must have hit them hard.

My father reckoned it might be more complex. So far, he seemed unwilling to discuss theories – although, being Falco, we could be certain he had them. What he did tell Tiberius as they had made their way home to the Aventine was that organised crime to the east of the Forum was changing.

Falco took an interest because it affected the Saepta Julia. The old man at the head of the Rabirii had been ailing for a long time, but Father said at last he had died. His body was being brought back from his country estate to Rome, arriving any day now. Old Rabirius was regarded in the underworld as the King of Kings. There might be a respectful mourning period, but his funeral would attract enemies as well as friends and associates; the occasion was bound to be used for plotting.

His empire would be inherited; it was looked after at present by his nephew, Young Roscius, and by the old man's powerful sister. I had met both. Rubria Theodosia was venomous, as were other female relatives. With most men in their family either dead or in exile, the women had grown used to wielding power. At the same time, Young Roscius was often at odds with their hard man, Gallo, so there were growing tensions within the organisation.

The cremation of Old Rabirius would provide an unmissable event. All the top racketeers in Rome would assemble, supposedly to show respect, but also to busy themselves with inter-clan manoeuvres. The time had come for key repositioning among the various factions that preyed upon our city.

Falco had mentioned that Old Rabirius and fellow mobster Balbinus Pius had been cousins. To me, it was significant. Balbinus fathered Balbina Milvia, who was still being acknowledged as the Roman wife of Florius. She kept in with her relatives, I knew; they were all in the same line of business. It was a safe bet that Milvia would be at the funeral.

His wife's position might cause anxiety for Florius. From babyhood, she had been dandled by sinister cronies of her parents, who treated her like fond uncles. Florius had no such pedigree. If he wanted to re-establish himself, he would have to come out of hiding. When the big rissoles gathered to take decisions on their future, he needed to join in. He must convince the other overlords that his exile was over and he had resumed control. He must show he was now personally running all the scams and stings he and Milvia had inherited. He, Florius Oppicus, was a very strong player, one for the rest to respect and honour.

To do that, he surely had no choice. Florius would be forced to show himself at the funeral of Old Rabirius, King of Kings.

16

I was now intrigued by the thought of Balbina Milvia. All I needed was an excuse to probe, and this fortuitously arrived. Our breakfast next morning was interrupted by Titus Morellus bustling in. 'Oh, oh! You do cause me trouble, Flavia!'

'Albia!' Tiberius corrected him, since my mouth was full of goat's cheese.

'Apologies, Aedile.'

I spluttered, still chewing. Morellus failed to take the hint. 'Your bright idea stirred up our old man. Scaurus has only ordered me to shift my fat arse to the Forum! I had to chalk up a sign on a general's statue, offering a pay-out for clues about Florius. Now we'll be inundated with twerps who have seen him scratching his warts at the amphitheatre. It won't be him, we all know that.'

'Which general?' asked Tiberius, pedantically curious. 'Acting as your notice board?'

'Any old baton-carrier, so long as he's dead and won't complain.'

Morellus moved children to make space on a couch, then stopped talking while he helped himself from our serving table. Little Gaius, uninhibited in his own way, sniffed at him, pulled a face, and ran off to play, followed by Lucius. During Morellus's busy munching, I mentioned my theory that his tribune had a canine phobia. After an open-mouthed swallow, he rejected this: all the vigiles were keen dog-lovers, which was why they were constantly rushing into fires to rescue puppies.

'If they are in the arms of pretty girls?' suggested Tiberius, with a wicked gleam.

Morellus declared proudly, 'My cohort is famous for pulling girls out of buildings – whether they are in any danger or not!' He was shameless.

After a time, when he had emptied the food platters, the reason for his visit emerged. Plotting Nicon's downfall, Scaurus and Morellus had decided that, while waiting for the public to cooperate, they should interview Balbina Milvia about her husband's return. 'Somebody needs to challenge her, in case she knows the beggar's whereabouts.'

I thought somebody should have done so before now. I also feared she would not tell them. 'Won't Florius be living at that house he used to have with Milvia?'

'No-go dwelling for us. Sixth Cohort. Those dodgy beggars.'

'If Milvia has any sense, it's a no-go dwelling for Florius too!' I scoffed. 'But I suppose she has to welcome him back. Other villains in exile will feel extremely nervous if they hear some wife has locked her man out on the doorstep alongside his travel-bags.'

'If she had any sense,' said Morellus, 'she would rifle the luggage for money, then opt for divorce and pass him straight into our kindly arms. All the kudos in that partnership came from her birth. But, Flavia, she needs a man. Milvia cannot depend for ever on being a Balbinus daughter. She had all her glory while Florius camped out in his provincial bivouac.'

'While the men are in exile, the women are in control.'

'Agreed. With a thousand miles between them, they made a good team. Couriers rode from Rome to Britannia, with profits relayed two ways; your crazy uncle used to track that, getting infuriated. Milvia posted off pocket money and home comforts. Florius passed back boxes of cash and goods to the home organisation.'

I growled, 'Until Britain finally noticed what a slimeball he is and shot him back here.'

'Florius is adaptable,' said Tiberius. 'He will pick up in Rome.'

Morellus agreed. 'The gangs will expect Milvia to return the reins to him. Her only way to be given any respect in their world is to be a well-behaved wife. Then she can at least keep the keys to the stores and cupboards.'

Morellus was giving me a stern stare, as a hint that this was how domesticity should be. My husband let out a snort of jovial laughter. I did hold our home keys, but Tiberius for one, and most of our household, I suspected, could pick locks.

The Fourth could not simply barge into where Milvia lived, because the area alongside the Circus Maximus was controlled by the Sixth Cohort, whom they viewed as cronies of the gangsters. Too pure to beg for their cooperation, Scaurus and Morellus had decided that approaching Milvia should be tackled indirectly; they embraced the idea that she was more likely to talk to another woman.

It was a myth. Still, I wanted this chance. 'Me, then?' I demanded, naming my day-rate. I heard a vague statement that the tribune would pay my invoice if I came back with something useful. I accepted that. If Milvia would talk to anyone, her family's code of silence said it would not be the vigiles. Even to me, would she ever admit that her husband had killed Claudia Deiana? Had she been living in happy innocence? Was Milvia even aware yet that the second wife ever existed?

'Well, you can have fun when you tell her! But I've been to see Fundanus and the pathetic second floozy has been despatched now. He may have squashed her onto a bier with some other customer to save firewood and incense, but the swine says the Brittuncula is reduced to ash. Her very expensive urn was placed in a row of basic loculi, in a public columbarium, where she will be forgotten.'

'Fundanus had said nobody was expected at her funeral,' I said.

'Nor did anybody come. No one's ever going to visit the tomb to dine with her spirit on the feast days for ancestors either. She's gone.'

Before Morellus left, I mentioned Old Rabirius and that other coming funeral. A conversation was held, where the men present elected that I should not go. I thanked these noble creatures for their concern, as if I would act obediently.

Another conversation occurred. Tiberius and Morellus belatedly recognised their decision was futile. They came around to allowing me freedom of choice, since I would exercise it anyway.

'Don't worry, Aedile. Nobody knows when the crook's ceremony is,' Morellus muttered. 'The Rabirii are saying it's private, family only.'

'If you believe that, you're nuts,' I cracked back at him. I said I would find out when it was due to happen.

17

Down in the valley of the Circus Maximus, within her closely guarded gorgeous home, Balbina Milvia was having her hair done. She always favoured high court fashion. She would not be following the republican tradition that mourners should cover their heads, but the imperial tenet that rich women showed off. A slave told us she was preparing for the Rabirius funeral; unaware that it was 'private', he let slip that it would be this afternoon, at the Horti Lamiani.

I would have liked to look around for evidence of Florius, but despite the hot curling irons, we were taken straight in to see the mistress. I tried not to think about Florius living here, though it made me shiver. My nightmares about him had ended long ago, yet I was now frightened they might start again. Was he here in this house, maybe hidden from view somewhere upstairs? Were food trays being taken to him? Water bowls and towels? Lamps in the evening? Could anyone go through the house and search for him? Not us, that was sure.

I say 'us' because for interviewing a gangster's wife I had brought my cousin Marcia. While I kept Milvia's attention, Marcia was supposed to be on watch for signs of her husband. I had worked with her on other occasions and back-up is good practice in any face-to-face with the corrupt. Also, my cousin could be tough – though not as tough, we found, as cutesy Milvia.

We met her in a lush salon. An elegant stylist was constructing on her client's head a huge semi-circular arc of tiny curls, some real, some fake, all well wired in, total effect ludicrous. In the province I came from, forest goddesses sat in sets of three wearing big hairstyles, though rarely this big. Product of the world's largest city, Milvia might have no idea what a forest was. And whatever spirit inhabited her was far from benign.

I had seen her before, though not close to. She was small, dark, sharp-featured, and had once been a very pretty girl. Now she was nearing forty. She patronised beauticians and showed off her bust. She might still believe she had striking looks. Slaves certainly told her so; otherwise they would risk being speared with dress pins. I had heard that Milvia had been spoiled all her life, also that she could have a temper. I saw her as an uncompromising staff-manager.

While I prepared to ask questions, Marcia was taking a good look at the décor and furnishings. Once in charge of the family fortune, Milvia had worked hard on her buying skills. I had already heard that her house was top-of-the-range in all respects. Outside, it was defended like a fortress. Inside, frescos were many and exquisite. There were books; there were statuettes; there was a cithara made from a tortoise shell, hung at an angle on a wall. I felt this was not to show someone's education and taste; it was set-dressing. A designer had placed those things.

The cost was conspicuous. Milvia, lucky woman, had been left with numerous bank-boxes; we had passed a selection in her atrium. She had always claimed she had no idea where her family's money came from. However, she certainly knew now. For fifteen years, with Florius away, she had controlled the family's businesses. Her horrible mother had been a large presence at first, but after Cornella Flaccida passed away, handling the organisation fell entirely into the perfectly manicured hands of her daughter, who never faltered.

When Marcia and I entered, Milvia greeted us in a friendly tone. We took off our cloaks, sat down uninvited and began like ladies from a temple who wanted to cadge charitable donations. She continued to sit still for the hairdresser, who carried on discreetly but was probably listening. As Milvia tilted her head for curl-fixture, her attention seemed to be on that, though I did wonder.

I told her my name; I hoped it meant nothing. I introduced my cousin only as my assistant. If I had called her Marcia Didia it could have signalled our connection with Falco. Milvia might know he and Petronius Longus had finished off her father, then spent years trying to chase down Florius. One thing she would not know was how I had met her husband.

'What does Marcia Didia assist you with?'

Io, this was a sharp witness.

Marcia, who could be a handful, answered for herself. 'I carry her handkerchief – and if it's required, I punch faces.' Most ladies with equestrian status would have been alarmed. Surrounded by violence all her life, Milvia barely blinked. Sensing reproof from me, Marcia looked smug.

'The authorities have invited me to see you, Balbina Milvia,' I said smoothly. 'It is a kind of welfare check.' In case she decided this was rubbish, I spoke with a wry smile. However, she seemed to think it perfectly normal that she should be looked after, even by the authorities. It reflected what was known about the attitude of the local vigiles cohort. I tried to ignore my cousin's frankly raucous chortle and beamed further reassurance. 'Please do not be alarmed. I'm sure people have been keeping an eye out for you since you and your late mother were living alone in what is, unfortunately, a rather rough neighbourhood.'

One reason for the district being rough was the enduring presence of this house, the long-term headquarters of multiple crime rackets. The proximity of the Circus Maximus added menace for most people. For the Balbini, that was merely a district of operation, though their biggest: they controlled the Circus, imposing persuasion and fear on the muggers and ticket scammers, the trinket and food shops, the betting fixers, the cheating chair-carriers, and all the tired drabs who offered bunk-ups beneath the outer arches.

'Oh, nobody ever bothers me!' No, I thought. Nobody would want to end up bleeding out in a gutter. 'Was that all?' Milvia had a high, little-girl voice. She was too old for it. I bet she wore a lot of pink. (She was in white today, as I was.)

'You live by yourself, which must be hard.'

'My husband went abroad.'

'Rather a long time ago!' I scoffed. Milvia acquiesced in silence. Cousin Marcia, who could be annoying, gazed at me brightly, as if openly suggesting, *Get out of this, then!* I did so by beefing up my approach: 'Florius is back. He was kicked out of Britain and returned to Rome.'

'Whoever told you that?'

'It is widely known. I even thought I glimpsed him myself once.' When Milvia made no comment, I noted that, despite her physical daintiness, she had hard eyes. 'Is he living with you?' I grilled her. 'Is he here? In your house?'

'We are married. It is his house too. But I have no idea where he may be.' She must be lying. She managed to look genuine, but she was blinking too fast.

Marcia suddenly leaned forwards, supporting me. 'Tell Albia! Owning up to Flavia Albia will be better than having your house searched by armed men.' Marcia was holding a richly decorated cushion from the couch where she was sitting; she smoothed the soft cloth on it as if suggesting how differently aggressive paramilitaries might treat valuable things.

A short cough of laughter shook Milvia. 'That wouldn't be the first time! None of them ever found anything. They will be disappointed again: Florius is not here.'

'Where, then?' I rapped, trying not to lose the argument.

'Find him yourselves, if you want him!' Milvia straightened up. The hairdresser stepped back momentarily. 'What is he needed for anyway?'

'I believe there are questions about his tax affairs,' I said.

'Florius never pays any tax.' She seemed proud of it.

That riled me. 'Of course not! He is a criminal. He only preys on society. He does not contribute.' Dear heavens, she was annoying. Turning on her was unplanned and unprofessional, but I could not help it. I toughened up more. 'He may have been pathetic when you married him, but he overcame his insignificance. He ran a vile mesh of scams in Britain. He is also being sought over a brutal death this week in Rome. A woman was abducted and drowned in the Tiber. The vigiles believe your Florius knew her. He knew her very well, in fact. They think she was causing him problems, so he threw her off a bridge.'

Milvia simpered, 'Oh, he turned into a naughty boy!'

'Be prepared. He will be arrested.'

'When they catch him!'

'Don't you want to ask me who has been killed?'

'Why should I?'

98

'Her name was Claudia Deiana. From Britain. She was looking for Florius. Did she come here to find him?'

'I know nothing about any woman from Britain. If you say she had something to do with us, then prove it.' These were classic criminal responses. She appended another: 'If she died, Florius had no part in it.'

'How can you be sure?'

'I know Florius!' Milvia immediately followed that cliché by indicating that she now wanted Marcia and me to leave.

We refused. Whether or not he drowned Claudia Deiana, I knew that Florius had murdered others, with no qualms over whether his victims were women. 'You cannot provide the wifely alibi – "He was with me" – unless you own up to seeing him,' I pointed out. 'Why do it? Why protect him? He fooled you, Milvia. Were you ever aware he was living with someone else, during all those years beyond civilisation? Did you know that they even had children?'

Marcia added more pressure, still playing the sympathetic one in our partnership: 'The authorities are sure Florius silenced this poor soul. So, aren't you at least a teensy bit worried, Balbina Milvia? Men who attack their families never change. Once they think they can get away with it, their violence becomes worse. If Florius has disposed of one wife, he might try the same again. Doesn't that scare you?'

'Florius has only ever had one wife – me!' decreed Balbina Milvia, complacently. 'And he will not raise a hand against me.' She was again signalling us to leave, this time more vigorously.

Now we did not linger. Neither Marcia nor I wanted to learn how they dealt with unwanted callers in this house.

As we were going, the hairdresser finalised her work; she helped Milvia add ear-rings to her neat little ears. I paused to watch, with some interest. Noticing me stop, Marcia took note too.

On the threshold of that beautifully designed salon, my maverick cousin could no longer restrain herself. I saw her intentions, but before I could stop her, Marcia turned back and cooed mischievously, 'So, Balbina Milvia – shall we give your regards to Lucius Petronius?' I could have kicked her legs and deposited Marcia on the fancy floor rugs.

Petronius was now living in what passed for harmony with Father's sister, Maia. His earlier life had been less settled. He once notoriously had an affair with this woman, Balbina Milvia. He must have been mad to stoop to it (as I believe my frank parents told him). The stupid entanglement cost him his first marriage, plus trouble about his job then a descent into wine and depression. The affair, not his first, had meant nothing to him. But Milvia had been a young, neglected wife who stupidly believed he was serious. Petro could hardly shake her off. Once Florius found out, a feud started. In Britain, Florius had tried hideously to kill Petronius, who had barely survived the incident.

There was an unspoken agreement that our family never spoke about any of it. But trust my cousin to ignore the pact.

'Get out of my house,' ordered Milvia, though she spoke as if merely shooing out two feral cats that had strolled in through an open door.

We washed our hands and faces at a street fountain, feeling tainted. Marcia gave her verdict: 'Juno's jawbone, Albia! That was one lying little cow!'

'Lying and wallowing in luxury. Did you clock her jewellery?'

Marcia listed: 'Gold and garnet ear-rings, boat-shaped.'

'Fine gold wires to form the closure. Each fronted,' I returned, 'by a disc featuring a big garnet cabochon, surrounded by seriously exquisite granulation.'

'Luscious!' agreed my cousin. 'You or I would wear those – if we were stringing along some idiot with huge pots of dosh! What of it, Albia?'

I said, whoever gave Milvia her shiny lobe-stoppers had bought them from the same fine jeweller who had made the pair owned by Claudia Deiana. A typical man, Marcia and I agreed, Florius must have given similar presents to both of his wives.

Ironically, in our family it was believed Petronius Longus, that rascal, used to do the same thing. My father said he would give his first wife and any girlfriend he was schmoozing identical presents. This was to fend off trouble. It saved him forgetting what each of them had had.

Florius might not be at Milvia's house right now. But the ear-rings suggested to me that his wife had seen him. For a coming grand occasion, as many women do, she was choosing to wear a recent gift.

He had been there. He had been in his fine-frescoed, bank-box-filled home. But if Milvia believed she had fooled me, she was wrong.

When I reported my suspicions to the Fourth Cohort, they decreed a full search, to be carried out by Nicon. Using him, a Castra Peregrina man, avoided problems with the Sixth. So, he and some troops he had at his disposal went in to give the house by the Circus a going-over. If Florius was living there, he must have decamped in time. They failed to find him.

I knew about the action, so went to watch what happened. I positioned myself, standing in the shadows, in one of the arches of the Circus Max. A group of vigiles were on observation too, I noticed, further down from me. I recognised none of the men, nor their officer. They must have been from the Sixth Cohort. I was aware of their presence, though confident they never spotted me.

If the soldiers were rough indoors, nothing of it was audible. It cannot have been the thumping roust most people receive when their homes are searched for fugitives. The troops emerged pretty soon; they sauntered out in an unhurried line, quiet, relaxed, well-disciplined. Balbina Milvia oversaw their departure, coming in person to her porch. Even with her crazy hairstyle threatening to topple her, she was fully the mobster's wife: defending her property, protecting her man, deriding the forces that were ranged against her.

Nicon left last. I saw him salute Milvia with much too much politeness. She even shook hands briefly.

Balbina Milvia turned back inside. The double doors closed. All the military disappeared off the scene, although Nicon first raised a fist to acknowledge the Sixth Cohort's officer. It looked comradely, no more, yet I thought their expressions held a message.

I stayed where I was for a while longer, staring at the house. Staring at the house – and wondering.

18

Over a hundred people must have come to the funeral of Old Rabirius, with more of the public ogling too. Then there were law-and-order troops: the vigiles for crowd control; the Urban Cohorts to prevent riots; Julius Karus, with men under cover as they observed the criminal element. I also identified tall men in uniform togas; beneath the bunched white woollen folds, each kept one fist upon something that was clearly not an oratorical scroll. Who wants their relatives departing from life under the eyes of armed Praetorians?

I was on my own special mission: looking for Florius.

The mass event was held in the Horti Lamiani. These gardens formed an imperial playground, part palace compound and part wildlife park, thrown out across the Esquiline Hill by a senatorial tycoon a hundred years before. He had bequeathed his spread to the Emperor Tiberius, who passed it to his heir, the following Emperor Gaius, popularly known as Caligula. He was supposed to be one heir of two but he made short work of the other, bumping him off as if culling co-heirs were a normal part of probate.

In rapid time, Caligula was himself assassinated for unspeakable acts – squandering, plundering, executing, bullying, giving lewd watchwords to his guards, incestuously screwing his sisters, claiming to be a living god: the usual

Julio-Claudian joy. His body was cremated here in the gardens, then originally buried under turf. Eventually the ashes were dug up by his sisters and carried to his family's tomb, the Mausoleum of Augustus. It was a big edifice, luckily: it came to be packed with scandal-making, sibling-murdering, politics-plotting Julio-Claudian relatives. Such an interesting family! Don't you wish yours was as scandalous?

When Augustus expanded Rome beyond its original sacred boundary, four or five great men seized upon this area near the Esquiline to make personal pleasure grounds. Outside the ancient Servian walls there had been a grave-yard, so paupers' bones kept being found whenever garden-ers tilled their flowerbeds, but the miasma had faded, and all the reputed witches had been kicked out to make room for gazebos. I had been to the Auditorium of Maecenas next door, but Lamia's Gardens had more craziness.

The beautiful setting was right for the glamour of a top mobster's funeral. Like Nero's infamous Golden House, which once sprawled over the heart of Rome, these Esquiline gardens included built features such as villas, shrines, banqueting halls and a bath-house. Also like Nero's extrava-gance, the exterior purported to be a natural landscape, though it had grandiose walks with orchards, fountain groups and tall urns, all set on terraces at two levels with formal flowerbeds. At one end there was a huge semi-circular swim-ming pool; a long porticus ran to it. Wild animals had once roamed free or were kept in cages, and there were still peacocks everywhere, which were very noisy.

I had made sure I arrived early. A garden area had been cleared, its topiary and rose bushes heaved out and kept in temporary pots, its herms, statues and urns lined up with them. Members of the Fourth Cohort arrived, mingling discreetly with curious onlookers, people who sometimes had little idea of the event. 'I thought I should come because somebody told me he was important,' I overheard one stupid woman saying.

Morellus brought his children; he thought carrying his baby on one shoulder would camouflage his profession. Tiberius, who was better at disguises, had looked out an extremely scruffy tunic in which he leaned on a rake as if he were a gardener. I had not spotted Nicon – though, to be frank, I wasn't looking. Nor had I seen Florius. It was well over ten years since I had consciously been in his presence; I was no longer sure how I would react.

Morellus soon found colleagues from the Second Cohort; the Esquiline gardens were part of their patch. Tiberius and I had worked with the Second and had low hopes of them today. Titianus, an unenthusiastic grunt, was their investigator; he bundled most of his casework notes straight into the cupboard of unsolvables, assuming he could find the key to it. Juventus, a worse nonentity, supposedly had a special task as an 'organised-crime liaison officer'; he went to bars, where he was constantly recognised by derisive waiters and passed a free beaker the cat had licked. I nodded but did not greet these characters.

There was a tedious wait. Tiberius filled it by actually raking up leaves; he made the terrace where we were extremely tidy.

At last, wending down through the Servian Walls, came an immense procession. In historic times, bringing a body to its place of cremation would have happened at night. Now, only the poor were sent to their gods then. It struck me that Fundanus had probably despatched Claudia Deiana during the hours of darkness, but for Rabirius that would never do. Most of Rome had to witness his departure, which would take place in a showy blaze of lights.

The wealthier and more famous the deceased, the flashier his funeral. This procession was even headed up by a *designator*, an appointed official who specialised in such occasions. He cut a portly figure; he must have eaten at far too many funeral feasts. I was astounded to see lictors with him, fakes of course, but clearing a path ahead of the bier as if they were state employees creating a route for a consul. After them crowded a battalion of musicians and mourning women. They were professionals, paid to participate – paid a lot, in this case. A fabulous orchestra of flautists and trumpeters puffed their hearts out, often in time and sometimes in key. The women went to extreme lengths, wailing loudly, ripping out hair and scratching their faces until they bled as if vying for the winner's crown in a drama competition. For Rabirius, Rome must have been sucked dry of hired celebrants. No one else would be buried today with such honours.

Before the corpse arrived, more actors represented his ancestors, wearing wax masks in their likenesses. If the masks were accurate, the old Rabirii had looked more like cushion-stuffers than vicious enforcers. I was hoping for cavorting and raucous satire, but jokes about cruel antecedents, let alone jokes about Rabirius himself, were not allowed. Normally the family's wishes were overridden; honesty about the dead was a traditional feature of Roman funerals. Today no professional mourner would risk reprisals. Even onlookers seemed nervous in case some nark accused them of not showing true respect.

As soon as the bier lurched to a stop, it was surrounded by elderly men, some with knife scars seaming their faces, all exuding heavyweight self-confidence. They walked like potentates. None of them spoke much, though they nodded recognition to one another or occasionally embraced like brothers. The wide-shouldered, bow-legged clique all wore dark clothes, some with vulgar gold necklets showing through the fronts of their cloaks.

I would have hated to get into a bar fight with any of them but, as far as I could tell, they carried no weapons. None were needed. The circle of mourners attending the bier to the pyre was visibly seeded with their minders and bodyguards.

The ageing crime lords gazed out into the crowds. I thought they were checking who else from their violent past had come. Occasionally, some younger man would step up and meaningfully shake hands; he would look humbled to be touching a hero, while his hatchet-featured patron stayed impassive.

I felt chilled. This was a gathering of the mighty in Rabirius's world. Without doubt, all would claim that their way of life was legitimate. Without doubt, it never had been. They had ordinary faces, plain looks that in a different context would belie their moral ugliness. The crooks were probably not even active nowadays, but I could see they were all making a mental connection with old times, longing to return to famous horrors. These were dedicated lawbreakers, men with gold in their coffers and blood on their consciences, men whose memories were black.

A large group of invited guests had come, walking together behind the bier. Significantly, few male mourners were in their middle years. The reason was simple: older ones were either living abroad – or, more often, they were dead. Their surviving families clustered in groups, looking strained.

Some of the old stagers helped the porters manhandle the bier towards the waiting pyre.

While Rabirius was posed for his final rest, the women hovered in a loose group, dry-eyed, the majority sombre in black, though some, like Balbina Milvia, looked more modern in white. I watched her air-kiss females she knew. One or two were dressed up foolishly: young trophies, teetering in ridiculous sandals and using handkerchiefs with great care so as not to smudge their eye colours. Most of the rest had lines or hollows under thick cosmetics, though some favoured austerity, as if being unadorned was a sign of the ideal gangster wife; no married crime lords allowed other men to cosy up to their women. It was not simple jealousy. They could never risk their secrets being revealed.

Wives had brought handsome children. They were well turned-out, with clean faces and neat hair; they stayed close to their mothers, looking bemused. These sons and daughters were normally shielded from the terrible way their fathers, uncles and grandfathers made their money. They were brought up strictly, with nurses, tutors, and promises of good future lives in establishment positions. The girls would marry young, within their clique. The boys expected to become lawyers and politicians. Some might do so. I thought wryly that 'respectable' careers do not debar their holders from criminality. A cynic might even say such a background helps.

Many who collected beside the pyre were strangers to me, although I had recognised Milvia and her relatives, the Cornellus brothers and their sister, who were all money-lenders over on the Aventine. Another of our locals, Appius Terentius, was missing, last seen travelling down to Brundisium on his way to a long overseas stay in a rocky province full of pirate towns and expatriate offenders like himself.

Among the Esquiline contingent I spotted Young Roscius, playing the main man among his younger siblings. At one point he exchanged a grim comment with the family's chief enforcer, Gallo; I wondered if they were remembering that murdered foot-soldier, Legsie Lucius. If he had not been shoved into the olive-oil dolium, he would presumably have been there, with other obvious members of the Rabirius organisation.

I knew their matriarchal leader, Rubria Theodosia. Since I had last seen her, the death of her long-ailing brother had brought a windfall of glittering jet jewellery (it must have been imported from Britain, as I knew). She moved among the mourners with authority, but slowly, like someone who had not worn in the new shoes she had bought for this occasion. Her veiled daughter-in-law, Veronica, kept to herself, like a pillar of bitter vengeance; she was still grieving a son who had been bloodily killed in the street in an inter-gang feud. And there was a surprise: beside the unyielding Veronica stood a tall, silent figure, funereally togate in black, who received honorific salutes.

Hello! People seemed to be welcoming back this gloomy ghoul. He kept his head covered as if for religious reasons, though it also conveniently hid his face. Surprised, I wondered if this could be Veronica's husband, who until now had lived far outside Rome's borders. With a murdered son and a dying father, had he risked sneaking home to Italy? People do travel long distances for funerals. It could be Rabirius Vincentius. If so, in Rome he was a marked man.

His presence might herald some destabilising of their clan. For one thing, his return from exile placed his cousin,

Roscius, in a much weaker position. Until Vincentius nipped away beyond a frontier again, if he ever did, Roscius, who was younger and considered a lightweight, could never hope to inherit their dead grandfather's position.

And what, I wondered, would be the outcome of any power-struggle that must start now between Rabirius Vincentius and that other ambitious returnee, Florius Oppicus?

There was still no sign of him.

19

I was thinking about these families' internal tussles, while flunkeys under direction of the *designator* lit lines of bitumen torches around the central gathering space. The sky above was still winter grey, but this ceremony would go on until well past dark. Flares had been attached to posts, arches and even statues. Sending this evil old man to the shades had become a sacred drama. We watchers huddled in our cloaks, like the audience in a particularly chilly theatre on some lonely Greek shore.

Family and associates pressed forward. Bystanders were unceremoniously pushed back. I found a space from which I could see the funeral pyre. A normal construction would be like a chest-high altar, simply made from logs set in layers at alternate angles. This beast must have taken days to build. I had previously taken the elaborate block for a garden feature, maybe a summerhouse. It stood about three storeys tall. Even hanging it with flower garlands would have been a full day's exercise. Ornate trellised sides held many carefully packed layers of firewood. Old Rabirius in his funeral state was to reside in his own roofed pavilion right at the top.

I had managed to squeeze close enough to see his bearers struggle up a ladder awkwardly, then haul the bier one stage further. I worked out that they must have tied down the corpse, or he would have slid backwards. He was dressed in robes, like a triumphing general, though if he had been kept at home on public view for the standard eight days, the embroidered fabric must be ruined. They had placed some kind of crown on him. Gold also glinted on the gorgeous bed where he lay. His mattress looked deeply comfortable; a silken pillow supported his lolling head.

Once the body was in place, the relieved bearers skedaddled back down to the ground. Next, a leather-clad falconer climbed to the top. He was valiantly lugging a heavy metal cage that contained a huge eagle. I do mean a live one. Nothing had prepared us for this: unbelievably, Old Rabirius was to be sent off with an imperial apotheosis. When the great golden bird was freed by some clever mechanism, this eagle would take off. A raptor rising swiftly skywards from the smoke is supposed to be a signal to the mortal world that an emperor is ascending to the heavens as a god. So: the Esquiline's filthiest extortionist was being treated as divine.

My husband had worked himself in beside me. Though normally mild-mannered, he was livid. He threatened to protest to the Urban Cohorts, raging that if this outrage failed to cause a general riot then he, Tiberius Manlius Faustus, was ready to start one all on his own. He had been angry enough that the sumptuary laws were flouted by dressing up Rabirius in a purple triumphal tunic, never mind that bloody crown. To suggest that a vile criminal would transmogrify into a constellation to be worshipped was an offence to the devout, an insult to real heroes and, in the spirited opinion of my Faustus, supplying that eagle was treason.

I pouted. 'Maybe the eagle was his treasured pet. Rabirius is taking it to the underworld.'

'Any eagle who knew its business would have pecked the bastard's eyes out.'

I calmed him down. There was no point in ranting. Even Tiberius slowly accepted that a man in a dirty one-armed tunic who was posing as a gardener would carry no clout with the Urbans. Saying he was on surveillance would not help. The Urbans were a maverick corps who had no concept of checking for guilt or innocence. They never wanted evidence; they simply bashed anyone who moved in their line of sight. At best they would fling Tiberius across a gravel path into a very thorny bush; at worst he would be seriously beaten up. If he managed to stay alive from that, he would be arrested.

'And another thing!' he grumbled bitterly. 'My bloody ex-brother-in-law is here! The bastard has an invitation. It's unspeakable.'

That would be his first wife's brother, no relative of mine. Salvius Gratus, a warehouse owner, had once admitted he leased space to the Rabirii. Whatever they stored in it was bound to be stolen goods. According to Gratus, in commerce men had to be flexible, closing their eyes to their customers' ethics, so long as denarii rolled in. That attitude had won him a place today, shaking hands with their enforcer Gallo, brushing shoulders with their crooked lawyer Mamillianus, lining up in the queue to show respect to Young Roscius. We knew Gratus. His behaviour here gave us a hint of how 'legitimate' people in business could become enmeshed with the criminal world.

Now there was animal sacrifice, though certainly not a modest gift to the Olympians carried out on a portable altar. At home Tiberius treated his little household gods to a scatter of grain on a fire each morning. On big occasions people might run to a chicken sacrificed on a block outside. Here, Rabirius had a massive marble altar that must have been specially dragged to the garden by ox cart; upon it a tame priest from the upper echelons of religion, distinguished by his spiked headdress and supercilious expression, stretched a whole farmyard of beasts: a pig, a sheep and an enormous bull – the full *suovetaurilia*. Each animal came with gilded horns and decorative streamers. Each was then sprinkled with wine, grains and flowers. Each, one by one, was despatched by bare-chested officiants with strong axe blows. The tame priest was then joined by a full-blown augur. Entrails were inspected thoughtfully. Tantalising scents of meats joined the heady aura of flowers.

A eulogy was given. A tottering old fellow clambered onto a small tribunal. He saw no need to give his name, though people near me murmured that he was Old Roscius, a brother of the dead man and father to the ambitious young nephew.

Only able to support himself with crutches, Old Roscius was too frail to maunder at us for long, though did his best. He had a turned-down mouth and fragile bones, so thin that his clothes hung off him. He croaked slowly, overcome with grief – even though people told me that he and his brother had never got on; they had feuded all their lives until Old Rabirius died.

We would never have known this from the eulogy. The brother's theme, intoned in a halting voice without notes, was that Old Rabirius had been a lovely man, a much-loved man, a true soul, the best of brothers, a father to all. Everybody who knew him liked him, everyone had loved to see him, he would always talk to anyone, he never did anybody any harm. He would be sadly missed by all. He was a good man, a great man, a lovely man, a hero who had died before his time.

Nobody jeered. Rather, there was pattering applause. I grabbed Tiberius by the hand, but he just pinched his lips in resignation.

Pungent incense began filling the cold air. Onto the pyre quantities of scented oil were being flung. Invited mourners who had not thought to bring any were handed little flasks from a laden container; we saw Salvius Gratus receive one. The incense and oils were joined by basket after basket of expensive flowers and scented herbs. Children, nervous of doing it wrong, were gently encouraged to add handfuls of rose petals. Women trussed in swathes of rich fabric patted at fake tears as they let the crowd observe their sorrow while they deposited their offerings. I scanned the group: still no sign of Florius.

By custom, the next part of a burial was led by one male relative with downcast head, who would light the pyre using a single torch. Here they imposed their own ceremony: a whole phalanx of those villains from the past was given burning brands to plunge into the layered branches. They staggered forward, only partially rehearsed; some forgot or were unwilling to follow instructions. None bothered to avert their gaze.

Then, while they were solemnly attending to that duty, and as the flickers of fire first crackled up, minders jumped into action: too late. Out of the crowd burst a woman who ran up to make a gesture. Meaning everyone to see it, she spat wildly into the flames.

20

Whoever the protester was, she was dragged off. Members of the Urban Cohorts rushed her, not the official minders; the Urbans dragged her away. This, it would be claimed officially, was for her own safety. From what I heard afterwards, she was a widow whose husband, a shopkeeper, had struggled to pay his dues to the Rabirii, until the strain caused by their threats became unendurable and he killed himself.

There was no chance the Urbans were going to treat that widow gently, but she would have known the risks beforehand. Many others from local industries, retail outlets and places of entertainment, who were being forced to pay protection money, must have been among the crowd. Those neighbours neither joined in her act of defiance nor dared show support.

The Rabirius associates all behaved as if they had not noticed the incident. I only saw their main enforcer, Gallo, snigger to Young Roscius; they glanced across at the man I took to be Rabirius Vincentius, who returned a wry look, then covered his head more with that black toga, religiously. Liquidising a widow can besmirch reputations: it would be reported later that they paid her off; gangsters can act benevolent if it looks good and silences complaints.

Meanwhile the pyre was so large that even though the wood had been kept dry in preparation, flames would take hours even to reach the corpse, then longer to consume it. Someone where I was standing informed us that fifty pounds of incense were known to have been deployed, but even that huge amount was not enough to speed up the process. It would take all night. Mourners could be waiting until morning to douse the remains with wine and collect the final ashes, so a select group slid away together, already off to hold their feast. Without bothering to collect Tiberius and Morellus, I made sure I followed.

Caligula had used the monumental royal residences on the Palatine, redesigning suites elaborately, but since no amount of luxury ever satisfied his family, he also lived here. Perhaps the Horti Lamiani had seemed more secluded; this area stood away from the city's ancient heart, allowing debauchery to take place out of sight. Buildings he had occupied remained, fifty years later, much as they had been. We passed through outside terraces lined with citron, apricot and acacia, imported trees never seen in Rome before they were brought by conquering legionaries. As we walked, I thought I heard shuffles and whinnies from horses that must have been hitched somewhere. Carefully descending marble steps, I was more surprised to hear sounds from wild animals. Big cats and other animals intended for bloody arena spectacles were normally kept at the imperial menagerie, outside one of the city gates; the old Horti Lamiani cages must still have been in use as an overflow. These beasts had sensed the unusual funeral activity. From the lions' growls and some large bird hooting, they clearly did not care for it.

The feast was set up in an underground cryptoporticus. This immense, richly decorated underground gallery stretched away for hundreds of feet. It would have been pitch dark, but expensive oil lamps were provided. They revealed a floor paved with the finest alabasters in elegant patterns. Slim columns of giallo antico, a beautiful patterned yellow marble, supported the ceiling, their bases and capitals sheened with gilded plaster. Walls were set with gemstones. Even though the old Julio-Claudian buildings were now unlived-in, the garnets, carnelians and rubies had never been gouged out and stolen. Nor had anyone lifted the statuary I saw everywhere, which still cluttered every possible corridor and niche: Bacchus, crowned with ivy and flowers, Tritons and Muses, a head of Priapus, a faun with grapes to gorge, a naked Venus tying a ribbon around her hair prior to bathing. These might be Roman copies of exquisite Greek originals, copies that had been here for a hundred years or so; much newer was the 'Genius' of our Emperor Domitian, wearing the aegis of Minerva, his patron goddess, and with a cornucopia. So the Gardens of Lamia were still imperial property. You could say they were still owned by a crazy emperor – but you would only say it quietly.

That cryptoporticus was gorgeous. Amongst the most refined effects, many dining couches had been prepared between the columns and statuary. In this cultured setting, the funeral meal would be served so his mourners could remember just what a powerful organiser of terror and bloodshed Old Rabirius had been.

I tried dutifully to insinuate myself among the flushed caterers, but when I saw how the diners were honouring their deceased as if he had been a man of merit, I felt sickened. There was so much respect, it might have been measured out in buckets. I could not bear to watch.

I almost left the gardens altogether, no longer caring. But outside again, I found Tiberius and Morellus hunting for me. The Morellus youngsters scampered nearby, wheeling the barrow Tiberius had filled with leaves. While we were grumbling about a thief and extortioner being commemorated with such glitz, a flurry caught our attention. More lictors. Men with bundles of axes seemed to be holding their annual convention today. Only two more arrived this time: it was less than Rabirius had had, although these were official; assigned to a genuine important person, they were bringing a big litter I had seen before. Out of it jumped a praetor, one of Rome's most senior magistrates.

He clambered down from his conveyance, broaching its thick curtaining like a dishevelled nymph parting the waves. Tiberius and I, and Morellus, all recognised him: Corvinus. Was he invited to the funeral as some cosy bribe? He was a fool and a bigot, who either refused to act when action was needed or else caused chaos with his incompetence. I had not previously thought him corrupt. His secretary, a dry wit called Lusius whom I recognised, ambled in his wake and told me his big-bellied, heavily becloaked employer had heard about the extravagant display; he had sailed up to express official views thereupon. Morellus winced. Tiberius cheered up. Needing no further cue, we sped after the praetor.

Corvinus found the feast. At the nearest end of the gallery, he even mounted a podium. It may have been where Caligula had once postured in effeminate silks and pearl-encrusted slippers, selling himself as a living Jupiter. Corvinus by contrast was savagely clean-shaven. He wore brilliant white traditional dress under his pseudo-military cloak, all topped off by an austere expression, like some goose-necked old republican. It would not have surprised me if he had shouted at us that Carthage had to be destroyed.

Without chamberlains to call for silence, the praetor could not immediately command attention. Waiters were haring in all directions, serving traditional highly spiced funeral food, while having to explain exactly what the dark canapés were. Entertainment by musicians and dancers was imminent. A screaming match started: since children were present, a mother had ordered the dancers to put on their clothes. This was a problem for performers whose dress code was castanets and nudity; they had brought no costumes with them. Mobster mothers hoisted their bosoms under deadweight necklaces and stalled the performance until cover-ups were found. Mobster children looked disappointed.

While the waiters ran out for new food and the dancers were sulking, Corvinus finally made himself heard. Perhaps all funerals should offer opposing versions of supposedly 'lovely' men. Corvinus wasted no time on Friends, Romans and Countrymen: 'Listen up! What I have witnessed today is disgusting!'

The mourners were shocked; they fell silent, as if uncertain whether they had been accused of a breach of banquet etiquette or of cheapskate catering. Wrong spoons? Too much cumin in the wheat cakes? No: too much flaunting in the display.

The praetor was brief. He had a loud voice. Pronouncing edicts was his role. At stentorian volume, he proclaimed his piece: all right-thinking citizens must find today's ostentation self-indulgent and luxurious. Such a send-off denied custom; it was un-Roman, a show of corrupt power. It sent out a message that criminals had immunity from the rule of law.

'Dressing up Rabirius as a tawdry god is unacceptable in a democratic state – one where we already have an emperor, Father of his Country, who in time – though we hope not for many more years – will be honoured with true divinity. I declare this appalling spectacle to be an insult to the Olympian gods and offensive to the Senate and People of Rome.'

Corvinus was a fool, though not as stupid as he sounded. Once he had spewed his outrage, he popped off his podium and beetled away.

Those present reacted uneasily. Apart from a handful who had probably tried to bribe Corvinus in the past, they did not know who he was. Nevertheless, his rousing speech started a colourful spurt of action.

The eight fake lictors from the Rabirius procession set about the praetor's two real ones eagerly. The odds looked uneven, but the real lictors' normal role was ceremonial, so for them a proper fight was a big treat. They weighed in with their rods; the rare outing for their symbolic accessories showed the rods worked and their owners had practised. The fakers must have chosen light batons, which quickly broke. Splinters flew around. Diners who had been hurt leaped off their couches angrily, some throwing plates.

All the subdued children came alive. Catching onto adults' bad behaviour, the bored brats hung with gold bullae threw bread rolls, then hurled burned titbits, skewered cinnamon bites and hard little spice cakes. Soon lads began experimenting with how far they could send the contents of full tureens flying through the gallery. Some had received discus-throwing classes at expensive gymnasia. Mothers vainly attempted rebuke. There were, of course, not enough fathers to be disciplinarians. You cannot use 'Wait until Papa gets home' if he has been done in by rivals or is camping out for legal reasons in furthermost Cappadocia.

Unaware of the spilled tureen contents, waiters shot across the beautiful alabaster floor with only lucky ones keeping upright and few saving their trayloads. Others scrabbled madly but skated into colleagues, whom they knocked over. It became worse. Girls who had watched their brothers' tureen game stopped looking like goody-goodies and made inventive use of wine flagons. Women, including me, squealed in horror as dark red liquid, the traditional funeral colour, flowed upon a highly absorbent alabaster pavement, which greedily sucked it in . . .

There were so many diners it had taken me some time to identify people I wanted to note. Now I realised that Rubria Theodosia and her daughter-in-law were both lying on a triple couch with an empty space between them. That tall man I had twigged to be Rabirius Vincentius, Theodosia's son and Veronica's husband, ought to have been with them. Scanning the room suggested other missing persons. Balbina Milvia was sharing a couch with a female she must know, but still minus Florius. Villains I had recognised before – the Cornellus brothers, for instance – and the old-timers I saw when the bier arrived were all absent. Gone, too, was Young Roscius. Gone was his ancient father, who had croaked out the eulogy.

These men should have been principal guests at the wake. Their vanishing act could mean only one thing: they had all slipped away, leaving the women to cover for them. The top mobsters were already in a secret room, plotting.

If he came tonight, as I believed he had to, their meeting would be also attended by Florius. Now my need was urgent: I had to find that hidden conclave.

21

I managed to grab a waiter, who promised me no other meeting was taking place in this building. They had enough to do, he snapped. He had never had to serve such rude people and would be glad when tonight's extravaganza was over. I left him trying to mop up wine with a cloth that was already sopping.

Outside I came upon more strife. Two of the most elderly crime lords, presumably distracted on their way to the conclave, were ducking and weaving. 'Bit of a scrap!' laughed a bystander. 'Look at the daft beggars falling over!'

One was the character on double crutches who had given the eulogy: Rabirius's brother, the elder Roscius. The other looked just as decrepit, though needed only one waggly walking stick. Rather than mayhem, it was a slow dance, about as vibrant as a snail race. They did possess the moves. They could have been arena boxers – a long, long time ago. Whenever one wanted to uppercut the other, he had to gather himself and steady his balance. Then, seizing his moment, he lunged. Too much effort would pull him around in a circle, with a crutch or a stick waving. The target had time to stagger out of reach. I never saw either make real contact. Even so, you could sense their aggression. Either would have bloodied the other, if only he could.

I asked what the fight was about, but the oldies had refused to say. The second combatant was one of the Ocelli. Who were they? Two gangsters who once controlled the turf along the river and the far part of the Campus Martius.

'I thought the Rabirii had wiped them all out?'

'Not the twins. They had to come out of retirement – no one else was left. But on a good day they can remember how to be villains.'

'What's this one's name?'

'Ocellus Gemellus.'

'He looks a hundred. Not many good days left. What's his brother called?'

'Ocellus Gemellus.'

Of course he was. They were twins.

'That's what Gemellus means, lady. Are you foreign or something?'

'Britain,' I admitted. Bystanders edged away, eyeing me as if I was a big spider in the lamp store.

The fight was about to be broken up. The praetor absolutely meant to expunge today's excess. Even with his lictors caught up in a scrum elsewhere, he was determined to impose decorum. He might be powerless to stop the Rabirius friends and family doing as they liked, but outside he would penalise the innocent crowd. For this, Corvinus had summoned all military units. He acted as traffic controller. He made apoplectic arm gestures to indicate that sightseers should be moved on. He crouched. He pointed. He even leaped into the air.

For the Urban Cohorts, moving people on meant knocking them down and stamping on them. They would judge their own performance by how many people they killed. The

124

Praetorians watched with superior sneers, not wanting to get their togas dirty.

For the vigiles, the Second Cohort, the call to arms could not be fully actioned since, officially, they were unarmed. In a praetor's presence, they were reduced to calling people names. Their victims included the Fourth Cohort's detachment, who had been in disguise, pretending not to recognise them; in response to bad-mouthing, the Fourth laid about, trying to hurt as many of the Second as they could before anyone used that worse insult, 'inter-cohort collaboration'.

Startled pedestrians fled. This was Domitian's Rome. Most had seen riot control before. They knew to run straight home and, when fists banged the door, persuade their mothers to insist they had been there eating porridge all night.

Corvinus kept gesticulating. Now warmed up nicely, he was thrilled by the arrival of mounted men, a unit on small speedy horses, led by the sinister Julius Karus with a long flag on a pole as his standard. They swept down the terrace, clearing it in one clean pass. All bystanders were now gone, and I had lost Tiberius and Morellus. I stood behind an obelisk, glumly hoping to stay safe.

During the cavalry mêlée, the walking-sticks duel ended. Someone had forced the oldsters apart. Gallo had brought a cart for the enfeebled elder Roscius; he was lifting Roscius in bodily when the doddering Ocellus twin leaped aboard too. He shoved the driver off, then whipped up a startled mule as if he hoped to hurl out his rival using speed and sudden turns. Old Roscius was pummelling him. Gallo shrugged and let them go. He strolled off on foot in the same direction.

I was unable to follow because Karus and the mounted auxiliaries swung back, kicking up dust and letting out wild cries as they performed dressage manoeuvres to impress

Corvinus. Karus, with his decorations from Domitian, knew how to suck up to top brass.

By the time they dispersed and I could safely move along the terrace, there was no sign of Gallo, let alone the maniacal cart. The air felt cold. I was anxiously conscious of lions' roars, quite close – a surreal touch. On my own, I walked along a gravel footpath, searching for any promise of a secret meeting. Herms were indifferent to my passing. Fountains glugged their neutral measures. I do not enjoy gardens at night, not since I investigated one in which a serial killer preyed on women. Failing and anxious, I wandered back closer to the pyre. It was burning in a desultory way, the task still far from finished.

My luck changed. Seated on a pile of empty baskets, I came upon the *designator*, the man who supervised funeral ceremonies. I sat on a low wall beside him and, in the informer's tradition, grunted at him gloomily to make friends.

His name was Corneolus. It sounded Latin, though not quite classic. His features were Italian, though not entirely. However, his depressed demeanour was pure workaday Rome.

I had seen him in operation at a distance, when he cut a commanding figure. Close to, his outfit, a tight long tunic, was not as clean as it had looked. He had a higher, weaker voice than his role required. 'Corneolus is my working name. We don't give it out in our neighbourhood. People can be funny about funeral workers, even though I never have to touch dead flesh.'

He confessed that his wife had not wanted him to do this event. I said she was a wise woman. He nodded gratefully: she had begged him and next time, he said, he intended to listen. I wondered how often in their marriage he had made that claim, yet I was pleased to see her influence working.

'Why was she against it?'

'She thinks they are common.' I was with her there.

Corneolus complained that the Rabirii had been monsters to deal with. They wanted a huge splash but were reluctant to pay for it. The women gave orders that the men counter-manded. The men refused to take vital decisions, so the women threw tantrums. It was nearly a disaster because the corpse was late arriving from the country. Important extra guests had come unexpectedly, requiring more conveyances from Theodosia's home to the gardens and messing up the order of the bier party (which had already taken three days to agree), altering the table plans for the feast, and making other mourners twitchy. Some guests had to be incognito. That was a real nightmare.

'Was that tall man I saw with Veronica her husband?'

Corneolus gave me a stern look. 'I am not supposed to say.'

'How much have they paid for your non-disclosure clause?'

'Not enough.'

'Well, then, go on!'

'Yes, he is. Rabirius Vincentius. Seems rather down in the dumps.'

'Understandable. His old father just died and his only son was murdered last year. Vincentius Theo was the boy.'

'I heard. The tall fellow is desolate. He blamed his wife, and when she gave him a mouthful, he blamed his mother. But I have to say that once he turned up, they all fell rather smartly into line.'

'Is he a tyrant?'

'He has been extremely polite to me!' Corneolus paused. 'I could almost like him. Some of these people are the dregs of society, but Vincentius has polish. I suspect if he wanted me exterminated, whoever stuck the dagger in would fulfil the contract in a good-mannered, even painless way. Possibly reciting an elegiac line of poetry above my corpse. The man shows his style.'

'Has he,' I asked, with interest, 'come home to Rome planning to exterminate many people?'

Corneolus pursed his lips. He liked to gossip. Even so, the long dark reach of the Rabirii made him cautious.

22

I let things rest temporarily. We watched the fire burning. Apart from us, and presumably the caged eagle, at the moment Old Rabirius was going to his next life unattended. Gentle flames reached up through the levels of his tall pyre with the relaxed crackle of an autumn bonfire. If any of the animal sacrifices had remained on that massive altar, we could have skewered them on tree branches and enjoyed toasted meats. All we then needed was a tray-slave coming around with warming tots of mulsum . . .

I mentioned that I knew a secret conclave was taking place. Corneolus had relaxed enough to confirm that in his *designator* role he had helped make arrangements. '*Sub rosa*, as the saying goes – so I suggested we literally hang roses from the ceiling.'

'Ooh, lovely!'

'Yes, I felt it was a nice touch.'

'I am sure even bullies and murderers appreciate a thoughtful gesture.'

He described how no food was being served, in case a line of waiters gave away the location. Drink would not be provided either, but anyone could bring his personal medicine. That included opium poppy, a popular restorative among the older mobsters.

Everyone had to arrive on foot, except the frail, whose transports would be kept inside, out of sight. Bodyguards and junior cadets were to wait close by, available if called upon. The rule was no weapons. It had also been agreed that no one would be searched. All parties had pledged they could be trusted. These were men of honour.

'Do you believe that, Corneolus?'

'Certainly not. I believe there will be violence. But not today. Today they are governed by a pact, in respect for the dead. They will merely arrange horrible deeds for the future.'

Corneolus had a way of sounding urbane and accepting, yet dour. He disapproved of these customers. He mentioned again that his wife had warned him off.

I asked how come he knew so much. He confessed his work allowed him to overhear a lot. *Designators* were assumed to use privilege, deaf to loose chatter. Mourners foolishly thought they were buying not just a procession and some sacks of rose petals, but that treasure, client confidentiality.

'No?'

'No, we are a chatty lot. Tittle-tattle flies on Rumour's wings.'

'Give me some! I don't suppose you saw their meeting agenda?'

I had overstepped a line. '*Flavia Albia!* Whatever those men are discussing was certainly not written down, especially in advance!'

'So sorry. Of course not. And no scribe will be taking minutes either.'

'Any scribe who tried it would expect a fatal aftermath.'

'Corneolus, don't worry, I won't ask you to say what those dangerous men are plotting.'

'No, you won't!' he returned hotly. I looked meek. He soon softened. 'All right, I cannot tell you anything. These people die off more frequently than most, and big funerals are my work.' He giggled. 'On the other hand, *you* could tell *me*. I can promise to stop you, if you've got it wrong.'

I gazed at him gratefully. This facilitator knew how to work with all kinds of people – including informers.

I had thought the subject through. Considering the facts I knew, I listed my ideas for meeting topics:

- The feud between the Rabirii and the Ocellus twins. Although the ancient twins had emerged from retirement today, the Rabirii would take control of the Ocellus territory along the river north of Tiber Island, plus neighbouring areas of the Campus Martius. The twins would probably demand a pay-off for yielding their traditional rights. It would have to be generous.
- The new player. The Rabirii and the Ocelli would be willing to settle, because it was in both their interests to join forces. They had acquired a new rival. A third party was after those lucrative rights and intended, if he could, to shove both other groups aside. He had a specific interest in the racehorse training up by Nero's Bridge.

Corneolus jumped in surprise. 'However do you know that? They are treating it as ultra secret!'

'Trust me. His name is Florius. He wants to take over race-fixing and betting scams. He wants to dose horses and nobble jockeys. Am I right or wrong?' Corneolus went white and did not speak. 'Is he expected to be at this conclave?'

'An invitation was discussed.'

'Where did they send it?' I demanded, quick thinking.

'His wife's house.'

'So, they think he is there?'

'No, they think he is not, but they know the wife is in contact with him.'

'Right. If you are comfortable sitting there on your basket, I shall carry on.'

- Reparation. The Rabirii would seek compensation from the Ocellus twins for the murder of young Vincentius Theo last year. Money might be included, but that would not count as full payment. Theo's parents and grandmother must have vengeance. There was a system: whoever slaughtered the young man in the street would be named and would pay for it with blood. A hitman would be commissioned. The Rabirii would pay the hitman, so the Ocelli would not be tainted by arranging the death of their own follower. Their culprit would honourably accept his fate.
- Further reparation. The Rabirii would also seek an admission from the Ocellus twins that more recently they murdered Young Roscius's runner, previously known as Legsie Lucius – now generally called the oil-pot man. If the Ocelli confessed, payment as cited above would be sought. Or with an Ocellus denial, their third-party rival might be blamed instead. As a gesture of brotherhood, the twins might offer to assist the Rabirii in obtaining vengeance against him. He would know nothing about that until it happened. Then he would know nothing about anything.
- Future. The Ocelli would retire again. The Rabirii would take over.
- Succession. A declaration would be made to name whomsoever Old Rabirius had designated his clan successor.

- Florius. Today Florius Oppicus would be solemnly welcomed as an honoured colleague. That did not make him 'family'. But neither did it signify a hitman would be sent out against him. He had the respect of all, they would say, giving him a kiss of reconciliation. If he was intelligent, he would know what they really meant.
- Balbina Milvia. Though not allowed to attend the meet, Milvia would be sent a message to assure her of honour due to her father for creating a climate in which all groups could flourish: respect for Balbinus Pius (a lovely man), his late wife Cornella Flaccida (an honest woman), and Milvia herself (a dutiful daughter), who had run the Balbinus group on the Aventine so staunchly, after the loss of her parents and in the absence of her husband. She *was* a child in the wider family. If anything ever happened to Florius, she would always be looked after; she could count on that.
- The Aventine. The Balbinus mob would retain their old turf and all its businesses with no interference. Ditto other honoured friends, the moneylending Cornellus brothers and their sister.
- Claudia Deiana. Neither the Brittuncula nor her death would even be mentioned. If Florius really had killed her, reprisal against a trouble-maker was these people's natural way of life. Nobody would care. Least of all Florius.

23

Corneolus had listened open-mouthed.

'You can guess what I want to know now, Corneolus?'

'Where is the conclave?' He still kept up the pretence that he ought not to tell me. So instead he took me. Of course, the crime lords, including Florius, were no longer there.

The day's luxury continued. They had met in a stunning room, paved with peacock-eye flooring and with walls faced in black slate, decorated with graceful gold-leaf arabesques. A series of throne-like chairs had been provided, all now empty, though cushions bore imprints of underworld back-sides. Rose garlands hung from the ceiling as a statement that anything said was secret.

Lurking just outside this fine venue we found someone: Juventus, the Second Cohort's 'specialised crime' officer. He was long-faced, vague and normally lackadaisical. His foot-wear used to be held together with string, but he had acquired different boots, clearly from an old-clothes stall. These had a strap missing on the left and the toe cover lost on the right. His dowdiness made Corneolus look smart despite his unlaundered tunic.

'I had better not introduce you two,' I joked. 'One goes only by his professional name and the other is deep under cover. This is a grand clash of the camouflaged with the incognito. I myself am feeling over-obvious.' The humour passed over their heads.

Corneolus faded from the scene once he had delivered me, but Juventus hung on. He was a lonely soul. He had been deserted by the rest of the Second, who had now returned to their station-house. It stood right outside the gardens so they could be recalled if needed, but it was time for them to hand over to the night shift.

I demanded to know about the conclave. Juventus started at the end. The attendees had dispersed in several directions so he could not tail them. This was a typically lame Second Cohort excuse. I growled back that he ought to have been able to follow at least one; I said I wished it had been Florius. 'Was Florius there?'

'Am I supposed to know Florius?'

'I do admire how you keep up-to-date, Juventus! He is the current head of the Balbinus clan. Finding him is urgent, a city-wide priority.'

'Nobody told me.'

'I am telling you.'

'I should have been sent a communiqué.'

'I can plug any gaps in your knowledge base. Just tell me if you saw Florius tonight.'

'He arrived after it started, then stayed to the end.'

'So you do know him?'

'I didn't know who he was, but when he turned up, they greeted him by name.'

'Then what?'

'The others asked him how he had enjoyed his holiday. He said it was fifteen years too long. They joked, "And in the wrong province." He laughed with them. He seems a very pleasant personality. They gave him a warm welcome.'

This was so detailed I wondered if Juventus had been sent on a positivity training course. 'Juventus! Were you hiding behind a pillar?'

'No, that never works.'

The idiot must have tried it. It can work, with a wide column and a skeletal informer, but since observing gangster activity took him to so many bars, Juventus was a chubby soul. His face was full, his chin plump, his arms and legs were growing fat with more than muscle, and his belly had swollen so it hung over his belt (another of his pieces of string).

I stayed patient. He would implode with a panic attack if I was too forceful. 'How come you overheard them? What did you do?'

'I went in with the wine servers.'

I gave him a suspicious look. 'Corneolus said they speci-fied no wine!'

Even Juventus, that sorry person, laughed. 'These are gangsters, Albia!'

I mimed shock. 'You mean, they broke the rules?'

'Absolutely. I saw all the drinks paraphernalia going in. Amphorae, goblets, herbs, sieves, and a great big metal heater for hot mixing water. I helped the slave who was staggering along with that, and stayed in the room to operate the tap.'

'Initiative!' I flattered him. He blushed. 'No vetting procedure?'

'Who needs it, when everyone is scared shitless of them? The wine waiters were from bars they control, so they all know me, Albia.'

If true, this was strange. Viewed by the waiters as a familiar face and by the gangsters as harmless, Juventus had heard everything? I must have shown my disbelief, so he took me into the meeting room, where the gormless lunk pointed out the water heater to prove his story.

It was a big tank, set on a tripod stand, topped with winged figures. You see them everywhere – everywhere with money. Someone would come to collect it, no doubt, but in the meantime it was safe, along with the rest of the serving gear. Only someone who wanted his throat cut would steal the favourite wine paraphernalia of Rome's top mobsters.

Though still sceptical, I made Juventus report all he had heard. Most matched my earlier guesswork. What Juventus added for me was the name of the Rabirius hitman: Turcus.

'Do you know him, Juventus?'

'Well, he's the Sixth's baby really. He was once pointed out to me – he was a smart businessman, of quiet bearing. He must have been sent on an errand into our district.'

'A contract?'

'I wouldn't know. He visited a bar I had just been to – he was asking where a local man lived. I was going that way, so I took him to the corner and showed him. It was no trouble.' Sadly, it did not surprise me that Juventus had let himself be dragged into showing a hitman where to find his mark – and presumably kill the person. 'So I can say,' he burbled innocently, 'Turcus and I are on hello terms. I was told he rarely socialises, but he seemed a decent character.'

This decent character had been summoned to the conclave room tonight. The gangsters commissioned Turcus to take out an Ocellus hood, one Castor, who had organised the death of young Vincentius Theo. However, Turcus could not be given another contract for avenging Legsie Lucius. The Ocellus twins denied responsibility. Legsie's killer remained unknown, as did the motive for his death.

'What are they planning to do about it?'

137

'Bide their time.'

'That sounds worrying! Who was named as the appointed heir of Old Rabirius?' I asked, thinking that whoever it was would still want revenge for their loss of Legsie.

'Rabirius Vincentius.'

'Tall man, dark toga? Wasn't he once facing criminal charges so has been exiled for years? How can he safely operate in Rome?'

'Protected, apparently. The lawyer, Mamillianus, told them it is all fixed with officials.'

'He was there? Which officials? Did Mamillianus say?'

'No, he was cagey, and they just laughed about it.' Juventus was squirming as I fixed him with more intensity. 'It sounded right, Flavia Albia. Vincentius is untouchable. He will run the Rabirius group, who will take over the Ocellus turf. The twins are bowing out. Young Roscius was given a baton as a deputy leader. Gallo will be their councillor. He will stand to one side as an adviser and make decisions for the good of all.'

'Or the bad . . . And Florius? You say he was greeted as a partner?'

'He leads the Balbinus mob,' Juventus confirmed. 'He went around the group one by one, very formally. Each of the men embraced him like a son or brother.'

'All good?'

'Not quite. Vincentius told Florius he could not have the racetrack scams and must stop his encroachment. He groaned, but he agreed. The decisions at the conclave will be upheld by all, Vincentius pronounced. That is the traditional way.'

Whether Florius believed their welcome, or they trusted his promises to comply, would become apparent in due course. Juventus said he left when they all did.

Florius would go back into hiding. I had lost my chance today.

24

Outside again, I absorbed the lonesome atmosphere of a large garden at night. Scents of woodsmoke, incense and flowers wafted on a chill breeze. Although there were lights everywhere, courtesy of the funeral, they only made the in-between shadows darker and more menacing. I could hear city sounds coming from the distance but they seemed otherworldly. The internal silence somehow suggested people might be watching, people with sinister intentions. I felt uneasy.

Juventus was still hovering. He was so useless he provided no sense of security. To cover my nervousness, I tackled him again about the meeting: 'I still cannot believe the crooks let you stay in the room.'

'I suppose they thought I must be all right – because of Vergelius.'

'Who is he?'

'Our tribune.'

'So that's his name. Wouldn't they think he had sent you to spy on them?'

'Oh, no, they are all friendly.'

'What does that mean?' I could guess, and it was doleful news.

'The tribune keeps on good terms. He used to go to the races with Old Rabirius.'

'Doesn't Vergelius fear that fraternising with scum puts him in a bad light?'

'What scum?'

'Gangsters, man! Extortioners. Powerful community predators, who put the squeeze on helpless victims.'

Juventus hung his head. 'He must know what he's doing. It's only the races anyway.'

Titan's testicles! It was so much more than that. If the corrupt lawyer boasted that the newly returned Rabirius Vincentius was untouchable, it was probably because this grubby Vergelius – Tribune of the Second Cohort of Vigiles, the very officer who ought to arrest him and send him to trial – had been paid off. No wonder those crooks gathered below the roses were complacent about having their wine watered by his dimwit special agent.

It also explained why Vergelius had ever assigned a clown like this to 'gangster liaison'. I could imagine the tribune jovially reassuring those in whose grimy pockets he resided, '*Operation Phoenix? The anti-vice initiative? Load of crap some stiff thought up . . . I'll put Juventus on it. He won't give you any trouble. Sit him down on a bench with a raisin bun and that's all the infiltration we'll bother you with.*'

'Was Vergelius at the conclave?'

'He sent kind regards. Gallo announced it to them all and they solemnly raised their wine cups.'

Dear gods. This was like listening to good-luck messages from distant relatives at a wedding.

Juventus had no more to give me and I was anxious to be rid of him. Luckily some members of the Second ran past us; they called out that the praetor had ordered them as firefighters to mount the pyre and retrieve the eagle.

Juventus asked if I wanted to come to watch them singeing their tunics, or would I be safe on my own? I waved him away. He galloped off after the others excitedly.

Alone, I began to wander. I was in a dingy mood because of hearing about the Second's tribune. This reminder of Rome's poisonous corruption left me feeling soiled.

There were too many buildings, which stood too far apart in the landscape, for me to search them all. Even so, taking the conclave room with its slate-adorned walls as an epicentre, I circled on a listless exploration in case Florius was still nearby. At one point I found myself in a room where the floor was made up of alabaster segments, framed by green glass borders. Water jets had been set into the walls at around three-foot intervals, their pathways crossing to create extraordinary light and sound effects, now even better by lamplight. There were indeed lamps, including expensive ones with five, six, seven flame-holes burning, and the jets were playing; someone had been using the room. Someone with clout.

A slave, presumably deemed invisible in the same way Juventus had been, attended the room in charge of the waterworks. As he began turning off taps so that the sprays coughed and died, it struck me their audio effects would have made a good cover for conversation.

'Who was here?'

'Men.'

'How many?'

'Two. Three, if you count the one hiding ten feet behind in the bushes.'

'Tailing them?' This was a new factor. 'Did he come in?'

141

'He lurked outside. They never knew. He was nipping along behind the three-tiered urns, but he froze if they glanced behind them. He was good!'

'Nice work spotting him. Who was he following? Know any names?'

I was talking to a long-haired skinny lad in a tired tunic. He said the man who had slipped him coins to set up the room was a stranger. He felt no allegiance, so told me straight out: 'Gallo.'

I took a guess: who might want a meeting with Gallo, away from other eyes? 'Was the second called Florius?'

'Could have been.'

'What was their purpose?'

'Talking.'

'Conspiring? Did you listen in?'

'No, I stayed outside.' He then gave me a look we both understood.

'Walls and doorways are sometimes no barrier,' I commented, with a smile. 'If I give you extra money, might you remember anything you overheard?'

He lit with a gleam of acknowledgement. So I did open my purse for him, and he did show that he had a good memory.

His name was Petrus. He might be half starved, but people were wrong to assume that suffering equalled stupidity: this lad was bright. From the start he had recognised the kind of meeting Gallo wanted, so he made sure to acquire saleable information for later use. He was a lad with a plan: to save up and buy his freedom. For me, simple nosiness can be golden, but people with needs make the best witnesses.

As far as Petrus understood, Gallo and Florius had been in discussion about the Rabirius clan's new grouping. Gallo, whose role as their councillor was supposed to be impartial, nevertheless made an offer to lobby for Florius regarding the horse-race scams.

What was in this for Gallo? He wanted to know something. Gallo had tried to ascertain whether Florius was present at the killing of the Rabirius man, Legsie Lucius. Denying he was there, Florius was sardonic. He claimed he never laid hands on targets himself. I knew that was untrue if his victims were girls destined to work in his brothels. I had also seen him, in person, cold-bloodedly open up an opponent's guts with a sword. Still, he maintained that nowadays he had people to act for him. Gallo would understand that, since he worked in the same way. They made the choices; they gave the orders. Blood stayed on their menials' hands.

There was no denial of him ordering the death. Florius complained that he knew Legsie Lucius was a Rabirius runner and – although he said he spoke hypothetically – if Legsie had lured someone with Balbinus connections into danger and taken them out, as a move against Florius, Legsie's punishment was only a start. The dolium death sent a message, but the Rabirii should expect more reprisals. This was fair: this was the code.

'Who were they talking about, Petrus? Who had been "taken out"?'

'Not said.'

No need, I thought. Gallo fully understood. So Florius was exerting pressure to be allowed to share the racecourse scams in return for not further challenging the Rabirii over the death of Claudia Deiana. Petrus confirmed that had been said.

'Were threats exchanged? Did their conversation end badly?'

'Apparently not.' The slave had a sense of irony: 'They assured one another they were both men of honour.'

'Ha! You don't think so?'

'Well, I might have believed it but . . .' He tapped his nose. 'Gallo promised he would make enquiries, which should not take long. He told Florius to meet him later by our animal collection. As soon as Florius had gone – still with that secret tail behind him, incidentally – Gallo waved a denarius at me. He gave me a big wink and asked who kept the keys to the dangerous beasts' cages.'

'Do you know? Did you tell him?'

'I could have used the silver, but I pretended not to know. We don't want anyone letting out a lion or bear. It takes us days to catch them if they ever escape. I hate that. They enjoy a little romp too much and won't return to their proper places.'

'Gallo wants to unlock their cages so they will go for Florius?'

'If he thought he could harm his "honourable" colleague that way, I told him it wouldn't work. Our big beasts are here in retirement because they are too friendly. They have no teeth. They loll around. They come up to you because they think people bring food.' Petrus dropped his voice confidentially: 'The only creature I'd never go near is Struthio.'

Who was Struthio? I enquired gently.

'The ostrich.'

Well, he sounded harmless. Just a big birdie.

Surely?

25

Struthio was indeed big.

Hurrying to the menagerie, we had heard him let out a deep booming call, at which my companion speeded up anxiously. We reached a row of cages where, along with other creatures, a very old lion and a half-mad bear were also loudly protesting.

As we approached, Petrus had gasped that the ostrich was easily upset. If anyone disturbed him in territory that he viewed as his own, he went for them. He could not fly, but would easily outrun anything on earth. 'He's not very bright, but so strong he can kill a lion if he wants to. If he's out and he spots you, lie down behind a bush and cover your face. You have to hope that if he can't see you he will lose interest and wander off.'

I did not ask what he would do when he was still interested in someone. We were about to witness that.

The ostrich stood over eight feet tall when gazing around. He must have weighed three hundred pounds, twice as much as the average Roman. He was a massive bundle of black feathers, with white wingtips and tail. His long, sturdy, pinkish-coloured legs had two-toed hoof-like feet, with intimidating four-inch talons that were made for ripping flesh. With his bendy neck, the bird looked goofy, but he meant business.

Torches lit the scene with a dull glow. Struthio was still inside his cage but Gallo must have broken the lock. With the door open, he was trying to aggravate the bird. He cannot have guessed how fast the ostrich would react. Petrus and I watched in horror. Struthio spread his wings in warning. Gallo was within reach at that point. Struthio kicked out. A massive claw tore half of Gallo's arm open. Next moment, blood was also pouring down his face where Struthio had nipped at his eye with his beak.

Gallo tried to cower behind the cage door. He ended up on the ground, howling with pain. Struthio, frightened and furious, ran past because he had seen someone else. A terrified man had leaped up from the cover of a large, three-tiered urn across the terrace path. He ought to have stayed there; he would have been safe.

Seeing him run away, Struthio launched into a pursuit. The fugitive turned back to look. Twice as tall, the ostrich caught up, then rammed him in the body with its strong bony breastbone. When he fell, the giant bird jumped straight on top. Petrus and I began shouting, but the ostrich kept giving the man devastating kicks in the stomach, aiming forwards and using those terrifying talons to lacerate his body. All the victim's internal organs were soon deeply mangled. He was done for.

Drawn by our shouts and the animals' alarm calls, men came running. Some were keepers, who knew what to do. A long plank was utilised, with people on both ends, so they pushed back the ostrich from its victim then manoeuvred Struthio inside the cage.

Helpers went to the victims. I had no interest in Gallo. I made myself walk over and join those who were looking at the man with the torn flesh and bloody guts.

I knew it could not be Florius, but must be the tail Petrus had seen following Florius and Gallo.

Now I could see whose corpse it was. Struthio had killed the special agent, Nicon.

26

Back in his cage, Struthio was rattling to and fro, lifting his wings and letting out agitated cries. Through the bars, a keeper soothed him, but the ostrich refused to settle. Other animals in a row alongside were drawn in by his intense anxiety. A lion yawned a desultory roar, while bears paced and ran short distances between the bars that confined them.

Someone threw an old blanket over the dead man, hiding the mess of his stomach cavity yet leaving that round face visible. I had despised him, but I could not bear to look any more.

Julius Karus materialised, with auxiliaries. I could hear the champing horses they had all leaped off. Karus raced in the lead. He let out a disgusted snarl when he saw what had happened to Nicon. A lifetime legionary, his watchword would be 'diligence' or similar. Although this was his own agent, he kicked at him in frustration.

Some idiot told him Petrus and I had been witnesses. My presence put Karus on his mettle. He knew who I was, though: I greeted him by name to emphasise we had had previous encounters.

The slave had collapsed, sobbing with distress. While the Varduli were inspecting Gallo, I managed a sly nod to Petrus. To Karus he was just a slave, to be tortured to oblivion if there was no other lead. Since I knew all the boy had overheard, I encouraged him to escape a pointless beating. He understood my signal, so he slid off. I hoped he could seek refuge with friends.

Karus ordered his men to carry Gallo to the Castra Peregrina. There, he said, they 'had the best medical facilities'. I suspected the wounded man was being sent for a beating, but Gallo's own people were perfectly capable of retrieving him. I had seen it before. Their expensive lawyer, Mamillianus, would skitter into that dark barracks to extract him with clinking sacks of joy. Money talks. Corruption wins. I wasted no anxiety on him.

'Nicon was tailing Florius,' I said to Karus.

'I don't believe that.'

'It's true,' I insisted. 'He had been seen following.'

'I doubt it! Nicon was my best man.' That said little for the rest of his squad. 'So where is Florius now?' Karus mused, a stagey remark to himself. 'He attended the warlords' meet. My guess is he's long gone.' I stayed quiet. With angry bullies, patience is best practice. If Karus meant to turn ugly, nothing in my repertoire would stop him. 'He is with his wife,' Karus decided. 'No question. That's where he holes up.'

'Her place was searched.'

'Someone must have warned him, then. He toddled off out for an hour while the squaddies were there. I know it in my water ... But why was Nicon looking for him by these cages?'

'Florius and Gallo had agreed to rendezvous,' I explained. 'Florius was a no-show. Too canny. Florius has been hiding from the authorities for years. You were in Britain. You must have seen how well he did that. The others have sworn an oath of brotherhood, but he won't trust them; if he approached and spotted Gallo planning an ambush, he will have swiftly backed out. Nicon got himself stuck behind a garden feature. When the bird attacked Gallo, Nicon tried to flee.' Karus tossed his head contemptuously: his men were trained to stay cool whatever horror unfolded in front of them. Still, this one was dead. Training had failed to save him.

I stopped talking. I felt exhausted.

Karus gave me his power-crazed, man-in-charge look. He said my husband was waiting for me by the Old Rabirius pyre. I did not ask how Karus knew that. Spying on people was his business. Still, as a comparative newcomer to Rome, he acted cautiously near a city magistrate, even one whose rank was time-expired. Oddly enough, I never felt he would start a feud with us; he was more subtle. He knew we had influence, which he might one day want to exploit. He collected contacts for future use. I suppose informers are no different, though we'd say our motives are cleaner.

In shock after what I had witnessed, I was no longer sure how to find the pyre. Karus solved my dilemma. It was probably to stop me interfering, though he may have seen me shivering. One of his men received a clipped direction to take me to shelter. I was beyond arguing. I wanted to be with my husband, so I let myself be steered to a nearby building to wait for him. Automatically, the Varduloran escort eyed me up. I gave him a stare that was straight from the old days in Londinium. He sloped off, though I kept in mind that he might lurk nearby. I nursed an oil lamp back to life so I would not be in darkness.

To calm myself, I stared at frescos in the room where I had been left. All the elements were familiar, yet subtly unusual. The field had been painted in blocks, a classic red colour, yet placed against a white background, with panels that looked like carpets hung up on the candelabra posts from their corners; their edges – fringed with ivy-like foliage instead of tassels – were curved. Birds perched on the top. The dado below was fairly normal, with rural, maritime and mythological emblems in squares and rectangles against a blue background; the frieze above had rows of intricate detail unlike any I had seen before, with the regularity of Greek key or egg and dart, yet freer curls and roundels that were almost Celtic.

On a different occasion I might have made sketches. Maybe those painters who hung around our house could be sent to look. Delicate Claudian designs would be better than the decorators' own dumb idea of a *Battle of Salamis*.

Home seemed very far away. I dropped my art appreciation. All I could think of was the dead face of that agent after the ostrich had ripped him inside out.

Impatient for Tiberius, I walked back outside. All was quiet by the cages. Struthio gawked through the bars at me but did not take fright. The dead man and the wounded Gallo had been taken away. Karus and all his men were gone.

Tiberius came hurrying along soon afterwards, with a big chair he had commandeered; it had a louche odour – macerated iris? – but the bearers were speedy and ran without jolting. As we set off, we heard a loud crash as the three-storey pyre collapsed, dropping the top pavilion down into its fiery heart. Even through the chair's skimpy curtains, light flickered briefly. Now Old Rabirius would be transformed from a feared villain into urn fodder: harmless ash and lumps of inert material. His soul would wander some glade where the spirits of dead gangsters had their way paid by ghostly associates, making his feral existence in Hades as easy as his life on earth had been.

No eagle marked his passage. Tiberius told me the Second Cohort had dodged the praetor's rescue order, so the Fourth showed their own heroics; they climbed up through the flames and retrieved the raptor, at the cost of only one broken leg, a strained back and burns to most participants. I found out later where the eagle and his handler went.

At that point, I did not tell Tiberius Manlius what I had seen before he came for me.

I had been standing in an ornate porch. Four or five noisy men came up the terrace path in a group, almost at a marching pace. I saw they were in cloaks, a couple of which were hooded as if the wearers were northern. They jostled one another, shifting positions. It looked casual but may have been a cover for one man in their midst.

I could not see him properly. He had better boots than the rest and I thought he was bare-headed. Balding, perhaps. Not contributing to the noise. I never saw his face, but even half hidden by his companions, the way he walked was unforgettable to me.

I felt sick. I was also physically spent. There were too many in that group for me to approach them. For once I was not so daft as to try. Longing only for Tiberius, I could not even bring myself to follow them. They were leaving the gardens, but I never saw where they went afterwards.

Sometimes you have to give up and reconvene another day. Nobody else seemed to think Claudia Deiana mattered, but the vigiles still thought she was murdered when she went up against her husband on her own. Though often rash, I would not do the same and make myself a second victim. I accepted the danger. In despair, I let him go.

But I knew that the man I saw leaving was Florius.

27

My husband had squashed into the chair with me. As always, his solidity and quiet air were comforting. I told him in a few sentences what I had learned from Corneolus and Juventus. Details could wait. Tiberius said Morellus had taken his children home, leaving him by the pyre until Karus's men had told him where to find me. All we wanted now was to be at home.

When we arrived, our household were managing to amuse themselves. The low barrow Tiberius had deployed in his disguise as a gardener was standing in our courtyard. Lamps glowed; a brazier was burning gently. A strange man in leather clothes had made himself a bed; he was lying on a mat he must have filched from Dromo. Dromo was whittling a stick disconsolately. Other members of our staff were leaning over the balcony, watching.

Little Gaius and Lucius had gone right up close. Sitting cross-legged on the ground, they were intent on what the stranger was guarding: no other boys in our neighbourhood had anything like this.

On the garden barrow stood a large cage. In the cage, eyeing the scene in baleful silence, perched an enormous eagle.

28

Next morning, I rose early, bracing myself for having to explain to small boys with big ideas that we could not keep their new friend.

Fortunately, the falconer had done my work. He was a miserable expert with a pock-marked face and constipated attitude. Sounding country-born, he said the eagle had been taken as a chick from the mountains. It used to be kept as a status symbol at the country estate of Old Rabirius, but the falconer refused to go back there. The bird had to stay with him, because nobody else would know how to look after it.

'What's his name?'

'A noble bird like this never has a pet name.'

The falconer had shown Gaius and Lucius a hole in his cheek where this mean raptor had nearly cost him an eye. He intoned dourly that birds of prey can never be domesticated. The boys kept asking hopefully, so he said it several times. He stressed that eagles may look handsome but are not fluffy, will not allow stroking, loathe soppy conversation, hate everyone, expect to be treated like gods. They require endless feeding. Their manners are foul; they are by nature aggressive and spiteful; they call for serious protective clothing.

'Don't try to give him titbits. He'll have your fingers off.'

'Rather like Flavia Albia!' commented Tiberius. Being a wise man, he murmured it. He and I exchanged a private smile.

The falconer, who shared his bird's malevolence, further enjoyed himself threatening the children that the eagle would love to get its mighty claws into them, carry them off and eat them. Not as scared as he might have wanted, Gaius and Lucius decided we would be upset if that happened, so they edged back from the cage to preserve themselves for Tiberius and me. I tried not to take the wicked foster-mother attitude.

What settled the matter for our boys was that they already knew the rule of law – established in my family for my brother's ferret and long before that when a young Tiberius had wanted to keep a crocodile: children were allowed unusual pets, so long as they were responsible for serving obnoxious foodstuffs and mucking out cages. Gaius and Lucius finally turned tail when they saw that the eagle had not only vomited pellets of bone, fur and who-knew-what ghastliness that morning – they were intrigued by the pellets – but that it regularly ejected a whitewashy deluge of filthy-smelling excrement.

Tiberius pointed out that even the vigiles, who had plenty of water for sluicing away smelly bird poo, had refused to give the eagle shelter overnight. Morellus had promised he and the lads would come to fetch the bird, but it was starting to look as if he might forget.

Now we had to find something else to do with it.

I was exempted from that discussion because Julius Karus came knocking. Rodan, seeming to recognise fellow vermin, abandoned his porridge bowl to let him in. Karus announced

154

his intention of interviewing me. He gazed around as if noting our house's layout and escape routes in case he ever came to arrest us.

Tiberius asked whether Karus would like to present the eagle as a gift to his patron, the Emperor. Karus strutted up to inspect it, sniffed at its mess once, then, toady though he was, he declined. In any case Domitian would want to know where it had come from. Explaining origins would start too many difficult lines of enquiry. Even Our Master's fixer shrank from fixing that. Like the best and worst of them, he knew his limits.

Self-knowledge made him dangerous. As a hard man, Karus might be deemed stupid, but I saw more to him: he had an intense capacity for organisation, which he used in the darkest ways. Turn your back and he would stab you in it. He was bound to be carrying a secret knife, and not for coring winter pears.

Gaius and Lucius amused themselves walking stiffly around the courtyard, mimicking his sniff. I had moved Karus to the room where I held client meetings, so he might not have seen this.

Tiberius joined us. This pleased Karus, an inevitable traditionalist who only approved of women answering questions in the presence of their heads of household.

'Actually,' my husband demurred, 'if you were interviewing me instead, I should ask Flavia Albia to be present. We are a team.' Karus hated that, of course. In the context of wives, the verb 'ask' made him bilious. (Could he be married? Was she a harridan?) Tiberius sounded obliging as he carried on, 'I was sorry to hear about your agent. What a terrible fate! Nicon came here from Britain, didn't he? On secondment to the Castra Peregrina? What was his legion?'

Karus could find no good reason to refuse an answer, though he squirmed with reluctance. 'The Second, the Second Augusta.'

'Same as your father!' Tiberius exclaimed to me, as if this was a joyous discovery. 'And Petronius Longus . . . I do wish we had known.' He managed to imply that my relatives, those two perpetual lads, might have used their old army connection to winkle out information about Nicon, especially information that was not supposed to surface.

Karus thought he should move on before he lost control. He took a breath. I plunged in before he could start: 'What happened on the Claudia Deiana inquiry before Nicon died? I assume he had reported to you? Had he managed to inspect where she stayed, Itia's lodging house? Her luggage was still there. I assume it has been searched now. Was there anything significant?'

Grumpily Karus conceded that Auntie Itia's had been visited, with nothing found. 'She'd got rid of the stuff. Still, her place could have been a good lead.'

I held back that I myself had suggested it.

He did tell us Nicon had confirmed that Claudia Deiana was called out from Itia's on the night she was murdered: a message, supposedly from Florius, was brought by a man who had since been identified as Legsie Lucius. Claudia had gone with Legsie willingly.

'You still think Florius is hiding up with Balbina Milvia?' I prodded.

Karus had had a big idea about that. 'Maybe not. The bugger holds equestrian rank, doesn't he? That means property!' he exclaimed. 'Four hundred thou sesterces, minimum, just to jump over the qualification bar. I've called up his files. I'll have any place he ever owned marked on a map and riddled through so not a woodlouse escapes discovery.'

Tiberius and I looked admiring. We said well done, and please let us know if he found anything . . .

I pursed my lips. 'Given that the oil-pot man was a Rabirius runner,' I suggested, 'if Florius wanted her dead because she was a nuisance, do you think he had done a deal with them to borrow Legsie that night? Hadn't he messengers in the Balbinus organisation? Or did he not want to use his own people, because it might lead back to him? Yet why would Florius arrange to have Legsie killed afterwards? Was it simply to silence him?'

'Who knows?' Karus shrugged noncommittally.

'Somebody does know,' Tiberius observed. 'I saw the scene. Several men must have been deployed to pickle the runner. Someone with a lot of clout arranged it.'

'Florius!' decreed Karus.

'Yes,' I put to both of them. 'But Florius is trying to set up a brotherhood with the Rabirii, He pretends he is a colleague they can work with. To murder a favourite operative of theirs – and to do so very publicly – fails to fit. It is starting a war, not an alliance.'

Tiberius nodded. 'What do you think, then, Albia?'

'I think putting the runner in the dolium shows Florius was deeply exercised over Claudia Deiana. He was warning the Rabirii with the strongest possible message. He doesn't want them interfering in his business – but he also believes they didn't simply lure Claudia out. For some reason it was they who killed her.'

'That seems stupid!' Tiberius commented.

'It does. She was his to deal with. And this has made a festering wound for all parties. Gallo was seriously trying to find out yesterday whether or not Florius arranged Legsie's murder. When Florius virtually admitted it, Gallo tried to get him fatally jumped by that ostrich.'

157

'So,' Tiberius pondered, 'the runner was never "borrowed", the Rabirii finished Claudia off. We don't know why but we do know Florius is intent on revenge?'

'Yes, there is blame on both sides and both sides want reprisals.'

Karus was running a stage behind. 'Why, if she was badgering him, would Florius object to how or by whom the nuisance woman was abducted?' It was a fair question, even if he had asked it pompously. 'And why would the Rabirii know anything about her in the first place?'

'That I cannot say,' I answered honestly. 'The other question has to be, if they arranged her hijack from Itia's, who actually threw her off the bridge?'

'Their people.'

'So were they trying to make Florius grateful because they got rid of her? Was it a "welcome home" present? Or, were they intentionally upsetting him? Perhaps your unit's surveillance of the gangs will throw up a reason, Karus? Gallo or Young Roscius must know.'

'How is Gallo?' Tiberius interjected. 'Will he survive?'

'He should, but we lost our grip on him last night. That bent lawyer fixed a *very* slick pick-up from the Castra.' Karus sounded as if he admired Mamillianus and his jail-busting methods. He went on blandly, 'I am not too worried. Inter-clan strife could work. If Gallo does take out Florius it will solve our problem the easy way.'

Tiberius propped his chin on his linked fingers. 'And what about Nicon? You had him working the Florius inquiry. Now he's gone, will you reassign his commission?'

'No one of the right calibre available,' Karus replied, sounding open: officer to magistrate. 'I wanted a man with past experience in Britain. Not too many of those afloat in

Rome! I have my own workload, looking at the wider picture. No choice left, so I shall be relying on the Fourth Cohort, at least in the interim. What I really want to say to you,' he was leaning hard towards my husband, deliberately ignoring me, 'is that you need to stop your wife pottering where it isn't suitable. This all calls for official action, with armed back-up. Great gods, man – a few moments earlier last evening, and it could have been Flavia Albia having her liver and spleen torn out by that bloody great bird's talons!'

Tiberius did not look at me. He had not seen what Struthio had done, but I had described it. I knew the thought had been worrying him ever since. He nodded. I made no protest. I would come to an appeasement with him later, privately.

Nothing further was discussed. We managed to push Karus off to annoy other people. He was going to see Scaurus at the Fourth Cohort's main station-house, intending to dump the Florius search on them. We happily lent him our runabout Paris to show him the best way to the Via Piscinae Publicae. Paris came back, reporting that on the way Karus had been asking him questions about us, to which he had spun silly answers.

I never found out what Karus had intended to question me about.

29

Some days you have to behave. Tiberius was returning to the new marble yard on the Campus Martius; now it had reopened after the oil-pot crime, there might be better stock on view. I sweetly said I would accompany him. He gave me a narrow look, fully aware that compliance had never been my style. When we first met, I was throwing defiance at him; I saw no reason to go soft now he had given me his store-cupboard keys. We were married. He had known what that would mean.

We went to the yard. While Tiberius was rootling among their lines of stone, I strolled on the riverbank with Barley. Tiberius had no great hopes of finding what he wanted, so said he would not be long. I teased that this is what husbands always promise, then tend to be hours. He grinned, looking insecure. 'Don't get in any trouble!' he warned.

'Oh, no, darling!'

He quickened his step as he left me, like a man who needed to scurry in case his girl ran off with the first no-good bumboat-rower who came sculling along.

However, the man I took up with was perfectly decent. Pottering aboard his vessel, it was the dredger captain. His ship's activity below Tiber Island had brought Claudia Deiana's body to the surface after she drowned. Now the dredger was moored further upriver, though once again not currently working.

I hailed him at once. He remembered me. His dog recognised my dog, which cemented our acquaintance. I tied up Barley on the wharf. The beagly barker, who never seemed to leave the boat, was maddened for a few moments by her presence out of his reach, then gave up and sat down on the deck in a huff. Barley seated herself demurely to wait for me, batting her eyelashes like a nymph in a myth who had escaped rape. I skipped up the gangway.

I asked where the crew were: gone ahead to their usual lodging house, since the landlady would supply a fish supper if they let her know they were coming ashore. They had previously held suckling-pig barbecues, with a firepit in the back yard, but that had been stopped after the next-door premises were set on fire. The captain smirked over the incident. 'Slightly unfortunate. The red tunics tried to whack a hefty fine on the landlady.'

We laughed. No doubt we were both remembering how feebly the vigiles had behaved the other day. 'Did she ever pay?'

'No, but she gave their chief a black eye, so we were in credit for cheering her on.'

'You don't like him?'

'He's all right – for an esparto-mat lobber. He thinks his big fire axe makes him special. He'll be even more special when he cuts off his own foot with it.'

I didn't bother to ask about the landlady, since she sounded true to type.

I had assumed there would be little more known about Claudia Deiana. Surprisingly, the skipper told me he had been asking his own questions among the riverside community. Turning up the body like that had given him a feeling of responsibility. But he had found no one who witnessed the woman being kidnapped or going off the bridge – 'At least, no one will own up to seeing anything.'

I tightened my cloak. 'Frightened? People know her history? That she had been a gangster's live-in woman?'

He made no reply. In itself it was affirmative.

The skipper had a chunky build, wide rather than tall in the way of Roman working men. He was tanned from a life in the open air, and bow-legged. He shifted on his feet as if standing still for our conversation gave him arthritis pains after years of hauling ropes and heavy-duty shovelling. For all I knew, he was a complete villain and cruel to his mother, but he had a solid aura of wisdom and honesty.

I told him about Nicon's death by ostrich. He had already heard. News had whistled around the wharfside shanties, where Nicon was already a byword. Nobody had liked him. 'And it wasn't because he was a foreigner. Well, not only that.'

'His officer-in-charge seems to think he was competent,' I said. 'I never saw it.'

'Searching for that fellow, he came whistling around the bars and lock-ups. Pushing in where people were having a quiet bite, asking his stupid questions. But when something really shocking occurred, he didn't want to know.' The skipper seemed more bitter than I expected if he was complaining about an official's harassment.

'Something shocking? You mean the man in the dolium?'

'Oh, him too!'

I picked up the hint. 'Was there something else?'

The skipper was reluctant to speak. I let enough time pass to show respect for this situation. Patience generally works.

The dredger captain's name was Scribonius. While we were marking this pause, I asked him. Scribonius began today's story obliquely. Going back to Nicon, he said that when the funeral director, Fundanus, had come to remove Claudia's body, Nicon already knew her name.

'The swine never said!' I was furious. If Nicon had known who she was, he must have understood all along why she was visiting Rome, not to mention who might have had a motive for disposing of her and what that motive could be.

Claudia had visited the Fourth Cohort's station-house, so Nicon might have seen her there. I wondered: when the vigiles were told that a corpse had been churned up in the river, was it perhaps no coincidence that Nicon had come down to the wharf to take charge? A routine body being dragged out would only have called for a few basic troops. He was an officer. In any case, during his commission to investigate Florius for tax dodging, he was supposed to be working under cover, which should have prevented him wandering into normal business.

'So Nicon realised who she was,' I mused to Scribonius. 'How could he have known in advance?'

'He knew, and he did not care about her,' returned the skipper, sounding angry again. 'Nicon and his men were even laughing about it later, when that man Fundanus picked up the corpse and took her off on his horrible meat-wagon.'

The funeral director really did collect her. The skipper confirmed that, and I could see it was making him angry. What he said next became all the more shocking: yesterday at first light – which would have been while people on our side were assembling in the Horti Lamiani for the Rabirius funeral – there was a horrible discovery. Across on the Transtiberina bank a woman's body was seen, washed ashore. 'And it was the same body! Claudia Deiana.'

Observers had seen odd similarities. Another plaid cloak, for instance. People hailed the dredger, which was out on the water. Scribonius took the boat over; he and the crew paddled ashore in their dinghy.

'It was unbelievable. She had been beached by the current this time. But there we found her, lying on her back staring up at us, as if to say, "Here I am, fellows. It's me all over again."'

To be drowned in a river once was unfortunate. To be regurgitated by the same river twice defied belief. To have been supposedly cremated but to turn up, untouched by fire but sodden with yet more muddy water, was an outrage.

I could not grasp this. Fundanus was a man I found revolting at the best of times. How could he have decided that since nobody would mourn her, he would steal the money he had been given, keep the urn, abandon responsibility and simply return Claudia Deiana to the river?

'He ought to have done it better,' said Scribonius, heavily. 'He knows where to deposit a corpse, if he wants it to remain secret. Undertakers learn where to slide one in, so it travels all the way to the sea and never winds up on the bank. You just have to understand the current.' He was speaking, with distaste, of a recognised skill among funeral directors.

'Is this regular?' I gasped.

'They all do it. When they have bodies found in the streets that no one will claim, or a corpse with no friends or relatives so nobody is paying. Slaves. Vagrants. Babies, quite often . . . They know where to drop them. They must think we don't know.'

I was appalled. 'Bodies end up on the salt marshes, at the port, or even out in the ocean?'

'You just be glad you don't live further downstream, my girl. We know about the ones that bump against a prow, or someone's oar hits them. Who can say how many others leave Rome behind and disappear that way?'

'So if Claudia Deiana had not encountered your dredging scoop that first time, we might never have known anything about her. It's horrible, Scribonius. You don't feel you can report these crimes?'

'What's the point? If the authorities were to put one lot out of business, another firm would spring up. The dead have to be buried.' The skipper shuddered. 'I'd rather work with mud any day! Well, if I find the poor souls, I pull them out. If there is time. If they surge up within easy reach.' Not perhaps otherwise, I gathered, feeling squeamish.

Finding Claudia Deiana again yesterday was a special horror. Scribonius and his crew had felt they could not leave her. Nobody in the Transtiberina wanted any involvement, especially once they realised she had been found once before. Because the dredgermen hauled her up the first time, in some way she belonged to them. So, after her second immersion they took her back into custody. Wrapping her in an old sail – a task that was not pleasant – they put her back in the hopper barge, where she was now once more berthed alongside the dredger. She had been there a day; they could not keep her any longer. For one thing, with her lying in the barge that should carry silt away, the dredger could not work.

I gathered there had been disagreements about what they ought to do. The crew favoured replacing the corpse in the Tiber, in some position where she definitely would not come bobbing up again. They would have to submerge her quietly, making sure they were not seen.

The skipper wanted to find a better solution. Words had been exchanged. That was why his men had gone to the lodging house without him, while he stayed behind on the boat, brooding.

'Scribonius, I think you are right.'

'I am.' He had a stubbornness to him; I could see why his crew might find him difficult to budge. I wondered if his wife found life easier during periods when his job took him away from home.

It was deemed unsuitable for me to deal with this. Laying out the dead was often women's work, but week-old decaying remains were off limits. A lad was sent into the marble yard to fetch my husband. As if summoned by magic the crew returned too. Scribonius sent me off the dredger onto the wharf. Even though he had told me Claudia was covered, he would not even let me look over into the hopper barge.

I stood on the bank of the Tiber, staring at the fast flow of its muddy water. It was the straight stretch that runs between Nero's and Agrippa's Bridges, above Tiber Island. This was where Legsie Lucius had been found stuffed into the olive jar, although there was no sign of it now. Gardens and new warehouses were being built on the northern side opposite. That seemed somehow remote from life on this bank.

Here, much older, seedier hutments, stores, stables and food serveries hunched and slumped in a dark fringe that was unwelcoming by day, evil at night. Distanced from the grand monuments on the Field of Mars and long ignored by officialdom, everything here spoke of outlaw activities, endemic trickery, despairing lives. A snack-seller wandered by; he cursed angrily when I waved away his tray, where the wizened offerings looked as if he had dug them up from a midden heap. Gulls screamed aggressively. If the hectic wharves on the Marble Embankment, full of commercial action, had been a sad place for Claudia Deiana to end up the first time, this was worse.

I saw none of it. I was lost in my thoughts. I was deploring how Claudia had been treated like an unwanted object, abandoned in life then misused in death, not only disposed of like rubbish, but now abused again. When Scribonius told me Fundanus ought to know where to dump a corpse, perhaps what he had said was significant. Perhaps the way in which she had been deposited this time had been intentional. Was her body deliberately sent where it was bound to come ashore and be visible? Word of the same corpse turning up twice would soon flash around the city.

I could not yet say who had done this to her, yet I began to sense how and why she had been made to suffer her double drowning. While I waited for others to gather and take decisions, I was pondering the plight of women.

I had decided Claudia Deiana had been used not only once, but again on this second occasion, to send a message of hate between men.

30

This time she did have a funeral. Tiberius devised a plan. Others fell in with it, grateful for his lead. He still had the air of a magistrate but he was plebeian, practical and sensible. He could organise a group to undertake a task willingly. The wrapped corpse was lifted gingerly from the hopper barge, then carried across the dredger and laid upon a cart they commandeered. I was still not allowed to look at her. Whatever was left of the drowned woman had been seriously roped up; the sad parcel stayed that way. No one needed to explain.

We brought Claudia Deiana all across the northern part of the city. She had no music to announce her coming. No hired mourners attended. No actors pretended to be her ancestors, not least because nobody knew who her ancestors were. Our small group, hardly a procession, accompanied her all the way through the Campus Martius and across the Via Flaminia, over the lower ends of the Quirinal, Viminal and Esquiline Hills, down through the ancient Servian Walls at the Porta Esquilina, into the Horti Lamiani. It was a long journey, but we knew at the end of it a pyre would be burning.

It was there, large enough and still just crackling hot enough to take another corpse. Three storeys and the pavilion room that contained Rabirius had collapsed last night, folding into a huge new pile that was still burning away like a gentle autumn bonfire.

Corneolus the *designator* remained in attendance. Given a quiet explanation, he cooperated. Crewmen from the dredger carefully took Claudia Deiana's body from the cart that had served as her bier, then swung the wrapped bundle over the sunken remains of the fire. Heat made their faces glow as they deposited her. Corneolus ordered his assistants to bring up more wood. Then he produced unused incense and other oils from some store he had, which we sloshed over the pyre until renewed flames reached skywards for a time, then gradually died. Claudia Deiana, known as the Brittuncula, went to her final abode in a blazing haze of sweet, expensive oils.

Tiberius wanted to give her a eulogy. We knew so little about her there was nothing he could say. 'You might speak something in her own language, Albia.'

All I knew in Britano-Celtic was 'Piss off, you pervert!' From the little I had grasped of this woman's history, she might have laughed over that with me, if she had a sense of humour, but in case it offended her ghost circling around us, I spared her.

'To the shades of the underworld, we send this soul as an act of friendship. On behalf of her children, far away, let her be received gently and remembered well. May her spirit not linger. May Claudia Deiana go to whatever gods she honoured, finally at peace.'

We stayed with her long enough to be certain nothing recognisable would be left. Nobody could mistreat her remains ever again. At last, somebody had given her respectful rites.

31

Sad and exhausted, Tiberius and I made our way home, following the line of the Aqua Marcia. This dank route below the aqueduct took us eventually up the southern side of the Aventine, past the main station-house of the Fourth Cohort of Vigiles. In my eyes they had become tainted by their role in employing Fundanus; I refused to go inside. Tiberius stepped through the gates alone. Scaurus, the tribune, was absent. My husband left a message. He claimed he made it factual and short, though he admitted the clerk was rather frightened by his tone as he dictated.

We spent much of the afternoon at home. Tiberius had earlier sent our runabout, Paris, to ask my father to lend his auction cart so the eagle could be taken out to Fidenae. The bird would be given a home, with its falconer, on his late sister's estate. The eldest of her three boys had chosen to live there with his father; Tiberius viewed his brother-in-law as despicable lowlife. Imposing the eagle's torrents of excrement on Antistius, who had made his sister unhappy, gave Tiberius Manlius satisfying pleasure.

My father had come up the hill to inspect the proposed cargo, aiming to protect what he called his high-class conveyance. It was a ramshackle, two-wheeled, heavy-duty carrier, inclusive of a morose driver called Felix and a mule called Kicker. The mule's lashing feet were only one reason Felix was morose. A miserable character, he could be annoying in other ways, but passed himself off so well as uninteresting that the cart had never been robbed, even when transporting valuable antiques. Anything smaller than life-sized statues would be disguised as farm implements under cloths that looked very off-putting, as if dung had been sprayed over them by mad-eyed beasts with no stable-training. During journeys, Felix played the part of a brain-dead yokel until he himself had come to believe in it.

Two chickens normally lived in the cart: Piddle and Willikins (the third, Diddle, had been sent to peck grain with her ancestors by my brother's ferret). Once Falco had let himself be won over, and the eagle was loaded, Gaius and Lucius burst into tears; they were distracted by being asked to look after the chickens instead while the cart was away. My father had his methods. He said that if Piddle and Willikins remained near the eagle, they were liable to follow Diddle's fate. This was no future for chucks that were, when they felt like it, still good layers. Felix would not take kindly to losing his omelettes either.

Gaius and Lucius were soon each carrying a chicken around happily. There had been a tense conversation about whether they should accompany the eagle to Fidenae, since it was a chance to visit their father and elder brother. Tiberius had gathered them up after their mother died; he was glad they now showed no interest in going back. He had been afraid they might be subverted by their ghastly father and kept at Fidenae; for my part, I had dreaded that their equally ghastly brother would decide to join them with us.

Our chef took a close look at the stay-over chickens, muttering that he could dress them with Vardana sauce. Winter savory was available, and they might lay the hard-boiled eggs . . . I told him not to be so cruel. Fornix said he could do Parthian instead, though he had run out of caraway because our steward had failed to reorder any. After I let him grumble on, he safely changed and began to talk about pork with almonds and figs.

At this point Titus Morellus arrived.

Tiberius and I had been acting as if we were not expecting a visit, even though we were ready to explode if no official action was taken about Fundanus. He should be called to account – and we wanted to see it done soon.

Morellus shambled in. He tried waiting for someone to offer him refreshments. It never happened. Morellus gave up on that. Since they deal with the public, the vigiles are realists.

He made the official excuses. For the Fourth Cohort, using Fundanus was often convenient; experience had proved him reliable, even when the vigiles had to ask him to handle truly terrible goods. Morellus looked at me when he said that, implying it was my fault that I sometimes came across dead bodies after horrific crimes. I glared back, unmoved. Morellus pretended to duck, as if I had hurled a palaestra weight at him.

Fundanus had certainly collected the remains of Claudia Deiana when she was first found. Nicon had stayed on the Embankment that day for a formal victim handover. From that point Fundanus acquired sole responsibility. No blame could be attached to the Fourth for whatever happened next. It was, murmured Morellus, a bit of a mystery.

So many unclaimed corpses turned up on the Aventine that Fundanus operated on a retainer. Although he might not make money from it, his basic costs were often met from the public purse. It would be miserly, but just adequate. This time, as Fundanus had already admitted, an unknown man turned up at his premises, viewed the deceased, then stumped up a good screw for formalities and funeral goods.

We all assumed that Fundanus chose to steal the money, then ditch the body on the sly. He was loathsome. Such a deed fitted our rock-bottom expectations. However, Morellus had more to say about what had actually happened.

As soon as the honest Fourth were alerted by my husband, they sprang into action. 'We rushed down to his place, full of curiosity! She floats up twice? Listen, this is official business, but I'll give you all the gen, Legate.'

'I left my note for Scaurus,' Tiberius pointed out.

'Scaurus has had to dash off – he's got unbearable tooth-ache. The man is in agony.'

'That's what he always says!' I snapped. 'He was scared. Tiberius Manlius does compose a good letter of complaint.'

'Yes, I read it,' Morellus answered, in a hollow voice. 'You have a true man of literature, Flavia. He could be a Greek intellectual. It must be a trial for you! We all passed the docket around and said among ourselves how glad we are not to be our tribune, having to answer your husband when he is angry.'

'Manlius Faustus *is* angry, and he will want an answer.'

'And he will get one.'

'Now, please.'

'Yes, Domina!'

'I am not your *domina*, thank you, Juno, Queen of Heaven. Pullia has that privilege.'

'She does, poor bloody woman! I feel sorry for her myself. All our kiddywinkles came home with phlegmy coughs after I took them to that funeral—'

173

'Fundanus!' Tiberius reminded him.

Morellus knew when to sharpen up. In sombre tones, he related that a group of troops had quick-marched to the funeral premises. He caught wind of the situation, so went with them himself. The Circus Maximus district, beside which Fundanus was situated, belonged to the Sixth Cohort, although Scaurus was fired up enough (even with his jaw inflamed) that he overruled demarcation issues. His men thundered in. Nobody liaised with the Sixth. That is, nobody even mentioned to those sad boys that the Fourth had come calling. The filthy Sixth had probably not even noticed yet. Anyway, if there was any trouble afterwards, the Fourth would say the Sixth did it. (This all seemed even more important to Morellus than what Fundanus had done with the corpse.)

The Fourth's lads found the funeral premises locked up. They broke in: first the yard, then the interior. Warrants are not usual in Rome: when the authorities come to beat you up and trash your home, you are expected to respond with admiration for their diligence. To escape having your savings pinched and your daughters groped, better pretend you are enjoying the whole experience.

Best of all, leave town. Drop a note with the number of your Forum bank-box onto a lamp-table before you flee, to save Domitian's agents any bother when they want to commandeer your loot.

Fundanus was not at home. Indoors, only pale, dead people were present. Undeterred, the troops embarked on a search, which they conducted with what Morellus called their customary thoroughness. That may have meant they removed wedding rings from corpses. They found nothing . . . that is, nothing else.

'Also customary!' I sneered.

'Your black opinion grieves me, Flavia.'

The Fourth wondered if Fundanus was out on a call to the recently bereaved; then one of their lads happened to notice that his donkey was residing in its stable. Fundanus, the overweight lump, was not famous for walking, so this said he could not be working. They gave the donkey a carrot, parked him in the yard, and searched his living quarters. Behind a bale of hay, buried well, they turned up the very expensive urn I had described.

'A few fleas jumped out of it. Obviously, the Brittuncula was not contained within this notable piece of agate art.'

'No, she was back lying in the hopper barge.'

'Well, be fair, Flavia, she had been there before. By now that barge would seem like home to her.'

'Cut it, Morellus,' Tiberius said. 'Tell us what the Fourth are planning to do.'

More or less their usual inaction. Plan Alpha, Morellus told us, was to warn the Sixth to watch for Fundanus so they could arrest him on a charge of defiling a corpse. 'They need the collar. Their crime numbers stink, they do need help—'

'Buck up!' Tiberius chopped in.

Morellus sighed but told us more: as the Fourth's troops were leaving the yard, they came across the young assistant Fundanus used nowadays. He was gibbering and trauma-tised. Once they knocked sense into him, he blurted out that violent men had visited the premises. They had crashed in and told the boy, whom they found grooming the donkey, they were going to 'do' Fundanus. Word had reached Florius that Claudia Deiana had been dumped back in the Tiber. He had come to exact revenge.

'Did the boy know it was Florius?'

'Saw him. Recognised him from the other time.' I remembered it was the boy who had recited what Claudia's memorial was supposed to say. 'This time Florius identified himself. Named himself as wanting a reckoning.'

Florius had personally pinned the terrified boy to the donkey cart. Why had not Fundanus cremated the Brittuncula, as he had been paid to do? The boy did not know. Fundanus was secretive, especially when he was up to something sordid.

Furious, Florius cruelly described what he intended to enact in return. He and his men would tie up Fundanus and spread him out on the slab where he prepared bodies. While he was still alive, they would ram embalming plugs very hard into every orifice he had. After committing other indecencies, they would stuff him into a coffin, one that was too small for him, then pile all the other bodies on top. The more decayed the better. Finally, they would lock up the building and leave Fundanus still trussed up to die all on his own. That would be slow, Florius had emphasised, grinning. Very, very slow.

It sounded typical. Florius had inventive cruelty. Once, years ago in Britain, when he tried to kill my uncle, he left Lucius Petronius tied up alone in a warehouse with a huge weight set up that would fall and crush him if he dared to move. It was a close call, but my uncle was rescued. Fundanus might not have been so lucky.

'So what happened? Did the Fourth find Fundanus departing life in agony and fear?'

'No. Our lads never saw any trace of him.'

Why not? Where was he? The boy could not say. The men who came with Florius had instructed him to scarper, to tell nobody or they would kill him too; he was not to come back until the smell of dead, decaying funeral director was so strong it reached the other side of the Circus Max and offended the toffs on the Palatine. The boy took refuge with a neighbour, who sent him back when the vigiles were seen arriving.

So! cried Morellus, triumphantly, we could guess Plan Beta. The Fourth Cohort were looking for the funeral director. Dead or alive, they thought they had better find him.

However, he added glumly, if Florius had found him first, we should assume that Fundanus was now dead.

32

The funeral of Old Rabirius and the warlords' conclave ought to have produced a period of quiet. Demarcation disputes had been sorted. The gangs regrouped. Their leaders had either retired or acquired new territory. Extortion, violence, burglary and bribery of public officials should have continued smoothly according to the old etiquette.

Gallo's unfortunate slip-up with the ostrich put him out of action, so the Rabirii would need to reallocate his work as their enforcer. They had Young Roscius. He was dim and crass, yet local people knew him, his backside stuck out with self-confidence and he reckoned himself experienced. He would be no worse than the ambitious junior administrators who were appointed by Rome's establishment. He strode around with the same swank and probably knew more about life than most of them. For his clan's needs, he would suffice.

As the Rabirii prepared for expansion, their worst problem was that their women had become much too dominant. With Rabirius Vincentius returning to Rome, he would need to conciliate both his callous mother, Rubria Theodosia, and his bitter wife, Veronica. Curbing their influence was not something he would be able to do simply by slashing their dress allowances and ordering them to stay indoors.

From what I had glimpsed at the funeral, Rabirius looked a broody presence. Was he reflecting on how the same dilemma must be affecting Florius, also now a one-time fugitive who had to reinstate himself? I wondered if either man realised that Balbina Milvia bought high-end cosmetics from the fashion boutique on the Esquiline that was owned by Rubria Theodosia? I had seen them together on the doorstep, air-kissing devotedly.

Families are rarely sources of joy. While the women were busily bonding, their men were hard at it, feuding. The Horti Lamiani conclave might have solved problems with the Ocellus twins, but not other ingrained rivalries. While Rabirius and Young Roscius must have been heading for a tussle, they faced the encroaching tentacles of the Balbinus mob. How much of the recent violence derived from that?

It was Morellus who told Tiberius and me how things were already awry. He was probably hoping some gossip would settle our complaints about Fundanus. By the usual unconscious osmosis, or by standing at bar counters talking to informants, the vigiles had gathered that, after failing to find Fundanus at his premises, Florius had dashed off to search elsewhere. Fundanus was doomed, the rumour went, though alive – so far. Everyone believed he had done a bunk, although nobody had seen him.

It made sense. Fundanus lacked many attributes though never stinted on self-preservation. The unscrupulous fool had stolen money from a gangster, then had not even managed to dump Claudia Deiana so Florius never found out. He must sensibly have run away. He had left his donkey behind as unconvincing cover. It spoke of panic.

He must be loopy to think he could keep his head down until Florius lost interest. Florius pursued grievances to the death. In fact death was most often the result. Florius had a fondness for death. He would keep hunting until he found the fugitive.

Morellus agreed with me: Fundanus was a dead man walking. 'Well, he may be walking *pro tem*. Soon he will be a dead man who is buried in a bloody big hole! If Florius digs his hole deep enough, we may never come across the evidence. To be honest, Flavia, I would prefer that. Once Fundanus is pulped by a vice-ball like Florius, I do not want to look at his ghastly remains.'

Meanwhile, there was a second rumour that Florius wanted other vengeance. His anger had been fired up by Gallo. Gallo, people were saying, was trying to square things, as an apology for setting up the ostrich to kill Florius. Still battling horrendous pain in his arm and eye, Gallo sent the lawyer Mamillianus to buy off Florius. The bribe was this: they would reveal what had really happened to Claudia Deiana.

I jumped. 'So it's definite that Florius did not kill her?'

Morellus accepted that with the leisurely disinterest of a child forcing down gruel. 'Well, yes, I suppose if he had done it himself, he wouldn't need Gallo to provide him with answers . . .'

'Exactly. Get a grip. Even from his sickbed, Gallo will use meaningful currency. Mamillianus went to Florius with a real bribe.'

Morellus grimaced but explained what Gallo was supposed to have confessed: Claudia Deiana had indeed been lured from Itia's lodgings by Legsie Lucius. Gallo denied any involvement: he blamed Young Roscius, obviously aiming to turn Florius against him. After she was seized, Gallo said that Claudia had been killed by the Rabirius hitman.

It was the second time I had heard of this expert in two days.

I spelled out what I knew. His name was Turcus. Juventus, the Second Cohort's 'special liaison' stooge, had once met him. 'A "pleasant fellow", Juventus says, though Juventus is not sharp enough to cut up lard. Turcus never socialises, it is claimed, although I presume anybody he kills is assigned a brief meeting. Non-convivial, short on chatter, definitely no slice of apricot tart.'

'Flavia, you are a treasure!'

'I am happy in my work. You should try it.'

'Pullia would think I was up to something.'

Juventus had told me that while he was spying on the warlords Turcus had been summoned to the *sub rosa* room. He was given a contract to eliminate a man called Castor. Castor had worked for the Ocellus twins, while they were active, and last year he arranged the death of the Rabirius rising star, Vincentius Theo.

'I can never imagine where your lovely wife gets her insights! She's as right as a pregnant goat,' Morellus congratulated Tiberius, who weakly smiled acknowledgement of this curious metaphor. 'Flavia, a horrid little hood called Castor, who indeed used to clear up human crud for those twins, appeared by the Trigeminal Gate at dawn today. "Oh, Titus Morellus, what happened?" Hanged on a crane. Like a washed loincloth in a back entry, Castor was left swaying in plain sight, while the meat-market cattle kept lowing unhappily and all the locals scuttled off fast the other way. We had to go and pull him down – he was hovering above our bit of the Trigeminal, worse luck. Nowhere to store him, with Fundanus doing a flit. We've propped him up at the station-house, in a cell, like somebody under arrest.'

'Jupiter!' muttered Tiberius, a fastidious man.

Morellus continued blithely, 'I took a look, pulled him about a bit. Hauling him up on the pulley had broken his wicked neck. Execution gangland-style. All the cohorts have been issued a warning that it heralds more.'

'Possibly not.' Tiberius roused himself to join in. 'If Castor's death had been arranged as a pay-off for the young man he mowed down in the street, does this not satisfy the Rabirii?'

'They are not so easily paid. And they are about to be even more unhappy,' I reminded him, 'if Florius goes after their tame assassin. Turcus is a valuable asset. Florius may manage to pick him off, but if he does they will hate it.'

'Right. There's not exactly a seasonal glut of reliable hitmen. But when that young man was killed last year, it had nothing to do with Florius or his crew.'

Tiberius and Morellus nodded away together. I folded my arms. 'No, that was a ghastly incident.' Morellus perked up, as if he longed to hear me give grisly details. I didn't. 'But you are right: Florius is indifferent to the dead cadet. He will be going after Turcus for despatching Claudia Deiana.'

'After that, there is the complication of Gallo turning. He is deviously implicating Young Roscius,' Tiberius continued.

'Such loyalty! In the meantime, Claudia matters,' I insisted. 'She matters so much to Florius that Gallo thought he could use her fate to make Florius overlook the ostrich incident.'

'Why, though?' Tiberius pressed me doggedly. 'What was so crucial about her?'

'I imagine Florius regarded her as his property. He might have deserted her, but another clan involving themselves was unacceptable. And it's very, very personal.'

'Killing his mistress? That's a gesture against his manhood!' Morellus probably thought the same way. 'Anyway, if the

Rabirii used Turcus for it then it's one contract Turcus will dearly pay for.'

According to Morellus, that was his misfortune. Nobody on our side of Rome had even known the hitman's name until I had said it just now. There was no chance of us finding Turcus to warn him – assuming we wanted to. Anyway, now Florius knew, the hitman deserved what came.

Florius would get to him, I was sure. So Turcus would be the next unpleasant corpse that turned up in Rome. Until then, all anyone could do was wait.

33

The only part of 'wait' that I really conceded was that it was too late that day to start. I was crazy, but not enough to set off after dark to find a man who strung up people like wet washing on the hooks of harbour cranes. He must have fulfilled his contract against Castor during the night watch. This was a creature who came out to prowl while the city slept. I preferred not to meet him then.

Next morning I rose early. While the household remained silent, I washed my face, dressed myself in a conventional outfit, put on walking shoes, and heated myself a beaker of honeyed mulsum.

Tiberius found me sipping my drink in the courtyard. 'Is there any point me asking you not to do this?'

'No. But thank you, and there is no need to ask me to be careful. Remember, a hitman works when he is issued with orders – and when he will be paid. In between, he is probably a sweetie.'

Tiberius humphed at that, though he was in the process of sneaking my beaker off me for a share.

'Besides,' I added gently, letting him take the mulsum, 'sometimes what he does appeals to me. You and I saw what Castor and his cronies inflicted on the Rabirius boy. It was ghastly. So breaking Castor's neck by hanging was too easy – too quick. He deserved the arena lions. He should have been tossed from claw to claw playfully for a long time. I shall only warn Turcus that Florius is looking for him. My quiet hope is that he may spot Florius coming and alert the authorities.'

'Meanwhile, he will tell you who wanted Claudia Deiana dead?'

'Yes. I need him to say who issued his orders.'

'You have a way,' Tiberius marvelled, 'of making ludicrous and dangerous ideas sound wise and safe . . . May I come with you?'

'You know you can't. There will be no matronly presence in this house. You need to stay and supervise. Make sure your dynamic nephews look after my father's chickens gently.'

'And the cook keeps his hands off them?'

'Exactly. Do not let Fornix pot roast either – boys or chickens.'

Tiberius looked rueful but let me go by myself. You do have to admire a man who allows his fairly new wife to trot out in her second-best cloak, looking for a professional hitman.

I did know someone who had met him.

Although he supposedly never did anything useful, Juventus was the member of the Second Cohort who arrived early at the office. The rest of the day shift were still buying their breakfasts in streets nearby. It was their custom not to hurry. Never being party to their heated discussions about why the Greens were crap and the short-arse Reds should all be sent to the silver mines, Juventus turned up at their station-house on his own.

I was still passing the time of day with their night-shift clerk. My mind was not fully on pleasantries. It had given me a jar to come back through the Horti Lamiani to the Second's base. On the way I had passed the blackened pyre. Everyone connected with the funeral had now dispersed. Ashes of Old Rabirius and Claudia Deiana must have been collected, but scents of burning hung around. Gardeners were beginning reinstatement tasks. They were replanting shrubs among white candelabra, gorgeous great marble things that had ivy carved on them. When I enquired, these workers confirmed that a small family group had been to collect what was left of Old Rabirius and, unknown to them, Claudia Deiana. So she had gone to eternal rest intermingled with the King of Kings. I hoped it would be more peaceful than her life with Florius.

At the barracks, even Juventus could tell how my walk through the gardens had affected me. With an innocent lack of guile, he tried to cheer me up. He was unexpectedly help-ful. I was the first person who had ever asked him to look through his many notebooks. His record of what he had overheard or persuaded people to tell him was mainly a waste of effort; no officers ever let him make reports or asked him for factual information. Wanting my nugget of detail, I became his favourite.

It took him a while to hunt through screeds of spidery observation notes. But stuck in the room where the cohort shut him away on his own, he had organised a filing system; it even contained an index. He found what I wanted.

Like all hitmen, Turcus protected himself with secrecy. However, Juventus had taken an interest after he had met the man. He once heard a salami-seller's wife telling a garland-making florist the district where Turcus lived with his family.

The district was enough for me. I went there. I made enquiries. Everyone locally thought Turcus was a decent businessman – so to them it was no secret where he lived. He supported the local temple. He served as a neighbourhood officer. His team (that key mark of character in Rome) was the Blues.

Tiberius supported the Golds, on the kindly grounds that somebody had to, but my father also preferred the Blues so I warmed to this killer in advance. Rome is a city of tradition, where your chariot loyalty is inherited with your eyesight and your bunions. Even though I was adopted, it had always been explained to me whom I must shout for in a stadium.

I had had to take a long hike across three hills, from the eastern side of the Servian Walls to the west. It meant passing through traditional Rabirius territory to within sight of the Baths of Titus. Turcus housed his family in a larger than average apartment in a good street. It was dressed up with drapes and doilies. You came indoors over a clean doormat, and were stationed in a comfortable reception room, where children's toys were kept in a big square basket, a large, well-behaved dog lay on a neat rug and dried lavender stems scented the air.

For this man, killing was a second job: he needed to be within striking distance of the river because he had a government franchise to organise imperial insurance to traders who intended to finance grain shipments. He vetted those who came forward, then made sure their cargoes were legitimate and their ships sound. If you passed him in the street, an insurance agent was exactly what he looked like, balding and mildly prosperous. He wore a below-the-knee beige tunic over a solid frame. He was heavy, though I could imagine him being active.

His children were not in the apartment; I never saw them, and couldn't judge how many he had. His wife was there when I arrived; she was a good-looking, steady woman, though her eyes seemed wary and she barely spoke. I noticed she wore a gold necklace and fancy sandals. He told her to go out. In other situations he and I would have gone somewhere outside the home, but if he was prepared to talk to me it called for greater privacy.

I had persuaded him to open up by offering him information about his safety. I made it clear I knew quite a lot about the Rabirii. I was fully aware of what he did for them. I wanted his story.

Hitmen do not usually write their memoirs. Nevertheless, they have adventures. Once we were alone, Turcus spoke with pride about his life as a hired killer. He knew he was good. He discussed everything, quite matter-of-factly. I managed to show no animosity, despite my feelings about Claudia Deiana.

How it worked was that Turcus would be sent a message that someone had 'business' for him, if he wanted to accept their offer. I noticed that he did have choice. If he accepted, he was told a name. From that moment, the person targeted would count as dead. Unless Turcus already knew the victim, information on what they looked like and where they hung out would be supplied. Rarely would he contract to kill women. He told me so, though I knew, because of Claudia Deiana, that it happened.

Sometimes there were other instructions, but in general he could choose his time and his method. After the victim was dead, if the mobster who commissioned the deed was pleased by how things went, a 'package' would be given to Turcus. It was treated as a friendly present, but consisted of a great deal of money. He did specialist work; he had earned a fortune from it, starting when he was very young.

He said he had killed thirty-eight people. Only the first caused a wobble; after that he felt no emotion. He had a detailed memory of each, and knew where the bodies were, if they had been concealed. Sometimes leaving the corpse in public view was an essential part of the 'message'.

'Like Castor, yesterday?'

Turcus only tightened the corner of his mouth. I left that and asked whether he had a preferred method. 'Stabbing. They used to call me Turcus the Knife. Through the ear or the eye, or by cutting the throat.'

'Most people in your line have a trademark weapon?'

'Some do. A knife is quick and gives you surprise, or you can make a different wound or more than one, so they die slowly, if blood and suffering have been requested.' I imagined him with a schedule, a catalogue of obliteration methods with his personal branding, options to select . . . 'I can use any tool,' he said, confirming this. 'If mutilation or dismemberment is wanted, it can be done.'

'What about the law that nobody can go armed inside the city boundary?'

Turcus laughed. 'What about it?'

I decided against asking whether he cut off and posted body parts, for extra messages. 'Do you have a preferred place for the act?'

'In the street.'

'Out in the open? And at night?'

'Fewer people about. Even if someone nearby hears anything, they will be slow to look out. I can do what I am doing, then disappear into the darkness.'

'Do you only work in Rome?'

'No.'

'Visiting a town where nobody knows you has its appeal?'

189

'Yes. Some quiet little place where nothing ever happens . . .'

'Eyeing up retirement spots? Have you prepared a secret bolthole?'

'No comment!'

He told me he never asked why a killing had been ordered. He assumed a head man 'failed to see eye to eye with someone', as they called it. Some kind of betrayal might have happened.

He had no conscience about what he did. He slept well afterwards. Nor did he concern himself with the wives and children of his victims. He never told his own wife what he was going out to do. She knew his profession, but never specific details, so nobody could harm her to gain information. I presumed his children only ever heard about the shipping insurance.

None of his money was wasted; he invested it carefully. He was conscious that what he did to other people might be done one day to him. In case anything happened, he had to provide for his family.

We reached our formal data exchange. When I asked him to confirm that he had killed Claudia Deiana, he admitted it calmly. She was brought to him on the bridge. He strangled her then threw her body over the parapet into the Tiber.

I explained how Florius now knew and was coming after him. Turcus expressed neither fear nor surprise. He seemed to think an attack on him was bound to happen one day. When it came, he would have to accept it. Obviously, he had upset a lot of people.

'Who gave you the contract for the British woman?' For me, this was the crucial supplementary. For him, it was the first time he hesitated. 'Who paid you, Turcus?'

Until then he had told me whatever I asked. He had waited for me to pose my questions rather than putting himself forward with a boastful narrative, but he replied frankly and in full. He had spoken in a level voice, almost verging on dullness. It might have seemed monotonous, were it not for his shocking subject matter. 'Who made you the offer?' I put to him again, trying not to overstress its importance. 'Was it Gallo, or Young Roscius?'

Turcus only said, 'A runner they used.'

'Legsie Lucius? The man who brought Claudia to you? Who was later killed near the river?'

'Him.'

'It wasn't you who dunked him in olive oil?' I had learned enough to believe that the dolium murder would not be his style; besides, Turcus worked for the Rabirii, so a death that was meant to send a message to them would hardly be carried out by him.

'Not me. Florius and his people must have done it.'

'Florius, who is now after you,' I reminded him. 'Don't walk near any giant storage pots! My father knew the Balbinus gang years ago and has some colourful stories. I believe that tribe has a history of killing people in containers. So let me ask you again. When Legsie Lucius collected Claudia Deiana for you, who had sent him to do that?'

'Not Gallo.' Turcus was definite. 'Legsie worked for Young Roscius, but Roscius seemed surprised at what happened to his runner. He really lost it afterwards. Legsie being found in the dolium was a shock.'

'If he didn't send Legsie to pick up Claudia, then who?'

'I was never told. Even though he denied it, organising the Brittuncula contract looked like Roscius. Rabirius Vincentius had not arrived in Rome then.'

'If it was Young Roscius, Gallo used to supervise him before the ostrich incident; Gallo might have been aware of what was happening.'

'Neither of them seemed to claim responsibility,' Turcus insisted.

'So who could it be? Listen – afterwards, who sent you your payment?' I demanded. That ought to solve this. I could see that Turcus knew. It looked as if he would refuse to say. The interview had become much harder. Even so, Turcus deliberated, reached a decision, then in his own way gave me the answer.

He rose from his seat and went into another room. When he returned shortly, he was carrying a woven straw box. He put it on a lamp-table beside me, lifting its squashed-on lid. Packed inside I could see several small soapstone pots. They were of a kind I recognised. I opened one; fingermarks showed where someone had dug in to lift out a slathering of sweet-smelling waxy cream.

Now I understood. For killing Claudia Deiana, Turcus must have received money as well; his price for a death would be much higher. But this was the clue: I was looking at an extra gift sent for his wife, a thank-you included with his payment. These pots would have been filled with luxury cosmetics from the beauty salon that went by the name of Pandora's. Pandora was the business name of the ageing sister of Old Rabirius.

Claudia Deiana's murder had been ordered by Rubria Theodosia, the most feared, most controlling woman in the crime clan.

34

I had met her before: I would visit her now.

Rubria Theodosia lived not far from the hitman, south of the station-house of the First Cohort of Vigiles. They generally tried to make out they could not find her address in their records. It saved them from difficult confrontations. Those were rare: few brave souls ever made accusations against her, though if they did it would be for magic, love potions, abortions, or simply having people beaten up. She lived parallel with the Saepta Julia, where my father had his antiques warehouse, so she could look across the Via Lata to the Campus Martius, and on to the river, where her clan were now diversifying. With this useful oversight of their new turf, her home was not far from the New Temples of Fortune and Hope. Since the Rabirii traded in misfortune and despair, that could be seen as ironical.

I had been in her apartment. Cleopatra might have thought it plain, but Cleo's taste was eastern opulence with bare-chested fan-wafters. Rubria Theodosia might sell sooty eyeliner, but not to slithery Egyptian eunuchs. At hers, it was enough to blind your visitors with a dazzle of purple and gold. Accompanying that colour palette came furniture which smart designers had certainly not bought at some downbeat Falco auction over the way. These items looked like special client commissions.

Downstairs was her streetside beauty shop although most trade, I knew, was carried out through personal visits to women who could afford to stay at home and have fancy merchandise brought to them. Sometimes sales did happen on the premises; immaculate young stylists organised pedicures or beanmeal facials while pushing their products to helpless clients trapped in long chairs set out on the pavement. I didn't waste time on Meröe and Kalmis, with their seductive talk of beneficial palm oil. I had yet to reach thirty, so felt I could manage without blocking up my character lines with brightening balms.

Polemaena admitted me. I remembered her. This ugly human watchdog was six feet tall, all foul buck teeth and wiry hair; an encounter with her was as nasty as having a pigeon shit on your tunic when you were too far from home to change your clothes.

She let me enter the gilded purple suite. A grandiose porphyry urn stood on a massive ebony table. It had gold handles. No surprise. I wanted to stand that urn on a mat, lest it scratch the fancy table. Inside the dense marble, without doubt, was whatever remained of Old Rabirius, plus indiscriminate chunks of wood ash, garden leaves and the carbonised bones of Claudia Deiana. I nodded to her secretly.

Rubria Theodosia stomped in. She was still wearing formal black but had exchanged her tight funeral shoes for slippers. It was a human touch from a woman who came across as a domineering old witch.

I had once put her in her sixties but if her brother had been in his eighties, she must have been older. In fairness, she managed to cover that up. Although a girlish glow on a mature face might look fine in the blur of a silver mirror, it never truly works. Hades, I've seen adolescents who make themselves look fake with too much brightener. From beneath a mask of her products, small eyes whose meanness could never be disguised peered out. She had one of those large mouths from which, when she spoke, came a rasping voice that suggested a long life of giving orders to make other people suffer.

She never bothered to emphasise how dangerous she was. People would cross the road to avoid her – if they dared offend her by doing so. I came visiting with a tingle of apprehension. Mentally I worked out how best to run past her if I wanted to reach the exit in a hurry.

As she plumped herself on an overstuffed couch, she acknowledged our past meetings. 'Oh, it's you! What do you want?'

'Greetings! Let me start with condolences for your brother.' I perched on a separate couch, upright, with my feet together. The upholstery was so packed with filling, it was hard not to slide off. I felt like a country cousin, coming fresh from the farm on an onion cart, with mud on my skirt.

I said I had been at the funeral. Theodosia thanked me for my respect. I did not say I had found the luxury grotesque. I kept quiet about the eagle. Nor did I ask whether that was Old Rabirius in the fabulous porphyry.

'Skip the chit-chat. What do you want?' she demanded again.

'A talk about Florius.'

'Never heard of him.'

'Cobnuts. His wife is your relative. I have seen you two hugging on your doorstep. Now Florius is back in Rome, eyeing up Rabirius territory.'

She snorted. 'Well, that's what he thinks!'

'I heard there was a conclave, where he was fended off.'

'You heard that?' I could see Theodosia thinking someone had talked: if she ever found out who, it would go badly for them. 'Florius always had his beady sights on the gee-gees. But he will wait a long time to get in there.'

'Racetrack scams,' I agreed. 'He wants the lucre.' Since she was not intending to say more, I spelled it out. 'Your group intends to invade the riverbank north of Tiber Island. You kicked out the Ocellus twins, poor tottering old souls. You can't like the fact the Balbinus mob are keen to expand northwards as well. There is bound to be a face-off.'

'If you think so.'

'I do! While Milvia was in charge of their outfit, you would have been safe. She seems content with her father's old manor. Florius is a different animal, very aggressive. He always was a betting freak, and now he's hankering to control the gallops and stables up by Nero's Bridge. Perhaps he thinks he can slide in, while the Rabirii are weakened by bereavement and you're newcomers there.'

'Let him dream!'

'Yes, you see it differently. You will resist.'

'We have fixed him.'

'Well, you've started a warning process. But will he be true to his word? I doubt it. He's an outsider. He doesn't follow rules.'

'He'll have to learn!'

'He lies like a fleecing stall-holder. I've seen him in action.'

Theodosia finally looked surprised. 'When?'

'He won't remember – but I shall never forget! So why,' I demanded, 'was Gallo schmoozing him at the funeral? Did you know they met up privately?' I guessed that Gallo pursuing his own affairs was not unusual, but if Theodosia was angry, I could not tell. I left a pause, then picked at the subject again. 'Can you be sure of Gallo's own allegiance? Of course he's been scratched half to death by a vicious ball of feathers – but convalescence will give him plotting time. You may find that dangerous. Your son must feel very suspicious of him. And Young Roscius? There's a loose ballista! Gallo must have kept him in hand, but Gallo's out of action. If I were Florius, I'd buy Roscius in and take a stand together against your son. I'd do it right now. Before Rabirius Vincentius can find his feet again in Rome.'

She might agree, but Rubria Theodosia would not be drawn in on how her late brother's heirs were in conflict. Instead, she fell back on proclaiming how they were planning big new moves. She admitted their intention was to take on the Balbinus Pius mob. So, she said, as well as developing the northern stretch of the riverbank, the Rabirii were looking at the lucrative area *south* of Tiber Island.

That would cause a huge upheaval. That centre of international trade had traditionally been the other clan's turf. 'I live there,' I said. 'The Balbini won't like this. They traditionally control all the rackets around the Emporium and associated stores and granaries – plus brothels, rooming houses, gambling dens, thievery and fencing stolen goods.'

'They had a free run long enough!' Theodosia growled.

'I cannot imagine them giving way.'

'We can handle anything they put up against us.'

'What about your family links? What about Milvia?'

'Milvia had better come in with us, like a good girl.' In my own family Balbina Milvia had never been seen as a 'good girl'.

Internally, I groaned. If the Rabirii did percolate south, a massive, two-way turf war would start, with enormous sums at stake. 'Florius will try to stop you,' I warned.

'Florius is an amateur.'

'He *was*. He has had practice. Do not underestimate what he has been up to in Britain.'

'How would you know?'

'It's where I come from.'

'Oh, yes – Flavia Albia, the druid!'

I ignored her thrust. Always in my heart was Claudia Deiana. I brought the conversation round to her: 'So is this why the Rabirii wanted to upset Florius? You went for his lover on purpose? A personal attack, using Claudia Deiana, to destabilise him? That was why you sent your own hitman to dispose of his British woman?'

Rubria Theodosia gave me a savage glare. 'What hitman? What woman? Prove it!' she commanded defiantly.

Before I had a chance to reply, we were interrupted.

35

I recognised the newcomer.

After Polemaena let me in, the wild maid must have hared off to fetch the daughter-in-law. Veronica, the hard-worn wife of Rabirius Vincentius, was a thin, short, determined woman. Loyally domesticated, she had run things for her exiled husband, a man she might never have expected to see again. Now she had the same problem as Milvia with Florius: her man had resumed his previous life, very unexpectedly.

How would this go? On the surface she had always appeared downtrodden, ingrained with unhappiness like a tarry plank, quite different from Rubria Theodosia. However, I had heard her speak out boldly in defence of her own. She was unsmiling and raw, her face defiant.

On behalf of Vincentius she had handled money, protected secrets, maintained the lie that her husband's sojourn abroad was unfair, kept the flame burning. He had been away for years but, thanks to her, he must have stepped back into his old position with full honours. I had seen how he was greeted at his father's funeral. Veronica had helped preserve his place. Would he respect her guardianship? I had always thought she could be a powerful woman. I could not envisage her giving up whatever independence she had scraped together in his absence. There might have to be fighting in that home.

For years Veronica must in theory have been 'looked after'. Left in Rome, she would have been under the patronage of Old Rabirius, sufficient to live apart from her mother-in-law. I had once knocked at her apartment, which was above a mean street in a dingy area. I was not allowed in, but when glimpsed from outside the interior had looked immaculate. The fact she kept her own home might be telling. Even so, she had had to share her boy. I knew he had treated this purple apartment of his grandmother's as his second home, and I suspected there had been jealousy.

The handsome son had been Veronica's life. Theodosia and she had brought up that intelligent charmer between them, teaching him to be like his father, while preparing him to head up their organisation. I had known him briefly. He had a clean record and was full of promise, but the women's ambitions made him a target. On the day he was killed, I had seen Veronica kneeling in the street with road grit grazing her legs, cradling the young man's bloody corpse while she screamed to the skies her anguish and her curses on all who had caused her loss.

Well, Castor had been removed from life now, as reparation.

Would that be enough?

Polemaena, who worked for the older woman, was close to Veronica as well, through passionate devotion to her son. Polemaena saw me as trouble. To help her stand up to me, she had fetched the angry Veronica.

She and Theodosia glanced at each other quickly when she came in, as if conferring about why I had come here. They had no need to allow me to continue this conversation. They were testing me; they wanted to find out how much I knew.

'Veronica,' I said at once, grasping the initiative. 'I saw your husband has returned! Shouldn't he be ensconced in a safe house in Cilicia, while you cover for him?'

'He was never charged with anything!' came the automatic response. Her voice told me this woman had come up from the streets without troubling herself with elocution. She looked tired out by bad experiences, but she might have been attractive once, perhaps a daughter of a foot-soldier in the Rabirius organisation. Vincentius must have married her because her people were loyal and she would know how to keep her lip buttoned.

I smiled. 'He has had a dull old stay in the provinces for a man who claims he is innocent. Won't the authorities in Rome be looking for him? Aren't you afraid of some crack investigation officer, waiting to pounce? Scrolls of affidavits, witnesses promised protection, Domitian's pet lawyers drooling over how much collateral they can confiscate?' Closely watched by her mother-in-law, Veronica looked derisive, saying nothing. I lowered my voice. 'And suddenly you must relinquish the keys to him?' She was still silent, so I kept pushing: 'Is it safe for your husband to stay? Or has he ensured he has nothing to worry about? High-level shielding? A spokesman inside the law-and-order machine? Paid-for indemnities from arrest?'

Rubria Theodosia intervened: 'My son and his wife are a tight family unit. Bonded by our double grief.'

That did not entirely fit my point, but I pretended to discuss the situation sympathetically. 'Well, your son will need his wife's support in the coming days. I prophesy a tussle. It's obvious Vincentius has to curb Young Roscius – he should manage that, although, as the poet says, I see the Tiber foaming with blood.'

'Ridiculous!' scoffed Theodosia.

'Really? All your crew on the streets have become used to working with Roscius, whereas they have not seen Vincentius for years. But there's Gallo. He is tough and very aware of his position. He was a loyal supporter in your leader's absence, when – I am sure – your foot-soldiers were reluctant to take orders from women.'

Both Theodosia and Veronica humphed so I knew I was right.

'Ultimately, it needed a hard man on the streets. Gallo,' I suggested, 'must think he is owed a return. Will Vincentius try to oust him – assuming Gallo survives his accident?' I was ignoring the women's fixed angry scowls. 'Interesting times on the Esquiline and Viminal!' I flexed my feet. 'And now there is Florius Oppicus. Still, Vincentius needn't bestir himself, while his women are making all the moves ... Veronica, I was talking to your mother-in-law, before you joined us, about exactly that. Rumour has identified who tried to undermine Florius by murdering his lover: your runner, your hitman – and you as the financiers.'

Theodosia flicked a glance at Veronica, then said quickly, 'I told her we don't know him. And we had no idea he brought his floozy to Rome.'

Veronica demanded of me bluntly, 'What is it to you, anyway?'

'I knew him in Britain years ago. I hate him.' I saw no point in disguising my position.

'What has he done to you?'

'What vicious men do to the innocent.'

'His wife says he is charming!' mouthed Veronica.

'His wife hasn't seen him for fifteen years!' I countered, my voice hard. 'Everything is changed. Milvia doesn't need him now. He was a wimp her father bought in for social climbing – that's if someone can climb from the gutter to the middle rank. Florius left. She took over her parents' position. Now she barely knows the man and she likes being in charge.' I straightened up, ready to attack. 'Well, you must know all about this situation, Veronica! Over such a long time, it must be easy to forget a husband's bad habits and his filthy table manners. You write polite letters while he is in exile, but when the rover reappears, expecting to fart around the house again and demanding his old bedtime privileges, it's a shock.' I suddenly threw in a new idea: 'Let alone the inconvenience if, suppose, you had filled his place with a lover. Do you think Balbina Milvia did that?'

Was it my imagination, or did Veronica's expression shadow briefly? Any give-away was gone before I could check, but was it even about Milvia? Veronica had always struck me as a one-man woman, isolated and virtually friend-less, but now I wondered. There might be another reason for her to live apart from her mother-in-law, though I stuck with my first thought for the time being.

'Did Milvia,' I demanded, 'persuade you to have her husband's lover killed? To prevent him guessing she was behind the murder?'

'Balbina Milvia comes from a close-knit family,' Theodosia announced. 'She was brought up to honour our ways. She is a dedicated wife who believes in traditional virtues.'

I chortled. 'You are suggesting she supports Florius? All the more reason for her to eliminate a rival. Maybe she is hurt and jealous. But she's no innocent. Balbina Milvia had an affair with one of the vigiles – while Florius was still living here.'

'She was young. The man was using her.'

'An excuse!' Although we were talking about my uncle, Lucius Petronius, interestingly no one named him. I reprised the old details: 'Maybe it was just a fling for him, but Milvia convinced herself he meant to marry her. If she was ready to leave her husband then, what might she have been up to since? What "traditional values" has she been buffing up in her boudoir, while Florius was squinting into the mist at the end of the world? She will have had no time to cover her tracks if she has been betraying him again. I heard that the British authorities have kicked him out – but neither he nor Milvia can have been expecting it.'

'She needs to get used to it. He is back!' commented Veronica. I wondered if she relished the news that another wife was in her own position.

'Yes, he is back,' I agreed. 'Trailed by another woman, whom somebody here callously disposed of. Worse for her – let me give you the latest news – Claudia Deiana was not allowed the dignity of a funeral, but her poor corpse has been heaved back into the Tiber a second time.'

The two women looked astonished, though they might have been feigning.

'Hideous, isn't it?' I returned gently. 'Her rotting body must have been stolen from the funeral premises.' That was letting off Fundanus lightly, but I wanted to sound lurid. 'It's sacrilege. I didn't think even gangsters like your family would sink so low. What remained of her was thrown off a bridge again yesterday night, this time where the current would deposit her in plain sight. So, I don't only wonder who killed her in the first place – but who wants to send that new kind of message to Florius?'

Rubria Theodosia smirked. 'It almost makes you feel sorry for him!'

'Not me.' I sounded bleak. 'But perhaps I do feel sorry for *her.*'

'Don't waste your pity!' Veronica commanded.

'Why? Because she was an outsider? Foreign? Not what people like you call "family"?' Neither answered me. 'Then, of course,' I carried on, 'there might have been a direct reason to get rid of her. They must have been together a long time. They had children, I believe, so I am assuming they shared a household for years. Claudia Deiana could have learned all kinds of secrets from Florius. When she arrived here, she went to see the authorities. Was she threatening to tell them something?'

'What?' snapped Theodosia, sounding contemptuous.

I had no idea. I sat upright on my hard seat, smiling at them gently.

According to the code, Florius should never have told Claudia anything. Turcus, the hitman, had said how it worked: a criminal protected his partner by keeping her in ignorance of his specific activities. Only if he had to leave her in charge would she need to be given insights into his business to keep it afloat.

Was that the case?

I wondered how Florius had intended to leave his British affairs when he was driven out so precipitously. Had he made arrangements? When the armed men picked him up, had there even been time? Was Claudia Deiana supposed to stay behind, running those stupendously grim brothels and bars for him? Was she capable? I knew nothing about any talents she had, nor whether she came from a criminal background. Would she have wanted to take over? The implication was that she did not. It looked as if she had dropped everything and come to Rome to rail at him.

By following Florius, had Claudia disobeyed him? Maybe she abandoned his British business empire, so there was nobody to steer it, with nobody (more importantly) to send the profits here for him? That was an empire he had personally created. His own: not inherited from Milvia and her family. I would guess the filthy enterprise he built up at the proverbial end of the road held special meaning for him.

'I believe we have no more to say.' Rubria Theodosia was terminating my interview. She used a fake elegant voice. 'Always a joy to speak to you, Flavia Albia – but we must force ourselves to let you go now!'

36

Never one to linger in an environment where the hostess might boil me in toads' blood, I graciously left. Polemaena slammed the door behind me pointedly. Informers need to be thick-skinned.

Outside, as I shook any contaminating aura from my skirts, I began to notice that war had broken out. Impedimenta had been sucked from the streets. Meröe and Kalmis, Pandora's silken young saleswomen, had dragged their recliners indoors and locked their shutters. Other shops were hauling in goods. Pottery, brassware and baskets were hooked off the pavements they usually blocked, to clutter up spaces behind counters indoors and it was not because some magistrate had come round enforcing portico legislation. Mothers called in scab-kneed urchins. Dogs stood up, stretching; they sniffed the air, preparing to find reasons to bark. Barrows were parked down safer alleys. Barrow-handlers clustered, muttering.

Pigeons that flew up for a look at the situation would have seen a diorama around the apartment where Turcus lived, now peopled with static figures that crouched behind barrels or loafed alongside pillars. I hurried up to a corner just in time to see three men with scarves covering their faces run out from the building. They waved their arms to the rest and shook their heads as if they had failed to find anyone. A glint by a belt told me they were armed. I moved up a level into a staircase, putting myself back from the street.

All the local dogs began baying loudly. Some trotted up in high-stepping excitement, like generals leading an incursion. In their wake a swarm of men raced in from the Via Lata. They were all shapes and sizes – but all had weapons. Window shutters opened up above, then closed swiftly. One old crone even dragged her washing from a high line, cursing.

The two groups of men met at an angle, foaming together, like currents in a tidal estuary. Momentum carried the fight up the street, away from where I was. I stayed put. The street dogs had slunk back to the sidelines, though occasionally a brave mange-carrier would bark hoarsely on principle.

No one asked questions. I only heard grunts of effort. They all fought as if maddened by drink; they all fought dirty. Some simply enjoyed fighting, though others seemed more specifically driven. Punches and kicks hammered. No knives flashed, but I could see fresh blood on tunics, and blood on the street too, wet and red, enough to cause boots to slip.

Someone came down the stone steps behind me. There was room so I drew aside, leaving him space to pass. '*Io!* It's kicking off!'

'Do you know who they are?' I asked, although I reckoned I knew.

'Madhats came looking for Turcus. If he or his wife had been at home, they would have been thrown out of a window. There's Young Roscius.' I saw him now, urging on the Rabirius men, while cheerily kicking one of the invaders, who was curled up on the ground. The man beside me winced and muttered, '*Spleen!*'

I glanced at him. He wore a long white tunic and was carrying a leather bag. He said he was a doctor; with a head jerk up the stairs he told me he had been visiting Gallo, who lived there.

'How is he?'

'Touch and go.' Taking advantage of a momentary lull, the man slipped out past me and quickly went on his way.

I kept back. A third group suddenly clattered up on horse-back. I recognised their ordered dismount from when Karus and his troops had arrived at the Rabirius funeral. He seemed to be scanning the fighters, presumably looking for Florius.

Any other unit in Rome would have rushed into the fray, hurling combatants apart. The Varduli used different tactics. They encircled the scene but stayed at a distance. At first I had no idea why. When I heard the sounds, I ducked. A bizarre buzzing came from nowhere, a repeated, unsettling *zizz, zizz, zizz*!

They had slings. These are very old weapons, weapons of utter simplicity, yet deadly. Like many auxiliaries in the Roman army, the Varduli must be trained to fire off shots; they were usually silent – unnerving – until some inventive soul, in Britain I think, devised a newer kind. With circular holes painstakingly bored into some of their projectiles, they produced a sound that was as disturbing as tinnitus. It would be bad enough while defending a fort, but in a city the noise bounced off the stone buildings with an unearthly effect.

The auxiliaries were firing off several missiles in each swing. They had different sizes. Spun at tremendous veloc-ity, even the shots as small as nuts penetrated and drew blood. Larger ones were even more powerful. They cracked right through dry old window shutters. A street dog ran off, flesh in tatters; he looked fatally hurt. I wanted to help him but could not possibly get there. As the slingshots slammed into the fighting pack, the screaming of projectiles turned into the screaming of men. All the time came that unceasing *zizz, zizz, zizz!*

These sound effects had disorientated those fighting. At the eerie whistling overhead, many covered their craniums, ducking. Others began to run away.

As the group thinned out, I saw Karus point to Young Roscius. One of the Varduli put a shot into the leather pouch of his sling; it was one of their largest missiles, almost too big to fit into his hand. He cupped the pouch around it, took a rocking step back and forward, raised the sling, circled it above his head slowly while he took aim. Abruptly, he whipped his arm faster and lashed off the shot.

He missed Roscius, who had unexpectedly moved. But the man standing beside him had the top of his skull sliced off.

That was it for everyone. The fight was over.

37

Home to the Aventine.

'Hit-to-kill!' exclaimed my uncle, Lucius Petronius, with the envious admiration of an old soldier, glumly retired.

'Super dense, super fast,' agreed my pa. His tone was positively loving.

'Bloody kinetic!'

'Terminal.'

Heads together over a missile I had picked up and brought home, they spoke further, of mobility, accuracy, target and impact. My cousin's partner, Corellius, who was normally a loner, came to join in. Our courtyard was crowded. Marcia rolled her eyes at Tiberius and me as we pretended to listen respectfully. My mother was present, playing with Gaius and Lucius to give their nursemaid a break; Helena had stopped Gaius and Lucius putting Piddle and Willikins into Barley's kennel so the dog would rush out chasing them. She and Marcia had exchanged a nod, though for some reason they had never been close.

Fascinated by the slingshot, Falco, Petro and Corellius were barely aware of the rest of us. 'Handful of auxiliaries scampering around, swinging their arms with these babies – barbarians will start dropping like fleas off a dead rat.'

'Lead?' Corellius was itching to get hold of it. 'That would be my preferred combat ammo . . .'

'Cast. Lovely little almond shape. None of your digging a finger in the ground to make a hole and pouring a rough nugget with molten metal,' Petro was carolling happily.

Corellius wanted to better him. 'Melt in flight from the heat, if it's got off fast enough.'

'Too bloody right. Faster than arrows any day. Gods, we used to love these babies. Devastating. Penetrate armour at four hundred strides. Cripple limbs, no problem. Light, portable – *cheap!*'

'Cheap as a gob of fish pickle,' Falco agreed with his old tent-mate. 'And accurate – in the right hands, spot on, squash the wart between a man's eyebrows. Brutal!'

As one, all three men turned to look at me. 'So, who fields these beauties?' Petronius demanded.

'Unit from the Strangers' Camp. Secret ops. Varduli.' I pretended to be watching Piddle and Willikins chasing Barley around, terrorising the dog.

Corellius sniffed. 'Where the fuck are they from?'

Picking up my dog to save her from the chickens, I glanced at Tiberius. He had previously researched Karus and his troops. He let me discuss the geography, while he shooed the chucks. 'North-eastern Spain. Far end of the Pyrenees. Celtic. Cavalry.'

'Cavalry? Bugger that. I thought slingers always came from the Balearics,' Petronius argued. 'Everyone knows that. Trained up to it from toddlers. Tough tots, not allowed to eat anything unless they shoot it.'

'Thin people?' I suggested quietly. That was daft of me. For these fellows, jokes about training systems were out of order.

'Face it,' said Father, like the realist he never had been. 'Anyone can learn to fire off a pebble with a piece of string.'

'In Rome, though? Slingshots in the street? Nutters!'

'Who leads them?' asked Corellius.

'Gaius Julius Karus,' I answered.

'That bandit!'

Falco and Petro gave Corellius the hard stare. They were both aware he had been a spy. Marcia had come in for banter over hitching herself to one of those. 'Know him?' asked Petro, in a cool voice. 'Who is this bastard?'

'Intelligence. A complete goon.'

'Domitian loves him,' I inserted. 'Three crowns and a silver spear. Special agent.' I hoped Petro was unaware that Karus now had charge of Operation Phoenix, the offshoot of Operation Bandit King, which had once been his personal project.

My father came over to me. 'And what,' he asked, loading it with patriarchal significance (a persona he rarely carried off), 'were *you* up to, crazy daughter, wandering into a bunch of mad Iberian slingers?'

'Not wandering. Being very careful.'

His loyal crony, Uncle Petro, backed him: 'Women these days – ought to be locked in the house for their own safety. I blame the husband!'

Tiberius made his helpless gesture. 'Don't put it on me. I was left at home, minding the children.'

That went down well with three ex-military crusties.

Why were they here? Falco and Petro had found out that Rome had been reinfected. They had come up the hill for an indignant rant about the criminal pustulance called Florius. According to them, he was theirs to find, which they would. After all, they had been looking for him for more than ten years, call it fifteen, so clearly they were the boys for this job.

Nobody pointed out that they missed how he had stayed in Britain after they thought they had chased him out.

Petro gave me a suffocating hug. He was, as always, solid, calm and full of manly kindness. 'Don't you worry, pet. Don't think any more about that creep. We'll get him.' Over his big shoulder I looked at my mother; she was giving my father her *change the subject* stare. He knew when to gaze up idly at the sky.

It soon emerged the veterans knew less about the current situation than I did. However, I let the old fraudsters congratulate themselves on their acumen. Then they took off, dragging my husband to a bar, where they promised to give him useful lectures on wife control. Tiberius went with them quietly, playing a helpless duffer whom everybody shoved around.

That was untrue. Otherwise, I would never have had anything to do with him.

We had a small crisis when Gaius claimed that Lucius had swallowed the slingshot. Fortunately my mother found it on a lamp-table.

38

Some time later Helena and I emerged from a room where we had been chatting as mother and daughter, though curiously she never mentioned Florius. Neither did I.

I could hear my steward bickering with my chef in the kitchen on the far side of the yard, and Paris the runabout was whistling somewhere. My father had collapsed on a bench on the drinkers' return. Breaking his peaceful silence, Falco said Tiberius had gone upstairs for a rest.

Glaphyra had returned to us from Mother's but she thought someone else was entertaining the boys. And, indeed, someone was.

'Show us, show!'

'Look, I've braided it myself for you. The loop on the first cord has to sit here, like this, on the back of your index finger.'

'Let me, let me!'

'No, hold off so I can show you first. Then you tie a knot in the end of the other cord, so you can clamp it between your finger and thumb. The shot goes into the pouch, so the soft leather cups around it.'

'Why?'

'So it won't fall out. Now you hold both ends in your one hand and begin gently twirling . . .'

Mother and I both started forward.

'Don't blame me!' cried Falco.

'True, for once!' agreed Helena, a blunt woman.

'The man has a false leg.'

'That's no excuse. You stop him!'

Too late. A shot was whipped off. Marcia had stepped out of their room onto the upper balcony. The fast projectile cracked into the wall beside her, two inches from her head. It dug a deep hole in the stonework. She saw that neither of the boys was responsible. Corellius had done it.

Nothing put him off. 'Whirl, step, they're dead!'

'*Io!* You nearly got her!'

'Give it, give it! I want a go!'

'See if you can get Willikins. *Pow!*'

I did not have to intervene. My mother had had two younger brothers and she was now bringing up a twelve-year-old son. '*Not* in the house, Gaius Corellius!' Helena snapped icily. The sling was confiscated, no argument. Corellius accepted that this woman, if she chose, could eat a spy on a toasted bun with fish pickle.

Marcia started giving him a mouthful. The boys, yelling with indignation, were carried off by Glaphyra, big hips swinging, at a practised waddle. Other staff looked out, then vanished. Tiberius inspected the wall in annoyance. Gloomily he spoke of masonry filler. He sounded as if he knew that nobody listens to building specialists. My father winked at my mother; they each picked up one of their chickens in a coordinated movement, ready to slink off home. 'We'll leave you to it, Albia.'

'Those overused domestic words!'

'Don't be bitter, darling.'

I declared the time had come for Marcia and Corellius to pack their bags, not forgetting his beautifully modelled, highly polished, bronze prosthetic leg. They were to go as 'innocent lodgers', staying at Auntie Itia's boarding house until they found out something useful for me.

39

While my home was so busy, something had happened. Over on the far side of the Forum, somebody had visited the Rabirius hitman when he came in from his insurance work and 'invited him to go for a drive'.

This was a well-known expression. It might not be refused. If the Emperor ever made a similar request, whoever had to accompany him knew he would torment them with friendly-sounding chat while enjoying their discomfiture because they had guessed what came next. An officer would be waiting with a sword. Even the 'good' Emperor Titus was an execution tease: people who went to a banquet with Titus might not need their transport home. Now his brother Domitian had become a legend for sinister walks, and it seemed criminals must have their own version.

Neighbours said Turcus had looked neither surprised nor visibly apprehensive, though clearly he knew what the invitation meant. He had been collected in a small carriage, disregarding the wheeled-vehicle curfew. A Vestal Virgin might use such a carriage; nobody thought Turcus was being picked up by a priestess. Whoever took him believed they were above the law.

Immediately after he went out, his wife grabbed the children and that large dog of theirs. Taking little luggage, they all left too. They had not returned. Nobody expected that they would. It was believed the couple owned a place some-where else in Italy, though she had never told anybody where it was. She was a pleasant woman, all agreed. The children were extremely well brought-up.

A couple more men with their faces covered came to the neat apartment, like those who had run in there on the day of the street fight. They made a cursory search, then departed, shrugging. They spoke to no one. They stole nothing, nor did they trash the joint. It would stand empty until the land-lord gave up and sold whatever was there so he could re-let the rooms.

Turcus was never seen again.

40

For a time, I could see no way forwards. I still wanted to be the sleuth who found Florius; I wanted to hand him to the authorities and make them give me a receipt. Still, he was never going to saunter up saying, 'Flavia Albia, I believe you want a word?'

He could have been anywhere. Milvia's house had been searched officially, for what that was worth. I remembered obsessively what I had seen then: Nicon and a group of his own men had gone inside, while watched by Sixth Cohort troops who stayed in the street. I saw Nicon being polite to Milvia, then giving a quiet nod to the Sixth's officer. Some kind of understanding had been going on there, but with Nicon dead I could only speculate. Morellus always disparaged the Sixth, though could be cautious about saying they allowed the Balbinus mob licence deliberately.

My father and uncle, on the other hand, always came straight out and said the Sixth were corrupt. In Petro's opinion, they used to let the Balbini operate at will around the Circus Maximus. Petro was certain the Sixth took bribes. Did the farcical search at Milvia's prove illegal payments still occurred?

The situation felt so murky, any officials I contacted might be too close to the gangs. Also, too many units were involved. Across the north of Rome, the long fingers of the traditional hills were divided up. The Pincian and Quirinal belonged to the First Cohort; they always claimed the Forum took up all their time and manpower, though their record was pathetic on pickpockets. The adjacent region included the Campus Martius; that meant the Seventh Cohort would be very much affected by any redistribution of gangster activity, now the Ocellus twins' power had declined. The Viminal was assigned to the Third Cohort, apparently keeping their heads down; likewise the Fifth on the Caelian. That left the Second Cohort to grapple with the Esquiline, home base of the Rabirii. I had worked with them and merely thought they were lazy, which meant lazily led. After the Rabirius funeral, I did suspect they were headed up by a tribune – named as Vergelius – who might be on the take. In my head I could hear Pa and Petro guffawing at 'might'. They would believe the Second were as bent as the despised Sixth.

With gang warfare flaring, it was a mistake to spread resources in this way. Jurisdictions might look sensibly fanned on a map, but if the units failed to work together – as they would – the result was a shambles. Control needed to be tightened, with a master plan and consolidated leadership. Hence the Karus appointment, I supposed. Some city prefect or Palace bureaucrat had got that right. Whatever anyone thought of Karus, if a task could fit his own ambitions, he was brutally efficient.

Even so, as a newcomer he had limitations. There was a bolthole in Fountain Court on the Aventine that the Balbinus family had used on occasions; I wondered if Karus knew about it. Morellus tried to keep the place under surveillance. He claimed lack of resources, but we gave him additional eyes. My husband had just won a contract to dismantle the old Eagle Laundry, so his men would spot anything that moved in the alley. Larcius, the clerk-of-works, would be gathering materials; reclamation rights were part of our tender. One of the lads would have to be stationed down where the skip and handcarts were, on permanent watch. Otherwise, as my father always said, in Fountain Court pilferers would steal your snot if you had a cold.

I doubted whether our men would see Florius. I ruled out the bolthole. The Balbini used their nasty nook to store stolen goods and melt down silver. It comprised a dingy shopfront and a shed beside a ginnel. Florius might hide up there briefly, but he would want a more luxurious billet to live in for any length of time. So where was he bedding down?

If this man had a permanent address specified in his unpaid-tax scrolls, it had to be the house he shared with Milvia. Didn't the vigiles reckon he had been there, at least until Nicon searched it? Nicon might have allowed Florius to escape, but after the troops left he might soon have slid back – believing himself safer than ever. A new, unannounced, raid by Karus might pick him up, though Karus seemed slow to think of it. I might have queried his slack attitude to searching, but Karus was Domitian's hard man; such a beast would not be slipped cash in return for favours.

Well, would he?

Florius was with Milvia, I felt sure. Her fancy place had to be his home. 'Business travel' was one thing. If he formally stopped living with his wife while in Rome, it would be equivalent to divorce. As I saw it, such a separation was in neither of their interests; divorce meant division of property, for one thing. For them, too, it entailed loss of face. If he ever split from her, he would lose position as the Balbinus heir; as a single woman in a masculine environment, she would lose clout. She might be respected as a widow, but never if she had been dumped. They had to stick together, and on that basis, I decided to make another surprise visit to Milvia's house.

Even I was too sensible to go alone into the citadel of a violent gang. Last time I had taken Marcia, but she was too much of a stirrer. Anyway, I had deposited her and Corellius at Auntie Itia's. I opted for my young maid Suza, who would love to gaze at fashionable furnishings. 'And Milvia has the latest high-top curls.' Suza was thrilled. Too late, I foresaw disaster. She would be so busy taking hairstyle notes, she would be no use for anything else. The daft girl, with her fancy ambitions, would probably try to move in as Milvia's beautician. 'Check out any jewellery she's wearing.' At least I could rely on her for that.

In the event we were accompanied by my aunt, too. Maia Favonia had called at our house, trying to find out what Falco and Petro were up to; she had overheard them agitating about Florius. She brought Petro's baby grandson, a stalwart little bundle of chubbiness who kicked a lot; she dumped him on Glaphyra. Maia decided to see inside her husband's one-time secret rendezvous (it was before he and Maia got together). Apart from scrutinising Milvia, she thought a peek at the old love nest would put one over on Petro's first wife.

'For Heaven's sake, Maia! Arria Silvia won't care. She would never have soiled her sandals crossing that threshold.'

'More fool her!' Maia was one of the strong, nosy, easily angered, shamelessly frank Didius women. I chose to respect her for it. That was better than starting a feud.

Listen: if the Sabine women had been as scary as ours, Romulus would have told his men not to bother trying to people Rome through a mass rape, but to stay safely single and vanish from history.

222

'She wasn't a fool, Maia. Silvia felt she needn't have a face-off. As mother of his children, she owned rights of possession.'

At that, Maia was off: 'Silvia should have marched right in and tweaked the ditsy floret's little nose.'

'Well, don't come with me, if you're planning to do it.'

'Not my rumble. If he had two-timed me, I'd have killed her. Come to think of it, I might have killed him.'

'Maia, face the truth. Petronius Longus had been hankering after you since our rascals came back from the army and he was introduced to you. Father says so. If you hadn't been already married to your drunken horse-vet and popping out children, yours would be one of the great love stories. Lucius Petronius would never have wandered.'

Maia assumed a crabby expression as if she thought seizing chances to wander was that sneak's natural state of mind, at least when he was younger and had the energy. 'I don't want him and your clown of a father getting involved again with those people.'

'Then help me track down Florius, so the creaky oldsters never have to.'

Maia took no exception to me insulting them. 'You are right. They are not what they were.'

'No,' I answered her baldly. 'And it may be those self-styled heroes never were!'

But a softer look came into Maia's eyes. 'Wrong! They used to be a gorgeous pair. Helena and I knew to grab them when we had the chance. They were all heart – and had everything to go with it!'

Unimpressed, I said Balbina Milvia must have liked what she saw too. Maia had to promise me she would not quarrel over Petro's murky past. Simpering, she made the vow. Like me, the person she wanted to batter was Florius, for trying to kill Petronius. In that cruel incident back in Britain, she had arrived on the scene while my uncle was still gasping and shocked. The next minute they were both teary in each other's arms, and had been laminated partners ever since. Maia knew how close she had come to losing him. She bore her grudges bitterly. Hades, I hadn't been present, but I was angry myself.

I do admit that reminiscence of griefs you have harboured for fifteen years breaks the informers' code. Good interviews are conducted on the basis of measured preparation, a neutral position and cogent questions, quietly put.

Still, when did informers do anything that sensible?

41

I had to change my mind about Julius Karus. Forget probity. He and a friend were making a social call. I was amazed. Chatting up a gangster's wife was not merely uncharacteristic; it cannot be in the hard men's rulebook. Karus's canoodling comrade was a stranger to me, but as they left the house, I recognised his cocky swagger: the proverbial 'officer material' – where officers were men my own associates loved to despise.

Everything about these swine said they had been deliberately barbered in preparation. Slaves with boot oil had done duty. Their neckerchiefs bore mercilessly neat knots.

I managed to drag my companions back into the shadow of an arch.

'She's still at it, then!' hissed Maia. Since Suza, our teenaged chaperone, looked puzzled, Maia elucidated savagely, 'Milvia. Entertaining soldiers on the sly!'

The men certainly looked as if they would have taken a flask of raisin wine and a parcel of sweet fritters as hostess-gifts, aiming for the kind of afternoon that good mothers would advise against. I asked a passing sausage-seller; he did not know Karus but growled that the playmate was a local tribune, a right picky bastard, might his balls drop off and his pizzle wither.

'Sixth Cohort?'

'If you say so. Aren't they all the same?'

'No, most are bad, but some are worse.'

So, the Sixth's top man was cosying up to the king of special ops, coming to flirt with Milvia as a horrible double act. I bet neither he nor Karus had troubled to tell their unit clerks where they were going, or why. I was wondering whether 'purchase of flask and fritters' would feature in their expense claims. Probably. Men on top salaries are generally brazen.

'That's for the *Daily Gazette* scandal column!' Maia decided. 'Who was seen calling on a certain housewife by the Circus whose husband is conveniently "away from home" . . .'

'Don't try notifying scribes,' I advised. 'I've been to enough funerals recently.'

After their exit, the men held a brief pavement conversation. It looked more businesslike than gloating over a conquest; I had seen clients leaving brothels just as deeply immersed, but in talk of wet-fish prices or the weather. They departed in different directions, loosening their neckerchief knots with identical gestures.

I hauled Maia and Suza straight across the road.

Balbina Milvia was having a busy afternoon. It must be her At Home day. We were admitted without a quibble. As we went in, I winked at Suza, muttering that she should note whether our hostess was dishevelled. Maia narrowed her big brown eyes. 'No chance. She's had too much practice!'

Milvia, pert and pretty in girlish green, was inspecting a packet of *globi*. Yes, her gift was sweet fritters, poppyseed-topped. Men on the hunt never change.

Women can surprise. Not at all hostile towards us, Milvia offered them round. I knew she had been an only child, so sharing was unexpected. She pulled a face as she bit into one, exclaiming, 'Ooh! They didn't pay enough!'

'On a budget. Who brought them?'

'People.'

'Family?'

'Friends.'

'Friends of yours? Or your husband's?'

No comment.

I took one. I put half back, agreeing these must have been the stale sweets from under a shop counter, on special offer due to old age. Maia, tight-lipped, refused. Suza managed to grab the packet, through which she then chomped happily, including the half-piece I had rejected. While she munched, she inspected Milvia, noting outfit, cosmetics and curls. Different ear-rings today. Three pearl drops: a fashion cliché, Suza's expression said. She was an opinionated lass. I liked her lack of social skills. So refreshing.

Milvia had noticed my different companion, Maia. Nothing wrong with those wide, free-of-guile eyes. 'New colleague? I hope she's less rude than the other one! And you brought your maid. Do I need to summon mine?'

'Not unless you want them to play gladiators with hair-pins.' Maia kept up the family rudeness, although she finished with a fake smile. That smile, with her unusual confidence, had once melted men across both peaks of the Aventine.

I noticed that she and Milvia were roughly the same height, while both would have been dainty when younger. Petro's first wife was similar. They were all his type, the reprobate. But the youngest sister of his crony Falco had been the real catch.

I introduced her. 'My aunt, Maia Favonia. Marcia's aunt as well. I expect you can see the resemblance.' Maia was a generation older and rounder, but she had the same stunning looks as our niece, with dark curls tumbling around a cloth headband she had stylishly devised herself – plus, of course, the free-flowing Didius truculence. 'She came to keep the peace.' I meant the joke as affectionate. Maia was mature enough to be amused. Suza rolled her eyes. Milvia failed to get it. 'We noticed your previous visitors. What did they want?'

'Hard to tell.' Milvia seemed truly puzzled. She came out with a blunt 'So what do *you* want?'

'Same as them, I expect – unless their visit took a romantic turn.' She did not bother to take offence, though I saw one foot kick at her dress hem. I specified: 'Where is your husband, Milvia? Isn't that what they asked?'

She gave us a stagey yawn. 'All too boring! Same answer: I have no idea. He can go wherever he likes. I threw him out.'

'Because of Claudia Deiana?'

'Is that her name?'

'It was. As I told you before, people say your husband killed her.'

'As *I* told *you*, I don't believe he could have done,' retorted Milvia.

'Too soft-hearted? Some called her the Brittuncula,' I pressed on relentlessly. 'She and Florius clearly had a long, close relationship. Rubria Theodosia tells me, Milvia, you were brought up to honour a code of loyalty, "a dedicated wife who believes in traditional virtues". Florius apparently follows the same lousy rules, where dedicated wives lead a closeted existence, while their men display no loyalty at all and traditionally bed down with someone else.'

'They had offspring, didn't they?' Maia asked me brightly. 'I heard no one can say how many, or who is looking after them. They may not even know their mother is murdered.' She was acting as a full Roman wife, mother and grandmother, quizzing Milvia blatantly, as they do. 'Have you children yourself, dear? You've left it a bit late, if you don't mind me mentioning it.'

I took a gentler line. 'Milvia and Florius were parted by legal difficulties a long time ago.'

'Oh, that must be hard!' flipped back Maia, still tough. 'Mind you, women do follow their husbands around when they travel, don't they?'

'Claudia Deiana, for instance.' I hauled the conversation to where I wanted it: 'Milvia, I know it was the Rabirius gang who organised the Brittuncula's watery death in Rome. Roscius had a runner who picked her up for them, then delivered her to their hitman for a contract killing.'

Maia sucked her teeth. 'Gruesome!'

'Yes, and there is terrible speculation that she was still alive when she was pushed off the bridge. The runner himself died a hideous death afterwards, the kind your father's old crew specialised in, Milvia dear. Florius planned that reprisal. People came after the hitman too, though one attack was broken up by Julius Karus. You know him, he brings you stale gifties.'

Suza thought she had better pause in chewing the *globi*.

'Have you finished?' demanded Milvia.

For a moment Suza was confused, clearly thinking the question was meant for her, not me. I was spending all my effort on my companions. I wished I had come by myself.

'I haven't even started. Milvia, I want to ask about the Rabirii. Their disposing of Claudia Deiana makes no sense. Have you any idea why they would do that?'

Milvia posed and pretended to think about it. She placed her neat chin on one index finger, with her crazily coiffed head on one side. 'Because they want to stop Florius moving in on the racing scene?'

'He may be a great gambler,' I agreed, 'and they certainly say he is placing the wrong bets!' Instead of posturing like her, I just considered what she said. 'So, are you telling me that strangling his lady love – and now tipping her off a bridge a second time – was a threat? "This is what happens to people who annoy Roscius and Vincentius"? In that case,' I suggested, 'why would the Rabirius mob not simply have killed Florius himself?'

Milvia pouted in a way that once-attractive women think is still pretty and luminous. 'Because he is married to me? And they are my relatives?'

'Well,' I agreed, 'female cousins of yours contracted and paid the hitman. I mean Pandora, with or without Veronica. Either might want to make Florius suffer, to beef up Rabirius Vincentius.'

'Oh – more family love!' Maia chortled, addressing me. Maia and I rattled our bangles and folded our hands in the way of two wise matrons. 'Mother and wife, fighting for their son and husband?'

'Clan etiquette too,' I rasped back. 'No one wants to kill the son-in-law of the late Balbinus Pius, so they murder his lover instead. Her being in Rome was inconvenient for him, yet a very convenient gift to them? Does that seem right?'

'No, it sounds as if they would be doing him a favour – and his wifey too.'

'Perhaps they couldn't get to Florius himself. We know he is hiding from the authorities, who want to discuss his taxes.'

'I have no knowledge of that,' chimed in Milvia. She was blinking too much for this to be true.

'Florius will be picked up one day,' Maia pronounced, with a subtle stiffening of her posture. This was how she tackled awkward children or battled my father over his unreliable auction records. 'The coward cannot hide for ever.' Petronius must have briefed her, because Maia knew as much as me: 'Florius already has his work cut out with rival gangsters, the vigiles, the special inquiry . . .'

'Headed up by an officer who brings his wife presents!' I inserted.

'So, Karus is bought off?'

'Karus isn't stupid.' Maia and I kept addressing each other as if holding a private conversation. 'I'd guess he just came along here with the other man. Who knows how far the vigiles tribune goes in collaboration, but I have contacts. I can easily find out.'

I had no connections with the Sixth. Maia pretended to accept the bluff, but said, 'If Florius hears about today's house call, that's bad. He will think his wife is playing around – again. He must remember past history. With him back in Rome, those old scores are back on. Two really big boys will be coming after him – your father and my husband.'

Balbina Milvia must have remembered that my father was Falco, so she only queried the other: 'Why? Who is your husband, Maia Favonia?'

'Petronius Longus.'

'That must be a worry for you!' Milvia immediately fought back.

So did Maia. 'Not at all. After he escaped your clutches, he found me. He knew what he really wanted in a woman. He is happily retired now and a grandfather, well beyond your

231

nasty reach. Thank your stars that sordid dalliance happened before I married him. You wouldn't want to have to deal with me!'

Balbina Milvia stood up. At this point she did call attendants, frantically using a tinkly bell so people came running. Milvia made a small gesture they must have recognised, barely a finger twitch. They were going to throw us out. She smirked at my aunt. 'Do give my regards to Lucius Petronius! What a charmer! If he ever wants to drop in again, I would love to see him.'

Maia shook off the advancing staff and regally swept out first, which gave Milvia a chance to grumble: 'Don't waste your energy harassing me, Flavia Albia. My life is blameless. If you think someone is playing footsie with the authorities, you should be looking at Veronica!'

After we were hustled outside, I reviewed the situation in my mind. It had always been much too easy to dismiss Milvia as soft. Falco called her slippery. Every claim of simple-minded innocence was a lie. She loved the money. She knew where the dirty denarii all came from; nowadays, she was personally counting it in. After her father died and Florius fled, she and her mother ran the Balbinus organisation together, until Cornella Flaccida lost her sense of reality. Milvia seamlessly took over. It was suspected that during her mother's final, feeble years this not-so-loving daughter actually helped Flaccida's journey to Hades; true or not, the idea may even have enhanced her standing. The Balbinus crew might never have feared her as they feared her father, but she consolidated her position so the whole organisation remained in her personal control. She seemed more successful even than the Rabirii, with their internal feuds.

That was her house. Floors were groaning under her strongboxes and it was decorated to her expensive taste. She was the queen ant. Everything revolved around the mistress; there was no sense that she ever had to answer to a master. I still doubted that their marriage had formally ended but I did begin to believe that Florius was no longer sharing the home.

'Albia, what did that little episode achieve?' groaned Maia.

'The sweeties were quite nice,' murmured Suza, happily.

42

We stood back in the arch of the Circus where we had paused before, now stung by the interview and need-ing recovery. After so many *globi*, Suza complained of a stomach-ache. Maia, a long-term mother, snapped that it was her own fault.

I ignored their bickering. I was watching the house. Milvia already had another visitor.

Nothing new there. Regular doorstep traffic would be quite usual. At certain hours of the day and night, all the ambient sneak thieves, bath-house clothes-manger raiders, step-inside burglars, delivery fiddlers, rent racketeers, fake fortune-tellers, change-table rushers, dropped-purse scammers, back-alley muggers, porch crawlers, brothel blackmailers, specialist temple larcenists, everyday portico plug-uglies and general-duty granny-bashers would bring their profits. Neighbours would not dare to complain about their activity.

Come on, agitated locals, you must have known what you were letting yourselves in for. Did nobody mention you lived near the headquarters of the big-time, famously violent Balbinus crew? You won't want to knock on that armoured door asking to borrow a crock of honey. You won't even mention how their lamp-boy stole your mule, and you will never court trouble by suggesting it's all unfair because this used to be such a nice area. Do you want your head kicked in? Anti-social behaviour is the slime in which those people crawl.

So, just as we had followed the two paramilitaries, another man had turned up to replace us. He was on his own. Something about the way he walked and his stance told me he was not born a native of this city. That could have placed him as just one of the multitude of slaves, traders, ambassadors or other transients who came to Rome. There was no reason for him to attract my attention – yet everything about him struck a chord, faint but plangent as an accidentally knocked harp.

He was solid, fairly tall, upright carriage. Seen from behind, he looked in his middle years. Not high status. A commoner. A workman. Trusted to go out and about on his own but quite possibly someone's slave.

He wore a workaday brown tunic, topped by a rough cloak fixed on one shoulder with a brooch I could not see. His clothing had long crumpled sleeves and ankle-tied leggings; neither was traditional in Rome, though in February nor were they rare.

Hair more light than dark – it might even be red. He had had a ruthless trim from a Roman barber, which would have disguised a foreign origin; any wild dreadlocks had been lopped out of existence, and if he had ever owned a big moustache, it had been shaved off. That might be deliberate on his part, or else he had been given no choice; Roman barbers were notoriously single-minded. You don't argue with a man who has a razor at your throat.

His doorstep wait took longer than he wanted, perhaps because our own visit had made the occupants defensive. In the moments while I was staring at him, he glanced around jumpily. Then that heavy door opened; he was swallowed inside. He seemed to have something in his hand, as if he was delivering a letter.

I waited. I sent the others home while I stayed there on watch for a long time, but he never came out again.

From across the road, I had made out no blue tattoos, no torque, no arm bangles. No checked material. Naturally there were no weapons. Even so, I thought I knew him. His name would not immediately come to mind. I might have tried shouting in his own language – except that, as before mentioned, all I really knew in Celtic was 'Piss off, you pervert!' Never the best social introduction.

If Milvia had him, there was no chance I might manage to see or speak to him. Finally I remembered that someone – Onocles, the tourist guide? – had told me his name was Ulatugnus.

That man had been Claudia Deiana's British slave.

43

How long did I wait? Too long.

Informers expect to be stuck in dank porticos or doorways for many hours of our sad working lives, hoping a witness or suspect will emerge, while doomed by past experience to know they will not. I was surveying the street long enough to notice that the Balbini had other observers. A bootshine boy never bothered to solicit customers. A couple of fellows spent far too long leaning against the counter of a food stall without buying.

They had probably noticed me too. We had almost reached the point of acknowledging we were colleagues. I had done it before.

'What's yours?'

'Unpaid rent. You?'

'Subpoena, when I can grab him.'

'Best of luck!'

'You too.'

Sometimes other agents would cover for me while I quickly fetched a snack, or I'd watch for them while they dashed to a public latrine.

I would not risk cooperation here. The people I had spotted might be on observation for Milvia, or they could be working for themselves on spec, hoping something would happen near her house so they could earn a snitching fee. I didn't want them to report that I was loitering.

The sun moved round. People I had seen go out on errands came back. Pigeons sank their heads into their shoulders and slept. It was nearing the time when a lone woman standing below an arch could be there only for one reason. I had already been mildly propositioned several times. In that situation anyone in a skirt was expected to be ready to lift it.

Around me all the noise and smells of Rome spread like a muffling carpet. From my high home on the Aventine, the city would have seemed remote. In the enormous long basin that held the Circus, the great stadium's empty, dusty centre diminished effects slightly, yet a low-grade murmur was always present; people would have missed it if it stopped. Workshops sited close to me under the arches made their racket; from much further away I could hear gulls and even distant creaks from ships and cranes along the river; animals lowed in the meat market. Other cities have different sounds and odours. Here the background might seem a normal mix of domesticity and commerce, yet I had travelled enough to know Rome had its special spikes of swearing and song, its distinctive wafts of fish scales and Lucanian sausage, its own unexpected moments of clatter.

I remembered Londinium. That gave me an unhappy moment.

Normally in this area I was heading elsewhere. Today I had plenty of time for reflection. There had always been crises at the Circus. A blaze fifty years before was supposed to have started in basket shops, then roared through from the apsidal end. The great city fire in Nero's reign was another disaster, and Domitian was still repairing damaged public stands after a more recent incident. Floods were an equal risk. Every thirty years or so the river pushed in, as if seeking to reinstate ancient swampland. If the Year of the

238

Four Emperors had not been ghastly enough, the Tiber then flooded the densely inhabited low areas, surging into places that were normally dry. People out of doors were swept away in a sudden inundation; people indoors were trapped in buildings, some even dying in their beds. Buildings collapsed; many still suffered the effects of mud and stagnant water rotting their fabric and foundations.

Yet the Circus had always been repaired or rebuilt, always on its same footprint. It was too old, too big, too deeply revered to surrender. Nowhere else in Rome was there such a large site to provide ceremonial occasions. Festivals were regularly centred here. The stands would resound many times a year. Even on days when there were no races, the building's underbelly was alive with shops, stalls, cabins and ateliers. Fortune-tellers and jugglers plied their trades. With arches and dark corridors, it was a notorious hangout for prostitutes – and, of course, criminals festered.

If that had been Ulatugnus who went into Milvia's, what in Hades was he doing? He appeared to feel no anxiety about entering the house. Any nerves he had felt were beforehand, standing on the step in full view, waiting to be let in. Was he now living with Milvia, as if she had inherited her murdered rival's possessions? Or was he with Florius – so Florius must be, after all, staying there opposite? I had been told that when Claudia Deiana died, Ulatugnus ran away from Auntie Itia's. Had he known where Florius could be found? Had they already met up in Rome? I even considered a theory that the slave might have put himself here on purpose, out of loyalty to Claudia, yearning for a way to obtain justice for his mistress. Was Ulatugnus working under cover? No, that was ridiculous.

239

More likely, after Claudia went missing Ulatugnus had sought out Florius, whom he knew from Britain. The slave told Florius what had happened to Claudia, accompanied him when he went to see Fundanus about a funeral, then stayed with him. If Florius was in fact living somewhere else, Ulatugnus passed to and fro, used by his old master as a messenger. Today he had brought something for Milvia, a letter, I thought. If Fate had been with me, he would have been sent back with a reply; I could have tailed him on his return to Florius.

No luck.

I slowly accepted that gangsters who had lived in a property for a couple of generations would not have possessed only one entrance. Ulatugnus had arrived at the front door. That was where visitors were screened. He might have noticed me, or from some other source Milvia knew I was still outside. She might simply be keeping the slave there until I gave up watching and went home.

Alternatively, Ulatugnus had done whatever he came for and left long ago, using a secret exit. There was probably a walkway behind the building, tucked in tight along the foot of the Aventine. There could even be old passages dug under the street to emerge in different premises. My uncle would know. He had spent years fruitlessly trying to gain evidence against Balbinus Pius, who had spent the same time merrily evading detection.

I was reasonably certain no one had left in disguise, nor had anyone jumped out and smartly hidden in a passing cart. The short winter day was moving on, but the wheeled-vehicle curfew had not yet allowed transports into Rome. No one had carried out any big chest, barrel or basket that could contain a man. I had not missed the slave leaving, not from the front entrance.

It was probable that Florius and any messengers routinely came in one way then left by another route. He and Milvia were bound to be security-conscious. Even at my own house, we had a grand entrance door in a porch on Lesser Laurel Street, plus a secluded back exit that the cook and other staff could use, then the builder's yard on the side with its own wider gates.

The plain fact was I had been daft to stand here.

It was stupid and dangerous in several ways. The hour had come when a lone woman lurking by the Circus became a distinct target. Even saying no carried risks. It was time to scarper.

'Hello, darling. What's your price?' Here came a stubbly skink in a one-arm tunic and half-boots. I could smell his sweat-rotting clothes from more than two strides away. Too sure of himself to accept rebuff. Now I was stuck.

Luckily another man slid off a donkey, pushing in ahead. He was covered with dust and looked harassed but determined. 'Sorry, fellow! I saw her first.'

'Get lost, Legate. Take your turn!'

'Prior arrangement.'

'What arrangement?'

'This do?' Tiberius Manlius held up his left hand, one finger separated to show his wedding ring. 'Still new enough not have gone green yet. She's mine. Sorry, my friend.'

The other man walked off, cursing me for a bitch and my husband for a pimp.

'Spoilsport!' I admonished gently.

'They told me where you were. I finished with my team at the site. Hit a snag and the light was going . . . It's coming up to dinner time. What's happening?'

I provided a fast résumé. Tiberius listened. After absorbing it patiently, he stood and stroked the donkey's ears, making no comment.

Of my own accord, I suggested, 'Is this when you give me a lecture about not letting my obsession with Florius ruin the rest of my life?'

'Sounds as if I have no need to.'

I kept going anyway. What is the point of being married if you can neither bang on nor state the obvious? 'I cannot forget or forgive. I owe this to the suffering child I once was.'

'I know,' he said, still not judging me. Some people might have found it aggravating. Still, that was marriage too. He had the right to be reasonable. I had the right to be stroppy with him, not to mention my right to be in the wrong and never admit it.

I quoted what I assumed he wanted to say: 'Is revenge all that matters to me? Don't I see that if he affects me so strongly right to this day, Florius will win? Can I never let the past go – or will I allow it to destroy my married happiness and well-being?'

Wise, though not exactly passive, old Grey Eyes assented.

'All right, be restrained,' I responded to his amiable silence. 'I am impressed. It is a while since you felt the need to rant at me.'

He did then mutter, 'It's a while since I felt so anxious.' Then he huffed. 'I didn't know you very well then. Will you come to dinner?'

'Yes, I am ready.' I was chilled, weary and depressed. My spine ached from hours of standing. I knew I was a lucky girl. After such a day, few informers can expect the luxury of being picked up by a loyal friend and safely taken home.

He climbed back aboard our donkey; I scrambled up behind him. Almost before she felt the weight of us both,

Merky set off. We had only owned her a few months but, like the rest of our household, she was learning to do as she pleased. She would head back to her stable without requiring guidance. In fact, if we had wanted her to go somewhere else, she would have headed for her stable anyway.

Tiberius was a steady driver. As in life, he aimed where he intended to go, refusing to deviate. If other riders or pedestrians bumbled into his way, he only slowed up until they moved, or he was able to overtake them. I could have lightly kept my balance with two hands on his leather belt. Instead, I wrapped both arms tightly around him, put my face against his warm back and let myself enjoy the security that, in defiance of past history, I had somehow acquired.

That hand with his wedding ring was covering mine heavily. I could not see his expression, though it would be a frown of apprehension.

He did know me now. There would be no fooling Tiberius Manlius that I might abandon my quest for revenge. He understood how, wherever this hunt led me, I would have to continue.

When we reached home, he went straight indoors by himself. There was no suggestion we had quarrelled, yet he took himself off without a word. I stabled the donkey. After unfastening her bridle and filling her manger, I fetched a heavy bucket of water, then pulled her ears the way she liked and stood there talking to her, which she also enjoyed. Home duties. I did know what a wife was for.

It was the dog who came to find me before dinner. But through the open yard gate I had heard Tiberius sending her. 'Where is she? Where's our girl, Barley? Go fetch!'

44

When I sent them off without me, Aunt Maia had stormed off home, telling Suza someone would collect the little grandson from our house later. I suspected that their apartment was to host ructions over Milvia, so nobody came that evening. Fortunately, Glaphyra loved looking after a baby – she was good with children of all ages, 'Even your hoity-toity mother and that right pair, her brothers,' but took special delight in this happy bundle. He must have a name, but his family all called him the Bug. His mother came for him next morning.

This was Petronilla, an interesting character. She had spent parts of her childhood with her mother in Ostia but had always been a father's girl. Her younger siblings had died of a childhood illness, after which Petro and she had a special bond. She had told me once, 'Being an only child may be a trial, but it's hell being the only one left.'

Later, when she fell pregnant, she refused to name the guilty party. Her furious mother disowned her, but her father allowed her and the baby to share the cramped apartment where he and Maia lived with some of Maia's brood. Petronilla had made a mistake but she never made a fuss about it. Whatever had happened to her, she bore the baby and started bringing him up, found a job to contribute financially, and got on with life.

As the daughter of a tall, well-built father and a petite mother, she could have followed either but had ended up tall. She had light bones and was pleasant-looking rather than pretty. As stubborn as Petronius, more placid than Maia, she was hard-working, a good mother, a quiet personality. I liked her.

She must have been a few years younger than me. Her natural confidante in our family was my mother. Helena had known Petronilla since she was an infant, some time before Maia met her. Today Helena would not do, however. The young woman was looking anxious but preferred talking to me, it seemed. There was a problem she needed to share.

Tiberius had left for his temple site. Everyone else was absorbed in normal activities. The young mother changed her baby's loincloth then she and I sat pretending to watch the Bug thrashing his chubby legs and waving his hands about.

Petronilla came out with her fears: she had overheard a messenger inviting her father to visit Balbina Milvia.

Crud in a bucket. That poisonous sneak Milvia had wasted no time. 'Don't worry,' I soothed, because the truth was not an option here. 'He will never go.'

'But he has gone! I saw him leave home, with that up-to-nothing-in-particular look.'

'All that stuff between them was years ago, love. Things will be different now.'

Or would they?

I understood Petronilla's dread. It might only be an invitation, which anybody sensible could easily ignore, but a man – all right, or a woman – who is suddenly contacted by an old lover will always be curious and vulnerable to flattery. If this involved a client of mine, I would be taking the most pessimistic view.

It had to be kept secret from Maia – not least because Maia had probably caused the situation by goading Milvia yesterday. Our Maia would never accept any blame for that. Even a consultation with Helena Justina was ruled out, because of Falco. His and Petro's close bond made this complicated. Anyway, he always told Petronius he had been stupid over Milvia, so there was no hope of them having a reasoned discussion. Even if they talked it through over a drink, Petronius would take a decision on his own, just as he had done when he first unwisely visited the gangster's wife. If other people called his decision crazy, he was more likely to dive in.

'Albia, we have to stop him!'

True. True, though it looked hardly possible. His daughter was sure he would not listen to an appeal from her. As a father he had hidebound attitudes. He would probably shout at her for eavesdropping and spying, then make loud proclamations about her lack of trust.

I told Petronilla to take the Bug home, not to mention anything to anybody else, and go to work as usual.

There was no way out for me. Counter-measures were urgently needed. I would have to organise them.

After yesterday, I had not intended to return to Milvia's in the near future, but I threw on a cloak and was soon back there. So that I looked different, it was a different cloak. Simple disguises are best. At least, they are fast to throw on.

I took our donkey, fitted out with panniers so I could appear to be shopping. Once I was at the Circus, I even bought some items. I had allowed the dog to come, to act as extra camouflage. While I was on surveillance, Barley climbed out of her pannier and stood on Merky's back. This was some game they had devised recently. It had the disadvantage for me that passers-by kept stopping to look at the unusual charming scene, with the clever dog on guard and gazing around from her vantage point . . . So much for discreet undercover work.

I managed not to think about how Tiberius would view me coming here again. So now there were two households with secrets.

There is a rule of thumb for this. If he does it, he is a despicable cheat. If you do it, you are taking silly risks. If I do it, there is a perfectly good reason. Besides, nothing will happen anyway.

Oh yes it will. Petronius Longus did visit, of course. My plan had been to jump out and confront him. But at the moment I spotted my uncle turning up, a gooey woman in a flouncy tunic insisted on telling me how charming and clever my unusual dog was, demanding to know how I had managed to train her to do this wonderful trick. Was it my idea in the first place, or had Barley devised it herself? Would I sell her? By the time I persuaded the crank to lose herself, it was too late.

Petro, thank the gods, was more sophisticated than Karus and the tribune; he had not visibly brought a parcel of reduced-price fritters. But however long ago their affair had been, when he strolled up at Milvia's the door smoothly opened for him. He barely had to knock. Like a man who was expected at the house, he stepped in. The door closed. Without going over there, I knew it would stay barred against me.

Someone had to fetch Petro out of there. Only one course of action remained. This was a father-and-daughter argument. Petronilla could not run to hers or even tell him she was aware of him philandering – but I jumped on my donkey and galloped to mine.

45

Falco was at the Saepta Julia. Chunky and wily, with fur in his boots for the winter, I found him outside, sniffing the air.

He had just received a message about something interesting that had happened on the far side of the Campus, up by the Neronian Bridge. He was about to rush off there because the rumour was of somebody dying unpleasantly. A horse was involved; it was a valuable horse, much fancied for a coming race, even if nobody doctored it. The vigiles were there, but special forces were in attendance too, so clearly this called for an informer to take a proper interest.

However, I had caught him in time. A short speech sufficed: 'Lucius Petronius was invited to Milvia's. I have seen the crackpot going in there!'

'Pigshit!' responded my noble papa, not even pausing for thought. If he was surprised, it immediately turned to acknowledgement that his old pal used to behave like this. He added, in the traditional way of his own father, Geminus, when faced with a situation, 'Pigshit! Pigshit! Pigshit!'

I found that solidly reassuring. When a Roman uses farm-yard imagery, he is reverting to his ancient roots. Our crisis called for slurry not philosophy. It needed a man who would leave his plough, defeat the enemy, then stomp home for root-vegetable soup.

My father always denied it, but he liked having subordinates. He rattled off instructions, as he dragged on a cloak: 'Whatever you do, don't tell Maia or you'll break her heart. Don't tell your mother or she will blame me. That idiot, he never learns. He always was a soft touch for kittens. If Milvia has got her little claws in him again, he won't listen. I'll have to go and drag him out by force.'

I would have loaned him my donkey, but he took the auction-house mule, Kicker. He told my cousin Cornelius, his under-manager – 'Call me the underdog' – to follow with a good length of rope, in case Petronius had to be tied up in the extraction process.

He raced off. Since he could never pass up a chance for a good inquiry, he left me to cover the Pons Neronianus incident.

'If it's viable, do not pinch my case!' he yelled at me, over his shoulder, as he left.

'And keep your mitts off mine at Milvia's!' I roared back.

This was father-and-daughter banter. Falco and I had worked together for a few years, while he was training me in my craft. He thought none of his other children would want to follow him as an informer, so I had a special place in his heart. We were both too strong-willed for a permanent partnership. But when we were able to work together again for a short period, it was a joy to us both.

So, with orders only to look at the scene and report back, I made my way over to the horse gallops by the bridge.

46

The northern part of the Campus still contained open space, despite imperial encroachments. In some parts a wide quay fronted the river, with a road that ambled as gently as a footpath, little used and marred by occasional weeds. Above loomed a low grey sky where clouds raced powerfully. Against the quay rolled the Tiber, almost in full winter flood, churning down from the hills into this outlying area as if bearing a haughty god who would not deign to pause to gaze at human incidents.

Across the water lay imperial gardens, a circus, a graveyard, all looking lonely from this shore. On this side, away to the north before the city boundary, the great cylindrical drum of the Mausoleum of Augustus kept its isolated state. To the south, butting into the heart of the city below the peak of the Capitol, were crowded monuments – theatres, stadia, porticos and temples. Between them and the river a rough district housed the riders and staff of the chariot factions, once four colours and more recently six. Jostling for precedence, the teams regularly brought horses to exercise along what remained of the ancient mustering ground, in the long berm beside the river, between the bridges of Agrippa and Nero. They used a windy stretch called the Trigarium.

Nero's Bridge crossed over from the upper bend in the Tiber; alongside it on the city side, at the far end of the Trigarium, was a space called the Tarentum, a shrine with altars that was supposed to be an underground gate to the Underworld. For one man it had indeed become the site of his entry to hell.

'You keep out of this!' ordered Karus, as soon as he saw me. He had men with him, looking aggressive, and a few vigiles, whom his men had displaced, looking lost. They were all standing around a small scene of devastation, like skittles in a back alley, none of them doing much. Even Karus seemed uncertain as to what to do next.

I made no reply, gently blowing out air in a silent shadow of the long whistle my father would have given. A nasty death had occurred. I was happy not to approach the wreckage. A chariot had been used as a murder weapon. That takes inventiveness – and money.

Two black horses with white socks were already cut loose from it, frothing and tossing hysterically. Although grooms were standing near in subdued groups, the Varduli were taking it upon themselves to calm the upset beasts. Those auxiliaries originated in the coastal part of Spain, where the land met the wildest sea; their own mounts were almost as small and tough as ponies, but they were interested in these larger, easy-moving, intelligent, agile animals. They might have thought they were also Iberian – Spanish horses are supposed to fly like the wind.

The man on the ground was indisputably dead, so the Varduli took no interest in him.

I tried to concentrate on the chariot instead. It had ended up tangled as in the worst kind of racing disaster, but this one had not smashed into a stadium spina. From the wreck's placement I could just work out which way it had travelled: up along the riverbank track from south to north. It must have come thundering through the Trigarium, a place that historically might have been named after three-horse vehicles, though this vehicle was a *biga*, with two. Small wheels, five feet apart, a basket that was little more than a base with a front guard-rail, set directly on the axle. Fast, light, open, manoeuvrable. A battle machine for barbarians, though used by the Romans only for races and triumphs.

Room for one driver; a passenger would be a squeeze. I could tell who the driver had been. He was crouched with his head in his hands, by himself now, close to the water's edge, weeping.

'Shock!' commented Karus, when he saw me looking. I wondered whether to approach the man and comfort him. A member of the vigiles went over instead. The red tunic put a hand on the driver's shoulder; I could hear him speaking in a low voice.

'Was the accident his fault?'

For once Julius Karus showed emotion. 'What accident?' he shouted angrily. 'No, this was not the driver's fault! There was nothing he could do about it. Somebody put a blindfold on him, then forced him to drive with a knife at his throat.' He controlled his stress somewhat. 'The man will remember this. He will never get over what he was forced to do today. My troops say that even the horses will have permanent nightmares – and it was not their fault either. The people who contrived this are animals.'

What people? 'Gangsters?' I presumed. That would explain the presence of Karus, the special initiative head.

'Who else would do something like this – or even want to?'

Karus grabbed my arm above the elbow, then pulled me across to where the body lay. He kicked it, the same way he had kicked Nicon. He intended to make me look, but I did so of my own accord. I needed to know who it was.

The man who had died was dressed only in an undertunic. Under the dust and damage, he was in his middle twenties, paunch, hairy arms and legs, barbered brown hair. It was evident what had been done to him. One of his bare feet had been tied with a rope around the ankle. The rope, so tight it had dug into flesh, was still attached. The other end, now cut free, had been attached to the back of the chariot. Judging by the filthy, bloody wounds all over his head and body, the victim must have been face-down at least part of the time, as he was dragged along at high speed, towed behind the vehicle. With its sightless driver, but with horses who knew the gallops well, the chariot had careered all along the Trigarium to finish here by Nero's Bridge. Somewhere on that long mad journey, not soon enough for him, the victim had died.

Karus said, 'I'm guessing it was meant to be Florius.'

It was not him and I disagreed. I thought it was never supposed to be. This must be a message *from* him.

'Cover the body,' I instructed urgently, keeping my voice quiet. I looked around. As well as the Varduli and desultory vigiles, there were onlookers from the chariot factions and a few curious locals. 'Be quick! Hide him from view as long as possible. Too many ghouls are ogling, and some will already have recognised him.'

'You know who it is?'

'I do, I'm afraid.' I kept him waiting a moment on purpose, so he would pay more attention. 'Karus, this is not Florius, but it bodes worse for the peace of Rome. You need to start planning. There is going to be a riot.'

Karus was signalling to his men, even before he demanded my explanation.

I gave him the bad news. I had recognised one of the heirs of the Rabirius crew, the dim, cocky one. 'This is Young Roscius.'

253

47

Trotting fast on their small horses, the Varduli set off. I urged my donkey to follow, though Merky failed to see the point of rushing. The corpse, tightly trussed in sacking, had been slung over a spare mount. A couple of messengers rode off in another direction, but the main party dashed down the road to the Agrippan Bridge, crossed the river to the far side, then knocked people aside as they swept through the northern Transtiberina and into the out-station of the First Cohort of Vigiles. The troops who attended the crash were also from the First, so whisking Roscius over to their secondary barracks had been their idea.

The body was flung down in the yard. It would be some time before anyone would think of this as a place to come to claim him. With luck, that meant it would also be some time before his family's calls for vengeance started.

Karus strode about. It seemed even he had to wait for further orders. The First's day-shift politely produced benches. Their duty officer woke up and offered to send out for pastries. He was instructed to get lost.

I knew this cohort; I approached for a friendly chat. That made Karus look jealous, unable to match the range of my contacts. He wanted to be the man who knew everything, not pipped by an informer.

The Varduli had dismounted; some watered their horses at the cohort's fountain, the rest sat silent on the benches. My donkey muscled in with the horses. My dog jumped up into the fountain, then scrambled out and shook herself over the cavalrymen. I called her, before some tough fellow who hated being wet lashed out.

Karus eventually calmed down. 'This was a bloody violation!' he exclaimed to me. Apparently he felt I could be talked to. 'Somebody thinks he's Achilles, dragging Hector around the walls of Troy.'

'Hector had been killed in combat first,' I pointed out, in a dull voice.

'Ha! So Florius doesn't know his epics?'

'Too Greek? Isn't it Virgil that people quote in Britain? That's the effect of sending imperial emissaries to supervise an official education programme.' I could tell Karus thought plugging a Roman poet over Homer was entirely proper. 'What's the grand declamation we're supposed to learn? "The Greeks shape bronze statues so real they seem to breathe, carve cold marble until it almost comes to life. The Greeks compose great orations and measure the heavens so well they can predict the rising of the stars. Romans, your great arts are to govern peoples with authority, to establish peace under the rule of law, to conquer the mighty, and show them mercy . . ."' What was I doing, talking literature to the hard man? Hades, what was he doing, listening to me? 'Florius has no truck with mercy or the rule of law. I believe he did this to Roscius.'

'Who else?' Karus now agreed. 'Picking off opponents. He has an elimination programme.' That was when I first learned about the hitman, Turcus. It was Karus who unbent and told me of his invitation 'to go for a drive'. He thought Florius must have been behind that too. Turcus would now be dead, he said. Karus was livid; after his earlier intervention at the hitman's apartment, it was a damned waste of slingshots.

While I sat quiet, still mentally affected by the Roscius death, Karus salivated over his theories: 'Now he has wiped out their contract killer, Florius becomes a much bigger target himself. The Rabirii will have to react. He must be aware. It looks as if he has gone for Young Roscius before any of them can go for him.'

I concentrated on what, to me, really mattered: 'Perhaps he supposes Roscius sent the people who killed Claudia Deiana.'

'Right.'

'No. He's wrong. It was the women. Rubria Theodosia paid for the hit.'

'Who told you that?'

'Turcus himself.'

'You talked to Turcus?'

'Of course.' I left 'Didn't you?' unsaid. No point in aggravating him.

Karus snarled. 'What has the Brittuncula to do with anything anyway?'

'She matters.'

'She matters to *you*, maybe.'

She mattered to me, and I believed she might have mattered to Florius much more than anyone else was allowing.

Julius Karus was a bigot. Destined to be half right, but half blind to the obvious. I turned away.

The First's out-stationed personnel always pretended to sneer at their colleagues in the main base on the Campus Martius, but they knew them, of course. I found some locals I knew here talking with cohort members who had been by the Pons Neronianus. Karus had not questioned any vigiles, but I took an interest. They lapped it up. Bursting to look efficient, they gave me the background.

The two black horses with white socks were a team people favoured to win an upcoming race.

'For which faction?'

'The Purples.'

'*The Purples?* Aren't they rubbish?' Everyone despised the new chariot faction. 'They are worse than my husband's team, who I hardly dare admit are the Golds. Are you joking? Or . . .' A thought struck me. 'My father heard that a horse, well, it must have been the pair, has some big bets placed. Know anything about that?'

The vigiles were not supposed to gamble, which meant they did so avidly. They explained that the prospect of a Purples' *biga* winning was not only an outrage but it affected the odds. Popular interest was steaming hot.

'Is there a racket involved? The poor beasts were hysterical when I saw them just now, but looked pretty good horses.'

The vigiles thought the Purples must have bought them by accident. Apparently, the crack team might even win, although it would depend on whether anyone either nobbled the horses or the driver. Either would be routine. This was Rome. Some tipsters even encouraged bets on whether nobbling had or had not happened.

'Today's driver is so shaken up he may have to be rested anyway.'

'That's going to bugger up the probability!'

'Well, the horses may not be fit to run, after what's gone on today.'

'Shambles!'

Nobody could say whether Young Roscius had been involved in a dodgy bets fiddle. Ever since the Rabirii had taken over control from the Ocellus twins, the new mob must have been heading into organised interference, though probably it was too soon yet. But Roscius had liked to visit and show off. Invitations to special viewings at the stables or on the gallops were a very old element in keeping gang leaders happy.

'And what about Florius?'

Florius also hung around; he was more of an expert than Roscius. It never helped him to make good bets, though. He was the kind of gambler that tipsters adored. He would make a wrong stab, dumping a lot of money on a stupid whim. He could afford it, of course. I asked if he had been seen at the Trigarium today: not that anyone knew – though the vigiles looked speculative.

When the crash happened, it was so loud it drew troops from nearby. Before Karus and the Varduli sped up and took over – so how did the specials know about it? – the red tunics had proceeded as they normally would. They found witnesses and asked questions. They had ascertained that Roscius came to the Trigarium today because he had been given celebrity access; he wanted to see the Purples' fabulous horses being exercised.

It was very early in the morning when not many people were about. The driver and team arrived first. Somebody jumped him. The driver never saw who; he thought there was more than one assailant. He failed to recognise voices – 'Or perhaps he did,' suggested the vigiles, 'but he was too frightened of retaliation to tell us.'

'Was he behaving as if he knew more than he said?'

'Don't they always?'

'Had he been coerced in advance into helping, do you think?'

'If so, he never expected what actually happened.'

His assailants put a blindfold on him. They held him at knifepoint until Roscius came. He was either alone or anyone with him soon spotted the situation and scrammed. From what the driver could hear, Roscius was grabbed, partially stripped and his ankle tied. One assailant crowded into the chariot, then forced the driver to set off. He could tell his chariot was towing a substantial weight. He heard Roscius screaming. Then the screams stopped.

The thought of what must be happening made the driver hysterical. At some point, the horses slowed enough so the knifeman took a leap out and was gone. By then the terrified driver had lost control. The reins slipped from his hands. He clung to the front of the chariot, still blindfolded, sobbing. The horses kept running, as far as the bridge. One tried to turn and their panic brought about the crash. The vigiles were sure Roscius must have been already dead.

All the men at the station-house had seemed to be waiting for someone. Now a commotion by the big gates announced a big rissole was marching in.

Julius Karus decided I had no business in the presence of the great. 'Get lost! Go and be a nuisance to your husband, like a proper wife.'

That was never going to happen. A more significant figure stalked into the yard and I knew who it was. A deep voice exclaimed, 'Whose is the piss-artist dog doing tricks on a donkey?'

'Mine,' I piped up meekly.

I stepped forward and was enveloped in a giant hug. It had the mingled reek of tack-oil and spearmint that went with a soldier who kept scrupulous kit and a very clean body to go inside his sacred armour. He was in full dress uniform, ignoring the ban on daggers and swords. When I could wriggle free, I tapped the space on his metalled chest where eight existing gold medals awaited their final companion. 'Number nine is still held up with despatches, is it?'

He roared with laughter. 'Cheeky minx. Give Uncle Titus a big kiss!'

Karus must have despaired. Not only was I a mascot with the First Cohort, I was being squashed breathless by the mighty commander of the Castra Peregrina, the Strangers' Camp on the Caelian. That was where legionaries on detachment from all over the empire were gathered in a dark fortress that no one was supposed to know existed. They carried out mysterious tasks under the control of this highly dangerous man, ironically referred to in service as 'Uncle'. At the Castra, even with imperial backing, Karus himself was merely a new boy on secondment, an interloper. I had really topped him now.

I cheekily called the Princeps Peregrinorum 'Nearly Nine Gongs', and he let me get away with it. He was nobody's uncle and 'Titus' was a fake identity – or so he had once told me. But I had the special privilege of calling him by his cover name.

48

A s I gave him the requested kiss, chastely on the well-
shaved cheek, I tried not to stagger under the arm
around my shoulders.

'This is a turn-up – me having to come over the river
where horrible misfits and foreigners lurk. I wasn't expecting
to find you here among the boys. What are you doing with
these roughnecks, Flavia?' Titus turned me around to present
me to Karus and the rest as if he was showing an athletics
prize-winner to a cheering crowd. 'This is our little pet sparrow,' he announced proudly. 'When something at the Castra
looks impossible, she hops in and solves it. Then the dear
little bird has to fly out again to that husband she adores for
some reason. Even the gods are jealous of him – they tried to
smite him with a lightning bolt but Flavia picked it up and
threw it back.'

All the men in the yard had straightened up on his arrival;
even Karus had produced a weakling salute. Loosing me, the
Princeps inspected the vigiles. These men were not in his
command. Nevertheless, he had the status to overrule that
day's officer, who tripped along behind him nervously. The
Varduli only rated a curt nod.

Whether Karus was a subordinate was unclear although,
face to face, the two men avoided a stand-off. Titus was not
giving an inch to the imperial favourite. He saw no threat to

his position, even though it could be argued whether three gold crowns and a silver spear from Domitian really over-topped standard service medallions, even eight of them.

'No refreshments?' he demanded of the First's duty officer. He would say his rule was positively fatherly, he would call himself hands-off, yet he wallowed in power like a hippo in mud.

I stepped in. 'He was sending out for pastries, but he waited to find out what kind you like.'

Titus gave me a fond look. I was certain he realised what had gone on before.

'Pine-nut custards,' I suggested demurely to the officer. 'Please, not poppyseed fritters. I had some of those yesterday that were old as Time.' Titus was listening. He was bright enough to pick up that this was meant to be significant. I kept talking to him while the vigiles scrambled away to fetch in an order. 'I do hate a man who takes a love-gift for a lady but settles for sweetmeats they are selling off as past it. Belittles him and insults her, don't you agree?'

'Oh, I always agree with you, Flavia! Who was the love-rat?' he growled.

'No names.'

'Why not? You can tell me.'

'Some tribune. I don't actually know his name.'

'Not like you! Who was being smooched?'

'A gangster's wife.'

'Husband anyone interesting?'

'The one we are all looking for.'

'Oho!' he returned gleefully. Then to Karus: 'Were you aware of a scandal with the moll?' Without waiting, he exclaimed blithely, 'Of course he is! He knows the score. Don't you worry your little head about it, Flavia.'

I had been hoping for an ally, but he dismissed me. That is the trouble with contacts: they are useless if they brush aside your concerns.

'Have you two been introduced?' he asked me, as if suddenly remembering that we might not have been. 'Flavia Albia, my favourite snoop. Gaius Julius Karus, I call him my optio.'

He winked at me. The title had a double edge. An optio was an officer selected for promotion or someone's personally chosen successor. As such, 'optio' could carry the suggestion that its holder was still inexperienced or not yet fully trained.

'Princeps, you cannot be intending to retire?' I returned, to cover any insult Karus felt. 'It's surely not time for a gout stool at some little cottage in the hills?'

'Too right!' boomed Titus. 'Mine is a whopping villa with a vineyard and so many sheep that when you herd them together you can see nothing but wool as far as the horizon.' It sounded like a joke but I guessed it was real. 'You'll have to come for a holiday – without your husband! – when I agree to go,' he finished, implying he was not yet ready.

Custards were brought, along with beer. The First must have a supplier right outside their barracks. The Princeps appeared to lose interest in anything else. However, I wondered if he was just getting a feel for the men who were assembled there.

All the Varduli must have had a sweet tooth; eyeing Karus, their leader, the auxiliaries plunged in. Karus refused to eat. The intriguing tussle for dominance continued, with the Princeps easily winning. 'That's the job!' He beamed, still taking the lead even with his mouth full. He was good. He knew it. He was older and grizzlier, dripping with the sense that his service covered faraway places with hellish conditions and very hard fighting; Karus only knew Spain and Britain, with but a single useful action on his record. It had been *very* useful, but the Princeps was not intending to go easy. To him, Karus was a comparative lightweight. 'We need energy, if there's going to be a riot over this Roscius being taken out. First rule of combat. Let's get some tuck under our belts before we start jawing.'

'Would you like to use our clerk to write minutes?' quavered the vigiles duty officer.

Titus gave it solemn consideration. 'Oh, I don't think so, son! I do not think what we shall be discussing can be written down!'

'Now you are here, Princeps, let's get on. We need a plan!' urged Julius Karus, finding it unbearable to wait for pastries while they could be fixing up aims and objectives. This man was itching for orders and lists, preferably assigning him full use of siege engines.

'Hang about!' The Princeps was wiping the crumbs from his mouth. Then, with his easy confidence, he launched straight into an action plan that he must already have devised. I could imagine him thinking about it while he marched here earlier. Titus had known what he intended to do before he ever came inside the barracks gates. 'Call in the Urbans.' He gave me another of his winks. 'Big stuff! That request can only come from me.' But he graciously said to Karus, 'I'll let you go and fix it. Tell their prefect I sent you – he'll give us some of his spares.' I continued to be fascinated by the tussle between these men, and the quiet way the Princeps had obtained not just leverage but a full grip.

Karus made the mistake of speculating whether the Urban Cohorts' prefect would be at the Praetorian Camp.

'No, he hangs out at his house on the Esquiline,' I murmured. Titus gave me a wide-eyed gleam. 'My husband had a conference with him there, about Florius.'

'Esquiline it is!' Titus confirmed to Karus. 'Grab us as many as you can. Dot the riot troops through the Rabirius turf. Keep them visible. Maintain a physical presence until any rumpus stops smouldering. Have your own men placed where they can swoop whenever something kicks off.'

'Right. What about the stiff?'

Titus strolled over to take a look at Roscius. He used his own impeccable dagger to rip open the sacking around the corpse. The messenger who fetched him must have described what had happened. 'That's ugly! When somebody comes to pick him up – as they will – the body can be released, but I want an out-of-town funeral. I'll organise an edict: that orgy on the Esquiline is not to be repeated. So: lonely necropolis. Close family only, minimal fuss, bare expense. All details to be approved in advance by the Castra commissariat.'

'I assume we have to be diplomatic?' queried Karus.

The Princeps leaped back in exaggerated shock. 'What obscenity is "diplomatic"? Never mind how the legions tiptoe around in Britannia, soldier, you are in Rome now. *Be diplomatic?* No, we bloody don't. This criminal object gets a quiet, quick send-off or the riot troops go in. The family can either keep it private, like I say – or, if they choose to be annoying, big cruel boyos will cast his worthless cadaver on the Gemonian Stairs until it's putrid.'

'Suits me!' said Karus, cheering up for once. 'Then he gets scraped up and shovelled into the Tiber?'

Titus gave him an approving look. 'You've got the hang of it. Grave in the river. Goodbye, Roscius!'

'What about Florius?' I put in.

'Oh, the returnee. Give me a position report,' Titus instructed Karus.

Karus said dourly, 'He must have done for Roscius. My thoughts are that the Rabirius crew will come out howling for his blood. That will be the next round of slaughter. Either they will finish Florius themselves, or they will flush him out for me. I am on to it.'

'Karus is on it!' Titus assured me. End of issue. My whole body tightened, but I made no answer. 'Time you went home, Sparrow. Go and cuddle that husband, if you don't like the look of us. Karus, have one of your boys take her back over the river, see she gets out of this rough district safely.'

That was the last thing I needed. I said so, but these were men making their own plans for a big new project. None of them was listening.

49

That then altered.

The Princeps had arrived at the station-house alone. Immediately on receipt of a message about Roscius and the threat of trouble on the streets, he must have left his office and marched over the river, solo. Now a flurry at the gates announced that his official escort had finally worked out where he was. I wondered if they were used to him losing them.

His panoply included a very smart honour guard, a signal bearer with a wolfskin and a metal hand on a pole, a trumpeter and even a secretary. Titus unbuckled his sword and let one of his troops carry it. 'Makes him feel big.'

An order was given that Julius Karus could take things forward, facing the gang warfare unsupervised. If Karus got it wrong, grinned the commander, blame would affix itself to him.

Titus decided he would take me home himself. His bodyguards would bring my dog and donkey. 'Are they tame?'

'The dog will run away if you talk to her. Watch the donk; I don't want her stolen, so I've trained her to go for strangers.'

Barley was licking the trumpeter, persuading him to pick her up; Merky was nibbling someone's cloak while the secretary petted her. Karus, of course, was horrified. This was all unmilitary. Besides, he did not want me talking privately with the Princeps.

It happened. Titus must have planned it all along. As soon as we emerged from the shadow of the station-house I got, 'So, Flavia! What are you getting your girdle in a twizzle over? What the fornicating fairy was your big fat hint about fritters?'

It was a short step along from the First's barracks to the Aemilian Bridge, then cross over, turn right, a quick trip through the meat market, pass the corn dole station and, since Merky could not mount steps, trot along to the Clivus Publicius for the climb up the Aventine. This gave me time to mention everything I wanted: my misgivings about Karus; my suspicion that the tribune of the Sixth Cohort was going easy on the Balbinus gang and even up to no good with Milvia; Milvia's claim that Veronica was also having an affair, in her case with the Second's tribune, Vergelius; my observation that Vergelius might be innocent of that but was certainly too deeply enmeshed with the Rabirius gang; my personal determination to track down Florius.

'What has the unspeakable Florius done to you, Flavia?'

'Never mind.'

'Oh!' The Princeps had either heard something already, or he now guessed.

He said he would stop for a moment to rest his corns. His escort stayed back, trained in his ways. We stood in the street near the starting-gates end of the Circus, while I talked about the death of Claudia Deiana: how I thought it had been mishandled, how Nicon had been a pompous idiot and Julius Karus still missed the point. I said that if I found Florius myself, I would let the Fourth Cohort have him. They had

268

been after him for decades and, in so far as anyone could be trusted, those boys would handle the situation properly.

'Never mind them,' mused the Princeps. He had listened and was responding much more quietly than he had in his top-man pose at the station-house. 'Anything turns up, you come over to the Castra and say you have a message for Uncle.'

'The Fourth have promised to pay me.'

'Bull's balls. They have no money. Bring me your findings; I can give you decent smackeroos.'

'You have a budget for informers?'

'Does a duck swim? I'll take it out of the bonus I'm supposed to give Karus when he sorts out the gangs.'

'Will he sort them?'

'Oh, he knows his stuff. A gold crown from the Emperor does not lie, my darling.'

'Three. And, don't forget, a silver spear!'

'And his bloody silver spear! Unheard-of. Well, that was the British fiasco, we both know it, don't we, Flavia? It nails him as a "British specialist", so he gets a mandate on a bronze tablet to keep pursuing Florius – who, after all, is only a tax dodger—'

I stopped him. 'No, Florius is much worse than that.'

He surveyed me, looking grave.

Before we parted at the bottom of the Clivus Publicius slope, I told him I had come up with one further theory. It concerned Karus.

'You think he's stuffing Milvia?'

'No, I don't,' I answered honestly. 'He would probably say, and I would probably believe him, that he visited her with that tribune because the tribune already had access and

Karus wanted to soft-talk her, instead of conducting another pointless house search.'

'Nothing scandalous?'

'I don't know. But I'll give him the benefit of the doubt. Titus my friend, consider: Karus makes out he is livid that the Rabirius hitman, Turcus, has been taken off the scene, presumably by Florius. That assumes Turcus really is dead. I met him and he was so very well organised, it would not surprise me if he quietly escaped and disappeared into retirement.' *Some quiet little place where nothing ever happens …* 'But Roscius is a fatality. I wonder, could it have been Karus himself who organised the chariot crash?'

'Reason?'

'Hoping to lure out Florius.'

'Oh?'

'Karus swims in from Britain,' I suggested, 'the back of beyond, as people here think. He is loved by the Emperor, but that diddle's done. Anyway, it was Britain, so count it as crap. He needs new glory. For that, he decides he will capture a man the authorities in Rome have long failed to find. He implicates Florius in at least one death, maybe two if he killed Turcus, or three with Legsie Lucius, then waits for him to come out shouting that he didn't do it. At that point, Karus plans to snatch him. He virtually said that's what he is intending.'

The Princeps accepted I might be right about the hitman disappearing. He thought I was wrong about Young Roscius. I noted that he must have mulled all this over himself. He offered his own take: he implicated Rabirius Vincentius. Now Vincentius had returned to Rome, he was ominously gaining power. He intended to remain – perhaps protected by the tribune Vergelius – whose collaboration Titus would look into, after my suggestion. For Titus, the advent of Vincentius made the murder of Roscius simpler. 'Vincentius has taken out his rival. To cover himself with the rest of his group, *he* will place blame on Florius.'

Once he had said it, I had to agree.

I suggested how to check: the driver of the Purples' chariot might be able to confirm whether the men who attacked Young Roscius were from his own gang. If so, Vincentius almost certainly sent them. 'The vigiles think the driver knew the people involved but is terrified to admit it. He needs a proper interrogation.' I recommended Scorpus at the First Cohort's main barracks: he would find the driver and question him efficiently. The Princeps guffawed, trust me to know the right connection, he couldn't have got that nugget from Karus – though if Scorpus should fail with his genteel vigiles questioning, some technical work with red-hot implements at the Castra ought to squeeze out proof . . .

He gave me another smothering hug. Then he lifted me onto my donkey, put Barley up into my arms, and sent me up the Clivus Publicius, telling me to keep out of trouble.

'I shall try,' I promised insincerely. 'Will I need a password for the guards at the Castra if I bring you any news?'

He bared his teeth in a horrible shark's smile. 'Don't you worry!' His reassurance was intended to worry me. 'Every man of mine knows who you are, Flavia Albia!'

As I rode up the dogleg towards Lesser Laurel Street, coming home to my husband, I decided not to pass on that remark to Tiberius.

50

Riding up the hill, I reflected that today I had seen as much tension pulling at the military groups as there was among the crooks they were ranged against. Anyone at headquarters despised the legions in the provinces. The vigiles hated the Urban Cohorts; the Urbans were jealous of the Praetorian Guards. Everyone looked sideways at the Castra Peregrina: everyone was suspicious of anyone else who had been granted special powers. This was just like the infighting between the Balbini, the Rabirii and the ancient Ocellus twins. It was no different from Vincentius eyeballing Young Roscius or Gallo, or from any gang leader trying to resist the women in his family.

Different factions strove against one another; different men jostled for dominance. They took it for granted mostly, but it could flare up bitterly. The reason the Princeps Peregrinorum could visualise the motives of Rabirius Vincentius was that he would have done the same. Pick off your rival. Keep quiet. Look innocent. Enjoy results.

If Uncle was not yet ready for his retirement bonus and land enough for a thousand sheep, was Julius Karus really secure in dreaming of that big office deep inside the Castra, with a collection of legionaries, the fiendish torturer, and his own trophies displayed on the wall? Or would Karus yet find himself sent on some long march to a dead-end posting?

I thought he was bright enough to see the risk. 'Titus' had command; he could put the boot in. No wonder Karus behaved tetchily. No wonder he had no intention of letting me sidestep him to find Florius myself.

Would even Titus allow a role for me? Or might he accept my information, then any suggestion of payment for my work would wither on the vine, in the time-honoured manner of most bureaucratic promises?

These thoughts carried me as far as my own house. Then, as I approached the elegant porch, I recalled a much more pressing matter. My father's last words when I saw *him* had been 'Do not pinch my case!'

51

Our door porter let me in.

'Too much coming and going!' he bellyached.

'That's what you are for,' I slapped back relentlessly. 'To collect their details. Who came? Are they still here? Who went? Are they coming back?'

Sniffing, Rodan gave me a sullen stare. He agreed to stable the donkey for me, while muttering that he had already been forced to look after my father's mule Kicker who had, true to his reputation, kicked him. Gladiator training had not made Rodan immune to pain. The porter unhappily told me that Falco had made his usual snide comments about Rodan's zero skills – they had a twenty-year feud, in which this was a primary insult – before Pa hurled himself back on Kicker and left.

'Was Lucius Petronius with him?'

'No!' Rodan looked surprised.

'Falco had not been able to find him?'

'How do you know he was looking?'

'Intuition.'

'Your father was stewing. He roared, "Petronius was not at the house". Falco has been chasing all over for him but has given up and gone home.'

'Did he ask about his case?'

'What case?'

*   *   *

274

It was a cold day so nobody else was visible in the deserted courtyard, where only a growing scent of Chicken Vardana reminded me I had had no lunch except a vigiles pastry that was giving me heartburn. I found my husband in my interview room, quietly reading. I let him grumble about being still stuck with no column for the temple job, but the demolition work at Fountain Court had begun on schedule, so his overall mood was placid.

Tiberius had last seen me piling up breakfast bowls, like a *domina* dutifully planning household tasks. He asked, carefully, where I had been instead. I described everything. It seemed a long time since Petronilla had come here so anxiously.

'So, you didn't think twice,' murmured Tiberius. 'You did steal your father's case?'

My logic was that Young Roscius being murdered affected my own case, so no theft was involved. Tiberius replied that he would be keen to hear how Falco viewed this. 'Will you go down the hill to tell him? Cosy father-and-daughter chat?'

'No, I shall write a note that Paris can take for me.'

'Smart girl!'

Tiberius returned to his reading. I had been brought olives and nuts from Fornix to keep me going. I applied myself to those, sitting still with a quiet smile as if dinner was the only thing on my mind. Tiberius leaned over sometimes to grab one of my treats, but he never looked up; he seemed fully absorbed in his scroll. All the same, I guessed he knew I was wondering.

If the Princeps was right about Rabirius Vincentius falsely putting blame on Florius, what could Florius do about it? Even if he was innocent of killing Legsie, Turcus or Roscius,

I thought Florius was stuck. What could possibly be his next move?

Then I thought about my uncle. What a sly risk-taker Lucius Petronius was. For a man who had always carried a reputation as steady and true, he really took the oatcake. By comparison my father, supposedly the feckless clown in that pair, was more reliable.

I had seen the rascal go into Milvia's house. So, if Petro had already left when Father arrived, it was a very short tryst, especially after fifteen years. Otherwise, when Falco turned up on the doorstep, was the guilty party hiding inside, abetted by a giggly Milvia? The thought was horrible.

I wrote a note for Father. He refused to send one back; he raved at Paris, my runabout, that he would not waste a wax tablet on me, let alone ink. Paris had to tell me Petronius had reappeared. He had stormed to my parents' house, violently complaining about being spied upon. His story was that he went to the gangsters' lair with the sole purpose of ordering Balbina Milvia to back off.

Oh, really?

Falco had asked whether Petro was intending to inform Maia. Petro snarled back that of course he would damn well give her a full formal notification because they had no secrets – which gained Falco's response that it was the first he had heard of that.

'Did they cool off over wine and nuts, Paris?'

'No, they were the only nuts present. Petronius declared that having a drink with a nosy, disloyal, interfering bastard would poison him – anyway, it was Cretan muck from an auction so he wouldn't touch the stuff. By the way,' added Paris, with a grin, 'your father says he's furious about you pinching his case!'

Despite that, he had sent my husband some Cretan wine. Although it must have come back from a sale unsold, it was perfectly decent. Tiberius unplugged it to try as a pre-dinner aperitif. He poured none for me, but it was understood I would share his beaker.

Before we ate that evening, I stood on our courtyard balcony, my face turned into the Aventine breeze, listening. Our house was quiet. Tiberius was still reading, trying to finish his scroll before he was called to the dining couch. Everyone who lived here was absorbed in their own activity. Despite recent differences, I could hear my steward and cook talking to one another. None of the others was venting complaints. Even the children must have been engaged in solemn play. Barley pattered up the stairs to nag me for fuss, but since I was absorbed in my thoughts, she only leaned against my leg and nudged me silently.

In our home tonight we had no stress. The master and mistress ran their house with quiet routines. The violence, deception and seething ambitions I had been witnessing all day faded from me.

Some hours later, I was back outside. I had slipped from a marital embrace when I thought I heard a desolate child. Little Lucius regularly woke in the night; he would start whimpering, then if nobody heard he would come out onto the balcony and howl. But either I was mistaken, or he had fallen back to sleep by the time I reached him.

Once again, for a moment alone I listened to the sounds of Rome: the city by the river, almost asleep now yet never entirely silent. Above me soared a wind-tossed sky where clouds covered the stars. As the clamour of delivery vehicles died to near nothing, I heard the Aventine owls and foxes in places where wild vegetation remained. Much further away, perhaps on the Quirinal, some bad neighbour had a cockerel that crowed all night. Somewhere else a heartless dog, tied up outside by a mindless owner, barked relentlessly. All over the city were voices from those people who live their lives long after daylight and seem never to sleep. Loud conversations continued through the tedious hours; sometimes a woman shouted or a man shrieked. Drifts of faint music started, then died away. Inevitably, rubbish carts set up their pre-dawn cacophony.

Still, most of the city was at rest. Only in some dark places wakeful deviants with blacker souls were plotting. I knew it. I was ready for them, waiting.

52

Pandora wanted to see me. Naturally she would not come to my house; I was to attend on her. I told her thuggish messenger that I would go. The death of Roscius was bound to have an effect. With the nephew gone, she would be a more controlling matriarch than ever – assuming her son let her retain her old influence. This odd request seemed promising.

I took Paris. We went down from the hill on the river side. As we walked, I was more aware than ever of the colourful Tiber environs. Along the Embankment, then up past the Pons Aemilius to the Trigeminal Porticus and Gate, we had to push through the daily crowd: thronging port workers and traders, shoppers, tourists, priests from exotic temples, hang-dog bar-keepers, snack-sellers, rowers, loaders and unloaders, and small-time crooks who were looking to steal goods off the back of boats. This was the habitat where I grew up, but I had always been taught it could be dangerous. You could be felled by a deadweight bale or crushed under falling marble; you might be preyed upon by thieves who would hack gemstone rings from your fingers or rip your arm off if you foolishly tried to hang onto your purse. Tiber Island has a hospital, but you have to be alive to be admitted.

We cut around the Theatre of Marcellus. After skirting the Capitol, it was up the Via Lata, where I first kept going past

Pandora's shop and apartment because I wanted a pre-meeting with the First Cohort. This was unscheduled. I was intending to warn Scorpus, their investigator, that he might be approached by the Princeps Peregrinorum. I was too late; the First had already had a visitation.

Scorpus told me a high-powered party had swept across the Campus Martius trying to find the Purples' driver. This Castra posse had been eager to subject the witness to inventive measures in the bowels of their camp; even Scorpus was looking forward to watching, if they allowed it, in case he learned something of their techniques. Unfortunately, a search of racing-faction premises, stables and chariot sheds came up empty. A subsequent rattle through local speakeasies produced no better results. The driver had done a runner – or somebody wanted it to look that way.

'What do you think, Scorpus?'

'He has been whisked out of sight.'

'A fatal disappearance, or a fix for his own good?'

'Just a protective move ... Unless he has had his tongue cut out.'

I walked back to see Pandora.

When we reached her premises, I remembered that these gangsters made Paris sweat. Last year, he had witnessed his previous master being murdered on the orders of the Rabirii; it had happened right in front of him, inside their house, after the master merely outbid Pandora in some property speculation. After Tiberius and I took on Paris as our own runabout, I used him in my investigations but here, rather than take him upstairs where the matriarch ruled, I left him at street level.

'She's just an old woman. I don't need a bodyguard. She may try to tell my fortune, but she thinks I'm a druid with my own guardian spirits.'

The two young beauticians, with their long white dresses and perfect skin, were there. Paris was fairly personable, and always up for gossip. When I trod the stairs to their mistress's lair, Meröe and Kalmis were coaxing him to their couch, offering balms. My runabout might now be in more danger than me.

'Don't worry, I'll come and rescue you soon.'

'No hurry!'

Meröe and Kalmis were extremely pretty.

Pandora was reading the future. In a metal cup she had molten wax, which she was casting into a bowl of cold water. This was held by her outspoken maid, Polemaena, whose glare alone was enough to twist the wax strands into hideous portents. I could have reported the pair for using magic, but I knew all the vigiles were scared of having an occult torque applied to their manly tackle if they attempted an arrest here.

'You want to speak to me!' I challenged, in forthright mode. 'Should I have brought my divining spoons? I take it you are looking into your gang's fortunes, after losing Young Roscius?'

It appeared the abruptly cooled wax was prophesying ill. Polemaena whisked the bowl away. Ugly and awkward as ever, she muttered, as if imposing the evil eye. Supernatural beings, good or evil, would have their work cut out trying to spook this one.

Without turning a hair at being observed in an illegal practice, Pandora bemoaned yesterday's death. He was young, he had such promise, he was subjected to such cruelty. Roscius had left five young brothers and sisters to fend for themselves. His father was a pitiful old man, who could hardly bear more trouble, but the authorities had dumped the body right outside his door. 'Dear gods, what do we pay our taxes for?'

I was waiting for her to complain about the meagre funeral rites that were to be allowed by the Princeps, but she was curiously silent. Perhaps even the Rabirii could see they had overstepped decorum with the flashy, trashy obsequies of Old Rabirius.

'Rubria Theodosia, what do you want from me?'

She came right out with it. She demanded to know whether I had a bead on the whereabouts of Florius. I said nobody knew where he was, though I wanted to see him pay for his crimes so I was still looking. Theodosia stared, as if checking whether she could trust me. At least that was a compliment: she believed I might already have found him. When I gazed back coldly, she made her offer: if I brought her his head, she would give me a villa in Neapolis – and the money to pay for running it.

Covering bills was a nice touch. Gangsters can be very aware of life's realities.

Without agreeing to work for her, I suggested that the one person who must know how to contact Florius was Balbina Milvia. They were relatives, so why was I needed? Theodosia retorted that Milvia was a venomous piece of work. Good news! The women had begun to fall out.

'I know you have been watching Milvia's house!' she snarled. It struck me that the people I had noticed on surveillance outside might have been put in position by the Rabirii. I asked about the boot-shiner and the men who leaned on bar counters. Theodosia openly admitted to the boot-boy, though she claimed the others were not hers. 'You've been inside to see her. Has that spiteful cow ever said anything to you about my daughter-in-law?'

'Such as?' I asked, hiding my anger at being observed.

'Milvia has spread some disgusting rumours.'

'About Veronica betraying her husband? Is it false?' The Veronica I knew was neither glamorous nor flirtatious, although that often means nothing. Plain dull women sometimes enjoy bed more than beauties.

I could have supported Milvia's claim, but it would have been pure mischief. Instead, I said quietly, 'I remember your daughter-in-law crouched on her knees, keening over her dead son, devastated. She has appalling griefs to bear. I cannot imagine her engaging in scandalous behaviour.'

'My son would never stand for it.'

'No, I presume not.' I kept my answer level. 'Who is the culprit, allegedly?'

'Does it matter?'

I thought it mattered if the supposed lover was the Second Cohort's tribune. Without more to go on, I decided not to mention him. 'Have you considered that if Balbina Milvia has begun to meddle, strife between Vincentius and Veronica may be her aim?'

'Oh, she is definitely meddling!'

Interfaction rivalry had become raw, I could see. There would be no more looking after Milvia for her parents' sake, no more calling her a decent member of the tight-knit crime family. Rubria Theodosia believed Milvia was determined to supplant Florius; his return to Rome had only sharpened her love of control – trust one controlling woman to despise that, especially in a younger model. Milvia intended to run the Balbinus mob herself. She, and not only Florius, was a new rival to the Rabirii. She, even more than Florius, would need taking down.

'So, if she is your problem, Pandora, why do you need to find him?' I scoffed. 'Can't you leave her to get him off the scene?'

'Oh, she is determined to finish him. We can't stop her.'

Why did she need me, then? Was Theodosia starting to show a decline, with family losses destabilising her? I wondered whether, if Rabirius Vincentius was annoyed with his wife, he had been flexing muscles with his mother too. And was there to be a battle between him and Milvia?

I said I would bear in mind her offer, then left. Polemaena glared after me, evidently calling down divine punishments as she slammed the upper door, almost catching my gown. Downstairs, I extracted Paris from the beauty girls, then took him away amidst a peculiar waft of skincare products.

I walked through Domitian's exotic complex of Isis and Serapis temples to see my father at the Saepta Julia. In the well-stuffed antiques warehouse he pretended to hide, but when I shouted for him to grow up and stop sulking, he duly emerged. We were still friends. He made me walk over to the river with him. I had to point out where the chariot had crashed beside Nero's Bridge. Most of the wreckage had been cleared away. We strolled back, part way along the gallops. Then he left me, saying he was going to make enquiries around the charioteers' faction houses.

'The Purples' driver has pulled a vanishing trick.' I had reported what Scorpus told me. 'But if he turns up, there's to be a Castra Peregrina interview. A specialist is already heating implements to poke into his organs.'

'You know some very odd people!' commented my father.

I said I picked up my contacts wherever I could find them. I had learned that from him.

53

When the next event occurred, Tiberius and I had gone for a family visit at my parents' house. We were all up on the roof terrace. My father loved it; even in the dead of winter he would make us sit out there wrapped in blankets. We would complain about the wind. He would gaze across the river, communing, he said, with the essence of his city. The Janiculan was too far away, more misty than mystical, while you could see interesting ships only if you walked right up to the parapet and looked down at the Embankment. We let him dream. Sometimes he bravely fired up a barbecue, but apart from the risk of windborne sparks setting fire to the house – or burning Rome – that meant fighting off a particularly scruffy seagull that had learned to wrestle for kebab skewers. Our house was only a little way down from the outlet of the Great Sewer. It rolled out from beneath the Forum and disgorged into the Tiber; in summer we could definitely smell its outflow.

On that evening there were no odours. Even Rome's constant breath of garlic frying in olive oil had been sucked away to the Alban Hills. The wind ripped across the terrace so hard my sisters in their flimsy drapes had already gone indoors. My brother, who was younger and more solid, was timing himself with an hourglass to see how long he could last out, to fulfil Falco's ruling that Romans were not softies.

Postumus loved a challenge; Father diligently set puzzles for him.

Suddenly we heard screams. 'Julia has had another curling-rod accident!' judged Mother, though I could see her straining to decipher the urgency.

'No, the girls are just comparing gladiators they lust after,' answered Father, lazily. 'I hope it's a phase.'

In case panic was justified, I was sent downstairs to investigate; I might be almost thirty, but in my parents' house I was still a teenager to be despatched on errands. At least indoors was out of the wind and warmer.

I had to skip all the way down to the hall. I found staff trying to calm Rhea, Maia's youngest. She was still in her cloak, so must have just arrived.

Rhea was coming up to twenty, still living at home due to several boyfriends' failings. Even Maia and Petro had thought at least one was positively honest and genuinely smitten, but parental approval is always a killer. Rhea had yelled back that he was a daft-head who would drive her wild with his dopiness. If they wanted to hitch her to anyone so boring, they should at least find a hundred-year-old lummox who would die on the wedding night. When Father had reminisced that Rhea reminded him of her mother, Rhea screamed and Maia kicked a wall so hard it was thought she might have broken a toe. Being Maia, she refused to let anyone look at it but the sore foot might be why she had not come running.

'I have to fetch Falco!' Rhea cried when she saw me. 'We need Falco. People tried to grab Tullus.'

'Father's coming. Who is Tullus?' I assumed it was the latest boyfriend.

She stared at me, then howled, 'The Bug!'

'No! Who would grab the Bug? He looks cute, but his poo and snot are legendary!' Rhea burst into tears. 'All right, Rhea, I do believe you.'

So: Petronilla's baby did have a name – and somebody wanted to snatch him. Stealing children was rare, open attempts in the street even rarer. I had only come across infant-kidnap when estranged fathers wanted to torment divorced mothers. Little Tullus had no known father, possibly because Petronilla had no idea who to blame. As far as we knew, she had never informed anyone of her baby's existence. No hangdog procreator would have come for his offspring now.

Other people were following me downstairs while I extracted the story. Petronilla had been out for a walk by the Armilustrium, carrying her son. Several men barged up and roughly demanded if he was the grandson of Petronius Longus. Then they tried to wrench the baby from her arms. Petronius had taught all his extended family how to resist violence. Petronilla shouted loudly, held onto her child, and kicked out like an embattled soldier. The baby was screaming – he was big for his age, with matching lungs. People came running from shops and stalls. The attackers fled.

Petronilla raced home. Everyone was in hysterics. The baby was sick. Petronius, who yesterday was never going to speak to my father again, instantly sent Rhea to fetch Falco.

Falco already had his cloak on. He left Rhea with my mother. Tiberius and I went with him. Before we left, he spoke only one word. It was 'Milvia!'

Despite the ensuing tension, for once our whole family swung into action with no faffing. By the time transport could move in the streets through the usual after-dark

287

delivery chaos, Petronius had taken his daughter and grandson out of Rome. If anyone asked, Petronilla and the baby had gone to visit her mother at Ostia.

That was a bluff. They had been sent secretly to my father's seaside villa. It was remote, well-staffed and discreetly fortified because Grandpa had often kept valuable antiques there. It was also large enough for others to join them. Maia and the two children she had at home, both my parents, with my young sisters and brother, Glaphyra with our two fosterlings, all followed for safety. Vulnerable youngsters were being hidden out of reach.

The oldsters had agreed it had to have been Milvia who organised the abduction attempt; Petronius was her real target. She would have hated Falco too, had she known he had killed her father, but – they hopefully told themselves – Milvia still believed Balbinus Pius had died in a housefire. All her anger was directed at Petro for spurning her. She aimed to punish him through his family.

Her husband's position in this was considered. Florius accounted Petronius as his rival from long ago; he would also know that Falco and Petro had hunted him for years. But since Milvia herself claimed she and Florius were at odds, Florius was exempt from blame in trying to grab the Petronius grandson. That did not mean he would not gloat. Neither did it make him less dangerous. Milvia's act could well have given him ideas.

Despite the danger, eventually our two patriarchs grew bored in hiding. Falco and Petronius decided together that they could leave their dependants on the coast. Since no gangsters had pursued them, they quietly returned to Rome. Helena stayed at the villa, taking charge; Maia came back to keep the menfolk out of trouble. They brought Suza. She had grown up working with shellfish near the coast and had become anxious in case we sent her back to her old life. I could sympathise with that.

Maia came over to harangue me. 'The lads have come back to Rome, but this is nowhere near over, Albia! That Milvia is deadly. She tried to harm my grandson and I don't intend to let it lie. I am expecting you to do something!'

'Like what, Maia?'

'Kill the bloody woman!'

'Right. I'll make a note in my calendar and do it the next time I have a free day.'

'I mean it. I want retribution.' Knowing Maia Favonia, she would obtain it.

Falco and Petronius stuck with what they had always done: working together in the way they considered so successful, they kept after Florius. They paid little attention to Milvia, despite her attempt on Tullus. They would punish the vindictive wife if it could easily be done, but in their eyes she had lost out enough already by failing to seduce Petro, that desirable dog.

So, they turned their main attention to Florius. It presented me with even more competitors in my own hunt to find him first. Forget the rest. Didius Falco and Petronius Longus were now the serious opposition.

54

When things started to move, it was indeed the old team who achieved the first coup: Falco and Petro found the Purples' driver.

I rushed down the hill to see Father. I won't say he and my uncle were crowing, but compared to them in bumptious mode, that noisy cockerel on the Quirinal would have sounded as discreet as a falling snowflake.

I let them see my annoyance. 'How have you done this? Everywhere had been searched!' One place had *not* been searched, they pointed out. 'What place? Where was he?'

Where would a man who was battered, terrified and shocked run to hide? They supplied the answer cheerily: 'He was curled up under his childhood bed at his mother's.'

All right. I agreed that it needed two supposedly retired investigators to think of looking there. The Castra Peregrina had no resources to compare. Even I had not thought of it. 'Good work, lads – but however did you find his mother?'

They glowed. 'Old trick. We went to the Purples' faction house in silly hats, calling ourselves the driver's relatives who had been dragged up from the country because his ma was hysterical over what had happened to him. "Uncle Lucius and Uncle Marcus" – a horrible pair of bumpkins, probably the product of incest. The Purples soon gave us directions to get rid of us.'

Unfortunately, their triumph ended after they hauled the driver out from under the bed and sat him on a wobbly stool with a pleasant request to talk to them. Using their we-don't-*really*-want-to-tear-out-your-fingernails technique, they were persuasive. He agreed that when Roscius was jumped at the Trigarium he did recognise men's voices. Falco and Petro grabbed his wrists and spread his hands as if choosing the first finger to damage, so he told them who it was. Sadly, neither my father nor his crony knew the two names he gave them.

While they had been discussing this, the driver's fond mother gave him the nod that her back door was open; he broke free and did a bunk. Falco and Petro had not been on manoeuvres together for years. No longer as slick, they knocked into each other in the rush to follow. They lost him.

'You two are not safe out of the house. What were the names?'

'Anthos and Neo.'

'Don't you worry about it, Albia. This is our lead, and we shall follow up.'

'We still have contacts. We can find them.'

'Nobody will talk to you,' I told them. 'Anthos and Neo are too scary.' I let it sink in, then took my turn, explaining conversationally: '*I* have met them. Anthos and Neo work for the Rabirius gang. They call themselves rent collectors, with all that it means. They go about on the Esquiline and Viminal, fetching in protection money. If people won't pay, they shove them onto their knees and garotte them with belts. There is no blood, so the pavements don't need washing.'

If Young Roscius had seen this pair coming at the gallops, he would have thought he was safe. They worked for him. It was even possible they went with him that morning, or had arranged to meet him. Either way, who had organised their involvement? In the past, I had seen them acting on orders from Gallo but, after Struthio, Gallo was in no state to take out Roscius or anybody else. More likely, Rabirius Vincentius fixed this. One thing was certain, Anthos and Neo would never have done the deed on behalf of Florius.

'Still, Florius will be exultant,' said Pa. 'Roscius dead is one less rival – bound to make him happy. Florius might have killed him himself if he had the right manpower.'

I suggested Milvia might not be letting him have access to their forces.

'When did he ever lack followers?' Petronius argued. 'We saw it in Britain. He could shunt together half an army when he wanted, whether they came from loyalty or fear, or they were simply following the money. He still has plenty of cash to buy in heavies. And we know he's a monster.'

My father disagreed. 'No. What he *does* is monstrous. As a man, he will be the same as always: a streak of flab with the moral incisiveness of jelly. Challenge him, he turns into a writhing worm. The first one of us who reaches him will be able to put a spade right through him.'

55

In the end it was me who found Florius. The old team had method, bravado and skills but I had luck and a good system in place.

My route into this mystery would be the same as ever. The death of Claudia Deiana was my starting point, still fixed. Whether Florius had killed her or the Rabirius clan had disposed of her to impose pain on him made no difference. I still wanted to understand what had happened to the woman who was fished out of the Tiber. I needed to find out why she had come to Rome. What had she thought was waiting for her in this faraway city, where all she really encountered was violence?

That had been my purpose when I kicked out my cousin and her partner and stationed them at Auntie Itia's lodging house. I sensed it was a key location. Marcia and Corellius had been there several days now. They were not enjoying it. Marcia left her partner swatting bugs in their cramped room, while she came up the hill to report. Apart from the fact I had meanly refused to pay their bills, the couple complained the place was noisy and full of unpleasant people. They had seen nothing of interest. Their verdict was that this was a dead end. Marcia enjoyed telling me that while busily scratching at a rash. She also said that although Corellius was trained to survive on military rations, he had developed troubling stomach upsets.

I caved in. If they had not managed to spot anything useful for me, they might as well start sorting out a new rental for themselves. 'I gather you don't intend us to stay here!' snorted Marcia.

'You would always be welcome to our house, darling. I just think you two need space of your own.'

I gave her a last description of Florius in case he showed up to collect his lover's belongings, if they were still there. 'Middle-aged, good boots, now probably balding.'

Marcia said they had seen no one like that. Then she corrected herself, because Itia's was full of middle-aged, slightly balding men with money for accessories. Most came for short stints in the company of young women – because there was no doubt the place I had foisted on my relatives was a brothel. Some lived there all the time. Some of those fellows could not manage more than chats with the working girls but they enjoyed the ambiance and as lodgers were treated like honoured clients, given titles like 'the decurion', while Itia's ran through all their money.

'Does Corellius talk to them?'

'He hates them. He says they are all frowsty old frauds. Decurions? Ha! They've spent their lives as gigolos and confidence tricksters preying on rich widows. Beautiful manners, but too keen on having Babylonian suppositories poked up their rear ends.'

'Ugh. Any sign of Claudia Deiana's British slave?' He must know Auntie Itia's: he stayed there with his mistress. After seeing him at Milvia's, I could describe him. Marcia automatically snapped that, no, they had not seen anyone like that.

Then she stopped. In fact there was a man attending to a master who stayed in what Itia called her premier suite; it must be rather comfortable as he never ventured out. His attendant seemed at a loose end; he was male, had red hair, an impossible name and not much Latin. Corellius had palled up with him. In the afternoon they played board games with the house's set of glass counters.

Dear gods. Our invalid with the prosthetic leg was teaching checkers to the slave, Ulatugnus.

56

Time for action.

There was no way I could manage the next move alone. Marcia was adamant that, despite his military background, Corellius would not want to be involved. I thought she was being protective but could not budge her. I was known at the lodging house. If I went there, I would likely be challenged. Even supposing I was allowed in, Corellius had said Ulatugnus always placed the board game so he could look out at whoever was passing the room where they played; he must be guarding the so-called premier suite, though Corellius had not been able to work out where in the huge rambly building it was situated.

This needed a proper raid. I talked to Tiberius; he brought in Morellus who reckoned he would have been up for intervention himself, if the building had stood in his area. He would come along anyway, and stuff the Sixth Cohort, but he wanted to be fronted by someone with clout. I was reluctant to hand this to Karus, so Tiberius suggested I invite my more powerful friend from the Castra. The Princeps would expect to take full command, but that might be no bad thing.

As soon as Morellus was told anything, Petronius Longus got wind of it. Once he heard, so did Falco. At this rate the whole of Rome would know we were coming.

Those who were to take part gathered unobtrusively just inside the nearby Circus Maximus. Before the start the men held a briefing.

Falco and Petronius announced that they were familiar with the building and its layout. 'It's Lalage's old place, biggest brothel west of the Circus – and somehow she always kept Balbinus Pius at arms' length.' They made a wild claim that they possessed this insight because my father, aged seven, had sat on the same school bench as the original proprietor, Lalage. They reckoned Falco had gone inside the brothel for old times' sake; Petro only went for work purposes. It was an unbelievable story, typical of them, but they did remember Itia used to work there.

'She was just one of the girls then.'

'Wasn't she the girl on the door?'

'No, Macra took the money on the door.'

'How would I know? We never paid any money—'

'What happened to Lalage?' I broke in.

My father said nothing. Petronius explained tersely: 'Balbinus got her. He was always trying to take over and cream off a percentage. Much like nowadays. Nothing changes. Lalage was tough. Balbinus put a knife in her ribs because she would not cooperate. She died in Falco's arms.'

To be an old acquaintance of my father could be dangerous. I had witnessed another one-time girlfriend die gruesomely at his feet: Chloris. She was killed by Florius, so Father really had his personal stake today.

He had seen terrible events in his time; I knew Mother would not want him coming on this exercise. Even so, if she wasn't at Ostia he would have told her about it. I was not so certain Petro had revealed his intentions to Maia.

'The main thing,' decreed the Princeps, weighing in, 'is to make sure that nobody dies today.' The old ones agreed that, for a new boy, he seemed to have grasped the essentials.

'Call me Uncle,' he condescended benignly.

Uncle would be in command, but he managed to win over other men who would normally want to take the lead. Respect hung around Titus like a swarm of flies; he only pretended to biff it away. Awareness of his worth was part of his personality. It was impossible to imagine him when he was young and nervous. He had brought a small, handpicked group, who definitely were apprehensive, but they looked keen to try their hands at emulating him.

There had been a curious moment when I introduced Uncle to my father and uncle, Morellus and Corellius. The old soldiers all narrowed their eyes to sum each other up. I saw none of them could decide what they thought. By the end of today, they would be in no doubt.

Tiberius came. He said he would not trust any of the others to look after me and there was no hope I would look after myself. He and I hung on the sidelines politely, lucky they allowed civilians a look-in.

Morellus had brought vigiles, though not their tribune. Rather than offend his opposite number in the Sixth, Scaurus was sitting it out. He had 'gone to Beneventum', a phrase for when 'grandfather's funeral' might sound too hackneyed. This way, if things went wrong, he could deny all knowledge, then take leave for a month claiming a tooth abscess, his other perennial excuse. Titus was supported by Julius Karus. He and the Varduli were sent off early, ready to infiltrate the building from behind. 'The bum-boy!' Uncle called after him rudely.

Everyone else would be at the front.

After Karus had left, Morellus primed us. The Princeps listened, while his clerk took notes to read back to their troops, who had in-the-field knowledge, not city experience. Uncle had lined them up on the Circus seats; they were neat and well-behaved. The vigiles milled around their own leader at will; the espartos looked amateur by comparison with the clean-cut Castra troops, but time would tell.

Titus Morellus gave out his spiel with pride: brothel raids were a vigiles specialism. However, he did say, 'Didius Falco and Petronius Longus will be in attendance, bringing their inside knowledge.'

They preened. 'There is one door,' announced Petro, 'a big cumbersome wooden thing, lolling on its hinges. Two others, either side, are blocked up.'

'Windows will be heavily shuttered,' added Falco. 'Brothels do not bother with natural light.'

'Thank you, Legates!' Morellus shut them up so he could describe the set procedure for what he called a full-on, fun-filled fandango. The main objective was containment – that was, not letting the rumpus spread outside to the local neighbourhood. The aim of that was simple: to avoid any excuse for the Urban Cohorts to come and mess things up. They were mad bastards. Legendary.

The lads, Morellus said, had to arrive suddenly, then go in fast and hard. The moment it became obvious that something was occurring, all the working girls would start to caterwaul; they would alert everyone else. Staff would bang on pots and pans. The madam would be yelling. Her language would make a drain-cleaner blush. His lads, tender souls, must not let lewd words disconcert them but should carry on, moving through the building as rapidly as possible.

299

Piss-pots would be thrown at them. 'Don't worry. It's only piss. It will be nice and weak; at places like this, the wine costs double but it's always watered.'

'Says he who knows!' cried one of the lads, throwing his voice so he was impossible to identify.

'Not me!' slammed back Morellus. 'I am true to the wife, that wonderful deserving woman.'

'Pullia – poor cow!' chorused several more of his lads.

Soldiers from the Castra were listening to this banter, with the air of fast learners. Scowling, their Princeps gave Morellus the sign to carry on.

All customers would try to evacuate fast. Spotting them would be easy due to their wearing no clothes, or hardly any, or perhaps cross-dressing in outfits with very strange appendages – plus the fact they would be sweating madly as they rushed to the exit. In panic, some would forget where the exit was. Grab as many as possible while they flittered around. They could be released later without charges. Attending a brothel was legal, but punters would probably all have wives, which would be useful for subsequent bribery or, as it was known, 'contributions to the widows' fund'. For that it was vital to take names; then it was a good ploy to pretend to disbelieve them. A neat trick was to demand an address from which someone could be fetched to vouch for them. Tell them messengers would be provided. It never failed. The 'widows' fund' would be generously filled, ready for its other role: as the money pot for next year's Saturnalia drinks.

Anyone at or above the rank of aedile – 'Sorry, Aedile!' – should have his toga straightened and be sent on his way. Kind words should be spoken about his wonderful record of public service, with congratulations on his diligence in personally checking houses of ill-fame. It would be polite to find his litter for him, if he looked confused by the chaos.

All working women should be taken into custody, a temporary measure unless they tried to bite anyone, and even then, only if they looked rabid. Each should be checked against the registration records. Those records had already been fetched. Uncle's secretary was looking after them. If the girls offered free services, this was disgraceful and must be refused. (Well, only while the raid was in progress. What anyone chose to do later would be up to him. Reminder: the cohort doctor kept salves, if anybody caught anything.)

If the obnoxious Sixth Cohort turned up uninvited, let them join in if they wanted to.

If the Sixth kicked off about lack of liaison, refer them to Uncle.

If their tribune turned up, pretend to mistake him for a customer and keep him in custody until it was all over. He was unmissable: he was a pig who thought the world was his to trough in, stank of myrrh and was half deaf.

The Fourth Cohort had devised this strategy over many years, using it often to acquire gifts for cohort widows and top up their drinks pot. They were competent and eager troops. In his laid-back, drawling, foul-mouthed way, Morellus was a trustworthy officer. They were all extremely good at fighting fires. These boys knew what they were doing, or so it sounded. Uncle complimented them. Morellus blushed.

It was a good plan. Meticulous, based on experience, tailored to circumstances. Manpower, equipment and specialists had been provided. All necessary back-up was in place. Only one vital element was missing.

I had intended to keep quiet, but as they gathered for imminent action, I was forced to jump in. 'Hold on! Before you all go rushing off, please remember our reason for doing this. You may see any number of filthy practices being carried out, but suppression of vice is not why we are here today. Also, we know that perfectly decent tourists and other people rent rooms. There is no need to be rough with them. The principal object is to lay hands on Gaius Florius Oppicus, believed to be hiding within the building. A description has been circulated, based on recent sightings. Bear in mind that he and his family have been known to use disguises.'

Falco gave a steer on that: 'Turn any old woman upside down, have a look and make sure she is female!'

'That's going a bit far!'

'Necessary, trusting daughter. Listen to me, men. If you encounter anyone and are not sure, act as if the person in front of you could definitely be him.'

'Tie the bugger up, throw him onto the body pile, and we can sort out identities later,' Petronius backed him.

'Gods, they were hard nuts in the bad old days!' remarked Morellus, not quite under his breath.

My father and uncle assured him they still were. There was laughter, but mild. The assembled party could see these two had the aura of bitter experience. They might be coming up to fifty, but believed they were still eighteen. They had endured pain, unfairness, failure – but sometimes glorious triumph. They still held themselves well. When they spoke, it had a warning ring of truth and when they fell quiet, they seemed even more dangerous.

'Good luck, to all!' proclaimed the Princeps, as men in very senior positions have to do. I was only surprised he did not sacrifice sacred chickens and formally take the auguries.

'Luck,' commented Morellus, openly, 'will have no place where we are going!'

57

It would probably go wrong, of course. It would go wrong for the usual reason. Neither the woman whose business was being turned over nor any of the people in the building knew what the plan was – or that they were supposed to comply with it. We would meet a lot of protests.

Uncle had ordered there should be no fighting 'unless absolutely necessary'. No one took that seriously. Some men present thought the whole point of a brothel raid was to knock all Hades out of everyone they encountered. Male or female. 'Or child, if the lamp-boys argue,' grumbled Tiberius.

'Tut tut! I don't want to see child-battering!' Uncle corrected.

'You haven't met many brothel boys!' My husband chortled. Talking to an old soldier, it had to be classed as irony.

'And you have?' came back suggestively.

'When I was a magistrate, the others decided only I possessed the right gravitas. So, yes, I have walked through a few bowers of Venus, so help me gods.'

'At least one of us will feel at home in here!' mocked the Princeps, raising his arm to give the signal. We all moved out from the Circus into the narrow lane where Auntie Itia's stood.

My father and uncle were the first-footers. Having somehow swung this treat, they had brought with them an aid that

Father had extracted from the dusty jumble he called his archives; the oldsters claimed their pictogram was a map of the building. It looked to be scrawled on the back of an old bar bill. Falco claimed that had been the only thing to hand.

As our advance party, they had made an effort. They did not bother with cloaks, but were padded up with several layers of thick, long-sleeved, brown tunics. From the deep bottom of clothes-chests, stiff old belts had been dragged out and oiled; their boots looked like footwear on statues of seriously self-important generals. Possibly generals whose names people even knew. Our duo was undoubtedly armed, though no weaponry was apparent. Petronius, whose hair was thinning, wore a Phrygian cap. It was red, so if his height was not enough, he could be spotted by colleagues in any mêlée. 'And rescued!' I muttered.

Proceeding at the louche amble of reprobate ex-legionaries, Marcus Didius Falco and Lucius Petronius Longus went forwards into trouble as they must have done so many times. Not marching in step, because that would have given the game away. One taller in his red bonnet, one sturdier with untidy curls, both looking relaxed. This had to be done. They believed themselves the lads to do it.

Their expressions were of a twosome who had just had a naughty idea together. *Let's go to a brothel. Our wives will never know* ... It was a cold day with no festivals, at an hour when bored men could convince themselves it was coming up to lunch time and they often went out to the Oily Jug, so nobody would miss them. All over the empire, pairs of mates were getting up to this. Ours had the correct air of doing nothing wrong, plus the requisite half smirking.

They were good, I admit. I could easily have been proud of them.

Instead, I was wondering uneasily if their act was too well practised. You never knew with those two.

The rest of us parked further down the side road, waiting. Locals who spotted us scuttled indoors. I watched Falco and Petro glance around as anyone might, taking in the faded signboard over the door and the worn Priapus statue with its improbably mighty organ. They looked at one another and nodded, as if they were punters deciding this place would do. It could as easily have been a bar or a shop, where they had agreed to try out the stock. They heaved at the wonky door, leaving it open as if they could not be bothered. They walked in.

I was under orders to wait outside, but as soon as the troops began gently moving forwards, I had made sure I stayed among them. I thought I heard Tiberius sigh, but he made no move to grab me. He came too.

I shoved to the front, then quickstepped ahead. From just outside the building I overheard our emissaries talking to the meet-and-greet girl. They had been told to ignore the listless guard dog and lumpish porter. She was the one they must put out of action, and before she screamed an alarm.

'Hello, darling!'

'Someone told us about here. Is it Itia's place?'

'That's right. We are a travellers' rest.' She gave them the official line but was obviously trained to sum up people's desires very fast, because she immediately added, 'You can hire rooms by the hour if you are looking for a nice afternoon.' I had reached the door so saw her give them a knowing smile.

They smiled back. I could see why Aunt Maia had said that in their time they were a lovely pair. They considered they still had what it took. Maybe they were right.

305

'Will you be wanting company?' enquired the girl. Well-trained maybe, but not well enough. She ought to have caught on by now.

'No,' replied Lucius Petronius, in the grave, sad manner he once used when rearresting habitual pickpockets. 'We want a word with you, darling.'

Then he grabbed her, put a big hand over her mouth, got one of her arms up her back and manhandled her out of the door towards the troops whose job was to neutralise today's captures after they were passed from the building. A corral was being set up in the street; carts had been ordered to act as meat-wagons later.

The porter roused himself and began protesting. Falco knocked him down to make him stop. A gentle tap sufficed. 'He stinks. Why do I always get the worst tasks?'

'Luck of the dice,' Petro assured him, like a player whose dice were counterfeit. 'Where next? Where the hell are we? What's happened to this place?'

They produced their old map and tried to orientate them-selves: 'Bloody hell, there used to be a corridor there! Itia's been remodelling.' Since the empire's building trade thrived on people madly reconstructing room layouts, this ought not to have surprised them.

'Your map is useless.'

'Chuck it, then!'

Falco, with a wrinkled nose, began lifting the porter over his shoulder like a sack of wheat; that made the unkempt black dog with the spiked collar jump up. It was loose. The dog had a slow brain but had decided to stop us stealing the door porter, who probably filled its food bowl.

'Albia!' exclaimed Tiberius, either a plea to desist or to

offer assistance. I assumed the latter. I was supposed to be good with dogs.

In a brothel you can never be sure what an animal has been used for. It may be very wary of humans. This one looked to me like an Agassian. Though not as large as Molossian mastiffs from Greece, which would look you in the eye if they put their feet up on your shoulders (before they tore your face off), Agassians are hungry, hairy, inelegant beasts who live to work. Bred by British tribes for hunting and tracking, they never see themselves as lapdogs. They do not play. This one was heavy enough to knock me over. It had large paws furnished with powerful claws and when it yawned in a speculative way, it showed off two vicious rows of teeth.

Its collar looked too big, but the bronze spikes told their own story. I had been faced with worse menace, but I didn't want to hold out my palm to be sniffed, while coaxing 'Good doggie!' Most Agassians I ever met took a pride in being bad.

58

'Lie down, Skyla.'

A calm voice had the Agassian turning its back on trouble. Skyla humphed down onto her sleeping blanket, front paws over her snout, ears down, eyes closed, just a round shaggy pile of dusty fur. Not a dog I could love – I like them clean and more interested in life – but perhaps the door porter had nobody else to stroke.

The voice came from Itia, as always alert to the arrival of tricky visitors. Sheen on her gown, tasteful stole, hair in an up-do, clip-clop sandals, expression like the king rat when someone unexpectedly opened a grain store.

She had seen me. 'You again!' Then she took in Tiberius. I saw her gaze flick around, missing her receptionist and porter, though she made no comment.

Falco and Petro had already gone on a wander. Taking over from them, my husband introduced himself, in his calm cultured voice: 'Manlius Faustus. We met when I carried out a magistrate's inspection here last summer. I hope you are still following the rules I outlined.'

At no time during the briefing at the Circus had he mentioned that he had been in this specific place before. He had been content to look like my hanger-on. I loved him when he came up with surprises. And I liked the way he had listened to an elaborate plan, yet then went ahead with his own agenda. 'You have a private office?' Without waiting for permission, he strode to a door, and shepherded us all into the inner room, which he must have remembered.

Itia ran her businesses from a long chaise, like an empress. Automatically she took it, though kept one sandalled foot on the floor. I perched on a couch. Tiberius stood in front of the door, which he had closed firmly. It was a small room, with fresco panels of figures floating in air for no obvious reason, their garments decorously windblown. Some had musical instruments, others religious items. I shot Tiberius a glance to say wafting dancers would be much better for us than *The Battle of Salamis*. He looked, nodded, then tackled Itia.

'I shall not prevaricate. Whether this is a lodging house or a brothel, it is to be searched officially.' Itia made an abrupt move, but he held up his hand. 'Stay where you are.'

'You can't raid me!'

'Already happening.'

'You can't touch me!'

'Why? Do you imagine you have paid off the local cohort? Corruption will be investigated.'

'I don't think so! I am not to be messed with.'

'Save your threats.'

'Where is your warrant?'

'Our warrant is in our troops' boots, lady.'

'I have a right to observe what is done to my premises.'

'You have no rights,' Tiberius corrected her. His tone was level, almost pleasant. 'You are listed as running a large, long-established house for sexual purposes. Most of your staff are registered for prostitution, and observers have confirmed you still operate as a brothel. This is an inspection.'

'What observers?' We could now hear regular heavy footsteps passing along the outer corridor. Long practice made Itia curb her agitation, but she nagged, 'Let me go and see!'

'No. Listen. Flavia Albia came here once to ask about Claudia Deiana.' Forced to cooperate, Itia nodded rapidly, though she sent me an accusatory glare.

'Claudia Deiana was looking for the man she regarded as her husband,' I said, 'and now we are looking for him too. We believe he is living here.'

Tiberius dropped his voice. 'This is the deal, Itia. Big numbers of heavy-handed troops can disturb your genteel lodgers, arrest your girls, fine you for a multitude of infringements, and collar your by-the-hour customers – even the honest ones who just popped in for a quick screw. You will be accused of breaking edicts that only Romulus remembers. Your business will take years to recover, if it even survives. Or – take the better option – you can tell us exactly where Florius Oppicus is hiding. If we find him, the troops will be withdrawn.'

'If you damage my place, I shall want reparations!'

'Don't push it. Your place is one of infamy. Where is he?'

'I can show you—'

'Good try. But you will stay right here.' Tiberius remained very calm. 'Tell Albia how to find him. If you give her wrong directions, the penalty will be severe.'

'There are guards.'

'We have armed troops to deal with them.'

Itia jumped off her long chair. I jumped off the couch.

'Do not mess with Flavia Albia,' Tiberius warned, barely moving. He held up his hand, palm outwards, showing a scar. Then he turned his wrist to demonstrate that the wound had gone right through. 'She skewered me to a table once – and that was her way to show affection. She wants Florius for personal revenge, so I can't imagine what she will do to you if you prevent her.' Someone began battering at the door behind him. We knew from the racket through the panels that it was fragile. Its owner was anxious to prevent it being smashed. 'Sit down, Itia.'

Tiberius called a warning to stop the battery, opened the door enough to check, then let in a soldier. The man had a sword raised. Classic. How many houses, temples and ancient palace halls had been invaded by legionaries in that same posture? Capturing Cleopatra, murdering Archimedes, firing the temple in Jerusalem, finding Claudius whimpering behind a curtain . . . Now one came bursting into a small office, where a woman with a soiled reputation worked out her low-status accounts. She had a tired face beneath a skew-whiff hairband, but Rome was fair: Itia received the same treatment as wives of dethroned emperors and defeated foreign queens – chinking armour, stamping boots and a menacing gladius. I wondered if any famous ladies faced with Roman soldiery had noticed, too, the anxious expression and faintly mingled perfumes of sweat and patchouli beard oil.

'Where is he?' demanded Tiberius Manlius again. Restrained and intelligent, he represented a different side of Rome. He would write you a docket but leave you alive to pay the fine: he would not stab you in the ribs. Well, not unless you were a habitual defaulter.

Itia groaned, but she told me where to look.

'Take back-up!' Tiberius ordered. The soldier had saluted him, assumed that his honour was in charge of this, and abruptly withdrew in the hope of rib-sticking elsewhere. Tiberius would have to remain with Itia. We could not risk her running free.

'Of course,' I lied. 'I'll send a guard for the landlady.'

'Albiola, he is too dangerous; I mean it.'

'Yes, darling.' But by then I was gone.

Outside I found Falco's old map on the floor. I picked up the family heirloom. Father and Petro had gone. I had better hurry, in case they got into trouble while I was searching for Florius.

All the building, which the map said was in fact three conjoined old houses, now thrummed with heightened bustle. Even so, the activity was disciplined. Nobody was shouting. Men were moving about constantly, traversing corridors and stairs, clearing rooms methodically. To and fro they tramped, picking up whoever they came across. I really should have asked for an escort, but they were all too busy. Anyway, I would be quicker on my own.

On my previous visit, I had been shown rooms for travellers. Itia had just directed me through a curtained arch in another direction. I wondered if she had deliberately lied, especially when I saw I had walked into what must be the brothel. First, washing facilities: bowls of water and chamber pots. No visible towels. Two soldiers came through, carrying a young girl by the arms; she was naked apart from a bust-band. 'Put a blanket around her!' I ordered them, though Auntie Itia's did not provide blankets either.

Boy attendants were being rounded up by some of the Fourth Cohort. More women, not all young, not all slim, came out half clad; some were in see-through materials, though not enough to go round so they had split the robes and shared the pieces.

Another group of red tunics were standing, open-mouthed, as they stared at a set of advertising frescos above the cloak pegs. These showed couples engaged in various positions of intercourse – 'Pick and mix!' commented one of Morellus's lads, as if shopping at a nut selection. There were more scenes, with not merely couples but happy nudes who were joined up in triples and quadruples.

'Look – this one is the spitting image of the Second Cohort's tribune! Run and ask if there's a prize for spotting him!'

'Say the woman in the middle looks like his sister!'

Breaking in, I asked, 'Is Vergelius here?'

They pointed. 'Eastern massage. Second booth on the left.'

I cut off the chat. 'Have you checked all the rooms?'

'Course we have. And we've been nabbing all the men – well, if there was nothing going on. If they were halfway through, we just told them to hurry up. The poor sods have paid for it. Not Vergelius. He gets his rocks off on the house. Some will need a few more moments, after they caught sight of our shiny faces peering in at them and they drooped.' My expression must have been telling. 'No, honest, we're here, Albia, for the sole purpose of punter-nobbling.'

'And I thought you were holding an art-appreciation course!'

I felt sure this place was wrong and not where Florius would be. Still, I had to check. I strode down the nearest corridor, with its rows of little rooms. At one I whipped aside a door curtain. A vigorous young woman was riding her client, not crouched like a jockey but flagrant and upright as a bareback circus rider. All she needed was a hoop or a pair of peacock feathers for balance. I gave an admiring look for her horsemanship, then dragged the curtain closed again.

Most of the rooms had their doors ajar as if they had been emptied out already. I went back to the vigiles. They were still gawping at the erotica.

'I hope you are admiring the gorgeous beds and couches all these people are playing on.' I had noticed the artist had really loved arranging his sets. 'Look at that padding, the pillows, the swathes on the coverlets. Someone knew how to paint a big bolster! And look at his swags, lads. It's giving me lovely ideas for home furnishing!'

They blushed, unsure how to take this satire.

Behind me, where I had first come from, I thought I heard Itia shouting. My husband's voice cut her off. I backtracked to the corridor, where I glimpsed a ragged boy going up the stairs, running.

I followed, powering up after the boy. Soldiers were coming down with a few people who must be renting at the travellers' rest. They had pained expressions on white, worried faces. It seemed unnecessary to escort them at sword point, but I merely asked one of the troops to help Tiberius with Itia, so he would be able to follow me. I kept going.

I found a big hall, with small tables and stools like a drinking den. The troops were hauling out annoyed tradesmen and hangdog petty thieves. My cousin's partner Corellius was hopping in wide circles on his good leg, while the slave, Ulatugnus, had him by his prosthetic bronze foot and was pulling him around. Spilled glass counters lay on the floor. They were skidding on these as Corellius shouted at the slave to tell him where Florius was hiding.

Ulatugnus tore off the false leg. Corellius yowked with pain, muffled it, fell, then straight away began scrambling to get hold of a bench. He bucked strongly and forced himself upright off the floor. Nearby, holding down another man by his shoulders, stood the Princeps, who shot Corellius an admiring glance. Next minute, Corellius grabbed the heavy draughtsboard. Somehow balancing on one foot, he began hopping around and thrashing the slave. Uncle signalled to a soldier. Corellius, though barely managing to stay upright, angrily waved at the helper to stand back.

Marcia was not there; Corellius must have told her to keep away. He had always had a dangerous side and was allowing it full rein now. I winced as he kept battering.

I ran back to the stairs. I would not wait for the slave to reveal where his master was. Like Itia, he might lie anyway.

The further I strode, the fewer people I encountered. Troops must already have raided some upstairs rooms because doors stood open, revealing basic rentals. No one was in them now.

One door was closed, so I opened it. Inside I found more pornographic action. The young woman involved at least had all her clothes on, and a big swathing apron on top. She was playing 'nurse', presumably to one of the men that Marcia had called fake decurions, who enjoyed speciality enemas. As Nursey packed the rear end of her elderly client with an opium suppository, she looked up, saw my expression, and said conversationally, 'It makes him happy!' I left them.

I pushed up higher into silent spaces. It felt as if no one but me from our group had been here yet. Here the building had remained unaltered and my father's map became useful. Sordid bordello rooms were shuttered and dim. In an entertainment area with a sunken dancing floor stood a huge lewd statue. Goodness knows why cultured people on heritage tours imagined the stone copulating goat was there – or what past audiences might have done on the surrounding seats.

It became harder to search, because of side passages: other routes in – and, my fear was, other routes out. I never saw that boy again. If Florius had been alerted, I had probably lost him. Breathless, I tried to speed up.

I had come a long way now. I was on my own, in a part that seemed deserted. Right at the top of the building, my map showed a room, a big one, that Falco had marked with a cross and a Greek capital letter 'Λ', perhaps for the long-ago brothel-owner, Lalage. I headed there.

Hearing voices, I pulled up abruptly. In a sideroom, through an open door, I glimpsed two men, no doubt supposedly on guard, though they were just loafing. It confirmed I was near to my quarry. I dared not tackle them, alone and out of my companions' hearing. Sounds of the raid had not yet penetrated the solidly built old building, so the men were lazily chatting together, still unaware of what was happening on the floors below.

I might have been able to sneak past, but it would have been too risky. Silently I hastily returned to the travellers' corridor, in search of useful props. One of the regular renters must be paying for room service; I had noticed a food tray on the floor outside a door. I took off my cloak then picked up the tray, which I balanced on my hip, selecting a goblet and a flagon to furnish it. I retraced my steps, catching up my skirt slightly with my free hand. I put on a sour expression, as if annoyed at climbing stairs. I was playing a put-upon serving girl.

The guards must be used to service personel; they did not even look up as I passed.

Anxious though, I speeded up. I wondered if Corellius had ever limped this far, though I thought he would have mentioned it. I wondered too how Florius spent his time, now he was stuck way up here, hiding from the authorities, from rivals, and from the wife who claimed to have spurned him. If he was holed up indoors, everything he needed must be brought to him. It would be worse than provincial exile, a lonely penthouse prison. He must be full of anxiety. Whatever the relationship between Itia and the Balbinus gang, Florius had to trust Itia not to betray him – as she might, if she decided there was money in it, or from sheer vindictiveness if she ever lined up with Milvia against him. I guessed he must be paying her a great deal of money for this lodging and for secrecy.

My heart pounded. He was here, I was certain. For the first time after many years, I would come face to face with him. His presence was so palpable I could taste it.

I arrived at the room that I had decided was his.

59

I had guessed right, but when I went in, it was empty.

I felt devastated. He was not there. Nobody was. Yet I could tell someone had been, recently.

Awash with disappointment, I leaned back to close the door gently behind me. I walked forwards several steps, then stood motionless, taking it in. I realised I was shaking.

A large, elegant space seemed to have once been an expensive boudoir. A substantial, well-furnished bed, in an alcove behind a curtain, though the drapery was dropping off a badly fixed rail. An odd dark stain marred the wooden floor in front of it.

You could live in this room. There was a small couch with faded silken upholstery, once some reddish shade but now faded to dirty oystershell. Footstools. Lamp-tables. (I placed the tray on one.) Overhead was an ancient plastered ceiling, thickly ingrained with lamp smoke.

Someone had been occupying the room – I could smell him. Boots stood upright beside the bed, boots I believed I remembered from when I saw Florius leave the Rabirius funeral. Otherwise there was just one holdall. He seemed to travel light.

Outside I heard noises. Unable to move, I stayed where I was, tears trailing.

Men burst in. Men I knew. Three of them. Three men who all folded me in hugs. Falco, Petronius, Tiberius. 'Here she is. She's all right . . .'

They all had bruises, and split knuckles. Ahead of them they had kicked a boy, perhaps the one I had glimpsed earlier, scuttling up the stairs. 'Not here. He's gone!'

'The little beast warned him.' The boy broke free. Squealing, he fled.

'Don't cry, you're safe. We'll get him, pet.'

'He can't have gone far. Don't worry, we'll find him.'

They all held me, passing me between them, their strong hands spread on me, their strong arms full of comfort. For a brief moment my shock at not finding him, with my shock at them finding me, was so great my legs threatened to give way. A flashback to myself as a street child in Britain smote me. Then it was gone. I had a new life, my own life. Whatever had happened to me once, I was held safe; my Roman male relations were smothering me in their love, reassurance, and anger on account of Florius. My father, my uncle, my husband. By the Twelve Tables of Roman Law and under the Twelve Consenting Gods of the Pantheon, I belonged to them: my patriarchal family.

'Take her home, Faustus.'

'Let go of me, then. I do still have legs!'

They let go. I turned out of the room, walking ahead of them. They came with me. My father, my uncle and my husband: those dear lads with their legal rights of ownership. This is how patriarchy works: I gave them instructions. They followed me like lambs.

60

On the way out, Falco and Petronius detoured into an adjacent room. They seemed to know where they were going and what to expect. A window was open. Outside, a roof lay below that would allow someone to escape the building. They leaned out, cursing. Pantiles had been knocked askew, they reckoned. I could guess who, alerted to our presence, might have scrabbled down there. He would have landed in the alley, and even though he must have jarred himself, he had made a run for it.

We continued our exit through the interior, reaching the room the two guards occupied. Someone had battered them; I noticed that Petronius now had two daggers thrust through his belt. Soldiers from the Castra were collecting the men, not gently.

A terrific noise started elsewhere. 'Karus! Finally found a back passageway.'

'Well done, special agent!'

Where I had picked up the tray earlier, I collected my cloak. While Tiberius was pinning the brooch for me, a door opened. The occupant came out to put another empty flagon on his tray. Amazingly, I knew him.

When I yelped in surprise, the others jumped, thinking it might be Florius. Not this flabby, flatulent, pestilential lump. '*Fundanus!*' We had thought he was dead.

'You haven't seen me!'

'I see you plainly. You told me you would never set foot in this building.'

'If anyone asks, I haven't.'

'Dear gods, Auntie Itia can't care whom she allows to shelter in her horrible doss.'

I nearly marched on my way, ignoring the foul funeral director, yet I wanted to know just how bad his actions had been. With the flat of my palm, I pushed him backwards into the room he had come from. Then I shook my hand as if knocking off physical contamination. There was no escape for Fundanus. My male companions clustered in the doorway while I demanded to know why Claudia Deiana had not been given proper rites.

'Nothing to do with me!' Fundanus blustered.

'Rubbish. Someone must have paid him,' said Petro, dourly, behind me.

My father judged, 'Can there be a filthier sight than a fat man with some intelligence convincing himself he has done nothing wrong, then shamelessly braying his "innocence"?'

'Not enough intelligence even to pretend to have morals!' I growled. 'He was paid, he was given instructions, and a highly expensive urn. Even so, his idea of professional integrity was to chuck Claudia back in the Tiber.'

'Who bribed you to do that, Fundanus?' demanded Tiberius. At the same time, my father and uncle sighed loudly and deliberately advanced upon the man. The way they trod towards him was threatening enough. Fundanus wet himself. Then the putrid pushover owned up.

It was the Rabirius gang. They had come promising cash if he would dump Claudia's body in the river a second time, specifically at a place where the current would take her to a bank. They had waited until Fundanus had done it, before they explained to him what kind of man Florius was. Fundanus had packed a spare tunic, taken all the cash they had given him, and fled. Auntie Itia's was only a few minutes from his place.

We enjoyed revealing that the man who now wanted to murder him had been secreted along the corridor. Then, when a group of Varduli came into view, we told them they had arrived a day after the festival – but here was one despicable lawbreaker we would give them for free. They were unhappy that the building had been efficiently cleared by others, so they fell upon this last chance of a captive. Fundanus began offering them money, but I told him they were foreign auxiliaries who spoke no Latin. From their happy gleams, they fully understood me: tormenting Fundanus was going to be the best fun they had had in Rome.

We came across Karus downstairs. Members of the Fourth Cohort had presented him with his own prize: Vergelius, the tribune of the Second. They were saying, with honest looks and grave expressions, that they needed an officer to pronounce sentence on this prisoner they had found in a compromising situation. They kept telling Vergelius he was suspicious because his clothes seemed too good, as if they were stolen, and the girl he had been with had told them he never paid; Vergelius had claimed he was a sausage-seller called Boxos and swore he *had* paid although, when asked what price, he could not say.

Silent, the tribune bit his lip. He regretted it immediately because somebody had previously punched him in the mouth. As a brothel raid, ours was true to form.

Karus, who must have met him before, gave no sign he knew Vergelius was an officer. Instead, Karus instructed the Fourth that if this man had made a false declaration, they should march him to the Castra Peregrina where extraction of the truth could occur 'in the usual way'.

I piped up, 'Would that be the way you handled the Purple faction's driver? Did he tell you anything useful?'

'No,' answered Karus, with an unflinching look. 'He died.'

Vergelius might escape that, but he would probably be reassigned to a post in a desert thousands of miles away.

Inside the large hall two soldiers had positioned the bronze false leg on a table and were diligently tapping out dents. Corellius watched, massaging his stump. He called to me that Ulatugnus had escaped. 'He claimed he doesn't know where Florius has gone. He himself was just squatting here, awaiting a boat downriver to Ostia. I won't miss him as a partner – he was a lousy board-game player.'

The rest of the building was now empty. My friend Titus was out in the street in his full glory as Princeps, complete with an underarm baton he had acquired. 'Some noble officer must have forgotten his swagger stick after an evening of joy, Sparrow! I gave it a good wash. We don't know where anyone has poked it . . .'

His secretary was patting Skyla, the Agassian hound, who was thoroughly disturbed by what had happened in her building and crying wretchedly. Perhaps they would give her a new home at the Castra. Brutal men can form weird bonds with dogs.

Titus had Itia being held at sword point in front of him. Far from weeping at her loss of trade, she looked brash and truculent; the soldiers in charge were extremely nervous of this prisoner. Without notes (since his secretary was so busy on dog duty), the Princeps began listing all the edicts Itia was supposed to have broken in the conduct of her businesses. My father and Petronius went to listen in, ready to help if he missed any.

Tiberius looked at me gently. Neither of us needed to speak. Hand in hand, we started to walk, leaving the tangle of back lanes, then heading towards the end of the Circus Maximus, where we could take a main road up the hill to the Aventine, on our way home.

We passed some members of the Sixth Cohort, coming to check what had happened on their patch, now that it was all over.

61

My husband had given a part of his day to my project, in the process obtaining bloody knuckles and stress, so the least I could do was accompany him to check on his own work. The temple porch he was reconstructing had stalled, due to the ongoing lack of a new column. I let him fret aloud about that, managing not to say I would like to hear the last of it. Then, since it was on our way, we dropped in at Fountain Court.

Nobody seemed to be about. The alley lay as it always had been, dank and overcast under the tall buildings that were too close together either side. Most had more storeys than the law allowed so they were liable to collapse; anyone whose apartment or workshop was crushed was bound to receive inadequate compensation and, if they died, there would be none for their heirs. This threatening backwater had never been a joy to live in. It was home to people who had no choice, many so far gone in misery they had lost the ability even to realise their grim plight. At least near the old laundry our workmen had put down wooden hurdles so puddles in the roadway seeped noxious mud into your shoes only when the hurdles rocked. We had to walk by a dead pigeon, and whatever people with upstairs accommodation had thrown out of windows from their slop pails.

Heading for the decrepit Eagle Building, that one-time flawed gem in my family's portfolio, we passed through a slumped colonnade. Falco had told me it was loosely affixed to a property that Florius had inherited from his father-in-law, Balbinus Pius. There stood the tat-stuffed Lumber Room, which bleakly advertised 'Gifts of Charm'. In all the years I had known this cover-joint, I had never seen any customer buy anything charming. But I had seen crooks use it, and once I saw Florius leaving.

Unprompted, Tiberius said we should check the place in case Florius had come back. We knew there was no point in knocking. In Fountain Court people hid on principle, the principle that nobody friendly would be looking for them. Having tried and failed with his lock picks, Tiberius picked up a stave from his men's latest skip to jemmy the door open.

The metalware the Balbinus gang had installed for security was surprisingly robust. In the end Tiberius fetched a big cold chisel and lump hammer, working up a sweat as he smashed off half the door frame and the masonry around it. My husband was very practical for a man who read Plato and Pliny the Elder, neither of whom are known as break-in burglars. When I mentioned his talent (while he examined the door furniture, wondering whether to carry it off), he said he wasn't going to let a murderous, vice-peddling tax avoider lock him out of a fake junk shop.

The place was still crammed. It always had been full – of nothing you would ever want. Someone had once made an effort to place broken tools and unidentifiable fixtures in separate baskets but they gave up. Cracked oil lamps still teetered in stalagmite piles, half-dead curtains harboured mouse droppings, cauldrons swung from the ceiling ready to brain visitors, while down at ground level you could cut your shin open on items with sharp protrusions. Throughout, there was a distinct smell of mould. Thieves never bothered to break in. Fleas and moths fled and went on holiday.

Once again, we failed to find Florius. He might have been here last autumn, that time I believed he had walked past me outside, but there had been no criminal activity since and it was clear no one was living in either the shop or the dingy, danger-strewn workshop beyond. The yard at the back was waist-high with rank weeds, the kind that give you a three-day rash if you brush against them. The gate onto the lane had been chained on the inside. It was still locked.

I hated being there. 'Let's go. This is another dump someone ought to pull down.'

'Right! I'll just pinch those door bolts. Then we'll go and have a look at my site.'

The six-storey tenement I had once lived in now reared up only four and a half, though the stairs still went higher, like a fantasy route in a fresco. Taking off the top had failed to let in light.

The building looked decapitated and shaved. My father's old rooms, which I too had used as an office for a long time, were completely gone. Apparently, all spaces under the floorboards had been packed solid with empty amphorae. When Falco was chaffed about that, he had claimed it was from decades of contemplating *What is the point?*

Beneath windblown scaffolding, the front and back balconies had been removed. In the old laundry yard, once home to huge washtubs, drying frames and lines, I could see neatly stacked reclaimed materials: bricks, beams, partitions, buckets of nails, tubs of other hardware, even whole sheets of ceiling and wall plaster. At least these were protected from theft, because the iron grille was still in place across the porch beside what had been the porter's cubicle. He had been a wreck. Failing to learn, we had him at home now.

Inside the stripped building carcass, the old dusty atmosphere that had killed generations with lung diseases was inevitably worse; a pall of dust and dirt hung like bad smog everywhere. Our men were filthy and worked with scarves over their faces. Some even had woollen caps and ear-plugs.

Beside their demolition skip, Tiberius cursed. He had ordered a guard, even on rubbish, which scavengers might toss about in the street, causing extra work for a good-neighbour contractor like himself. Nobody was currently on watch. Anyone could have stolen the salvage or caused damage. More important, Tiberius wanted people with no business there to be kept away; when a building is being pulled down, there are too many opportunities for serious injuries. He did not want to feel responsible for mutilation or death. Tiberius was unusual in that.

In fact, nobody was about in Fountain Court, though it had its old air of hidden eyes watching, with inhabitants liable to prey on anyone who passed, regardless of whether they seemed vulnerable or tough. We worked out why our skip was temporarily unattended. Somewhere high up indoors, we could hear the particular noises of breathless men trying to carry heavy doors around corners on slippery stone steps. Tiberius called out to Larcius, his clerk-of-works. Receiving a testy answer from a man who was straining hard and had already had an idiot drop a large door on his foot, Tiberius went up to help.

I offered to stay with the skip. He said it only contained rubble, so not to bother. I would be no use with the doors. I was more likely to lose my temper as the men wrestled with their burdens, ignoring any advice I gave. (Yes, I had visited building sites before.) I was stuck, the way you are if you accompany a man to his workplace and he gets caught up. Going home on my own would be seen as disloyalty. Instead, I stepped into my old apartment, taking one last look before it disappeared for ever.

I entered via the double front doors. When it was my home, I never used to do that. For reasons of my own I had kept the entrance blocked with flower troughs, which had now been brought to our house. Coming in that way was disconcerting, and the bare interior gave me another shock. I had not been there since Father's sale of the building was signed off. I had never seen my apartment with all its furniture removed. Ridiculous not to realise today that the rooms would be empty. I knew perfectly well that anything I valued, from here and the top office, had been transferred to where I lived now.

Even denuded, this was a place of emotion for me. Fountain Court was where I first learned to be independent. It was where my adult character formed. These rooms, once the best-decorated in the block, had been my refuge from all kinds of unhappiness, a quiet place for recovery from weary days and lonely nights. Here I had stabilised. For one thing, this had been where I spent the three years of my short, happy first marriage. Much later, Tiberius came here, before we were lovers. I had been very ill at the time; he looked after me, while I was learning to love him. I knew in my heart he already loved me. That period also made a good memory.

I had left one front door open, so the others would know where I was. Muffled up against the dust, they would never notice me moving about. For a long time, I could hear the men arguing and groaning as they inched dead-weight old woodwork around bends in the stairs. It gave me time to sink into reverie.

A little mournful, I walked out to the back of the apartment, where a fire escape had supposedly allowed tenants to save their lives in an emergency. By some amazing piece of luck, fire had never engulfed this building. The back balconies and steps had been mostly used as a rat-run by thieves and adulterers. I lived on the second floor. For most of the time I was here, the ground-floor fire escape had been missing – torn down and used for kindling by Lenia, the old laundress – so the upper part was pointless because nobody could access it. I had devised a private way in and out through the first-floor rooms of a neighbour, then came up hidden stairs. I kept it a secret, so that nobody bothersome, nobody who had followed me home and was let in by that useless porter, no ridiculous boyfriends that I had decided to dump, ever knew where I lived within the building. Single women must develop strategies for their protection, especially at night. Now that I lived safely in a family, with staff, I had almost forgotten what that felt like.

Oops. The entire fire escape was gone. I nearly stepped out into empty space.

Chuckling to myself because a death-dive when I no longer had to live here would have been a stupid irony, I swayed in the back doorway for a moment, as I looked down for the last time at what had been the washing yard. The Eagle Laundry, Fountain Court: about to vanish and be replaced by a lavish private house. Now that, for anyone who had previously known this ghastly hovel, really was ironic. Thank you, Ulpius Trajanus, the gentrifying senator.

Behind me, I heard a footstep. Assuming it was Tiberius or one of the workmen, coming to find me, I turned back into the apartment. Then I saw someone else.

I was as startled as him. He had smooth pale skin, with a slight puffiness, and small dark eyes. He was glancing behind as if listening, at the same time stepping further in. When he walked, he always stepped on the balls of his feet, like a man who wanted to be admired for his physique, getting ready to spring. His arms hung slightly apart from his body, as if he was expectant of attack.

Well, that was right.

Down in Fountain Court, this creature might have come to the Lumber Room, where he saw that someone had broken in. He knew it would never have been thieves, unless they were insane. With the shop under observation, where else could he go? Ahead lay an apparently deserted building site. Hoping for a last-minute bunk hole, he slipped indoors. He started up the stairs, heard men struggling down towards him, so sidestepped in here, where I had left a door open. Had I been stupid, or was this our fate?

I knew who he was. Completely unprepared this time, I was standing in the same room as Florius.

62

Beyond the door, still somewhere overhead, grunts and sharp cries of 'Watch it!' marked Tiberius and his men slowly coming closer. It made an incongruous backdrop.

I found myself unable to make a sound. I had no weapons. There was no exit behind me. He could escape if he chose, but must be desperate for a new refuge. Now I had seen him he could not stay here, or not unless he silenced me. He was probably armed.

Still stunned, I heard myself croak, 'I have been looking for you!' My throat locked so I could not say his name, but I produced the formula for mine: 'I am Albia. Flavia Albia.'

You spend years thinking about a man who has done you wrong, inordinate wrong – only to find that he never thought of you at all. Quite simply, he does not remember you.

Perhaps he never knew any name for me. 'Flavia' came afterwards, for citizenship reasons. To him back then, I had been nothing more than a trading commodity, someone he had lured, groomed and intended to use for profit. He no more noticed my identity than a chandler would recall a particular wheat sack. Even the rape had been more for business reasons than lust. Everything to me – yet nothing to him.

'What do you want?' Florius had a weak voice. Until now I had forgotten how he sounded. In my bad dreams, he never spoke.

He was older; we all were. My father, who had known him younger and flabbier, always called him an untidy lump. We saw him in Britain after he had sharpened up, body-built in a period when he dallied with gladiating. Since then he had become an established racketeer, with money sluicing in for luxurious living so he verged on businessman's podge again. Seriously balding, he had moved into a new phase of life. But he was still physically dangerous.

My presence was annoying, though he wanted to concentrate on what we could hear going on outside. A crash, followed by curses, made him move as if to close the door. He had partly knocked it to, but was trying to keep back out of sight. 'Leave it open.' To be trapped in a room with him would be so hideous I felt sick. Somehow I spoke calmly; somehow he obeyed. 'Unlike the authorities, I am not interested in your tax status,' I told him. 'But I am curious to know who forced you to leave Britain?'

He was still so annoyed about it, he could not help himself: 'A bastard called Karus! Had it in for me. Went poking into archives. Found an old charge against me. Unearthed a deposition, prepared by the old procurator, Hilaris.'

I knew what that document must have been. I had seen it once. I was so surprised I laughed. He stared.

I took a deep breath. 'Rape of a virgin, was it? A female who was underage?'

'Utter piss!' Florius was too emphatic; he never thought to ask how I knew that.

'No. Highly dangerous for you. The deposition was addressed by Flavius Hilaris to the provincial governor, *legatus Augusti pro praetore*: Frontinus. He is still living – grand stuff! You really do not want anything so serious resurfacing.'

'Pig's pizzle. That charge is over ten years old.'

'Out of time? Is that what your lawyer told you? You need a new one.' My voice sounded very quiet. 'Karus may have been scratching around for evidence, but what he turned up is still valid. The scroll will have been kept, in case they ever laid hands on you.'

'It would be laughed out of court. They would never find the girl now. Who was she anyway?'

'They know who she was, Florius. They know where she is.'

Florius took stock, obviously furious. But he would not speak.

I gave him clues, spitting them out: 'The girl was adopted by an agent of the deified Vespasian and a senator's daughter. Could not be more respectable. Lives here in Rome. Wife of a magistrate. Knows all the top people – knows Karus, which is fatal for you. If he learns that he can call upon your victim, Karus won't believe his luck. No more trying to stuff you with unpaid tax bills while your accountants wriggle. No more elusive haze of racketeering, which no juries under-stand. *Rape of an untouched young girl?* You know what that means. He can confiscate every asset you have – and he has already been looking at your property, so he's right up there already, poised for forcible possession. You are a public enemy. Julius Karus makes his name executing those. Most of all, rape of a virgin is a capital crime. It's your death sentence.'

Florius was still failing to make connections.

'Florius Oppicus, you asked me what I want. For half my life, what I wanted was to kill you.'

Finally, that got his attention.

★　　★　　★

Recognition of the facts slowly penetrated, even if he still found no personal recall of me.

'How many others?' I mused, driving home my point. 'I cannot have been the only one. You were brutal. The people who worked for you were terrorising monsters. The places you owned were vile. I may have been the only girl who ever got away . . .' I let out a puff of bitter laughter. 'No? Still means nothing? I had always thought you were bound to remember. To bear a grudge against Didius Falco, because he and Helena Justina rescued me.' Even my parents' names seemed unfamiliar to him. 'I was sure you would bemoan that one little soul who managed to fight her way out of your clutches.' All the time I was accusing him, Florius remained expressionless. 'I see. You did not even bother to care about your loss! What was one gone, when you could always entrap more?'

Florius still had nothing to say. He had learned the criminal code. Never acknowledge anything.

Despite the increasing background noises as the workmen approached our level, he looked as if he intended to leave. He would run straight into them, so hesitated.

Remorseless, I ramped up pressure. 'I am thinking about a body I saw in a hopper barge, on the Embankment . . . Do you want Claudia Deiana's jewellery?'

At that, Florius did seem to react, though only to stare. I fumbled in the satchel I generally carried, managing to bring out the broken chain, the fine enamel brooch, the single highly expensive ear-ring.

When Florius first visited Fundanus, he had asked about jewellery. But now he shook his head, roughly refusing the items. At least I did not have to let him come any nearer. Closing my hand, I said, 'We know she had a plaque with a

335

portrait of your children. It has never been found, unfortunately. I cannot give you that memento.'

Finally, he spoke. 'No matter,' answered the father of those children harshly. 'I know what they looked like!' I noticed the past tense.

Even I was shocked by how callous he was. He had no intention of providing for the offspring he had left behind; he would not choose to see them, nor ever again seek news of them. Only Claudia had cared, and she was gone. I wondered if she ever realised how he felt towards her treasures. If so, it would have been one more grief for her.

I tried pushing him again: 'I supposed the Rabirius gang must have torn off her other ornaments to send as a message to you.'

'Oh, it was a message!' Florius agreed, at last growing heated. He had thought he was untouchable, or ought to be. 'They sent an ear-ring to my house. My wife was given the thing!'

'Did the Rabirii do that deliberately, to cause trouble between you and Milvia?'

'It caused trouble!' he repeated in a hollow voice, a man recalling harsh home strife.

'Was that when Milvia first heard you had a second wife?'

'Milvia knew,' stated Florius.

'She knew *before* Claudia was killed? I'm starting to think Milvia must have done. Most people assumed you killed Claudia Deiana – but I have another explanation. Wasn't it Milvia's own response? Rubria Theodosia arranged it for her, but Milvia made the request, after learning of your double life? So, the ear-ring was sent for Milvia – to confirm that her Rabirius relatives had ended the problem as she wanted?'

Florius refused to say, but the corners of his mouth tightened hard. That answered me.

I knew this conversation could not go on much longer. 'I want to understand.' He was so hard to engage, I was almost begging. 'I saw Claudia Deiana's corpse. She and I had a province in common. What kind of life had she experienced? I want to hear why she had come to Rome? *Why?* Did she know from the start about Milvia? Because, if so, she must have realised that could never end well. Why did she follow you? Had you given her instructions to remain in Britain without you, yet she was so angry at being deserted she chased you anyway?'

Florius scoffed quietly, almost to himself. 'That is what everybody thinks. Well, let them.'

'Is it true?' I persisted.

'It is none of your business.'

'I have made it my business.'

'And who are you?'

'Falco's daughter.'

'He is nothing!'

'Wrong, Florius!' My voice croaked. 'You nearly ruined my life.'

He looked me up and down. 'It doesn't look like it!' he sneered. 'I fail to see any damage.'

The past was irrelevant to him. He ignored the devastating internal grief, the nearly broken personality, the fear, the pain. He judged me as he saw me here: well-dressed, self-assured and prosperous. Suza was back in Rome, turning me out so that even for a brothel raid I had tight, elaborate plaits in my hair and the glint of gold in my ear tips. Florius heard my educated voice, my firm statements and informed questions. If I had still been the street scavenger, he would never

337

have recognised that pathetic mite, but neither did he accept that he ought to know me now, the new version.

Revenge was impossible. All the expectations I had carried for so long had come to nothing. He would never admit what he had done. He would never acknowledge why I had hated him for half of my life. He had a true villain's lack of conscience. His criminality was completely based on the simple rules used by most of them: seeing nothing wrong in what they did and never owning up.

Our confrontation was not supposed to be like this. I had always wanted to flay him with accusations, force him to admit how sinful he was. He had made his choice years ago, when he started out. What he did was his way of life; he denied any crimes.

Nevertheless, I tried. I had to be true to myself. I put my personal griefs aside and carried out my job as an informer.

I spoke in the level voice I used when interviewing suspects. 'This is what I think happened. Claudia Deiana followed you to Rome. She was looking for you; perhaps she found you. Only you can say whether Claudia caused trouble. But Milvia learned of her existence and had the Rabirius gang drown her. You tried exacting retribution from them. They snatched Claudia's poor corpse and threw her into the Tiber again to punish you a second time.'

Perhaps a shadow passed across the dark eyes of Florius, but it was impossible to tell.

I continued, staying cool: 'You were equally violent. You had Legsie Lucius brutally murdered, the runner who had lured Claudia into their hands. Someone – and it may have been you – had the hitman Turcus dealt with too. He confessed to me that he had carried out Claudia's killing and I suppose you had found out. Meanwhile, in the Horti Lamiani, the other gangsters pretended to be reconciled with you. Gallo offered collaboration, but then he tried to wipe you out. You saw what a threat the Rabirius gang were – but then was it you who removed Young Roscius? I do not think so!'

Automatically, Florius jarred, though he still made no comment. He steadied.

I spoke more softly: 'I suspect Rabirius Vincentius for that. With Gallo out of action, possibly for ever, Vincentius has erased all other rivalry, sacrificing Roscius, placing blame on you. Roscius was a thief and a wimp, but nobody loathed him, not enough to rejoice at his passing. If it is said that you killed him, people will believe it. They will *want* to because, frankly, that is less frightening than accusing Vincentius. In the world you inhabit, lording it over you gives Vincentius power and diminishes your status. What can you do about it? You don't have the strength to remove him. With his father no longer clinging to life, the son's influence can only grow. The women who support him are stronger than Milvia will ever be – though I concede she is more spiteful. She is cunning, vindictive – and, Florius, if you want to occupy *her* father's position, you are stuck with her.'

I had said enough – too much for him. The workmen were clearly passing right outside, though not in view because Florius had pushed the door part closed. Instinctively we stopped talking. They must be tackling the next flight down. Immersed in the task, they kept going with their load, though one called my name enquiringly. I did not answer. Florius and I stood silent, exhausted by our battle of words.

After they reached ground level, the men must have dropped their burden with relieved groans. The strong voice of Tiberius Manlius called from below: 'Albia, is somebody with you? Are you coming down or shall I come up?'

339

I saw a decision in Florius's eyes. I pushed Claudia Deiana's jewellery back into my satchel, using that as cover to bring out my knife. Every informer should carry a 'fruit knife'.

Known for sudden escapes, abruptly Florius spun around. He darted from the apartment. I tried to follow but he pushed the double doors together in my face. He seemed to do something to fasten the handles. Whatever it was, he had no time. When I heard him running down the stairs, I flung myself bodily against the doors, pushing and pulling until I broke out of the apartment. He had tried to fix the handles together with his belt, which rarely works. I rushed after him.

Florius had reached ground level. I could not see the other men, but Tiberius was waiting, one foot on the bottom step, head up. In one hand he grasped the big cold chisel, in the other the long-handled lump hammer. He was threatening Florius with these, but once I appeared he made a gesture: I could choose what he did next.

Florius grasped we had some kind of relationship. Undaunted, he exclaimed jokily, 'All good! As you see, she has not killed me!'

Tiberius moved his foot off the step. He was just taller than the other man; he looked more solid and mature. 'If Flavia Albia wants you dead, I shall kill you myself.'

Florius no longer controlled me. I had other options. *A streak of flab with the moral incisiveness of jelly* ... I gave the signal that Tiberius wanted: let the worm go.

Tiberius stepped aside. Florius scoffed. Racketeers have no truck with heroic gestures.

His attitude revived a terrible memory. I regretted my decision. I began to go after him, but Tiberius stopped me. 'Put your bloody knife away!' He wrapped both arms tight around me, though restraint was unnecessary. I dropped the knife as I heard him say, 'Leave it, love. Others are coming for him.'

Grasping my hand, Tiberius led me out into Fountain Court.

Doors had been placed across the alley to block it in one direction. In front of this barrier stood my husband's work team: Larcius, Serenus and Sparsus, Trypho, and a couple of others I did not know, who had been brought in for this job. Dressed in rough clothes, covered with dirt, heads muffled, they looked menacing.

His men must have known the circumstances. The young apprentice, Sparsus, stooped to pick up a bucket and a stubby stick. He held the bucket with one arm. Slowly at first, he began cracking out a single rhythm so it sounded like a funeral drum. Others took up tools and joined in. That made it menacing. Louder and louder, then faster, came the beats. Their meaning was obvious.

Florius laughed in their faces. The crime lord who believed he could not be brought to justice turned from them and walked away. Then he saw how he was trapped. Coming down Fountain Court from the other direction were four men on horseback: Varduloran cavalry.

63

The auxiliaries rode down towards Florius at a controlled slow pace. Between the tall, dark buildings, their horses stepped with small dainty paces as if in a circus, dancing. We learned afterwards how, back in the brothel, Morellus had told Julius Karus about the Lumber Room; a detachment must have come looking for him. The Varduli had seen Florius now, seen him come out of the Eagle Building, seen him with our workmen closing in from behind, as he slowed his pace. Holding their neat horses in check, the riders moved down the alley from the other direction, intent on arresting him. It would be done with caution but no fuss, and certainly no compromise.

Florius abruptly began to walk faster again, head down a little, a picture of a man who had lost his fight, submitting. I was the only person present who had seen him in such a pose before. I wanted to call out not to trust him, but no one was likely to take in my meaning. Only I was unsurprised when he acted.

With a long stride forwards, he bent down to one of the hurdles that our men had placed on the road surface. He seized it in his hands, lifted and flung it from him hard. He had more energy and must have been much stronger than he looked. I was suddenly back in the Londinium arena with him fighting, mocking, killing, triumphing – and escaping . . .

Edge on, the heavy piece of wood hit one of the Iberian horses full in the chest. The beast screamed and reared, plunging sideways so it crashed into its companions. Another horse stepped onto the fallen hurdle so lost its footing. Riders fell. Others were struggling to regain control. Men shouted.

There was a loose horse. Florius raced to it and rolled himself up into the saddle. He could ride. He had lived in Britain after all, where horseflesh is sacred; he had his own rural villa, where he must have owned stables, no doubt with expensive animals.

Escape had seemed impossible – yet he was achieving it. Of course he was. He always did.

At the far end of the alley two men on foot appeared. One was tall, wearing a red cap, the other sturdier with unkempt curls: Falco and Petronius. I heard their shouts. Florius kicked and drove the horse straight between them. They were both knocked aside. He galloped through and away.

Two of the Varduli recovered enough to wheel their mounts and chase him. Another would shortly be following. Florius knew the Aventine of old, whereas they were strangers to the city, let alone our characterful district. He could have lost them in the back lanes; instead, he seemed not to care. He pushed directly across the high road that crossed the hill's top, the Vicus Armilustrium. When he came to the Stairs of Cassius on the cliff's edge, high above the river, he actually forced the small horse to continue down. Those steps were notoriously steep; I often avoided using them. Florius rode well enough and that horse was brave, well schooled in tricksy battle moves, a tryer. Even so, the descent must have been terrifying.

He made it halfway before the horse panicked. A couple of old women coming up had bawled insults at this outrage, someone crazily riding on their daily route; they swung at him with the baskets they were carrying. Florius tried to shove past. His mount refused. He slid off, left it stuck there and carried on, now a hasty pedestrian. The auxiliaries followed him down on foot, but they were well behind.

In the bustle on the Embankment, they lost him. It was quite close to the Emporium, where Claudia Deiana's body had been first brought ashore by the dredger.

The authorities searched for several days but never found him.

64

There must have been private quarters in the Castra Peregrina that were well up to the standard of commanders' houses in legionary forts, perhaps even more luxurious. All the same, the Castra was not a place to accept a dinner invitation. So much could go wrong. Of course you would not fear being poisoned (although I knew it had happened). If your jovial host at a banquet went cold on you midway through the meal, he had much worse punishments at his disposal.

So when Uncle asked us over, we responded no, no: Titus, our dear friend, must absolutely come to us. We had a celebrity chef who had once worked at the legendary Fabulo's (now defunct, though not because we had poached its chef). And if Stertinius, the sought-after cithara player was free, we might call him in to give us a set afterwards.

The change of venue worked well because Uncle brought a thank-you present, which we could immediately stash. It was not a trained rose-tree in a pot or a beautifully wrapped packet of sweets with real gold shavings. There was no gold, in fact. A heavy Greek urn was packed with freshly minted silver coins.

These denarii were my fee for information that Titus said had led the authorities to Florius. 'I hope the posh pottery is all right, Sparrow. I got it from that curious old fellow you brought on the raid. Did you know he runs an auction house?

Apparently, all the top connoisseurs are desperate to buy his stuff.'

'He told you that?'

'Along those lines. Is he legit?'

'*Falco?* About as bona fide as I am, accepting money for a job where I failed.' Citing the fact Florius had not been caught, I felt I had earned nothing. Uncle waved this idea away. I had pointed them to the brothel, he said, then held the fugitive in conversation, at my personal risk. Once the Varduli arrived to collect him, my task was done. If they let him escape, that was their fault. Karus, grinned Titus, was having to write a report to justify the failure.

'Take the money!' Tiberius encouraged me. 'We have painters to pay.'

I commented that I had once believed I was marrying a pious man.

'Piety,' he explained, somehow reminding me of my father, who knows why? 'Piety means being dutiful when you cannot avoid it, while showing respect for the gods. Since the gods have showered this luck upon you, take it, darling!'

'Where did you find him?' asked Titus.

'Oh, I was hanging around one day, and I bumped into him.'

'Why doesn't it happen to me?'

'You must be hanging around the wrong places,' explained Tiberius, demurely.

We then had a good dinner, thanks to the excellent Fornix. The Princeps ate and drank heartily yet managed to trawl through plenty of gossip, mostly without spitting or spillage of food. First, however, he wanted to pick brains. 'What's the insider spec on that man Corellius? Is he any good?'

Our information was patchy because Corellius was as secretive as Uncle himself. Uncle liked that. We knew Corellius had been an army scout, which was how his leg was originally injured; more recently he was employed by the Palace to monitor foreign ambassadors, including Parthians whose deviousness was notorious.

'Important!'

'He was trusted.'

'He has languages?'

'I imagine he must.'

'Can he still ride?'

'Only on a donkey. He says he can just about grip a saddle with his thighs, but it tires him . . . Titus, what are you plotting?' I demanded, while Tiberius ladled me a generous serving of Fornix's main dish. It was little roundels of dough, which he had dried overnight then fried in oil, layered with pork-shoulder meatballs; he did another version with chicken cooked in milk that the boys loved.

The Princeps held out his own bowl, looking keen. Tiberius played host again. 'Corellius? I liked what I saw of him. My plot is to put Karus's big nose out of joint and choose someone else as my optio.'

'Corellius Musa has only one leg, Titus!'

'Yes – but did you see him on it, battering that red-haired slave? Knock him over, Corellius bobs upright as if he simply hasn't noticed he's face down on the floor. Holy crud, he could win the hopping Olympics. Panathenaic one-legged race.'

'Yes – but a major position in the Castra?'

Titus was philosophical. 'Commanding the Castra never needs route-marching. It's a sit-down job. I should know – I created it. You have to perch at the centre of your bloody big spider's web, spend time plotting devious manoeuvres, and order the legionaries to grab a few nonentities. Night times we do our torturing, but he could change that if his woman objected. He has got a woman?'

'My cousin. Are you intending to split them up?'

'Not for the world. She came in with him to see me for our little chat. One of the lads with old-fashioned attitudes said something out of turn. She socked him.'

'That's Marcia!'

'She'll do. Nothing broken. I've told her where they can find a little enclave of apartments with the wives my soldier boys are not allowed to have. Very nice neighbourhood. Even with my boys living it up there.'

We had not seen Marcia since the brothel raid. She must have been too busy house-hunting.

Titus picked up his foodbowl to drain it of sauce. The Princeps was perfectly attuned to the rule that you follow your hostess in matters of etiquette; he had already seen me doing this. I had told him my mother was a senator's daughter who had no truck with silly manners and my chef liked clean ceramics coming back from meals.

'Albia wants to see the back of the couple as visitors, but she may be concerned,' Tiberius reinforced me, 'as to whether a disabled man can impose as much authority as you do, Titus?'

'Oh, it's all bluff. Just have to fix himself up with a reputation. Parades – well, he could lean on a very fancy stick. If he wore an eyepatch as well, that would give him even more character. I could poke an eye out for him, if he wants – or else he could just make it a mystery, whether he really has lost one or not.'

'You seem to have spent time thinking about this,' Tiberius applauded.

'Stops me getting bored. I've got a big city map with location flags that I can fiddle with, but this is better. Planning how to get the notch on Karus. Keeping Karus down, blocking him from senior positions; well, I see that as for the good of Rome.'

'Dutiful and respectful of the gods!' I reiterated, smiling.

'Lovely fun!' agreed the Princeps, who was clearly not religious. 'More fun even than playing with yourself while scoffing a dirty great figgy tart.'

Fornix had included tarts in the dessert course: frangipane, luckily.

Titus continued talking about Karus, who, he said, was becoming dangerously comfortable, bigging it up as the gangster specialist. He had created a report about the new situation, confirming that Rabirius Vincentius was entrenching himself, and was behind the murder of his rival, Young Roscius.

'Vincentius has even been arrested for nephew-nobbling, but of course he will get off,' growled Titus. 'Half the lawyers in Rome are working for him like trireme rowers. Sweaty faces all round at the Basilica Julia. Those togate twisters have already fixed that he should only be held under kindly house arrest. Next move is complete rehabilitation, followed by compensation for inconvenience and an imperial apology.'

'He is the next big rissole?'

'Top snail on the wall. That's if he dodges the financial charges.'

'Charges? What is *his* tax situation?' asked Tiberius, comparing him to Florius.

'Looks as if Veronica paid up the occasional smidgeon. Not enough, but she made the gesture on his behalf. Auditors are poring over it. Of course it's going to take them years – you know auditors.'

I smiled and said, yes, I did know an excellent Census auditor.

Meanwhile, Vincentius had moved Gallo out of range. Gallo protested, but had been told that after the ostrich attack he must retire, for health reasons, to the country villa that was previously used by Old Rabirius. This piece of convalescent real estate was likely to be crowded, since Vincentius had moved his mother there too. He had said Pandora was becoming too frail to run her own business – meaning, interfere with his.

'But wasn't she backing him?' I asked.

'Does he need her? He probably wants to wipe her out, but nobody dares kill off Pandora. Even Rabirius Vincentius is scared of his mama.'

'In case she puts a curse on him and his organs all wither. But he'll be fighting back: "May worms, cancer and maggots invade the marrow of my mummy, who is horrible to me!" What about his wife?' I asked.

'Veronica? Who knows?'

'What do you mean?'

'Not been seen. Karus reckons she is either dead or dismissed to share endless country living with Rubria Theodosia.'

'That's a terrible punishment,' Tiberius said. 'My mother-in-law is a delight,' he then assured us hastily.

'Veronica has paid a penalty,' Titus said sombrely. 'Vincentius took it into his head that she had an affair with a vigiles' tribune. No crime lord can allow his wife to betray him, especially with a lawman.'

'Vergelius? Of the Second? Was the rumour true, then?' I asked.

350

'Truth may not come into it. Karus reckons Vincentius was informed of an affair by Balbina Milvia. Karus, who does have some subtlety, thinks it was *un*true, but it suited Vincentius to believe it.'

'So what's happened to Vergelius?' asked Tiberius.

The Princeps smiled. 'I had a little chat about his career structure. He came to my Castra all fired up, thinking he had been selected for the Praetorian Guard.'

'That's a very old cover story when upstarts are about to get what for! *Come and hear about your promotion* ... No?'

'No.'

'Small fort in Noricum?'

'Warm! Small fort in Pannonia. I let Karus pick the new postings, because anything Karus likes, Domitian will adore on principle. The Palace was thrilled we took the initiative – saved them having to draw up a position paper, expound ramifications, justify travel expenses ... Before you ask,' Titus added disingenuously, 'we thought the tribune of the Sixth deserves a little something too, in recognition of his many years' promoting good relations with the Balbinus gang around the Circus Max. Discharge on grounds of deafness – no doubt caused by listening to pleas for special treatment from unsavoury characters – discharge and land grant in Mauretania Tingitana.'

I pondered that. As far as I knew, Mauretanian land was desert. 'And what about Milvia?'

'Not seen either. Could be in bed with a lingering cold, but she's thought to be missing from home. A curious rumour says she has decamped – with her husband, if you believe fairy stories.'

I stared. '*Milvia is with Florius?* Marital love?' It was unbelievable.

Tiberius asked the key question. He phrased it gently. 'So where are these fugitives, noble Princeps? What is believed to have happened to Florius?'

'Gone, most excellent Faustus.'

'Gone? Taken time to depart?'

'Looks somewhat like it. Gone right out of Rome, we think, back into exile in some lonely hole where, Karus reckons, Florius will lie so low that this time nobody will ever find him. New spread. New identity. New woman, unless he really has taken Milvia with him. Same old financial methods, though. All the grime south of the Forum will be sending him holiday funds again.'

'Gone how?' I demanded, determined to hear details. 'Could it be that he slipped onto a boat he kept secretly waiting here, then sailed down the river, before anyone set up a marine alert?'

'Dear gods, you are good, Sparrow! That's right. The British slave croaked to Corellius it was their plan for emergencies. Karus has picked through a few muddy moorings and believes he found where the boat was. It has vanished. Needless to say, no witnesses.' Titus then wanted me to explain how I knew Florius had had this plan.

Because that was what he did years ago, when Falco and Petronius were chasing him in Londinium. They thought he had sailed for Gaul, evading the watch they had set up.

Of course, on that occasion – as we now knew – Florius had fooled them. He never left Britain.

'Well, Sparrow, you can forget about all this,' I was advised. Titus tipped back his head and dropped in a grape bunch, sucking in the individual berries as he worked down the clusters neatly. 'Florius has departed. Possibly shackled to the horrible Milvia. Let him go, girl!'

I said I would still like to know the truth about his wife who was pulled out of the river, Claudia Deiana.

'Never mind her. Trust your Uncle. Some questions in life are never meant to be answered. Not even by a crack investigator like you, sweetheart. Find a nice shelf for that old Greek vase I gave you. The fellow says it's a rare one – he's never seen another like it. Black figure he called it . . . or did he say red figure? Two Greek kings with their heads down, playing a board game – reminds me of your Corellius. Lovely vase. That auctioneer charged me enough for it. But I bet he has a little man in a pottery workshop who knocks out hundreds for him! What will you have painted with the silver treasure?'

Gloomily, Tiberius answered for me. 'Unless we can stop our workmen, *The Battle of Salamis.*'

The Princeps Peregrinorum reached for our smoked cheese. 'Greek again? Don't you worry, Aedile. You have Albia looking after you. There is no way those boyos with their fancy pots of cinnabar will be doing what she doesn't like.'

I smiled mildly, pretending to accept all that was said. My husband expressed no disagreement, though old Grey Eyes was privately twinkling.

I had grabbed the cheese first. So I took out my 'fruit knife' and cut it into three for us. I knew how to be a good *domina*. I ran the home, chaste and modest and frugal, a wife who loved her husband and his house. I ran it with pleasing conversation – and if ever, as that conversation rolled, I harboured different thoughts, I knew how to hide them.

The Fabulous Stertinius came to play his cithara, so then there was no need for chat.

65

Swollen with winter melt-water and heavy with alluvial silt, our river flowed through the last part of its two-hundred-mile journey. Modest when compared with the great water-ways of Europe, trivial in comparison with the Nile, nothing to the Euphrates or Indus, the Tiber pushed steadily down to the Tyrrhenian Sea. We took that route. We could have gone by road, fighting through massive traffic jams as my family traditionally did, but that February the river called. We were going down to Ostia because my husband, who never gave up on a quest, strange stubborn fellow, had decided that Ostia was where he might find a suitable column to repair the porch of the Little Temple of Hercules Gaditanus. It had been burned out twenty years before, but if Tiberius had any say, it would be rededicated to the Aventine's favourite demi-god this summer. Someone else had rebuilt the body of the temple about ten years ago, but left the crucial porch buried in props and scaffolding. Nobody could remember now, but I guessed that was because the previous contractor had been unable to find a replacement marble column.

I travelled with Tiberius Manlius. If he failed again, which he assured me was impossible, somebody would need to be on hand to stop him overheating.

I welcomed the gentle journey. I had a lot to think about. All the time, of course, I was pretending I was not thinking. I just sat watching the fields go by, while Tiberius gossiped with the crew, devouring facts about life on the river. He was loving that.

We went on a *codicaria*, a specially designed Tiber haulage boat. My husband found it interesting enough to calm his pent-up tension over the marble quandary. The sturdy craft had a forward-set mast on the foredeck with specially stepped cleats so the crew could climb it. This was because, unlike fixed masts, which were supplied with their own ladders for going aloft, the towing mast could be dismounted and laid flat when not needed. The boat also carried a spritsail, though the craft was not heavy enough to require a capstan aft to assist with the lines when dragging larger vessels. Ours nipped along, normally pulling small or medium vessels, though with trade at a low ebb in winter, it was now going back to the port empty.

Most haulage was literally manpower, though oxen and other animals were used. I had always believed there was a one-way system, so boats were drawn along in a single direction on a designated bank of the river. In practice this was Rome. There probably was a rule but nobody followed it.

Tow boats and the vessels dragged behind them had no brakes. Starting them in motion took a great deal of effort. Stopping them took a very long glide. If they met other boats coming towards them, there was another, extremely complicated, set of rules about the right of way when passing. In theory the larger boat took precedence, though in practice it seemed to depend on each captain's force of personality. One tow rope would be slackened, so it sank to the bottom of the river; those hauling in the opposite direction took the inner passage with their barge and stepped over the dropped rope without stopping. Then the others could pull up their rope and continue. Alternatively, since being dragged on the riverbed with its hidden obstructions damaged lines so much, sometimes a brave crew on the outer side would do it differently: they flicked up their line right over the inner boat, mast and all. This carried obvious risks. In fairness, we never saw an accident.

All the working boats had crew and many had animals, which meant an enormous number of places to stay had been built along both banks. At the end of each day, the hot and tired beasts had to be warmly stabled or they came to harm, while the men needed their own food and beds. A huge community of provisioners existed to service the river boats.

All of their rubbish went into the river, with the clearance of the mucked-out stables and anything that fell off boats. In the ports they had divers, specially trained to rescue lost cargoes, but plenty of other detritus remained in the water after it had been deposited in the long stretches of rural waterway. Agricultural waste found a natural home in the water. From Rome, upstream, came all the human effluent from the city sewage system. Nevertheless, fish were taken from the Tiber and fed to people. Children swam. Passengers on boats normally gave no thought to what they were floating over.

I did.

A burden had been lifted from me, without question. I had faced old fears and addressed years of emotional damage. Confronting Florius had been mysteriously therapeutic, even if it failed to go the way I had always expected. I could now live with what had happened, even though there had been no resolution. As we journeyed downriver, I sat mainly in silence, but I was re-establishing my bond with Tiberius. I was confirming to myself my decision was right: life with the man I had chosen over revenge against the man I had hated.

All the time, as I surveyed water with its characteristic yellow-green tinge of alluvial silt, I was thinking about what would have happened to Claudia Deiana, if her body had not been recovered that day by the dredger. I was remembering what Scribonius, the captain, had said about other corpses that were carried downstream amidst the muck and sand and unspeakable human rubbish that clogged and fouled this famous artery. Unknown people, in unknown numbers, suffering unknown fates.

Later, I would have even more cause to think about Claudia Deiana. But on the day, peacefully travelling with Tiberius, I was quiet for my own reasons. However much he enjoyed himself as he learned the lore of boating, he understood the situation. I was entirely his – yet my sad heart was once again with that woman from Britain. I would always yearn to discover how and why she had ended up in Rome, to die here and be deposited like just another piece of city rubbish in the Tiber.

66

Ostia never had a homely feel. As the entrepot for the greatest city, hub for the import of goods from all over the known world – and beyond – the place thronged with vessels and vehicles, all used by people who would never stay long. There must be native-born inhabitants, some Latin tribe that went back centuries, but those people were rarely in evidence. Everything here spoke of business. Grasping, preying and using were the chief means of flourishing; insincerity and bad faith were the ethics. This port was chock-a-block with consumables, all with their prices and quantities, their time limits for freshness, their end-dates for fashion, their references, their advertisements, their unsubtle grades of status, based always on price. Ostia was full of people too, from the anxiously lost to the frantically hurrying.

Mostly it was crammed with ships. In the couple of days we stayed there, we looked at the harbours, the old port at the mouth of the river where ocean-going vessels had to unload into shallow-draught lighters out on the open water, and the newer port of Claudius with its long arms and break-water, topped by the legendary lighthouse, lined with quays to which tugboats would bring incoming ships, once their masters had secured the right documents and paid the fees. Portus, as that was called, was supposed to provide sheltered mooring, though it had proved deficient; storms caused catastrophes. A newer basin, built according to better engineering principles, would have to be created. The only surprise was that Domitian, who was so greedy for veneration, had not begun it and put his name to it.

Even with many problems, into this humming hub came every kind of commodity, led by grain, then fine wine and olive oil, then heavy building materials. Among the latter were enormous timbers, and bulky stone, which was primarily marble from all the quarries of the world. Sometimes, while the clever but human unloaders were unloading it, they dropped a lump. No doubt occasionally some precious piece that had been carried hundreds of miles at staggering expense fell apart of its own accord, which would be what the harassed port operatives inevitably claimed. Either way, enough accidents occurred for special storage areas to be set aside; in them were collected beautiful items with horrendous scars, splits, flaked carving, shattered ends. They were laid out in pathetic lines. Anyone who wanted a short column on the cheap could have a look.

My husband came; he saw; he selected one.

Thank you, all twelve consenting gods of the wonderful Olympic pantheon.

Of course this was Rome, even worse it was Ostia, so there would be a process. Negotiating ownership, payment and arrangements for carriage would take almost as long as a peace treaty between international powers. Conducting business in the port was by an unhurried system with several layers of queuing for attention and dockets, followed by manly conversations with dubious officials-cum-asset-traders, before intricate verification of your references and banking details. Everyone you had to deal with assured you that he, unlike the others, was an honest man. You had to tell him

359

that so were you, while trying not to seem unreliable. Even when buying for a temple, bribery was standard. Tiberius knew how to do it (his uncle was a warehouse-owner) but he could not hurry the procedure. Bored, I went back on my own to the place where we were staying, telling my dear one I would pack our stuff.

We were staying at Onocles' cousin's place. That's right: Onocles, the weedy priest who led culture tours around Rome. This was deliberate. I had been perfectly open about it. Onocles had recommended his cousin Cleon to those travellers with whom Claudia Deiana had crossed Europe; to nobody's surprise, I had asked Onocles for the address because I hoped they would still be here. Tiberius, ever tolerant, went along with my scheme.

Fate, with its usual quirks, did not disappoint me. I was just too late. The tour people had gone.

Yes, they had been here, and they had stayed for some time, hoping to identify a ship for Athens or Alexandria. Two days ago they had found one. Cleon did not know its name or its berth in the harbour. He thought the tourists were all nuts to trust themselves to the ocean at this time of year, but he had not tried to dissuade them from going because by then he had absolutely had enough of them.

He was balding, with long straggles of hair, like his cousin, and with the same air of weary lack of hope. He was my kind of failure. I was glad we had stayed with him. I particularly liked the way he said that if the group had remained much longer, he might have cut short their travelogue, using exotic foreign weapons to murder them one at a time, after preparing clues written in hieroglyphs . . .

His place was clean and decent. There was a bakery opposite for breakfast rolls and they would give you a fish supper if you supplied two hours' notice. Downstairs, I made arrangements for Tiberius to bring the column here overnight. The cousin took an interest in us finding it. We could store the precious item in a space he was just emptying of luggage; he said some previous guest was arranging its collection.

Upstairs, I ran into a surprise. A woman, on her knees with her back to me, was prising up a floorboard in our room.

67

'If you are looking for my jewellery,' I announced loudly, 'I hid the box in a donkey pannier, but it wasn't my donkey and the damned animal has walked off.'

Red in the face, she jumped up, turning around. She was dressed in her own version of the Greek style, with a very long undertunic over which she nearly tripped. On top she had a shorter gown with a deep embroidered hem in an architectural pattern. Over that she had devised a double waterfall peplum with more antique scrollwork. I saw earrings, neck chains, bracelets coiling on both arms. Her head had a wrap-around scarf, side curls descending amidst fillets, and a bun falling apart on the back. Her arms were bare, and in the sandals she had chosen, her toes must have been freezing. To call her middle-aged would have been charitable.

In her arms she was desperately clinging to several scrolls. I gave them a cool look. 'Let's guess. Previous stay in the room, forgot your memoirs?'

'Novels!' she corrected me, with some pride. Despite the Greek get-up, she spoke Latin, with no odd accent. 'Adventure novels. I hid them for safety then, oh, my goodness, nearly left them behind.'

'You wrote them? That's unusual.'

'A woman has to have a job. Otherwise it would have been

selling fish on a quayside and wielding an abacus for some rich old miser who would grope me.'

'How many of your tales have been circulated?'

She blushed. 'None.' The fish cannot have earned her much travel money, I thought. The miser must have left her his bank-box. If he did, she must be persuasive in some way. I wondered how far she had let him go with the groping.

'And what are your stories?' I asked, though I knew it is risky to encourage a writer.

'The adventures of one of the Suiones, my hero, Boy Bonivir.'

'You don't look Suionian.'

'Of course not! I am from Gallia Narbonensis.'

'Ever been where the Suiones live?'

'Who needs to go? The Suiones are beyond the edge of the world. All I know is that they are fabulously blond with blue eyes, and inhabit the far, far north. I cannot even find out anything about their territory.'

'Very grey,' I guessed.

'You have been there?' she demanded, in delight.

'No, but I was born in the north. Grey and cold. What does Boy Bonivir do there?'

'He is a man of action, with characteristic thoughtfulness.' I managed not to groan. 'People view him as all-knowing,' declared his creator, defensively, 'if a little gloomy ... His sense of humour is supposed to be wondrous, though I am afraid I am not good at writing jokes.'

'Sounds a rare creature! All-knowing? Still, I bet he never remembers what time his wife will have his lunch ready. Does he have a wife?'

'No, he keeps the treasured memory of his long-lost love from many heart-breaking years before.'

'And while he is treasuring memories,' I quipped, 'what does he do for sex?'

The author blushed. Standing her ground, she carried on bravely: 'There must be another country, even beyond the territories of the Suiones,' she mused breathlessly, 'but so far I cannot discover anything about that either.'

'Hard luck! Invent a magical island?' I suggested.

She thought I was being facetious. 'I want to give readers realism. That is what they crave. I use creative imagination and knowledge of the human condition, including as much research as possible. Female intuition is a wonderful tool too. What we don't know, or what cannot justifiably be invented, I leave out. My readers will not have been among the Suiones either, so they won't need every minute detail. They will be seeking mental escape in a striking location with unusual weather, where unexpected adventures can happen. I only have to write with conviction, plus empathy. Empathy, empathy.'

'You write about a man?'

'It's quite easy. I have met some.'

'And a remote country?'

'The distance makes it seem exotic. The other useful premise is that my hero lived a long time ago.'

'Good cover!' I smiled falsely. I had had enough of this. Give her two more sentences and I would be extremely rude to this drapery-decked fantasist. 'You must be Agape – also known as Margarita.'

She looked startled. 'I had no idea I was so famous!'

I pulled her down off the pedestal. 'Don't get excited. I heard about you from the landlord's cousin in Rome, Onocles.'

'And who are you?'

'My name is Albia. Flavia Albia.' I gave it a beat. 'I am an investigator.'

At once she looked intrigued and burst out, 'I would love to ask you all about that! Is it hard? Do you love it? You must have to use female intuition a lot too?'

'No, I use facts.' I slapped her down, then had to make up for it. 'Onocles suggested that you, with your impressive knowledge of the human condition,' but, dear gods, please not your female bloody intuition, 'you might be the best person to ask about your travel companions.'

'Why?' Agape went straight to the point, looking deeply suspicious.

'One of them has died.'

'Horrible. In the river. We heard.'

'Heard? May I ask how?'

'The landlord told us. Onocles sent Cleon word. Of course, I cannot tell you anything. I could never break their confidence.'

'I wouldn't dream of asking!'

'But, of course, you are planning to?' This woman was less vague than she appeared. Well, shrewdness was good in a witness.

'I do want to ask about what happened on your group's journey to Rome,' I began. 'Onocles described your fellow travellers: the doting mother with her wastrel son, another who was cruel, the ex-tribune splurging his discharge funds, the widow who became sozzled every time you stopped at a *mansio*, the failed gambler, the drainage engineer, the man who was interested in Egyptology . . .'

'And the crazy lady who wants to write adventures, because she cannot help doing it, even though she lives in a dire society where writers must be masculine?' Agape smiled ruefully.

'Well, I was able to gather some colourful material so I shall press on!' That was when she told me the others on her tour were all bigamists, blackmailers and spongers. She gave me a few curious details. Finally, I brought her to mention Claudia Deiana. 'She was travelling on her own, with only a single attendant. I did have a long intimate conversation with her.'

'She had a husband called Florius.'

'Not travelling with her,' Agape admitted, but I thought she was holding back.

For the time being, I changed the subject. 'What was she like? As a person?'

'Guarded.'

'Do you mean afraid of Florius?'

'Definitely not.'

'A strong personality, then?'

'Oh, yes. Ulatugnus once told me she and Florius were as bad, or as good, as each other.'

'You spoke to Ulatugnus?'

'Only in passing.'

'I want to understand,' I pressed her. Agape ought to recognise that situation. 'Claudia Deiana came from the same province as me, so I felt we had something in common. The crude authorities in Rome dismiss her and her terrible fate. To me, she is like a character who has died before a story starts – yet her very existence is crucial to the plot. Can you see that?'

She nodded vigorously.

'So, Agape, at first all I knew was that Claudia Deiana saw herself as the wife of Florius Oppicus, a man I had met in the past coincidentally. He journeyed to Rome and she followed him, either knowing or not knowing that he had a wife here. On reaching the city she tried to find him. Somebody offered her news, and lured her to her death. It has been widely assumed that because he had a wife already, it must have been Florius who killed her.'

Agape started shaking her head, as if in disbelief, though she said nothing.

'No?' I kept going quietly. 'I always thought the law-and-order men were wrong and, indeed, now it looks as if rivals of Florius murdered Claudia. But at one time,' I suggested, with caution, 'I even wondered whether Claudia was so angry about the other woman Florius has that *she* wanted to kill *him.*'

More head-shaking. 'No, no, you really must not think that! She would never have done it!'

'Never? You talked to her about Florius, then?' It was time to lean hard on my informant about this. 'She was all alone on her enormously long journey, Agape, and must have needed somebody sympathetic to share her anxieties? I imagine she was desperate to confide.'

'We talked of many things, yes.'

'So why are you so certain she would not have attacked Florius? Too weak? Too innocent? Too *sensible?*'

Agape repeated her assertion that she could not break a confidence. I pleaded. She claimed someone else had an interest. I asked who. She ducked her head.

I was starting to understand what was going on here, and why a woman like her would choose to keep the situation from me. Very gently, I put to her, 'What was their relationship? Whose "interest" are you defending? You surely cannot mean Florius?'

She allowed herself to nod slightly.

'Agape, you cannot be protecting him?'

'She would have wanted me to.'

'Are you telling me everyone has got this wrong? Florius and Claudia – *it was true love?*'

Agape nodded more strongly. 'Life partners. Soul-mates. Meant to be together. Flavia Albia, it was indeed love.'

Story-telling was her life, so once she began it all came out convincingly. I made allowance for her own romantic attitudes but, even so, she made sense. According to her, Claudia and Florius had lived together in Britain for more than ten years and absolutely belonged together. Eventually he realised he was being watched by the authorities and was about to be pulled in by Julius Karus. But he had no intention of abandoning Claudia.

The couple had already made plans. They would leave Britain. They had intended to travel across Europe together, but Florius was suddenly taken to Londinium under armed guard. Perhaps Karus had suspected he was ready to flee. He was not allowed further contact with Claudia. However, she knew he was expelled back to Rome; he had thought that would happen because he had old charges to answer. They had discussed this. She was to follow him. They would meet up after Florius had discreetly gathered funds. He already owned a villa in another province. They would go there and start a new life.

'What went wrong?' I wondered. 'In Rome, did she ever find him?'

'No. That was awful. He was staying at the other woman's house because he had to collect funds. Claudia did find out where it was, but he told her not to go there. Ulatugnus, her slave, took him word of where we were staying. Our group was preparing to depart from Rome, but Claudia could keep her room—'

'At Auntie Itia's?'

'Yes, she would wait there for Florius to fetch her. Then the night before we left, a message came for Claudia to meet up with Florius. At least, that was what the message said. She was thrilled. I thought it unsafe. I wanted to go with her. She was determined and had left the lodging before I could do anything about it.'

'If you had gone, you would be dead too.'

'That's horrible!'

'No, count yourself fortunate . . .' I believed all this. It would fit the bitterness in how Florius had spoken to me when I confronted him at Fountain Court. Most of all, it chimed with his behaviour after Claudia died: how he had rushed to the funeral director; then his demand to see the body, as if to make sure it was her; wanting her jewellery initially, making arrangements to pay for her burial. 'What was the other province? Where did Claudia believe he was proposing to live after Rome?'

'Never said. They wanted it kept secret.'

'That's a nuisance.'

'Somewhere east, I presume.'

'You don't know that.'

'Yes, I do!' snapped Agape, tetchily. 'If they caught up with us, they were coming on the next leg of our tour with our group.'

Sailing on a heritage tour? At that point I stopped believing all this. 'Florius was fooling her. He would have stayed with Balbina Milvia.'

'Not at all,' Agape responded firmly. 'He sent luggage for when he joined Claudia. If they had met up in time, they would definitely have come with us together.'

'She had booked her room to continue at Itia's.'

'It was a bluff.'

369

'Your group is going towards Athens and Alexandria? Which?'

'Depending on sea conditions . . . We have a ship waiting. We sail tomorrow.'

'Without Claudia,' I said sorrowfully.

Margarita Agape made no reply. I grabbed a note tablet from my satchel, wrote quickly and handed it to her. 'Those directions will find me. Write to me! Write to tell me what happens.'

I breathed slowly. I had worked out what she had wanted to keep from me. Florius had come to Ostia. He was still going east. He was already on their ship.

I abandoned the author in our room with her scrolls. I ran lightly downstairs.

Most of the luggage I had seen Onocles' cousin lining up earlier was now on a donkey cart. It was being picked up by a red-haired man, whose face and limbs showed he had suffered a bad battering very recently.

By now I was expecting him: solid, tall, upright carriage, middle years. Workaday brown tunic, rough cloak fixed on one shoulder, long crumpled sleeves and ankle-tied leggings . . . 'You must be Ulatugnus. You belonged to Claudia.' I paused. 'Claudia and Florius.' He said nothing as he flung a bundle upon the cart. 'My name is Flavia Albia.'

'Oh, I heard about you!'

'None of this luggage is Claudia's?'

'No. He told the landlady she could have that.'

'This is his – and he is leaving. I take it he has boarded ship? Is he taking Milvia?'

'No chance. He wants nothing to do with her.' He was probably lying.

Margarita Agape came out of the building. She managed to climb on the cart beside the waiting driver, despite her clutch of Boy Bonivir scrolls. She nearly lost her grip and scattered the precious manuscript in the roadway. Ulatugnus did not help her. Neither did the driver.

Ulatugnus was squaring up for the last piece of luggage, a large, very heavy box that undoubtedly contained money. I told him I had hoped that, for the sake of his dead mistress, he would have gathered the fare home then stumped back to Britain, like a loyal old retainer, to care for the family's abandoned children with his honest kindness.

Ulatugnus sniffed. He thumped down the big money chest on the base of the cart. 'Not me. They must survive on their own. I shall take my chance with him.'

That's life. Whatever Florius had felt for Claudia, it was over; those children would be deserted, left to fend for themselves as poor urchins that nobody wanted, even perhaps sold into slavery. I knew all too well what their lives would be. People might have expected me to trace them – but they were the spawn of Florius. Their only hope would have been Ulatugnus, but you just cannot get retainers with kindly, honest hearts, these days.

As he readied himself to leave, he turned to me slyly. I said, 'You are meeting up with your master, the fugitive, and I have to decide what to do about that.'

'Do nothing. The ship's cleared to leave, the master paid. As soon as I roll this stuff on board, she's sailing. There's nothing in harbour that can outrun her. Don't even try,' Ulatugnus ordered, with a hint of threat.

I made a gesture of resignation. I had made my choice at Fountain Court. I stayed true to the decision, albeit with difficulty.

371

Before Ulatugnus jumped on the cart, he looked at me in the leery style every woman learns to recognise. He muttered a crude comment, in his own tongue. He may not have thought I would understand, but I answered at once with the one angry phrase I still knew in Britano-Celtic.

It is in every known language and bound for any that do not exist yet. I gave it to Ulatugnus straight, the retort that translates into Latin as 'Piss off, you pervert!'

68

Was it over? It felt that way. I devoted myself to the support of my husband, like a good middle-ranking wife. He definitely had unfinished business.

There was the usual agitation. Fortunately, Tiber boats are perfectly used to the carriage of marble columns. Ours was only a small piece, as crews kept remarking dismissively. Still Tiberius kept clucking over it, while they viewed him as an amateur.

We watched over the precious cargo all the way to Rome, saw it disembarked on the Embankment, yelled at rough treatment by a cavalier crane manager. Then I had to guard the thing while my husband went to organise a cart. Men always take three times as long to do that as they have promised when they leave you waiting. It was dark by the time we had the marble safely in our own yard. Even then, for a long time Tiberius was out there with his clerk-of-works and oil lamps, lovingly checking measurements, discussing their work programme, inspecting and reinspecting the piece of stone. Drax, the team's watchdog, was removed from Fountain Court and brought to sleep beside the column. He wee'd on it.

Next morning at first light that column was dragged to the temple porch where, once they managed to fit and install it, it would reside for the next few centuries. I leaned out of a window to call down the street helpfully, 'Don't drop it!'

Then I went back to bed, spreading myself like a starfish in the warm space Tiberius had vacated.

Quite a long time later, Suza was putting my hair up. We were doing it in the courtyard because indoors the light was poorer. Suza seemed quiet; I was vaguely enjoying that. It is bad enough having a hairdresser fiddling, but being made to engage in their nonsensical chatter is worse. I was enduring Suza, but I hate the way attendants make you look unrecognisable. I like the world to see me as I see myself.

Once she had whizzed the silver mirror past my head too quickly for me to check what she had done, I stayed there, thinking. I had told Tiberius about Florius going overseas among the tourist group. I could still alert the authorities, if I chose. In February it should be easy enough to track down a luggage carrier who had taken obnoxious people and their excessive chattels to the port, then learn which ship they were loaded onto. Fast signals would get the ship intercepted. I could do that. But I had decided not to.

Things would all go back to how they had been before, unless one day Margarita Agape sent word of Florius disembarking somewhere ... It was likely she would tell me, because she had already tested my address, sending me a scroll with a Boy Bonivir adventure: *Cold Winds from the North*. The chilly read must have been rushed along the Via Ostiensis while Tiberius and I were leisurely wending along the meanders of the Tiber. At least I would not have to meet her, expectantly waiting to hear compliments on her work ...

The group would have sailed now. I tried to imagine what might happen on that voyage. How would Agape, the great romantic, react if Florius had brought Milvia with him? If he moved shamelessly between wives, reinstalling Milvia and

374

betraying Claudia? Loyal to Claudia, her confidante, would Agape threaten trouble? Would Florius then murder her to stop her? Would sensible male passengers – the ex-military man, the spy, the engineer – apprehend and disarm him? Would the plump person from Belgica, who spoke in broken syntax of mystical truth, gather them all in the tiny galley, to lounge in graceful postures while he described who Florius was under his disguise (what disguise, Albia?), what he had done to cause so much unhappiness, and what punishment the law ought to impose on him?

Or would Florius jump overboard and swim for it, because those people were so awful he could not bear to go all the way to the Nile with them?

'Flavia Albia,' my steward broke in on my playful thoughts, 'has Suza told you anything about her adventure?'

Gratus was tall, slim and elegant, a smooth operator. He provided his own immaculate white tunics, with shoulder braids from neck to hem as a symbol of his office. He had the iced accent of a Palace flunkey, under which he concealed the aggressive vowels of a barrow boy. Normally he dealt with events himself and would not snitch on another household member.

'Adventure?' I queried cautiously.

Suza squirmed.

'Show Albia your new bangle, Suza.' I took the time to notice, while Suza pretended not to have anything she should not. I was expecting the inevitable snake, eating its own tail, with cheap glass eyes. This was a simple circle, but in neat twisted strands of what looked like real gold. Given to someone else's servant, it had to be a silencer. 'Was it,' Gratus asked, bright-eyed with interest, 'Maia Favonia or Marcia Didia who gave it to you, Suza?'

I had not seen my aunt since she came bellyaching about Milvia pursuing Petronius. I knew my cousin had been here, perhaps choosing her moment while we were away in Ostia. I had been told she had brought the cart from Father's warehouse, to take away some items of theirs now she and Corellius were setting up house. Maia, who did the auction accounts, could claim free use of the cart and must have got it for Marcia.

I stared at Suza until she began crying. Gratus looked the other way. As soon as I had mopped the waterworks, I sat down Suza for a talk. Gratus pretended to be putting new wicks in oil lamps so he could listen.

I explained to Suza that I would not be angry if I could help it, but I could not have people in my house who were keeping secrets.

'I never wanted to!'

'Well, that makes sense. I know Maia and Marcia only too well. What prank did they lure you into?'

'You can't imagine.'

'Then you had better tell me, Suza.'

'It's horrible. It's a secret!'

I said that I would have to see about that – although by the time she had finished, I agreed and indeed insisted on a rigid code of silence.

Suza had returned to Rome from the coast, because she hated to remember her life at a shellfish factory. I had left her behind when we went to Ostia in case the smell of the sea upset her again; this left her at a loose end in Rome. She happily spent time using my credit at Prisca's bath-house, having manicures at my expense, trying on my clothes and scarves.

Marcia had arrived first at our house; Suza obligingly helped her carry property she was collecting. Maia then turned up, not knowing we would be away; she was intending more complaints against the poisonous Balbina Milvia. Both women had accompanied me on interviews, so they sat down together, ordered snacks from my kitchen, and shared notes. Suza, a bold piece at the best of times, took it upon herself to join them, since she had been to Milvia's too.

'They asked for wine,' Gratus informed me, 'but I said you had all the cupboard keys.'

Even sober, my aunt and cousin had worked themselves up into more and more agitation, particularly Maia, who had never forgotten how Florius once nearly murdered Petronius Longus in Britain. She had discovered that Milvia recently tried to pursue him again. Petronius had fanned the flames of Maia's fury. He foolishly admitted Milvia had threatened him, saying she would never forgive his rejection and would make him suffer – hence the assault on Petronilla and little Tullus. In fact Petronius thought the attempt to abduct his grandson could well have been worse. Petronilla might easily have been hurt, and if she had loosened her grip, the Bug might have had his brains dashed out.

Maia and Marcia decided this could not continue.

They persuaded Suza to help them. At first they claimed they would try to fix a reconciliation, healing rifts through woman-to-woman peace negotiations, over delicious must cakes and almond biscuits. Too late, a more devious ploy emerged. By then Suza felt she could not back out. So, she was sent to Milvia's house with a fake invitation for the cutesy one to meet up with Lucius Petronius.

'But it wasn't that!' Suza wailed. 'He knew nothing about it!'

Too right. He would never have let Maia and Marcia tackle the mad adventure they were planning. First, they sent Suza with a hired chair, with room inside only for Milvia and her. No chaperone or maid. Suza had to say she knew where the assignation was to be, so she would show the way. Petronius supposedly wanted Milvia to come alone for secrecy.

I already dreaded what was to come next. 'You made it sound very exciting. You got her to come out in a chair with none of her own attendants. I hope,' I said, 'Balbina Milvia was never brought here to my house!'

No. First they went from Milvia's home by the Circus on a fairly short trip to an empty apartment on the Caelian. It was one that Marcia and Corellius had looked at in their search. They had rejected it, so would never live there. Still, Marcia had kept the keys overnight. 'She said to the agent, "While we are considering . . ." and he believed her.'

Milvia tripped inside the building, hoping to meet a repentant lover, only to find Maia and Marcia. She was immediately set upon. They tied her hands and gagged her with a scarf, reminding her that this was what had been done, on her orders, to Claudia Deiana. Ignoring her mostly, they kept her there until nightfall.

Once the traffic of Rome's deliveries had died down after curfew, Maia went somewhere nearby where she had been keeping Kicker and the auction cart. The women pushed Milvia out of the apartment, still tied up, then dragged her aboard and covered her with the nasty cloths that Felix used to disguise any large statues he was transporting.

'I hope,' I gasped faintly, 'the chickens were not forced to take part in this.'

'No, Piddle and Willikins were left behind.'

378

Maia, a confident driver, took the vehicle boldly down the Forum on the historic Sacred Way. Her destination was the Aemilian Bridge. It was dark; the riverbank appeared to be deserted. Anyone who was there thought it best not to know what was happening.

They drove through the Forum Boarium onto the bridge and halted. Maia was going to take the cart over the river, along the far bank and back across to the Campus Martius where Kicker would be stabled in his normal stall in the Saepta as if he had never been anywhere. First they would have a pause.

It was dark and very quiet. Right up until that point, my innocent Suza had no real understanding of what the others meant to do. Maia and Marcia now told her to get down and hold Kicker's head to stop him walking on. In horror, she watched them pull Milvia off the back of the cart. One at either side, so any witness would think they were holding up a drunken friend, they walked her to beside one of the ancient piers; they looked downstream at the silt-laden water with its rich burden of rubbish and sewerage. They talked. Milvia listened. Trussed up and held fast, that was all she could do. They told her that 'respectable' Roman housewives were much scarier and more vindictive than any gangster wife or mother. Milvia was hard. She was tough. She believed that she was powerful and dangerous. These were Didius women. They were harder and tougher, as they were about to demonstrate by ridding Rome of her.

While Suza stood with the mule, trembling, my aunt and cousin pointed out to Milvia where they believed the hitman she had hired had murdered Claudia Deiana. They reminded her of what had been done to her own victim on that other dark night.

She was already gagged and bound. Maia and Marcia stripped off her jewels so her body would not be identified, even if it was ever found. As a courtesy, Marcia punched her in the head once so she passed out and would be unconscious when she hit the water. She was a dainty woman. Between them, my aunt and my cousin picked her up in one strong movement, rolling her over the parapet of the Pons Aemilius.

So Balbina Milvia was thrown to her death in the Tiber.